PROOF OF *Love*

A PEMBERLEY TALE

Proof of Love

A Pemberley Tale

Some loves are meant to be

Brenda J. Webb

Proof of Love – A Pemberley Tale is a work of fiction. All characters are either from the author's imagination, or from Jane Austen's novel, *Pride and Prejudice.*

DarcyandLizzy@earthlink.net
www.darcyandlizzy.com/forum
ISBN-10:1721211799
ISBN-13:9781721211791

First Edition: June 2018

Cover design and formatting by Roseanna White

I dedicate this book, as usual, to those who helped me create this story. My friend and editor, Debbie Styne, whose expertise and encouragement are invaluable. My betas: Kathryn Begley, Janet Foster, Tracy Brown, Terri Merz and Wendy Delzell, who do everything within their power to make the story error free. Also, I would like to thank Janis Badarau for cold reading the story.

Lastly, I dedicate it to those of you who read my books and promote them by word of mouth and review. Without your help and support, I would not be writing.

Thank you all for being a part of my team.

Other Books by Brenda J. Webb

Fitzwilliam Darcy - An Honourable Man

Mr. Darcy's Forbidden Love

Darcy and Elizabeth – A Most Unlikely Couple

Darcy and Elizabeth – A Promise Kept

Passages – A Pemberley Tale

Chapter 1

The best proof of love is trust.
~ Dr. Joyce Brothers

Cambridge University
December 17, 1810

As he stared out the window of the house he had let for his time at the university, Fitzwilliam Darcy, the heir of Pemberley, envisioned how abandoned the frost-covered grounds would look the following day. Having stayed for weeks after the previous term ended, William, as his mother had called him, understood that most students AND professors would leave that day and he would be virtually alone until classes resumed in January. This meant that by tomorrow there would be no one left to challenge to a game of billiards or to share a glass of ale at the local pub.

"Are you going to stare out that window all day, old man?" John Lucas asked as he walked back into the room. Having shared the house with Darcy since last year, Lucas had grown accustomed to his roommate's idiosyncrasies. "I do not believe you have moved an inch in the last hour."

"How would you know?" William answered sombrely, not bothering to turn. "You have been in your room all morning trying to fit all the gifts you purchased for your family into one trunk."

"You pretend to be a curmudgeon, but you forget I saw the

trunk full of presents you purchased for Georgiana." William shrugged as Lucas continued. "How old is she now? I do not recall."

"She celebrated her thirteenth birthday last month."

"I would have thought her older, but I suppose that is because she is tall for her age."

"She inherited her height from our mother."

"What are your plans? Will you go home or stay here and feed your demons as you did after last term?"

William turned to scowl at his classmate, a pleasant looking fellow who favoured another friend, Charles Bingley, though his hair was brown whilst Charles' hair was flaming red. "My demons?"

"You know very well what I mean. Drowning your sorrows in a bottle of brandy will not change the fact that Lady Henrietta is now your father's wife and your new mother. You have to accept that at some point."

"She is *not* my mother! She is only two years older than I!"

"But she is eleven years older than Georgiana, and you said yourself that your sister is fond of her. Therefore, you must consider her feelings."

"My sister is fond of anyone who will notice her. God knows Father neglected to pay her any attention after Mother died. For all practical purposes, I neglected her, too, by being gone so much of the time."

"You had no say in the matter; you were in school. Besides, you do take care of Georgiana. I know of no other man who would make certain his sister had respectable clothes by escorting her to the modiste."

"I started after Mother died. Had I not, her gowns would have been far too short by the time Father noticed...if he noticed."

"There! You have proved my point."

William pictured his father's new wife. "All Father did during the last six years was cavort in London, drink and gamble. Is it any wonder he ended up marrying a—"

"No one says you have to like the woman, Darcy," Lucas interjected. "But you must accept her; she is at Pemberley to stay."

Watching William's frown deepen, Lucas clasped his friend's shoulder. "If you are not going to Pemberley, come home with me. A change of view may give you a new perspective on all of this."

"I fear I would not be civil company."

"You are too much of a gentleman to be very uncivil, and I promise you will not be required to carry the entire conversation. Your protégé will be there as well. You know how much he loves to talk."

"Bingley will be there? I thought he was off to London."

"He intends to stop at the Hursts' home and then come straight to Lucas Lodge. I expect him the day after tomorrow."

"I wonder at him staying away from that Bennet woman long enough to visit his family. She is all he talks about."

"Come now, you know the lady's name as well as I do. After all, I speak often enough of Jane and my other neighbours in Meryton."

Ignoring his reproof, William continued. "I have tried to reason with Charles, but he will not listen. He should be in no hurry to attach himself to any woman—at the least he should wait until he comes into his inheritance."

"Which I understand is not until after he completes Cambridge."

"Yes. Charles has three more years before he can access his funds. Even then, if he wishes to advance in society, he needs to choose a woman with a substantial dowry and connections, instead of one with no dowry, no connections, an estate entailed to the male line and four younger sisters. He might end up supporting the entire family should the father die."

"My friend, Charles and I are not like you. We are not slaves to the rules of the *ton* or the opinions of our relations, and if you met Jane Bennet, you would know why he is so smitten. She is not only the most beautiful girl in Meryton, but I dare say she is the kindest."

"If she is as wonderful as you say, why are you not besotted with her instead of her sister?"

"It is simple. At first glance, all eyes are drawn to Jane because she is so beautiful, but once you get to know the sisters, a clever man will discover that Lizzy is not only strikingly handsome, but she also has the most engaging personality. Behind the petite girl with such fine eyes, is a lively, intelligent woman. A man would never get bored with Lizzy as his wife."

"If you think so well of this woman, why do you not make her an offer? After all, we will graduate in another year. That would be the perfect length of time for an engagement."

"I have tried to convince her to marry me, believe me, but all I get for my trouble is a laugh. She says I am too much like a brother, and she is too young to think of marriage."

"How old is she?"

"Sixteen." Suddenly, Lucas smiled conspiratorially. "I do have a promise to fall back on, though—a longstanding agreement we made as children."

"Oh?"

"She agreed to marry me if she has not found a man she loves by the time she is two and twenty. However, should her parents try to force her to marry—"

William interrupted. "Force her?"

"If Mr. Bennet should die the estate passes to a cousin—a vicar whom Lizzy happens to loathe. Her greatest fear is that her parents will insist she marry this cousin to ensure Longbourn stays in the family."

"Is Jane not the eldest?"

"Yes, Jane is eighteen."

"Then why is she not set to marry the cousin."

"Mrs. Bennet maintains that Jane is too beautiful to sacrifice to a lowly vicar. She believes her eldest will eventually make an advantageous marriage and is fully prepared to sacrifice Lizzy, should it become necessary."

"So, the mother is a mercenary who is hedging her bets."

"You could put it that way."

"Now that you have explained so fully, tell me this: Why a well-situated, handsome fellow like you agreed to be any woman's last resort? That would be too degrading in my opinion."

"I have been in love with Elizabeth Bennet my entire life.

Whilst she may not be in love with me, I would welcome the chance to make her my wife and hopefully win her heart."

"But what happens if, whilst you are waiting, you meet another woman and fall madly in love?"

"I do not foresee that happening," Lucas replied confidently. "After all, I am already two and twenty, with no prospects in sight!"

William shook his head. "You are as daft as Bingley."

"When it comes to Lizzy, I am. Now, say you will come home with me. Whilst in Meryton you will undoubtedly meet the Bennets, which may give you a better perspective on why Bingley is besotted with Jane."

Or perhaps have a chance to change his mind, William thought. "I will agree if you will promise me one thing."

"What is that?"

"I am accustomed to riding out every morning alone. It gives me time to gather my thoughts without having to carry on a decent conversation until I am ready to do so."

"Only you would ask such a thing, Darcy!" Lucas said, guffawing. "But you have it! Now, since you gave Adams the week off, do you need help packing your trunk or shipping your packages to Pemberley?"

"I am perfectly capable of taking care of myself."

"Then why did you bring your valet back to Cambridge?"

"Father's new wife had started giving orders to Adams, and he could not stomach the thought of being left behind."

Lucas laughed. "I cannot say that I blame him!

"In any case, Adams considered it his duty to pack most of my things before he left, so there is little for me to do."

"Then let us hurry. The coach I hired could be here at any minute. We can drop your shipment at the post stop on our way out of town."

Meryton
Oakham Mount
The next day

Though frost was still on the grass, the sun was beginning to rise when Fitzwilliam Darcy reached the pinnacle of Oakham Mount astride one of the Lucas' stallions. His friend had assured him he would find the path up the mountain if he kept south, and that was the route he had taken. Thankful the snow that threatened yesterday had held off, William took in a breath of brisk air as he admired the azure sky and watched the earth come alive in the valley below. Suddenly unbidden, a feeling of despair washed over him.

He had hoped Lucas Lodge would prove a haven where he would be free of the machinations of women. Despite John Lucas' assurances to the contrary, his sister, who was one and twenty, had acted like a besotted schoolgirl the moment he alighted from their hired coach. Following him as the housekeeper led the way upstairs to his bedroom, Charlotte Lucas peppered him with questions until John stepped in, admonishing her to let him rest from the journey. However, the instant he came downstairs for the evening meal, he was again bombarded by a steady stream of questions not only from her, but from her mother as well.

Discovering that asking personal questions was a family trait, William answered as civilly as possible whilst attempting to preserve some degree of privacy. It had come as a great relief, however, when John began to relate his experiences at Cambridge during the last term, leaving William to eat in relative peace. Immediately after dinner, he pleaded fatigue and retired.

That morning, John had rapped on his door at daylight, suggesting William follow him to the stables straightaway if he wished to ride without being disturbed by his sister. Once there, a horse was saddled, and he was pointed in the direction of the highest peak in Meryton. Having now reached the spot his friend guaranteed was the most peaceful in all of Hertfordshire, William desired nothing more than to re-read his last letter from Georgiana in peaceful seclusion. After tying the stallion to a tree, he opened the missive.

Dearest Brother,

It saddens me to know we will not be spending Christmas together this year. Even if Lady Henrietta is not your favourite person, she cares for you. Of that I am certain, and I am equally certain that her feelings will be hurt if you do not come home for the first holiday that she and father will celebrate as a married couple.

Please consider visiting Pemberley before you return to Cambridge. That is all I ask.

Your loving sister,
Georgiana

Sighing, William placed the letter back into his pocket. Though he hated to disappoint Georgiana, he simply could not spend Christmas with his father's new wife. Not only was the new Mrs. Darcy young enough to be his sister, it was obvious she had married George Darcy merely for his money. Curiously, when William said as much to him in private, his father had found it amusing. His exact words came back to taunt William.

"Of course, she did, Fitzwilliam. What woman would not want to be mistress of Pemberley?" His father's eyes had twinkled in triumph. *"You do not have to like Henrietta, but I expect you to show her the respect she is due as my wife."*

Consequently, he had not shared Lady Henrietta's less than motherly comments upon their first private meeting. It would serve no purpose other than to broaden the gap between him and his father; therefore, William had kept that conversation to himself and stayed away from home as much as possible.

With these thoughts running through his mind, he walked over to the trunk of the largest tree on the mountain, removed his great coat and placed it across the frost-covered bark. Sitting down, he leaned back against the tree and closed his eyes, letting what sunlight filtered through the bare branches warm him. Suddenly something behind him moved. Standing abruptly, William noted a mound of rocks stacked to one side of the trunk had shifted, some falling to the ground. Further study revealed a split in the tree that had been hidden by the rocks—a split in which something was wedged. William tugged at the object until it loosened, slipped from his grasp and tumbled to the ground. Picking up a burlap-wrapped package, he unwound it to discover a small journal. Curiosity overrode prudence, and opening it, he began to read.

The Meryton Assembly, June 15, 1810

Mr. Bingley is what a young man ought to be—sensible, good-humoured, lively. I never saw such happy manners! So much ease, with such perfect good breeding. He is also handsome, which a young man ought likewise to be.

Jane was flattered when he asked her to dance a second time. She did not expect such a compliment, though I did. What could be more natural than asking her again? After all, he could not help seeing that she was five times prettier than every other woman in the room. No thanks to his gallantry for that. Well, he certainly is very agreeable, and I give her leave to like him, for Jane has liked many a stupider person.

Suddenly, a voice pierced the silence. "What right have you to read my diary?"

Startled, William whirled around. A petite, raven-haired beauty with hands on her hips glared at him. Her long dark hair was being whipped in every direction by the wind, and her eyes, dark as coals, were ablaze with fiery indignation. Lucas' words came to mind.

Behind that petite girl with such fine eyes is a lively, intelligent woman. A man would never get bored with Lizzy as his wife.

Elizabeth had been stunned when the man turned to face her. This stranger was not only taller than any man of her acquaintance, but so handsome that she was suddenly at a loss for words. Hair as black as night, eyes the colour of the morning sky, a patrician nose and perfectly formed lips held her mesmerised until his horse broke the spell by pawing the ground and snorting impatiently.

Chiding herself for being so easily overcome, Elizabeth struggled to keep her hand from trembling as she held it out. "I shall take that."

Handing her the journal, the stranger stuttered, "I...I did not mean to—"

"Did not mean to what, sir?" she demanded. "Read my private thoughts?"

A wave of righteous anger seemed to wash over him. "If you truly wished to keep your thoughts confidential, why did you store your journal where it could so easily be found?"

"Easily found? I have kept it here for years without it being discovered."

William took a deep breath and let it go slowly. "It was not my intent to discover your diary."

"Then what *was* your intent in reading it?"

All colour drained from his face. "I have no excuse. I apologise, Miss ..."

"Bennet...Elizabeth Bennet. And you are?"

"Fitzwilliam Darcy," William answered, dipping his head in a slight bow.

"John Lucas' friend from Cambridge?"

"Yes."

"I wonder what he will think when I tell him I caught you prying."

William winced, and the hurt in his eyes instantly convicted Elizabeth of being too harsh, yet conflicted as to why she should care, she continued. "Oakham Mount is too steep and rocky to be useful for riding; it is scarcely useful for walking. Hardly anyone bothers to come here; that is why I claimed this place for my sanctuary years ago. How did you manage to find it on horseback?"

William untied the horse. "I was simply following a path, and it led me here. I am sorry to have invaded your refuge." Mounting effortlessly, he donned his hat and addressed Elizabeth. "It will never happen again. Good day, Miss Bennet."

As Elizabeth watched him ride back down the mountain, one thought came to mind. *Let us hope your word is more reliable than your manners, Mr. Darcy.*

Lucas Lodge
The next day

Though Bingley arrived at Lucas Lodge with barely enough time to dress before the party the Lucases were hosting for the neighbourhood, William seized the opportunity to warn his friend again about raising expectations. Nevertheless, the second Charles was dressed, he rushed downstairs to find his *angel.*

From his place beside the mantel, William did not bother to disguise the frown on his face as he watched Bingley claim a second dance with the blonde-haired, blue-eyed woman. Across the room his displeasure did not go unnoticed by Elizabeth Bennet, who was enjoying a glass of punch with John Lucas.

"I confess I do not know why you invited *that* taciturn man to Meryton, much less to stay in your home."

"Now, Lizzy, it is not like you to dislike someone you hardly know. You could not possibly have sketched Darcy's character in the brief period of time he has been in Meryton, and, as I explained, it was my fault that he was on Oakham Mount. I thought he might enjoy the view."

"I accept that you sent him to invade the one place I consider my sanctuary, but I knew all that I needed to know about the man when I caught him reading my diary."

"That is not fair. If you found a book, would you not open it to determine the owner?"

"He was not looking for a name. He was reading!"

"You simply do not know Darcy as I know him. Once you do, you will find him a candid, loyal and trustworthy friend."

"A friend who is not only too proud to dance with any woman here, but one who disapproves when Mr. Bingley dances with

Jane. One has only to look at his expression to know what he is thinking."

Lucas glanced at his classmate who was, indeed, glaring at Bingley. "You do not know their history. I believe Bingley told you that his father is in trade."

"Yes, he did."

"The elder Mr. Bingley's fondest wish is for Charles to buy an estate, become a gentleman and leave trade behind. When he met Darcy, Bingley shared his father's dream with him. Darcy not only took Bingley under his wing, he went to a great deal of trouble to school him in managing an estate and to include him in his circle of friends."

"That is all well and good, but it is obvious he does not approve of Jane being part of Bingley's circle of friends."

"He worries that Bingley will raise expectations he cannot fulfil. After all, Charles will not inherit his fortune for three more years."

"Jane is besotted. She would be willing to wait for Mr. Bingley, if he is serious."

"Three years is a long time, Lizzy. Either party could change their mind in that length of time."

Elizabeth brows furrowed. "So, you are taking Mr. Darcy's side?"

"Do not look at me that way, Lizzy. I am not taking anyone's side. I simply concur with Darcy that Bingley is not financially able to marry at present. Furthermore, I think you should be benevolent enough to acknowledge that Darcy is only concerned for his friend."

"I might be more sympathetic if Mr. Darcy showed any concern for Jane."

Suddenly, Arthur Goulding appeared beside them. "May I have this dance, Miss Elizabeth?"

As Lucas watched her walk away, he decided it might be wise to speak to his guest, so he walked in William's direction.

"Darcy, let us take a turn in the garden. There is something I would like to discuss."

William gave him an exasperated look. "Can it not wait? If

Bingley dances with Miss Bennet one more time, they will be as good as engaged."

"No, it cannot wait."

Once they were several yards down one of the torch-lit gravel paths, Lucas stopped and turned.

Seeing the unease in his host's expression, William's anxiety rose. "Has something happened to Georgiana?"

"Heavens, no! It is nothing like that," Lucas replied. "It is only—I feel it my duty to warn you that the people of Meryton think very highly of Jane Bennet. Any attempt on your part to separate her from Mr. Bingley will not be taken lightly and could result in your being shunned by the entire neighbourhood."

"Just as Miss Elizabeth shuns me tonight?"

"You noticed."

"How could I not? Still, you know as well as I that Bingley cannot support a family at present. And, even if he could, why should he settle for someone with no dowry or connections just because the people of Meryton approve of her?"

"That is Bingley's choice and I strongly suspect your opposition has to do with the fact that you cannot do likewise. Your future wife will likely be chosen by your relations, whether you agree with their selection or not."

Lucas' words caused William's temper to flare. "Are you implying that, if left to my own devices, I would fall in love with someone as far beneath my station as Jane Bennet?"

Seeing he had touched on the truth, Lucas teased, "Or, perhaps my choice, Miss Elizabeth."

For some reason, Lucas' referral to Elizabeth as his choice annoyed William. "*Your* Elizabeth is tolerable, but not handsome enough to tempt me! I would not choose her even if I were looking for a wife decidedly inferior in rank!"

Lucas laughed. "Methinks thou dost protest too much."

William threw up his hands. "Am I the only one who suspects Jane Bennet may be pursuing Charles simply because her mother wishes it? Do not pretend you have not heard Mrs. Bennet boast tonight of a most advantageous marriage."

"I do not deny that her mother is impressed with Charles' fortune, but no more so than any mother of the *ton*. Fortune hunters are not limited to the lower classes, my friend, a fact you recently learned the hard way."

Seeing William recoil, Lucas quickly added, "I apologise. I should not have brought up your situation."

"Nonetheless, you made your point. My own father could not see past a pretty face, so why should I expect a man of Bingley's age to act any differently? It seems I have brought nothing but trouble with me to Meryton, so if you will excuse me, I will remove myself from your company."

As William disappeared in the darkness, Lucas called, "Darcy, wait!"

Seeing that his roommate was not going to stop and knowing there was no reasoning with Darcy when he was in one of his moods, Lucas went back inside.

Arthur Goulding was not a small man, nor was he an accomplished dancer. After that rotund gentleman had stepped on Elizabeth's toes for the third time, she pleaded a headache in order to escape him. Insisting that a little fresh air would be just the thing to help her recover, she declined Goulding's offer to escort her and quickly fled the dance floor through the double French doors leading onto the terrace. Intending to sit on one of the cement benches in the garden to take off her shoes and rub her aching toes, she was hurrying down the gravel path when the sound of men's voices brought her up short.

Recognising John Lucas and Mr. Darcy, she stepped off the gravel path into the shrubs where she hoped to remain unseen. Still able to hear every word, by the time William stalked away, she was seething.

She watched until his tall form passed completely out of sight. *As if this tolerable woman would ever consent to marry you!*

I would have you know, Fitzwilliam Darcy, that from the very beginning of our acquaintance, your manners were such as to form so immoveable a dislike that I knew you were the last man in the world whom I could ever be prevailed on to marry!

With that, Elizabeth went back into the house.

Chapter 2

Cambridge University
Seventeen months later – May, 1812

Thunder rolled, and the smell of rain assaulted William's senses as he walked out of the large two-storey brick house. Following his valet to the covered wagons packed with the furnishings he had accumulated at Cambridge, he studied the clouds forming to the west and as Adams placed his own box in the first wagon, William's brows furrowed anew. Heavy rains in the last two weeks had left the roads mired in mud except where rain-filled ruts ran like steams down the middle of them. Moreover, a good part of Cambridge was flooded, whilst rising rivers and streams threatened to wash away the bridges leading in and out of the city.

Adams, who at forty was so thin that he looked like a schoolboy, glanced in the same direction as his employer. "It seems that Cambridge is to be blessed with more rain."

"I fear you are right," William replied. Then, he added, "I appreciate your willingness to travel with the furniture to Pemberley. If my coach had not lost a wheel last week, that would not be necessary. You could have travelled to London with me and taken a coach from there."

"I do not mind, sir," the servant replied as he nodded towards the men waiting by the wagons. "Mr. Gaines and Mr. Rollins come highly recommended as drivers. Has the local blacksmith given you any indication of when your coach will be repaired?"

"With all the mud, they have been overwhelmed with repairs and cannot make any promises. If I am to leave anytime soon, it seems Zeus is my only option."

Knowing how high strung the stallion was, Adams asked, "Will you ride him all the way to Pemberley?"

"No. I will head to London and take one of the coaches there. I have business in Town."

As Adams nodded, William reached inside his coat and pulled out a piece of paper. "Here is the list of the inns where I have accounts. You are authorised to charge to them with this letter. I suggest you get started. Hopefully, you can gain Huntingdon by this evening."

The valet took the paper. "Thank you, sir. We shall do our best."

After shaking William's hand, he climbed aboard the front wagon, taking a seat beside the driver. As it began to lumber down the road, he looked over his shoulder and waved. William gave a nod in response and returned to the house just as the first drops of another shower began.

The place looked empty since the only furniture left was what was in the house when William rented the property. There was just a well-worn sofa and small table in the parlour, so he walked straight to the kitchen and sat down in one of three chairs left around the table. Tempted by the rolls that Adams had bought at the local bakery the day before, he pulled one from a cloth-covered bowl and opened the jar of plum jam on the table. Spreading a generous spoonful over the roll, he could not help but smile as he took a bite. Mrs. Lantrip had been the cook at Pemberley as long as he could remember, and she never let him run out of his favourite jam, even if she had to send it to him by post.

Pouring the last of a pot of lukewarm tea into a cup, he took a sip before grabbing a list lying on the table. Perusing the things that must be done before leaving Cambridge, he marked off the next-to-last item—*ship furniture.*

At that very moment, John Lucas stuck his head in the room. "Darcy, have you heard the news?"

William jumped. "Lucas, I did not hear you come in! Did you remove your boots in order to frighten me?"

Lucas laughed. "I did not. You must have been preoccupied. You never hear anything when you are lost in thought."

"I was not *that* preoccupied. To what news are you referring?"

"The bridge on the highway to New Market has washed away."

"Good heavens! Was anyone hurt?"

"None that I heard. Still, until a new one can be constructed, travellers going east will be forced to journey north or south and circle back, which will be very inconvenient."

"I pray Adams arrives at Pemberley safely."

"At least Adams is headed north. Word is that area has not suffered the storms we have. He should be safe. It is you and I who need to get out of Cambridge as quickly as possible. Market Street is beginning to flood, and all the shops are closed and boarded. Adams was fortunate to get the last of the rolls at the bake shop because Mr. Russell has closed it and left for London."

"Why would a merchant desert his business?"

"Have you been listening to me? The shops already have water in their basements and it is rising. Many of the residents of Cambridge have left for higher ground, and now that the bridge to the east has washed away, I think we should do likewise."

"You claimed you were not leaving until the end of this week."

"That was before we were blessed with more rain. Yesterday the water was nearly over the bridge to London, and another good soaking could sweep it away entirely."

"I wish I could leave, but I have to wait on Mrs. Thornhill. She is on her way to inspect the house and collect the last month's rent. She should arrive tomorrow or the next day."

"With all the repairs paid out of your pocket, I dare say this place is in better shape than when you leased it. Why would she need to inspect it? And in the past, your solicitor mailed the rent. Why not have him do so this time?"

"Since her son died, she may need the money immediately."

"You are too kind, Darcy. When I think of the dire circumstances you are facing, I am inspired by your consideration of others."

Whilst Lucas continued to chatter, William was transported to his father's study the day after that man's funeral. In his mind's eye, he watched the steward inform him of the sad state of the family's finances and felt his stomach lurch once more in protest. Totally unaware that his father had paid off his new mother's gambling debts, wiping out the better part of the family's coffers, he could not help reeling again whenever it came to mind.

"But as for me, I cannot wait," Lucas continued, completely ignorant that William had not been listening. "Lady Aileen expects me in Richmond tomorrow, and I am not going to disappoint her. I wish to make her an offer before I return to Meryton."

Hearing the word *offer*, William's mind instantly returned to the present. A vision of loveliness with fine eyes and long, dark locks stood before him, setting off a familiar ache. Would Elizabeth be hurt by Lucas' change of heart?

"I say, Darcy. Are you well? You look as though you have seen a ghost."

William's eyes narrowed. "How long have you known Lady Aileen? A fortnight? A month?"

"Six weeks. But the minute I spied her, I knew she was the one."

"And what of your promise to marry Miss Elizabeth? I realise that you believe she may never marry you, but should you not be certain first? Have you no concern how this could affect her?"

"I do not think Lizzy took those childish promises any more seriously than I did. Besides, the last time I was in Meryton she was enamoured with a member of the militia, and Mr. Bennet looked the picture of health. There is absolutely no reason to believe he should not live a long life. Moreover, Jane is now engaged to Bingley, so the Bennets' future is secure."

"A security obtained at Bingley's expense," William spit out cynically. "And who is to say Charles will not fall out of love again as he has in the past."

"In any case, Lizzy is not waiting for me to save her. She speaks very fondly of this Lieutenant Wickhampton—or something like that. According to her, he is quite the charmer and I understand he is from your area of the country."

"Wickham? George Wickham?"

"That is the name. He must be as charming as Lizzy claims, for Charlotte said the same thing."

William stood and walked over to a window. As he stared into space, he pictured the dark-haired beauty of Oakham Mount in that blackguard's arms. Everything within him shouted that he must warn her, but he doubted she would listen to anything he had to say. Sickened by the thought of Wickham working his schemes on Elizabeth, he turned with eyes ablaze.

"It is imperative that you act quickly to warn Mr. Bennet and all of Meryton that George Wickham is a gambler and a deceiver. He is not to be trusted around their daughters or with any loans."

"Are you certain you are not overreacting? Lizzy claims that he is—"

Angrily, William interrupted. "Wickham's father was my father's steward for more than thirty years. George and I grew up together; he has always been a cad and a liar. He cares nothing for the women he ruins. Tenants' daughters, shop clerks, maids and gentlewomen—they are all the same to him. My father never saw George's faults and subsequently bequeathed him the living at Kympton in his will. When Father died, George refused the living and demanded that I pay him three thousand pounds instead. I was happy to be rid of him, so I did so gladly. Four months later he returned without a farthing to his name, begging for the living. I refused, and he made threats. That is when I had him thrown off the estate."

Lucas looked shaken. "The moment I get to London, I shall inform Father straightaway via express post. He will make certain all of Meryton knows Wickham's character quickly."

"I hope it is not too late already."

Lucas walked over to grip his friend's shoulder. "If your worry is for Lizzy, keep in mind that she is no fool. She will sketch Wickham's character long before he realises it."

"I pray that you are right."

"I am. Now, if you are not coming with me, I must be off. After I leave Richmond, I plan to return to London to order new clothes. One should be well-dressed for one's wedding."

"Your family will not worry if you stay away that long?"

"As soon as I have my lady's consent, I will write to inform my parents. Still, I may not return to Meryton for another sennight. What say you join me at White's one evening for supper if you are in Town when I return from Richmond?"

"If possible, I will."

Longbourn
The next morning

Gloom had filled Longbourn like an early morning fog since Mr. Bennet was carried into the house after the accident. Witnesses said he was taking a fence on his stallion, lost his seat and fell on a broken fence post, impaling his leg. The injury was so severe that the local apothecary felt unqualified for the task and sent a servant to fetch the physician in the next village. Said physician was now trying to combat a rising fever on top of attempting to save his leg.

Mr. Bennet's misfortune sent Mrs. Bennet's nerves spiralling out of control. In between shouts for Hill to bring her smelling salts, she raged at Elizabeth for not securing their cousin, Mr. Collins, whilst he was at Longbourn. That gentleman had spent the last week bragging about his new patroness, how she required him to have a wife and that he intended to choose from among his cousins. His sights were first set on Jane, but upon learning she was not available, Elizabeth quickly became his prey.

Nonetheless, his visit only reinforced Elizabeth's opinion that her cousin was not only unattractive in every possible way, but totally ridiculous. Consequently, she had used all her ingenuity to keep out of his sight until it was time for his departure. Furious at her daughter's subterfuge, as Collins was preparing to leave for his new parish in Hunsford, Mrs. Bennet promised that the entire family would visit Kent shortly, presumably to give him another chance to offer for her least favourite child.

However, with Mr. Bennet's health now so precarious, all trips were out of the question. Consequently, Mrs. Bennet's anger at Elizabeth knew no bounds.

In a large linen closet on the third floor, the two oldest Bennet daughters sat on the floor, talking.

"Lizzy, what will you do?" Jane whispered. "I heard Mama tell Hill to send a footman after Mr. Collins in the morning. He is to explain that you have changed your mind and now wish to marry our cousin."

"I must speak to Papa."

"He may be too sick to be of any help."

"Still, I must try. If you can do something to distract Mama, I shall slip into his room."

Jane stood to leave. "I shall do my best. Count slowly to one hundred before leaving the closet."

Fortuitously, when Elizabeth reached her father's bedroom, she found only Hill with him. Since the housekeeper had always been fond of the Bennets' second daughter, when she saw Elizabeth peek into the room, she motioned her forwards whilst simultaneously signalling her to be quiet.

After she was inside, Hill said softly, "At present your mother is speaking to the physician downstairs. He left orders that no one is to disturb your father, but I know Mr. Bennet would want to see you. I will wait in the hall and let you know if I hear anyone coming."

Elizabeth took the old woman's hand. "Thank you. I will not be long."

Slipping over to the bed where her father lay with his eyes closed, Lizzy sat down on the edge. When she leaned over to kiss his forehead, Mr. Bennet's eyes flew open and with great difficulty, he rasped, "Lizzy, you must listen carefully. Your mother is determined to send for Collins, and I cannot protect you in my present state. She intends to force you to marry him."

"That leaves me with only one choice, Papa, and you know what that is."

"John Lucas' promise?"

"Yes. If I can get to Cambridge, I know he will marry me."

"Lucas is a good man," he murmured. Elizabeth nodded. "In the left bottom drawer of my desk is a hidden compartment. Inside it is ten pounds I saved for an emergency. That will buy a ticket on the post coach to Cambridge and help both of you get to Gretna Green. Cloaked in your mother's old mourning dress and bonnet you should be safe from harm whilst travelling alone."

Elizabeth began to cry. "I love you so much, Papa. I do not wish to leave with you so ill."

"I insist that you go." As she nodded her assent, more tears filled Elizabeth's eyes as well as her father's. "Knowing you are married to someone deserving and not that idiot Collins will help me to recover."

Elizabeth sniffled. "Please fight hard, Papa. I have to believe you will pull through; else I could not leave."

"And I have to believe you will be better off with Lucas; else I could not send you to him."

Suddenly the door opened. "Someone is coming," Hill whispered as she rushed to sit down in the chair she had previously occupied.

Quickly kissing her father again, Elizabeth smiled at Hill and ran to the door. Looking both ways and seeing no one, she ran to the stairs that led to the attic. Just as she made her way up them, the physician and her mother rounded the other end of the hall.

London
A Mayfair townhouse

George Wickham, a tall, handsome rogue with auburn hair

and brown eyes, was very proud of his looks. Whenever he was near a mirror, nothing would do but to admire his reflection, just as he was doing now in the gilt-edged mirror over the hearth. Satisfied he looked well turned-out in his newly purchased suit, he began to scour the parlour for items small enough to pinch and sell. Picking up a silver snuff box, he found it empty and quickly dropped it into his coat pocket.

He was examining a gold-trimmed china figurine on the mantel, when a decidedly feminine voice asked, "What are you stealing now, George?"

Wickham whirled around to find a handsome blond woman with green eyes watching him from the doorway. Lady Henrietta wore only a very thin, red silk nightgown that left little to the imagination. Her state of undress made him smile. "Is that any way to speak to an old friend?"

She held out a hand. "I shall take whatever you put in your pocket."

Wickham removed the snuff box and held it out.

"Are you my friend?" she asked, taking the box.

"I am probably one of the few *true* friends you have. And, tell me: Why should you care if I pocket a few things, as none of this belongs to you."

"What makes you think I am not the owner?"

Wickham looked about with a more discerning eye. "I had no reason to suspect it belonged to you. But, if it does, why do you stay at Darcy House? This may not be as grand, but it is certainly no hovel."

"Fitzwilliam is not aware I own this property, and I wish to keep it that way."

"How did—"

Knowing Wickham would not stop until she explained, Lady Henrietta interrupted. "It was left to my mother by a distant uncle shortly before she died. I inherited it from her. I allow my cousin, Lord Hartford, to occupy it when he is in Town, and in turn, he pays the staff and upkeep. People assume it is his, and I can use it whenever I desire privacy, such as today, whilst he pretends to be better off than he is."

"Lord Hartford? I am not familiar with the name. Besides, I thought you had no living relations."

"David is the only family I have left. His father was a second or third cousin of my father. I recall his mother was the only person on that side of the family who liked Mother. Thus, she visited several times a year, bringing him with her."

"Does he have an estate?"

"Spelling Park. It is in Liverpool."

"Now *that* I have heard of. I understand it is on the market because it is nearly bankrupt."

"It is not bankrupt yet, but David spends like a sailor on leave. That is why he comes in handy when I need a favour. He is willing to do almost anything to make a few pounds."

"Sounds like a fellow opportunist!"

"You do remind me of one another, except that he is not as wicked as you."

Wickham grabbed his heart. "You wound me."

"Liar! You have no heart to wound."

"Be that as it may, tell me—how did you manage to hide this property from old George Darcy?"

"He trusted me when I told him I owned no property." What Lady Henrietta would not mention was that she had a substantial bank account in Edinburgh that had also belonged to her mother, lest George expect to be paid all that she owed him right now.

Wickham laughed. "No fool like an old fool."

Or a young one, she thought. Aloud, she said, "Precisely."

"Speaking of your mother, I saw her once at the theatre. Lady Carmichael was quite the beauty in her day."

"My mother was very beautiful, but equally foolish," Lady Henrietta replied. Then, appearing to recall another time and place, she added, "Had she not rushed into marriage with the rogue who fathered me, she might still be alive. Instead, because of his dissolute ways, she and I were left in poverty long before he was killed in a duel. It was years before she rose above the disgrace and gained a modicum of respectability, and that shortened her life."

"It must have been hard on you, too."

Ignoring this statement, Lady Henrietta changed the subject. "I asked you here to explain that I am not ignoring you. I simply cannot pay you more at this point in time."

Wickham grew irritated. "I arranged for you to meet the most eligible man in England. I even provided you with witnesses touting your lineage and connections to impress him. Moreover, I did such an excellent job that he married you. I expect to be paid the entire three thousand pounds we agreed upon for my services.

"However, the most *desirable* man, then and now, is Fitzwilliam Darcy, not his father."

"Yes, but the son would never have given you the time of day."

"Seeing that George held the purse strings, I had no choice but to proceed from that angle. However, I am not convinced his son would not have been interested."

"Oh, I understand now! You have fallen under Fitzwilliam's spell. After all, why should you be any different than most women?"

"Jealously does not become you, George."

"Nor does lust for your *son* become you, *Mrs. Darcy*."

At that, Lady Henrietta could no longer hold back a laugh, and Wickham walked over to pull her into his embrace. Kissing her passionately, he was pleased with her response and whispered, "I have not had a woman in far too long."

"If I allow you to do whatever you wish, will you promise to stop hounding me about the money?"

"You have never refused me before, why bargain now? I know you want me as much as I want you."

"I do not deny it. After being bedded by a man old enough to be my father for far too long, I welcome someone virile. Still, how can I think of pleasure when you harass me so?"

"I harass you because I have received only a thousand pounds, which barely paid my most urgent gambling debts, whilst you are living in the lap of luxury at Pemberley."

Lady Henrietta pulled away and crossed to a liquor cabinet. Pouring a glass of brandy, she held the bottle up in a silent question. Wickham nodded. After pouring another glass, she handed it to him and drank the contents of her glass in a few swallows.

"I would be in the dower house right now if Georgiana had not insisted things continue as they were. Besides, had George not died suddenly, you would already have your money. He had finally trusted me with the combination to the safe holding the Darcy jewels. I made copies of several less noticeable pieces and sold the originals. That is how I got the thousand pounds."

"Were you not afraid George would notice the fakes?"

"George Darcy was a drunk and a pawn in my hand. If he had noticed, I could have persuaded him that he was mistaken. In fact, so great was his trust, that had he not died when he did, I might have completely ruined him before Fitzwilliam graduated from Cambridge."

"Really? I had always known George to be a prudent financier."

"He believed in gallant gestures. After we married, he paid off all my gambling debts, which almost wiped out all the profits from his stocks and bonds, and I never stopped gambling afterward."

"Pray tell me. On what did you wager, and being a woman, how did you place your bets?"

"Horse races. When I was but a child, my father frequented the race tracks and took me with him. He even let me choose his bets on occasion, so I became familiar with the man who placed them. Later, that man agreed to handle mine as well."

"So, you managed to lose even more after George paid off your original debts."

"Yes. It was all part of my plan to bankrupt Pemberley. I knew he would keep paying, even if he got angry when he learned I was still gambling. Then, when George's steward reported the week before he died that the bank had refused any future loans—"

"Why was the steward handling this?" Wickham interrupted.

"George did not feel well, so he sent his steward, Mr. Sturgis, to represent him and negotiate the terms of a new loan. When the loan did not materialise, Sturgis declared that, other than what revenue the tenants brought in, the family jewels were all George had left of any real value unless he began to sell the land. I believe the shock of the bank's refusal and my new debts brought on his death."

"Knowing how private old George was about his finances, I wonder at you knowing anything about it."

"The first thing I did when I moved into Pemberley was have my maid discover the best places for eavesdropping."

"There is one thing I do not understand. Why reduce the Darcys to paupers? If they lose everything, so will you. Why not reside at Pemberley for the rest of your days and enjoy their wealth whilst wreaking havoc with their personal lives? Would that not suffice for vengeance?"

Lady Henrietta's voice rose with indignation as she hissed, "I shall not only see them penniless, I plan to utterly destroy them like they destroyed—"

Realising she was about to say too much, she instantly went silent and, seeing Wickham's puzzled expression, assumed a mirthless smile. "Since George deprived me of the pleasure of seeing him disgraced, Fitzwilliam will take his place. And, do not worry. It is not my plan to leave Pemberley without any resources. I will still have this house and the money from the sale of the rest of the Darcy jewels as I replace them with paste."

"Need I remind you that I could always whisk Georgiana to Gretna Green, and we could walk away with her thirty-thousand-pound dowry?"

"And need I remind *you* that will be a last resort? You could push Fitzwilliam too far and wind up dead."

George smirked. "I am not the least bit worried about that conceited arse, but it is good to know that you are concerned for my health."

Henrietta laughed aloud. "My only concern is that he might learn of our relationship and trace the elopement scheme to me. No. The Darcy jewels are a safer solution."

"I care not how you get the money, so long as I get what is due me."

"Of course, but first I aim to have some amusement by testing Fitzwilliam's vaunted principles."

"No doubt, by coaxing him into your bed?"

"How else? He relishes being known for his sense of duty and being in complete control at all times. I wish to see if I can make him falter."

Wickham walked over to replenish his drink. "I fear I should warn you that Fitzwilliam Darcy is definitely *not* his father and not nearly as malleable. You will not be able to lead him so easily."

"He is a man. I am a woman. If I can convince him to let me satisfy his carnal nature, I can ruin him just as I did George."

Wickham snorted. "You may be a very desirable woman, my dear, but if you think Fitzwilliam Darcy would *ever* dally with his late father's wife, you are badly mistaken."

"Is any man strong enough to resist this?"

George watched as the silk nightgown floated to the floor. Slowly sliding her hands from her naked breasts to her flat abdomen, Lady Henrietta swayed enticingly. Wickham set his glass down and rushed to her. Crushing Henrietta in his embrace, he kissed her forcefully. Then picking her up, he stalked towards the door.

"I thought not," she murmured into his neck.

Whilst servants scampered left and right, Wickham carried their employer out of the parlour, across the foyer and up the grand staircase as naked as the day she was born. Having been witness to her seduction of George Darcy, the servants were accustomed to Lady Henrietta's debauchery, but not caring that the male servants saw her naked went far beyond anything they had witnessed before.

After she and Wickham were completely out of sight, the servants crept out of the surrounding rooms to congregate at the foot of the stairs. They stared up at the first floor where the sounds of their employer's amorous affair filled the air. At length they looked at one another, eyes meeting silently. One by one, they returned to their duties as though nothing had happened.

A post inn near Cambridge
Early evening

All the other passengers had long since vacated the post coach by the time it reached the stop nearest Cambridge. The rain had let up at their last change of horses, but as soon as the vehicle stopped in front of the building and the driver climbed down to help Elizabeth out, the rain began again in earnest. Pulling his hat down over his face, the driver took her elbow, picked up her bag and assisted her up the steps of the porch.

"I suggest you rent a room until your family can come for you," he said. "In this weather, it may take them quite some time to get here."

"But...but, I cannot possibly stay here," Elizabeth protested. With no choice but to lie, she added, "I must reach my brother's house in Cambridge today. I had no time to write, so he will not know to come for me. He lives on Crown Street...close to the university." At the concerned look on the driver's face, she added, "Surely, that is not too much farther is it?"

"I am sorry, but I can only transport passengers from one post stop to another. Besides, according to a driver at the last inn, the bridge to Cambridge is almost under water, and the roads are practically impassable."

At that moment, two people walked out of the inn—a tall man of about forty and an older man who was much shorter. Seeing Elizabeth and her bag, the taller one crossed to her. "I am Mr. Owens, the innkeeper. I apologise, ma'am, but we have no more rooms for rent; however, my wife will gladly make a place for you in the kitchen, if you do not mind sleeping on a bench."

Before Elizabeth could reply, the coach driver said, "She wants to go on to the university today, Clyde."

"That is impossible!" Owens exclaimed. "There are no carriages available for hire, and the water is almost over the bridge. No horse will cross it."

"I tried to explain that to her," the driver interjected, adding, "I plan to sleep in the stables tonight, so I will see you in the morning." With that, he ran to the coach, climbed up on the seat and whipped the horses forward. Man and beasts rushed towards the stables, leaving Elizabeth staring after them.

Taking a deep breath, she lifted her head as she addressed the innkeeper. "Sir, I must get to Cambridge today. If I must walk, I will."

"Excuse me, but I could not help but overhear," the older man said, stepping forward. "I live in Cambridge, and I plan to return home today. If I may be so bold, you may ride with me if you wish."

As Elizabeth studied him, he doffed his hat and bowed. "Percy Crumley at your service. I have no choice but to get home since my mother depends on me. Besides, old Sam is not afraid of the water. He will cross the bridge."

At this pronouncement, Elizabeth studied the largest grey horse she had ever seen hitched to a wagon covered with a tarp that extended over the driver's seat. The animal seemed unfazed by the pouring rain.

"It is dangerous enough for you, Percy," the innkeeper cautioned. "Surely you are not suggesting that this young lady take the risk?"

"It is less dangerous than walking."

With no way to argue that point, the proprietor addressed Elizabeth. "It is entirely up to you, ma'am. I do not advise it, but if you are determined to get there today, Percy is likely your last hope. And I can vouch for him. I would trust him with my wife or daughter."

Elizabeth picked up her bag. "I am ready if you are, Mr. Crumley."

Chapter 3

Cambridge

William was miserable. Rainy days saddened him, and he could not remember the last time the sun had shone. Moreover, Mrs. Thornhill had not arrived that day as he had hoped, leaving him no choice but to stay another night. Having already finished reading a book John Lucas had left behind—*L'école des femmes*[1] by the French playwright Molière[1]—he resorted to re-reading old newspapers left from a stack used for packing breakable items. Getting bored, he spent another hour poring over a map and calculating how long it would take to travel to London via a different route, should it become necessary. Concluding that most other routes would add several days to the trip, he became even gloomier, for he was eager to see Georgiana.

With nothing left to distract him, William was forced to face the two issues now threatening to crush him: Pemberley's dire finances and his desire for Miss Elizabeth Bennet. In his mind those issues were intertwined. For whilst he had fought his attraction to Lucas' neighbour because of her unsuitability, it was only a year before he met Elizabeth that his father had been unable, or unwilling, to fight a similar attraction to a woman young enough to be his daughter. Subsequently, George Darcy had

---

1 **L'école des femmes** (The School for Wives) is a theatrical comedy written by the seventeenth century French playwright Molière and considered by some critics to be one of his finest achievements.

married Lady Henrietta and mortgaged Pemberley to pay off her gambling debts. Once the end results of his father's indulgence with Lady Henrietta were revealed, it changed everything.

The arguments he used to conquer his interest in Elizabeth Bennet—that her circumstances had ill-prepared her to be his wife and that his relations' scorn would crush the *joie de vivre* he had found so refreshing—were now moot points. He now had to marry a woman with a large dowry to replenish Pemberley's coffers. Nonetheless, the debutantes the Matlocks had found to be suitable candidates for a wife made him cringe, and he was loath to dwell on that subject. Pulling a paper from his pocket, he attempted to concentrate on it.

His steward, Sturgis, had prepared a list of what he felt might help replenish Pemberley's reserves. It included selling all the excess horses, cattle and sheep, letting unproductive tenants and servants go, and increasing the variety of crops planted to have produce to market in the fall. Other than an aging, unproductive estate in Weymouth once owned by William's great-grandmother, there was nothing left to sell and that estate would take hundreds of pounds to renovate before it could be put on the market. In conclusion, the steward suggested that William meet with his bankers to consolidate the loans his father had taken out, using the Darcy jewels as collateral. To that end, those jewels had been sent to London with a trusted servant and two guards and awaited him there.

Another of Sturgis' suggestions was to allow Lady Henrietta to continue to reside under Pemberley's roof, something Georgiana had begged him to do. The steward's reasoning was that if William forced her into the dower house, it would require more outlay for additional staff, albeit a small one. Consequently, though William desired to show his new mother the door, he agreed to let things continue as they were for now. At least this decision had made his sister very happy.

Having gone over the entire list, William was weary of contemplating his predicament. Standing, he stretched and walked to the front door, opened it and stepped out onto the porch. A mist covered everything, for the slow drizzle of the morning had transformed into another downpour, lowering the temperature. Shivering, he peered down both sides of the street. Seeing no signs of life and satisfied that he was alone, William went back inside, locked the door and added more wood to the fire he had started.

Deciding to go to bed, he removed the blanket from his trunk, lay down on the dilapidated sofa and reached for a bottle of brandy on a table he planned to leave for the next occupant. Taking several swallows, he went to blow out the candle, but thought better of it. Lying back on the sofa, he covered himself with the blanket, closed his eyes and prayed not to meet Elizabeth Bennet in his dreams again.

In short order the rain blowing against the windows lulled him into a restless slumber where, despite his prayer, he was once again riding to the top of Oakham Mount.

The road to Cambridge

Though the tarp over the wagon covered the driver's seat, Elizabeth was soaked to the bone after the rain began to blow sideways. It was still early, but due to the cloud cover the sky was almost black with the only illumination provided by frequent bolts of lightning. Just as they reached the bridge, a large bolt revealed an inordinate amount of water pooling ahead. Pulling Sam to a stop, Mr. Crumley slid to the ground.

"Where are you going?" Elizabeth shouted.

"To get a better look!" Crumley yelled as he hobbled into the darkness with the help of his cane. After what seemed like an eternity, he returned.

"The water has not yet reached the middle of the bridge. We must act quickly."

Though her heart was in her throat, Elizabeth nodded. After all, was this not what she wanted? As Crumley whipped the reins, urging Sam forward, she willed herself not to scream. Despite her worst fears, the horse confidently stepped into the water running over the end of the bridge. At one point she felt the wagon slide sideways, but undaunted, Sam kept going until they were above water in the middle of the bridge. With no time to waste, Mr. Crumley slapped the reins again. The gelding responded, and before long they were safe on the other bank.

Crumley gave Elizabeth a water-soaked grin. "I told you we could trust Sam!"

"And you were right," Elizabeth said, smiling with relief.

When they began down the road to Cambridge, the wagon slid from side to side in the mud, though neither occupant seemed worried. It was only after they entered the town that Mr. Crumley spoke again.

"What is the street and house number?"

Since she had often sent covert letters to John, Elizabeth knew the address by heart. "It is on Crown Street—number twenty-five."

"That is the main road in and out of town."

"It is. Might I ask where you live?"

"Only a mile or so on the other side of Cambridge."

When they reached their destination, Crumley was relieved to see a faint light in the window. As he went to climb off the wagon, however, Elizabeth reached for his arm.

"Please, you must not try to navigate these steep steps with your cane. You might fall, and I would feel dreadful if you were hurt. Furthermore, we would never find a physician in this weather. Wait here, and I shall wave to let you know all is well."

Giving Crumley no time to object, Elizabeth was on the ground and climbing the steps in mere seconds. Reaching the front door, she took a deep breath and rapped as hard as she could on the ornate wood. There was no answer. She tried again, this time rapping for a longer period of time. Still, no one answered. Fearful that Mr. Crumley might join her at the door and discover her lies, she decided that the glass panes might create more of a racket. Just as she began rapping on them, the door swung open to reveal a very dishevelled Mr. Darcy.

Seemingly unaffected, Elizabeth turned to smile and wave at Mr. Crumley. However, the second the wagon lunged forward, her smile disappeared. Just as William called out for the driver to stop, she shot past him without a word of greeting.

"Close the door!" she ordered as she began removing her soaked cloak.

Her command brought William fully awake. "Madam, I do not know what your intentions are, but I will have you know—"

Elizabeth closed the door herself.

Immersed in another argument with Elizabeth Bennet in his dreams, it had taken some time before the persistent rapping on the front door penetrated William's senses. In a daze, he rolled over only to realise too late he was not in his own bed. Hitting the hard floor, he managed to get on all fours before sitting back on his heels. When at last he stood, he weaved groggily towards the door where the glass panes were still vibrating.

Opening it, he was stunned to be confronted by a woman wearing mourning clothes. She had obviously arrived aboard the wagon on the street below, for when she turned and waved, the vehicle began to leave. William called for the driver to stop since she was clearly at the wrong house. Apparently, the driver did not hear, but whilst William was thus occupied, the woman rushed past him into the house.

Her command to close the door brought William fully awake. "Madam, I do not know what your intentions are, but I will have you know—"

At that instant, Elizabeth removed the bonnet and veil, cutting short his reprimand. His next words were uncharacteristically tongue-tied. "Miss...Miss Bennet, why are you dressed as—"

"As a widow? I shall explain later. Please do not fear for your fortune, Mr. Darcy. I did not come to see you. I came to see John. Would you please be so kind as to inform him that I am here?"

When William did not immediately reply, she declared, "Never mind, I shall find him myself."

Taking the candlestick from the table, Elizabeth went up the stairs, leaving William staring after her. Once she was out of sight, he concentrated on the sounds of her footsteps as she went from room to room. It was not long before the candle crossed the landing and headed back down the steps. Reaching the bottom, Elizabeth walked straight to him.

"Where is John? I thought he was to receive his diploma in two days."

"Graduates may now choose not to receive their diplomas in person, but rather have them sent by post. With the recent floods, most of my classmates have chosen that option and have left the area already. That includes John."

"He...he is not here?" Elizabeth asked incredulously.

"He left for Richmond yesterday."

"Richmond? Why would he go there? One would think he would go home to celebrate." She tried to smile but could not. "Do you think he will be long in Richmond?"

William's conversation with Lucas regarding Lady Aileen ran through his mind, including the fact that he was going to have wedding clothes made in London after leaving Richmond. "I could not say, but he stated that he may go to London when he leaves there."

Without realising it, Elizabeth began to clutch William's arm in desperation. "It is imperative I find him. Can you tell me where he is staying in Richmond?"

"I apologise, Miss Bennet, but I feel it is not my place to inform anyone of his plans."

Wearily, Elizabeth sat down on the sofa, no longer able to hold back her tears. "You must understand. My father is gravely injured and may die. My mother is using his accident to force me to marry a cousin I despise." She wiped her tearstained cheeks with the backs of her hands. "Papa gave me the funds for a ticket to Cambridge, so John could keep his promise to marry me."

William closed his eyes. Knowing full well the pain of losing a parent and the grief of being betrayed, his heart ached for her. Deciding that he must soften the blow, he said, "I fear I should caution you not to depend on Lucas to save you."

"Mr. Darcy, please do not speak to me in riddles. Just tell me what you mean."

He reached for her hand and gave it a tender squeeze. Watching Elizabeth's innocent ebony eyes grow even larger, he said, "I am sorry to have to tell you that John has fallen in love with another. Lady Aileen lives in Richmond, and John has travelled there to make her an offer."

Being totally exhausted, the news was too much, and she fainted.

William managed to catch Elizabeth and turn her so she lay on the sofa. Since he had no smelling salts, he tried to wake her by patting her cheek and calling her name, but there was no response. Not only was she unconscious, but he felt certain she had a fever—a result, perhaps, of being in wet clothes. As was his wont, he argued with himself about what to do next.

He had undressed Georgiana often enough. *Yes, but Georgiana was a child, and Elizabeth is not.* If I do, she will be compromised. *Being alone with you means she is already compromised.* She will hate me when she awakens. *Would you not rather make certain she lives to argue the point?*

In the end, William felt he had no choice. Kneeling beside the sofa, he began by removing her boots and then sliding her stockings down her legs. After that he rolled Elizabeth on her side and unfastened the buttons on the back of the voluminous black dress and those on the sleeves. Since it was much too large for her small frame, it slid easily off her arms, and he was able to remove the balance by tugging the dress from the hem. Using the same method, he removed both petticoats she wore. Once down to her shift—a thin muslin piece that left little to the imagination—he tried not to stare whilst he dried her with a towel but was not successful. When finished, he wrapped her wet hair in one of his shirts and her feet in another before tucking a blanket around her body and placed his greatcoat over her.

After adding more wood to the fire, he hung Elizabeth's wet clothes over the backs of chairs he brought from the kitchen and moved a rug to the floor beside the sofa, where he lay down. Suddenly conscious of the fact that this might be his only opportunity, he rose on his knees to study the only woman he had ever desired.

Though her eyes were closed, long black lashes were a reminder of the *fine eyes* he admired. Grudgingly, his gaze dropped to her nose. Unlike many women of his acquaintance, Elizabeth's nose was small and turned up slightly at the end. Being so near, he could also see a light sprinkling of freckles across the bridge—doubtless a result of walking without a bonnet. He smiled at the realisation that no woman of the *ton* would walk if they could avoid it, much less without using a parasol.

Like her other features, her ears were small and well formed. And, as his eyes traced the outline of one, it dawned on him that Elizabeth was eighteen now—the same age as the majority of debutants Lady Matlock had introduced to him of late. Recalling that he was expected to attend one of his aunt's soirées next week, William grimaced. He despised the fawning that passed for conversation at those events.

As he swept a wet curl from Elizabeth's forehead, a thought rushed to mind. *I have no doubt that you would never fawn over me.* Then, in frustration, his vigilant conscience declared, *Enough! Elizabeth Bennet is not of your sphere, and she has no dowry with which to help Pemberley!*

Reaching for the brandy, William drank half of what was left before lying down on the rug on the cold floor. The liquor had the desired effect, and he soon fell asleep to dream once again of Elizabeth.

Longbourn

The very hour Edward Gardiner received his sister's express informing him of his brother's accident, he had set out for Meryton. Arriving at Longbourn not long after Lizzy had departed for Cambridge, howbeit without her mother's knowledge, he was able to talk to Thomas before one of the physician's draughts rendered him incapable of staying awake.

After listening to what precipitated Lizzy's flight, Gardiner replied, "Whilst I disagree with sending my niece across England alone, I would never wish for her to marry Collins. Lizzy has always loathed his sycophantic disposition. How could Fanny be so mercenary? With Jane engaged to Bingley, what has she to fear?"

"Bingley will have no fortune until he is four and twenty, which is two years hence."

"Surely Fanny knows I would never let my family go without a home."

"And I, for one, am grateful for your generous spirit. Still, we both know it would be very hard for you to take them all in."

"I would do it gladly, Thomas. You must know that."

"What I need at this moment is for you to follow Lizzy. Make certain she finds Lucas, and they marry. In the bottom right drawer of my desk, underneath other correspondence, is a legal document I had drawn up some time ago. It authorizes you to act in my stead. I had hoped it would never be necessary, but take it and do what you must to help my Lizzy. You have the power to sign for me."

"If I am to be of any assistance, I must get on the road. Rumour has it that Cambridge is almost cut off by rising flood-water as it is."

"Go quickly before Fanny realises Lizzy is gone, else she will insist you find my daughter for her own selfish reasons. Write to Jane as soon as you know something, Edward."

"I will do as you ask, and I will address the letter as though it was written by Caroline Bingley. Hopefully, Fanny will not suspect a thing." Then he grasped Thomas Bennet's hand. "Listen to your physician and fight with all your strength. Lizzy needs you, as do all my nieces."

"I will, Edward. I promise you, I will."

With that, he rushed to Mr. Bennet's study to find the letter. After he had located it, he explained to Fanny that he had made a quick trip just to check on her husband's progress and had to return to London straightaway.

In less than an hour, Edward Gardiner was on the way to Cambridge.

London
Darcy House

Mr. and Mrs. Barnes had served as the butler and housekeeper for the last twenty years at Darcy House and both had seen many changes, but nothing had been as disconcerting as the day Lady Henrietta arrived as the new mistress. Whilst they were fiercely loyal to the Darcys, neither liked George Darcy's new wife, and their relationship with her had deteriorated even further when they noticed her trying to capture the heir of Pemberley's attention. Though neither was prone to gossip, they kept a sharp eye on her, which was one reason Mrs. Barnes intercepted Lady Henrietta in the foyer upon her return that afternoon.

Noting that once again her mistress smelled of brandy mixed with a man's cologne, that her face was flushed and her hair dishevelled, the housekeeper tried not to show her disgust. "Where is Miss Darcy, madam? I was expecting her to return with you, so I instructed Cook to expect her for dinner."

Lady Henrietta did not acknowledge the housekeeper as she walked past her across the foyer, but suddenly she stopped and turned. "I have not spoken to Georgiana today, but I am certain that the Earl and Countess of Matlock will feed her before they send her home, no matter when that may be. You need not worry about her. Now, instruct the servants to prepare a bath, for I am exhausted. I plan to bathe, eat and retire early."

With that pronouncement, the brazen woman ascended the grand staircase unsteadily.

Watching until she was completely out of sight, Mrs. Barnes recalled Lady Henrietta declaring that morning that she was going to Matlock House to fetch Georgiana.

I imagine spending the day with the man who wears that awful cologne must be tiring.

Making a mental note to add this lie to the journal she kept on Mrs. Darcy, Mrs. Barnes went in search of her husband. It was his place to order the footmen to take water up for the bath, whilst it was her place to see that it was heated. Tonight she meant to make certain that when her mistress stepped into her bath it was barely warm.

A post inn near Cambridge

It was dark by the time Edward Gardiner stepped out of his coach at the last post inn before Cambridge. Had he not been in his own vehicle, he was certain he would not have made it this far since no other vehicles were foolish enough to be on the road. Furthermore, because of the mud and rain it had taken them longer than usual to travel this distance. Shouting for his driver and footmen to take the coach on to the stables, he walked into the inn. Noting that the common room was full of people resting in every conceivable spot, he was not surprised when the innkeeper said he had no rooms available.

Apologetic that he could not provide a man of his age with a bed, Mr. Owens said, "You are welcome to sleep wherever you can find a place. I believe there are a few blankets left, if you need one."

"That would be most kind of you," Mr. Gardiner replied. "And, if I could bother you for a moment more, I am trying to find my niece. She was just ahead of me on the road, and I hoped I might find her here."

As he began to describe Elizabeth in the mourning clothes, the proprietor's eyes lit up. "How could I forget? Even after I explained to her that the bridge was almost under water, the lady was determined to get to Cambridge today."

"Are you saying she is not here?"

"Precisely. An old friend who lives on the other side of Cambridge had to get home to his mother, and he offered to let her ride with him."

Gardiner's eyes went wide. "Do you know if they were successful in crossing?"

"I pray they were, but no one will know until the rain lets up.

Still, if anyone could do it, it would be old Crumley. That horse of his is not afraid of anything."

"How could you have allowed her to leave?"

The innkeeper recoiled. "I am not in charge of telling folk what they can and cannot do, sir. And I would trust my own mother with Percy Crumley."

Gardiner instantly calmed. "Forgive me. It is just—I am very fond of my niece and ..."

When he was unable to continue, Owens interjected. "I understand, sir. I did try to persuade her to remain, but she was determined."

"I suppose I have no choice but to wait until morning to see if the bridge held."

Just then, an older woman sitting nearby approached Mr. Gardiner. "Excuse me. Did I hear you say you were going to try to cross the bridge into Cambridge in the morning?"

"Yes."

"I must get to the university to collect the rent on a house I own." Her eyes fell to the floor. "With my son's death, it is left to me to handle such things. It would be a great help to me if my maid and I could cross with you."

Gardiner smiled. "Providing the water has receded and we are able to cross the bridge safely, I have no objections."

"I thank you. My name is Thornhill...Mrs. Thaddeus Thornhill. I will be at the table on the left all night. Please wake me if I should be asleep when you are ready to leave."

"I will."

When the old woman returned to her maid and sat down, Gardiner turned his attention back to the innkeeper. "Is it possible to get something to eat? I have not eaten in hours and neither have my servants."

"We are out of the pheasant and vegetables my wife cooked for dinner, but we usually have plenty of bread, cold chicken and cheese. How many servants do you have?"

"Just two."

"Tell them to come into the kitchen—they can use the back

door if they come from the stables. Would a fresh cup of tea help the food go down?"

"It would, indeed!"

"Your servants are welcome to sleep in the stables. I do not think they will mind, since there is plenty of fresh hay for bedding. You are welcome to stay in the common area with the others who do not have rooms."

"My servants will be glad to be out of the rain, as will I. Thank you for sheltering us."

"I am glad to be of service."

Chapter 4

Cambridge
The next morning

Winter had been harsh and lasted longer than usual. Spring followed its lead, for though it was the beginning of May, the weather was unseasonably cold. There was some food—bread, jam and cheese—but William had been so certain the water would recede as quickly as it had in the past that he had not bothered to stock the larder, which was nearly empty because he had planned to be on his way to London. Thankful that the house he had rented was on higher elevation, he feared that if the water did not recede soon he might have to trespass on the nearby houses to scavenge for provisions since the shops in town were closed because of the flooding.

Wood for the fire was nearly depleted, too. Though he had added some to the fire in the early morning hours, it had not been enough to provide any real warmth. Fearing Elizabeth's fever might grow worse if the house were any colder, he concluded that raiding his neighbours' woodsheds was preferable to having her suffer; thus, he decided he would appropriate what wood he could find today before riding out to check the bridge.

Crossing to the sofa where Elizabeth lay sleeping, a slight smile crossed his face as he realised she was still wearing his shirts wrapped around her head and feet, as well as his great coat. Glancing at his own apparel, he was embarrassed to note that the shirt he wore was smudged with dirt from carrying wood, and mud marred his breeches and boots. Even so, he resisted the urge to don clean clothes because Elizabeth might need the contents of his trunk to stay warm.

Noting how peaceful she looked, William's thoughts flew to the madness that would ensue if society learned they were here alone. Had she not arrived when she did, he would likely have forsaken Mrs. Thornhill and ridden Zeus north to find a way around the water. Now that was no longer an option. Even if Elizabeth could ride with him, her fever dictated she stay out of the weather, and each day they were trapped increased the chances of being discovered.

Deciding he had sufficient worries at present, William pushed the possibility of that happening to the back of his mind. Exiting the front door, he crossed the lawn to the woodshed next door.

When at last Elizabeth's eyes fluttered open, she became frightened. Lying perfectly still, it took a moment to remember where she was. When she did, she sat up, making the great coat fall to the floor. Mortified to discover that she wore only her shift, she grabbed the blanket, tied it around her like a cloak and stood up. With her heart racing like a drum, she walked barefooted to the black dress hanging over a nearby chair. It was still damp, as were the petticoats. Only her stockings were dry, and grabbing them, she sat back down and began hurriedly pulling them on.

At that instant, William came through the door from the kitchen with arms full of wood. Upon seeing Elizabeth, he froze. Incensed, Elizabeth left off donning the stockings and stood to face him with only the blanket for cover.

"I hope you have a good explanation as to why I am unclothed," she said frostily.

The sight of her long dark hair hanging almost to her waist rendered William speechless.

Seeing his expression, Elizabeth self-consciously pulled the blanket closer. "Sir, I asked for an explanation."

This declaration, louder than the first, garnered William's attention. "I...I have no explanation other than the fact that you were soaked to the bone. I feared you might become ill if—"

"That was not your decision to make!"

Instantly, William's Master of Pemberley persona surfaced. He placed the wood beside the hearth. "That is where you are mistaken, Miss Bennet. You were unable to speak for yourself; thus, I was required to act. I did what I thought was sensible after you fainted."

The change in his demeanour put Elizabeth off guard. "I ... I fainted?"

"You did."

"Still, I would have been perfectly fine wearing—"

"You already have a fever."

Elizabeth's hand flew to her flushed forehead. "Do I?" Then remembering that she was angry, she sputtered, "I...I feel well enough."

"We are trapped in this house with little food and one blanket. My worry is that your fever may worsen if you are not kept warm and fed." He went back into the kitchen and returned with a tray holding a cup of lukewarm tea and a roll with a piece of cheese in it. "You must eat if you are to recover."

Something about his manner made her reluctant to refuse and Elizabeth took the cup. Swallowing her pride, as well as the tea, she reached for the roll and took a bite. "Thank you."

William nodded. Whilst she ate, he watched. Unsettled under his gaze, she kept her eyes diverted until at length he spoke. "What will you do now? It will be impossible to leave until the water recedes."

"I have no idea." Trying not to tear up, she added, "I suppose I have no choice but to travel on to my uncle's home in Cheapside once I am able. He and my aunt have always been very kind. They will not turn their backs on me."

"But since your father is—" Seeing tears fill her eyes, he said gently, "In his current condition, your father may not be able to thwart your mother's plans. Will your uncle rise to the challenge and defend you?"

"I have no idea. But this I know—no one can force me to marry Mr. Collins."

"Collins? William Collins, the new vicar at Hunsford?"

"One and the same."

"I can certainly understand your reluctance. According to my cousin, he is a toadying fool."

His words elicited a smile. "Your cousin is very insightful."

"Colonel Fitzwilliam is that, as well as unafraid to speak his mind."

"He sounds like a gentleman after my own heart," Elizabeth said. Then she added, flippantly, "Is he married?"

Disappointed with where this conversation was going, William replied, "He is a second son; he must marry someone with a large dowry."

Elizabeth had been teasing, but William's answer immediately crushed her spirit. She needed no reminder of her place. "Would you please leave the room, so I may dress?"

"In what? Your clothes are still damp."

"I have other clothes in my bag."

"I did not see a bag," William stated, looking around. Then he spied something on the floor next to the front door. "Ah, there it is."

After bringing it to Elizabeth, she began removing the contents of the carpet covered bag. "Oh, dear! It got wet as well. All my clothes are damp."

"I have a nightshirt in my trunk. It is much too large for you, so I think it would make a satisfactory gown. That is, if you wish to use it."

"Show me."

After William fetched and held up the nightshirt, she nodded. He was right. It was almost as long as she was tall. Sighing, she said, "You have convinced me. Now, if you will leave, I will change clothes."

"After you are presentable you will find me in the kitchen."

The second he disappeared, Elizabeth donned the nightshirt, relieved once again to be in dry clothes. Then she went into the kitchen to find William putting on his gloves.

"Where are you going?"

"I wish to see how the bridge to London is faring."

Elizabeth ran back into the parlour and returned with his great coat. "You will need this," she said, holding it out.

"Thank you," William replied, giving her a slight smile. Donning the coat, he went to the back door. "I shall try not to be gone too long. Keep the doors locked."

A post inn near Cambridge
The stable

"There you are!" Clyde Owens cried as he approached Edward Gardiner. "I thought I would find you here."

Elizabeth's uncle, who had been conversing with his driver, turned to greet the innkeeper. "I simply cannot wait any longer for the rain to let up. The clouds will ensure darkness comes early again. My driver and I were trying to determine if the coach could handle the amount of mud on the road if we drive to the bridge."

"I have news for you," Owens said. "Mr. Crumley is at the inn. He crossed the bridge less than a half-hour ago, and he allows that although both ends are still under water, he was able to cross. Of course, he has the advantage of a heavy wagon and a sturdy horse."

"Is that the man who took my niece across?"

"It is. Percy is a good man, if sometimes a bit too brave for my taste. He will be returning to Cambridge after he rests for a while, and I suggest that if you are determined to go, you ride with him."

"Why would he risk crossing it repeatedly?"

"I own a small warehouse in Cambridge where I sell goods to the public, as well as store supplies for the inn. Whenever I need goods, I pay Crumley to transport them here. Knowing that a good many people might seek shelter from the storm under my roof, he feared I could run out of foodstuffs—flour, cornmeal and such; thus, he brought me a fresh supply. He must return to the city for the sake of his mother who is there. As soon as we are done unloading the wagon and he has had something to eat and a bit of rest, he will return home."

"I should be most grateful to meet him."

"If you will accompany me to the inn, I will introduce you."

In a few hours or so, Mr. Crumley, Mr. Gardiner, Mrs. Thornhill and her maid were heading towards the bridge in Crumley's wagon. Whilst the women sat under the tarp in the back of the wagon on benches, Mr. Gardiner sat on the seat beside the owner.

"Tell me," Edward Gardiner said, "was the water lower today than when you crossed the bridge with my niece?"

"I would say so. But to tell the truth, it was so dark when we crossed that I could not see well enough to make a fair comparison. I will say that the mud is much worse though. Sam is having more difficulty walking today."

Mr. Gardiner's heavy sigh garnered a sideways glace from Crumley. "I would never have taken the lady across except that she was determined to get there."

"My niece is nothing if not determined. She wanted to reach her fiancé who has just graduated from the university."

"Oh? She told me it was her brother she was trying to reach."

Fearing he had let too much slip, Edward added quickly, "Yes...well...her brother and her fiancé share the house."

Satisfied, Percy Crumley tilted his head towards those in the back, saying quietly, "I do not understand why Mrs. Thornhill could not wait until the floods subside."

Mr. Gardiner leaned closer to Crumley. "She said she needs to collect the rent from her tenant, a student, before he leaves for the term." [2]

"For her sake, I hope he is still there," Crumley said. "With the threat from the water rising, most of the students left days ago."

---

2 In researching terms at Cambridge, I found evidence that in 1819 an Easter term ended on July 9th. Cambridge seemed to have 3 terms as opposed to Oxford which had four, and the next term at Cambridge would start in October. For purposes of this story, I am ending the term at the end of April.

"I cannot say I blame them. By the way, when should I expect you to come back for us?"

"Are you certain you want to return to the inn?"

"I am certain I do not wish to be stranded in Cambridge."

"In that case, I shall attempt to return about this same time tomorrow. With any luck, the bridge may be above water. If I do not return, you will just have to wait until the water goes down."

It was almost an hour before the bridge in question loomed ahead. Edward Gardiner's heart began to beat faster as it became clear that water was still streaming over parts of it. He swallowed hard. "I pray your horse is as sure-footed as you say he is."

"Do not worry about old Sam! He will take us across safely, just you wait and see."

I am afraid I have no choice, Mr. Gardiner thought.

Cambridge
The rental house

Elizabeth stood at the front window for what seemed like hours. She had expected William back before now and could not help craning her neck in a bid to catch sight of him. Just as she began to think he may have run into trouble, a fit of coughing seized her. Pulling one of William's initialled handkerchiefs from a pocket, she covered her mouth.

Once the coughing ended, Elizabeth heaved a sigh of relief. *I am glad you are not here Mr. Darcy; else, along with this slight fever, you would insist I go straight to bed.*

Even though his officiousness annoyed her, thanks to John Lucas, she better understood his manners. After what happened in Meryton, she had been so vocal in her dislike of the man that Lucas had revealed the enormous number of servants and tenants who fell under William's protection, in addition to his family. Though she allowed that such responsibilities could make one overbearing, she did not appreciate when he acted as though everyone was under his authority, including Mr. Bingley and, of late, herself.

Suddenly, it came to mind that this evening would mark twenty-four hours in each other's company with no chaperone. Well versed in the price to be paid should they be found out, the thought of being forced to marry that gentleman caused her to shiver. Oddly enough, Elizabeth shivered not because she found him as despicable as she had at their first meeting. Though she would never forgive his opposition to Bingley's attachment to Jane or his disparagement of her family, that taciturn, prejudiced and authoritarian gentleman had been unfailingly kind to her throughout this entire ordeal—even insisting that she plunder his trunk to keep warm. Recalling his graciousness, Elizabeth looked down. The realisation that she was wearing one of his frock coats over one of her newly dried gowns made her smile at the absurdity of it all.

She looked back up just in time to see Zeus rounding the corner of the house. Rushing to the hearth, she removed a pot of water she had put on to boil and took it to the kitchen. Certain that William would appreciate something warm, she made a fresh pot of tea with what was left of the leaves. Not long afterwards he knocked on the back door, and she hurried to open it. She was shocked at how pale and gaunt he looked, but before she could enquire about his health, he began to explain.

"With all the water standing at the bridge, it is impossible to tell exactly where the road lies. Only the middle of the structure is visible, and Zeus was too on edge to press him to cross it."

As he was talking, William removed his hat, great coat, gloves and lastly a scarf he had wrapped around his neck since he had not bothered to don a cravat. Instantly mesmerized by the sight of his uncovered neck and chest, especially the dark hair visible above the first button of his shirt, Elizabeth stared unwittingly. When at last it dawned on her that she was staring, she quickly turned and began to pour the tea.

"I...I thought you might need this," she said, holding out the cup.

A slight smile lifted the corners of William's mouth. Taking the cup with both hands to warm them, he sat down. After a sip of the weak liquid, he said, "This may be the best tea I have ever tasted."

Elizabeth smiled crookedly. "Surely you jest."

"Given our current circumstances, it tastes heavenly."

She took a sip from the cup she poured for herself. "I agree." Then she glanced away. "This is the last of the tea, and the food will likely be gone tomorrow."

"If nothing changes, I will have no choice but to search the neighbouring houses. I know the residents on this street have left Cambridge, but perhaps there will be some tea or a tin of biscuits in one of them." More circumspectly, he added, "I despise taking things that are not mine, even if I may be starving."

"Surely, no one would begrudge a person food in similar circumstances."

"Someone kind would not. Still, I plan to leave payment if I find anything of use or damage a window gaining entrance."

Having said that, William dropped his head into his hands and rubbed his forehead wearily. Elizabeth took note of his appearance.

"You look exhausted."

"I am tired, but what of you? Do you still have a fever?"

Not wanting him to worry, Elizabeth lied. "No. I have only a slight cough to show for my foolishness, but I imagine you are weak from not having eaten whilst you made certain I did. And, your exhaustion comes from sleeping on the cold, hard floor, whilst I slept on the sofa. I insist that you eat right this minute. Then you will remove your coat and waistcoat and lie down on the sofa and rest."

Elizabeth offered William a sliced roll with cheese, as well as a stern glare that told him she would brook no opposition. Too weary to argue, he ate whilst she poured him another cup of tea.

"Whilst you rest, I plan to read a book with the help of this candle and what little light filters through the front windows." Grinning, she held up the candle. "At least we have lots of these."

"For that you can thank my valet. Adams brought enough candles for a year when he accompanied me last term," William said with a smile. Then his brows furrowed. "I am at a loss as to what you found to read though."

"I hope you do not mind, but I found this in your trunk. She held up Lucas' copy of *L'école des femmes*."

"But it is written in French."

"I know. There is one in my father's library. I have read it, but it is interesting enough to read again."

William smiled wryly. "I am amazed you read French and astonished you would find the subject interesting."

"Do not be, Mr. Darcy," she said, smiling mischievously. "My father provided me with a thorough education and I assure you that I have read far more *interesting* subject matter in both French and Italian."

Busily removing her things from the sofa, Elizabeth did not catch the look of admiration in his eyes. "There! Now lie down," she exclaimed, stepping aside.

William did as he was told. "Wake me if I am still asleep when night falls. I do not want you to sleep on the floor."

Elizabeth spread the blanket over him. "I will."

"Promise me," he murmured sleepily.

"I promise."

Later

Finished reading and growing drowsy, Elizabeth noticed there was no longer any light coming through the windows. Night would soon encompass them, and it was time to wake Mr. Darcy. Standing, she stretched, lifted her shoulders and rolled her head in every direction to loosen tight muscles. Then she walked into the parlour.

Astounded that William made no noises like her father did when he slept, Elizabeth crept closer. He was sleeping on his side and she had an unobstructed view of his face. Without the frown lines always present when he was awake, he looked so approachable that she was struck by how handsome he was. Charlotte Lucas had talked of nothing else for months after his visit to Lucas

Lodge, and only now could Elizabeth admit the truth to herself. She had dismissed her friend's adoration as schoolgirl infatuation, but though Fitzwilliam Darcy had many faults, being unattractive was not one of them.

Suddenly he moaned as though in pain. Feeling responsible for his present condition, Elizabeth decided she could not interrupt his rest. Then, out of the blue it dawned on her—there was enough room for her to lie beside him on the sofa if she was very careful.

Do I dare? After all, I promised him I would not sleep on the floor.

Deciding it was worth being embarrassed if he woke and found her, she lay down. His body was so warm that she had to resist the urge to get closer and, in only a few minutes, Elizabeth was as sound asleep as he.

Traversing through mud growing deeper by the day had slowed their progress and the day was quickly getting dark by the time Mr. Crumley's wagon entered the outskirts of Cambridge. He turned to address the lady inside his wagon. "Mrs. Thornhill, what address are you seeking? I must decide which is closer—your house or the one where I left Mr. Gardiner's niece."

"I happen to own two houses, but the one I rent is at twenty-five Crown Street,"

Crumley leaned back to hear more clearly. "Excuse me, but did you say twenty-five Crown?"

"I did."

Crumley laughed, catching Mr. Gardiner's attention. "May I ask why you find that amusing?"

"It is amusing because you and Mrs. Thornhill are headed to the same house. I left your niece at that residence yesterday!"

Anxiety overwhelmed Edward Gardiner. Quickly looking back to see if Mrs. Thornhill had overheard, he decided she had not. Still, by bringing along someone he had initially pitied, he had inadvertently jeopardised Lizzy's reputation. Mrs. Thornhill was not totally without funds, as he had first thought, but was, in fact, a member of a prominent family. He knew this because she had shared information that was none of his business, or anyone else's, last night as they sat at a table in the common room of the inn before he slept.

Mr. Gardiner's mind raced with thoughts of what to do when they reached the house where Lizzy was staying. However, he had little time to make plans before the wagon began rolling into Cambridge. They passed several cross streets before Mr. Crumley pulled the vehicle to a stop in front of a large, brick house on a hill.

"This is it!" Mr. Crumley proclaimed proudly. "Number twenty-five Crown!"

"I shall go to the door to ascertain that someone is present," Mr. Gardiner announced, adding with authority, "Wait here!"

As he climbed down from the wagon, he prayed that Mrs. Thornhill would obey. The instant he reached the door he began to knock. Getting no answer, he cupped his hands around his eyes and peered through a glass panel. It was useless, for the house was too dark inside.

Meanwhile, wondering why Mr. Gardiner had taken it upon himself to check on her tenant, Mrs. Thornhill also instructed Mr. Crumley to wait and followed Mr. Gardiner to the door. The second time he knocked Edward got no answer before Mrs. Thornhill declared, "Step aside."

Turning to find her right behind him, Mr. Gardiner had no choice but to do as she asked. Producing a key from the sleeve of her gown, she proceeded to open the door and walk in with Elizabeth's uncle right on her heels.

A faint light could be seen coming from another room. "Please wait here in case your tenant is not properly dressed. I shall see if I can rouse him," said Mr. Gardiner.

Once in the other room, he waited for his eyes to adjust to the flickering light from a candle almost burnt through. When they did, he could see the form of somebody lying on the sofa and crossed the room to there. Mr. Gardiner was about to address the occupant when he realised what he was looking at. Lizzy was lying on the sofa next to an unfamiliar man, who had one arm over her. Totally forgetting about Mrs. Thornhill, righteous indignation took control of his temper.

"Lizzy! What in the world is going on?"

At the commotion, both William and Elizabeth immediately sat up. First to her feet, Elizabeth looked dishevelled, her hair down and uncombed, her clothes a mixture of hers and Mr. Darcy's. Still drowsy, she swayed unsteadily.

"Un...Uncle? What are you doing here?"

"First, I think you had best explain what *you* are doing!" Mr. Gardiner declared. Then to the man now standing beside his niece in an equally dishevelled state, he asked, "Who, pray tell, are you?"

"Mr. Darcy!" came a cry from somewhere behind. That was followed by Mrs. Thornhill's entrance into the room.

Her shrill cry roused William completely. "Please, forgive my—*our* appearance. If we are not properly dressed, it is a result of being stranded here for so long without—"

"And this is your defence?" Mrs. Thornhill declared, cutting him off. "I am to believe that you were both lying on the sofa and nothing improper happened?"

William's reply was vehement. "Miss Bennet is not *that* kind of woman!"

"Miss Bennet, you say?" Eyeing Elizabeth, the landlady turned to Mr. Gardiner. "Is this your niece?"

"Yes, it is," Mr. Gardiner replied self-consciously. "Elizabeth, this is Mrs. Thornhill. She is the owner of this house."

Almost paralysed with apprehension, Elizabeth nodded.

"May I assume Mr. Darcy is not your brother, Miss Bennet?" the landlady said.

"You may."

"Then since John Lucas is the only other tenant authorized to be in the house, is it possible that *he* is your brother?"

Mr. Gardiner cringed as Elizabeth replied, "I have no brothers."

Giving Mr. Gardiner a sharp look, Mrs. Thornhill's head swung back to William. "On top of this entire matter being unseemly, Mr. Darcy, your lease states that no ladies of the—" William's expression grew darker, so she reconsidered what she was about to say. "That no *women* are allowed. The penalty is one hundred pounds and eviction."

"I will gladly accept the penalty to end this argument."

"Which is reasonable," Mrs. Thornhill said. She frowned at Elizabeth. "I hope you have learned a lesson, Miss Bennet. Your folly in coming to Cambridge without a chaperone was not without cost to Mr. Darcy."

William straightened to his full height. "Miss Bennet and I are engaged. Confusion about our plans to elope to Gretna Green after my graduation brought her here. That, and the fact that the weather had other plans, caused this entire fiasco."

Shocked at William's pronouncement, Elizabeth's mouth went dry, and she lost all ability to speak. Meanwhile, the landlady was suddenly all smiles.

"Oh, dear me!" she said, fanning herself with one hand. "An elopement—how romantic."

There was nothing for Edward Gardiner to do but support Mr. Darcy's account. Embellishing Mr. Bennet's instructions, he said, "Mr. Darcy, naturally Elizabeth's father was very upset when he learned she had left Longbourn. Still, he wants only her happiness. Therefore, he granted me permission to act in his stead when he sent me in search of my niece. I was instructed to observe the ceremony and sign as a witness in his place."

Panic-stricken, Elizabeth tried to change the direction in which the discussion was heading. "But, Uncle, we—Mr. Darcy and I—we decided to wait and be married with all our family present."

"Oh no, no, no!" Mrs. Thornhill said, clucking her tongue. "My dear, it is far too late for that. A young lady's reputation is very fragile and not to be trifled with. Though a romantic notion may have precipitated your journey here, the fact that you and Mr. Darcy have been without a chaperone for so long would create a scandal."

"But...but we are the only ones who know," Lizzy argued delicately. "If none of us say anything, then no one will be the wiser."

"Your youth betrays you," Mrs. Thornhill said authoritatively. "For you are badly mistaken. Everyone at the inn knows you were coming here, and Mr. Crumley let it be known he left you here with a man. Surely someone is aware that Mr. Darcy of Pemberley was stranded in Cambridge and—" she clucked her tongue again, "so you see that will never do. Mr. Gardiner said you are one of five sisters. You may not care about your reputation, but what about theirs? If you are ruined, you ruin their chances for a good match. Do not despair, however, for I insist on being a witness to your ceremony so I may personally thwart any gossip that may arise later."

"I am afraid she is right, Lizzy," Mr. Gardiner announced, sympathetically patting his niece's arm. He leaned closer. "I am sorry, but you left me no choice."

Addressing William, he said loudly, "Mr. Darcy, I should like to speak to you privately."

William glanced at Elizabeth, who implored him with her eyes to stop this madness. Yet as much as he wished to reassure her, he could not. There seemed no resolution to their predicament except to take the honourable route, even if it meant he would wed the only woman who had never wanted him. Taking a shaky breath, he followed her uncle into the kitchen.

As they left, Mrs. Thornhill declared, "Do not be too long, gentlemen. Mr. Crumley is waiting to take me to my house on University Street. It is well-stocked with firewood and supplies, and I insist that all of you come. At least there we will not starve whilst we wait for the water to recede."

Chapter 5

London
Four days later

As he exited Hoby's's[3] on St. James Street, Charles Bingley was so caught up in admiring his new boots that he ran right into another customer who was just arriving.

"Excuse me, sir, I was not—" Recognising the one he had assaulted, Bingley immediately ceased his apology. "Lucas! What in the world are you doing here? Just days ago you declared you were off to Richmond to propose to Lady Aileen. Do you require a new pair of court shoes for your wedding?"

With a grimace, Lucas looked away. "No. As it happens, I will not be in need of new shoes or clothes."

"Oh?"

"The lady refused my offer."

"I...I do not know what to say, old man, except that I am sorry."

"Do not be," Lucas replied with a sheepish smile. "In hind-

---

3 **Hoby** - Perhaps the most famous of all the London boot makers was George Hoby, whose shop was at the top of St James's Street. He was famous for producing the iconic Wellington boot to the duke's specific requirements. `https://janeaustenslondon.com/category/shopping/

sight, I believe I was very fortunate *not* to have secured the woman's hand."

"Then it has turned out for the best. May I ask, are you planning to return to Meryton soon?"

Lucas smiled wanly. "I believe you wish to see Jane Bennet more than you wish to visit my family."

Bingley smiled. "I do not deny it. Though I treasure your friendship, my purpose in going would be to see Miss Bennet."

"At least you are honest!" Lucas replied. "Alas, I am not ready to return yet. I had my solicitor draw up some papers which I must now cancel, and truthfully, I think a few days in London might lift my spirits."

"If anything can lift your spirits, it is London! By the way, I was just at Darcy House and Mrs. Barnes told me he is not in residence. I thought our friend was coming here directly after graduation."

"He likely got stuck in Cambridge awaiting his landlady. She insisted on inspecting the house and picking up the last month's rent. And you know Darcy. He can be much too accommodating at times."

"That is because Darcy takes his role as a gentleman seriously," Charles said with a laugh. "For my sake he even tolerates my sister's attempts to curry his favour. Lord knows I have tried to make Caroline cease her scheming, but I have had no success."

Recalling Bingley's sister, Lucas had to smile. "That is Darcy—decorous to a fault."

Suddenly Bingley's expression darkened. "Do you think him in any danger? Rumour has it all roads to Cambridge are flooded, with one bridge having washed away entirely—the one to Newmarket, if I remember correctly."

"Your memory serves you well. That bridge washed away before I left, and last I heard the bridge to London was almost under water."

"Darcy is nothing if not cautious. I fear we may not see him for a sennight or more then," Charles replied.

"I agree. He and I are to share a supper at White's once he arrives. Would you care to join us? I would be glad to let you know when the arrangements are made."

"What a splendid idea! I am staying at my brother's home on Grosvenor Street. He and Louisa are not in Town at present, and I have the house to myself. Just send a note around when the meeting is set."

"I shall see you then," Lucas said, giving Bingley a half-hearted smile before hurrying into the boot-maker's shop.

As Charles watched him leave, he recalled his newly purchased boots and glanced down at them. With a wide smile on his face, he strutted towards Hatchard's[4] to pick up a book Louisa had ordered. To say he was pleased when other occupants of London noticed his new footwear would be an understatement.

Darcy House

As Richard walked into the house, Mrs. Barnes hurried to greet him. "Major Fitzwilliam!" A hand flew to her mouth. "Forgive me. I meant to say Colonel Fitzwilliam."

"No need to apologise; I have not gotten used to my new rank either."

Mrs. Barnes smiled appreciatively. "I was so relieved when I heard Mr. Darcy had sent for you."

The colonel tensed at this pronouncement. "Relieved? Is something wrong with Darcy? Is he ill?"

"Not ill, no. But—" She hesitated.

Richard leaned in closer. "Mrs. Barnes, our collusion with regards to matters of importance concerning Darcy has been and will always be our secret."

"I do not doubt that. However, in this case I know so little

4 [4] **Hatchards** - is the oldest bookshop in the United Kingdom, founded at 173 Piccadilly, London, by John Hatchard in 1797. It moved within Piccadilly in 1801, to No.189–190. This shop had a numbering change to 187 in 1820. It still trades today from the same address. Hatchard's portrait can be seen on the staircase of the shop. https://en.wikipedia.org/wiki/Hatchards

about what is happening that I have no choice but to pray that he opens up to you."

"I understand. Is he in his study?"

"No, sir. He is in his suite. Do you wish me to announce you?"

"That is not necessary. I shall just go up and see what is so important that I missed a meeting with General Lassiter to rush over here."

As the colonel ascended the grand staircase, the housekeeper considered how different the cousins were in appearance. Whilst Mr. Darcy was tall and dark with light blue eyes, Richard was average height, with light brown hair and eyes. Still, they were as close as brothers and seeing the colonel this morning lifted a great weight from her shoulders. He had long been her ally in keeping circumstances beyond Darcy's control from sending him spiralling into the melancholy that had shadowed him most of his life. It had taken him years to recover from his mother's death, only to be battered again when his father married that calculating widow and all too quickly left him facing financial ruin upon his death.

Mrs. Barnes feared that she had never needed Richard more than now, for only this morning the Master had instructed her to prepare a wedding breakfast for a small party tomorrow. He offered no explanation, other than he was to marry an Elizabeth Bennet at eleven, and the wedding party would arrive shortly thereafter. Then he disappeared, leaving her to speculate on what might have occurred. As a result, several images were swirling in her head, not the least of which was that Mr. Darcy was being coerced into marriage by a fortune hunter.

Perhaps the colonel can talk some sense into him. I cannot believe my dear boy would marry a woman he has never once bothered to mention. And, with so few expected for the breakfast, it would seem that most of his relations will not be a party to it.

With a heavy sigh, she returned to the kitchen to supervise the preparations for the event she was dreading.

Reaching Darcy's bedroom, Richard knocked once before entering, as was his custom. Surprised to find his cousin's tailor taking measurements of his client at that hour, he crossed the room to a large, overstuffed chair, sank down into the comfortable fabric and placed his feet upon a stool. He watched silently as the tailor called out numbers whilst his apprentice wrote them down, and when at length the exercise halted, he spoke.

"Getting a new suit to impress the debutantes at mother's ball, Cousin?"

"No!" William replied sharply. "I lost weight, and Mr. Todd is simply altering this one." Removing the coat, he handed it to the tailor. "Do you have everything you need?"

"I do."

"Excellent. I expect you here precisely at seven in the morning."

Nodding, the tailor and his assistant hurried into the hall and closed the door.

"The reason you sent for me must be of great importance if you cannot speak of it in front of Todd. That man fitted you for your first pair of breeches."

"This is no occasion for levity, Richard. I have much to say and very little time in which to say it."

The colonel lowered his feet from the stool to sit up straight. "If I did not know better, I would think you were about to say you are planning an elopement to Gretna Green."

"More precisely, I am getting married, but in Cheapside, not Gretna Green."

"Good Lord, man!" Richard exclaimed, rising to his feet. "Have you lost your mind?"

Placing his hands on both shoulders, Darcy settled Richard back into the chair. "Let me explain before you get upset."

"I am already upset."

"Just listen. Do not speak until I have finished."

Relating to his cousin everything that had happened since

Elizabeth had arrived in Cambridge, the colonel was uncharacteristically silent when William finished.

It was an agonisingly long time before Richard responded. "Will my opinion matter? After all, you had your godfather arrange the special license with his cousin, the bishop, who also agreed to marry you. Obviously, you intend to go through with this."

William began to pace, as was his habit whenever he was anxious. "Elizabeth's uncle challenged me to do my duty. What was I to do? Refuse? As a gentleman, I had no choice. Still, you alone can help me clearly see both sides of the matter. That is why I asked you here today. I need your insight."

"What is on your mind?"

"One minute I am convinced this marriage could be my salvation; the next, I am certain it will be my undoing."

Richard saw the torment in his eyes. "Then calm down and let us sort this out." Pointing to another chair, he ordered, "Start by sitting down."

William sat in the chair across from him, though the tapping of his foot on the floor provided evidence of his anxiety.

"Let me begin by saying I was a fool not to have seen the signs sooner," Richard stated.

"What do you mean 'signs'?"

"You have been ranting about the Bennet sisters' unsuitability since the Christmas of 1810 when Bingley fell under the spell of the eldest. However, despite the fact that the family has a fortune-hunting mother, two out-of-control younger sisters, another who preaches Fordyce's sermons and a father who thinks it all hilarious, you spent an inordinate amount of time finding fault with Lucas' favourite: Miss Elizabeth. I missed that entirely. In my defence, I was convinced your ire was a result of your concern for Bingley. Well, that and the fact that I had never before seen you besotted with any woman."

"I am not besotted!"

"Darcy, you asked me to be honest. I expect the same of you."

William's head dropped, and he stared at the pattern in the carpet. "I...I cannot deny I have been unable to get her off my mind since the moment we met. If that means I am besotted, then I suppose I am. But I was never blind to her unsuitability. Why do you think I never visited Lucas' estate again? I feared Miss Elizabeth's circumstances had ill-prepared her to be the mistress of an estate the size of Pemberley, nor would she have the skills necessary to navigate the *ton*."

"Those things can be learned if one is not slow-witted."

"I never doubted her cleverness. While we were trapped in Cambridge, I discovered that, unlike the debutantes your mother advances, she is fluent in French and Italian, can converse on practically any subject and enjoys poetry, especially Thomas Moore and John Donne, as well as Shakespeare's writings."

"I am not surprised you find such accomplishments awe-inspiring," Richard said, trying not to smile, "but what would you do about her ridiculous family?"

"I have considered that. The only solution is to see them as little as possible."

Richard rose and walked to a chest where a bottle of brandy and several glasses sat on a tray. Pouring himself a drink, he took a large swallow. "And how do you think Miss Elizabeth will react to that?"

"I confess I had not thought about her reaction."

"As far back as I can remember, Mother has complained that Father never discusses anything with her. It has not made for a genial alliance. Whilst I am no expert on marriage, I do know that to maintain harmony, a wife must be consulted when something affects her." His cousin nodded, so he continued. "What is your greatest fear?"

William stood after Richard had and was now at one of the ornate windows overlooking the estate. With hands gripping both sides of the frame so hard his knuckles were white, he stared into the distance. Then, heaving a ragged sigh, he answered.

"Somewhere inside, a small fragment of my being still believes that love can conquer every obstacle." He smiled as a memory flooded him. "Mother often said that to me when I was a child. Still, by the time Elizabeth came into my life, I no longer knew if I believed it. She alone awakened that faint hope." His smile then vanished. "What I fear is that she may never return my affection."

"I cannot, in good faith, allay that fear, Darcy. You asked me to be honest, so I will. We are speaking of a woman who, when faced with marrying a lowly vicar, was mercenary enough to set her sights on someone of higher rank, even though, by her own admission, she did not love him."

"Yet she knows my wealth far exceeds what Lucas will inherit, and she never pursued me."

"Do you not think your objections to Jane the reason for that? Surely she knew you would not be open to a union with her if you were not open to Bingley marrying her sister."

"But once Bingley and Jane became engaged, she had to know it was with my approval, if not my blessing." What William did not mention was that he had loaned Bingley five hundred pounds against his inheritance so he might have the funds to purchase Jane an engagement ring and pay his travels to and from Meryton.

"You assume too much, my friend."

"Consider this! When her uncle stumbled upon us and insisted we marry, she disagreed with him. She only acquiesced when Mrs. Thornhill declared that a scandal would hurt her sisters' chances for a good match."

"Listen to yourself, Darcy! Whilst trying to convince me that Elizabeth Bennet is no fortune hunter, you made the case that she does not want you! There was no real harm done at Cambridge. You are not one of those cads who beds a woman and then refuses to marry her. Your only mistake was in helping a foolish young woman who turned up on your doorstep during a storm. And I would be remiss if I did not point out that you have another option."

"Which is?"

"Pay some poor squire a few thousand pounds to marry Miss Elizabeth. And, if it would make you feel less mercenary, give her and each of her sisters a small dowry. By your own admission, that is more than their father has provided. Then, get on with your life."

"I...I could not be that callous. And, in any case, I would be hard-pressed to come up with the funds at present."

Seeing the anguish in his cousin's expression, Richard clasped his shoulder. "I had to put it forth to gauge your reaction. Now I can say with certainty that I believe your heart has already chosen; thus, I will raise no more objections. Still, let me be clear about what I think. I would feel much better about the whole affair, if marrying her was simply your choice and not your duty."

"I imagine Miss Elizabeth feels the same way."

"Whether you meant to or not, you have convinced me that you are not merely acting out of duty. And I have faith in your ability to persuade her."

William smiled wanly.

"Obviously, you want to keep the wedding a secret so our family cannot raise objections beforehand. I assume that is also the reason the ceremony is to be at the Gardiners' residence."

"Elizabeth requested we marry there, though it will serve to keep the wedding secret for a time. You may tell Georgiana once you are in the carriage and on your way."

"My parents will be wounded when they realise I spirited my cousin away from their house to be at your wedding—an event they were not invited to attend."

"I apologise if by helping me, your relationship with them is strained."

"I do not think it could be any more strained than it already is," Richard said with a thin laugh. "Have you considered what Father will do? After all, he took your side when Lady Catherine asked him to insist that you marry Anne. I fear he will feel you betrayed his trust by not accepting one of the women he thought suitable. He may wash his hands of you."

"He only supported me in regards to Anne after a physician of his choosing declared her too sickly to bear children! And it is not as though I elected to defy him. I was trapped by circumstances and had no choice but to marry Elizabeth."

"For your sake, I hope he sees it that way," Richard said. "There is one thing, though, for which I am thankful."

"And that is?"

"I thank God that Lady *Harlot* is not here. I fear the trouble she might dream up if she knew what was about to take place." He looked around cautiously. "And I would not be surprised if she had spies listening to us right now."

"One day you will call her that in front of Georgiana."

"I shall endeavour not to. Still, given that she duped Uncle George into marriage, almost destroyed Pemberley with her gambling, and still has the daring to try to catch your eye, the name fits. And, at some point, Georgiana should be informed of her true nature."

"I fear she will learn Lady Henrietta's character soon enough. Now that Georgiana is older, I no longer care to conceal her behaviour in order to shield my sister."

"It cannot be too soon for my taste," Richard replied. He drained the last sip of brandy from his glass. "I must be on my way. I left General Lassiter wondering why I was not attending a briefing."

As he walked to the door, William called his name. Halting, Richard looked over his shoulder.

"I appreciate your frankness, my friend."

"If I have learned one thing in His Majesty's intelligence service, it is that one cannot deal with a situation unless one first faces the facts. As long as you are entering this marriage with your eyes wide open, I am satisfied."

Giving William a smile that did not reflect the disquiet roiling inside, Richard exited the room. Once in the hallway, he closed his eyes.

I pray you have chosen the right course, Darcy. You, of all people, do not deserve to be unhappy for the rest of your life.

The sound of a maid opening a door further down the hall brought him back to the present and Richard hurried on his way.

Colonel Fitzwilliam had no way of knowing his concerns regarding eavesdropping were not misplaced. Someone *was* listening to their conversation: Lady Henrietta's maid, Sarah Perry.

She was left at Darcy House with the sole aim of keeping her ladyship abreast of what happened whilst she visited friends on the outskirts of London.

Having risen from poverty to a lady's maid by sheer willpower and a stroke of good luck, Sarah had no intention of ever losing that position. A penniless gentleman's daughter, she had started as a maid and worked her way into a position as the senior upstairs maid in Lady Carmichael's house. When that woman's personal maid quit, she had convinced the mistress to give her the position. Lady Carmichael died shortly thereafter, and her daughter, Lady Henrietta, had taken her on. Having served Mrs. Darcy since shortly after her first marriage to the elderly Lord Wharton, Sarah knew her well.

Clever and unafraid, she was no one's fool, and when she realised what her conniving mistress wanted most of all—to spy on others—she set out to make it possible. Concealing holes in the wallpaper of particular rooms, she used wooden pegs to keep light from filtering into the servants' corridors. Consequently, all that was necessary for Sarah to spy on any given room was to remove the peg and replace it afterwards. Not only had she listened to private conversations here and at Pemberley, but she especially enjoyed observing the occupants unawares.

Eight and twenty and very plain, Sarah was under no illusions that she would ever marry, so she focused on one man in particular—Fitzwilliam Darcy. Seizing every opportunity to spy on him when he changed clothes or bathed, she enjoyed herself immensely until the day she forgot herself and gushed about his powerfully built body to her mistress. After that, Lady Henrietta had insisted on seeing the younger Darcy for herself, and to Sarah's chagrin, her ladyship claimed the best peepholes for herself, leaving her no choice but to create more.

After seeing her new son in all his glory, Lady Henrietta had begun to dream about Fitzwilliam Darcy as well, even going so far as to make inappropriate remarks to gauge his response. It was not until after George's death, however, that she told Sarah of her plan to become Fitzwilliam's lover, something the maid thought highly improbable. As she scurried back through the corridors to Lady Henrietta's bedroom today, all of these things ran through her mind.

"Her ladyship will be livid when she learns Mr. Darcy is to be married. How can she seduce him if he is enamoured of a wife?"

Rushing into the room, she closed the panel in the wall and leaned against it, catching her breath. "I had better pay extra to get my letter delivered straightaway."

Crossing to Lady Henrietta's writing desk, Sarah scribbled a hasty note and placed it in an envelope. Then she slipped out of the house to post it.

Cheapside
That same day

As Mrs. Gardiner hemmed the last section of Lizzy's hastily assembled wedding gown, she could not help but note the frown on her niece's face. Lizzy, who was standing on a small stool whilst Mrs. Gardiner stitched, had not said a word for the better part of half an hour. In truth, other than an occasional fit of coughing, she had been silent.

"I apologise for making you stand so long, but I am almost finished," Madeline Gardiner said. "Your fever is down, and your cough sounds much better than when you arrived, but it is still worrisome. Tell me, did the tea help?"

"It did, though my head still aches, and my throat is sore."

"If you would allow me to fix the draught Mr. Darcy's physician prescribed—"

"Neither Mr. Darcy nor his physician knows what is best for me!" Elizabeth interrupted emphatically, stepping from the stool. Then she said more softly, "Forgive me, Aunt, but I believe your remedies work just as well as the physician's and I detest that Mr. Darcy sent him here without asking my permission."

Mrs. Gardiner stood and embraced her niece. "I know why you are angry, but believe me, dearest, this is not the end of the world. In fact, I believe this is the beginning of a wonderful life for you. As Mrs. Darcy you will have the world at your feet."

"What benefit is that, if I have no feelings for my husband?"

"If your partner is a good man, love will follow. Do you know that when I was growing up in Lambton, the Darcys were revered for their benevolence? And Edward found your intended to be a very pleasant young man who wished to do what is best for you. In my opinion, any man who takes into consideration a woman's feelings will treat her well."

"He did not take my feelings into consideration before. Do you not recall what I once overheard him tell John? 'Elizabeth is tolerable, but not handsome enough to tempt me! I would not choose her even if I were looking for a wife decidedly inferior in rank, which I am not!'"

"I cannot deny that what he said was cruel, but we all say things we do not mean when we are upset and we think no one is listening. And from what you told me, he was arguing with John Lucas at the time."

"But sometimes what one says in anger is true."

"I saw the way Mr. Darcy looked at you when he helped you from the coach. I know a man who is besotted when I see one."

Elizabeth sighed. "You do not know him as well as you think."

With two fingers under her niece's chin, Mrs. Gardiner lifted her head until their eyes locked. "Was he unkind to you when you were alone with him?"

"No. It is just—" She dropped her head once more.

"Are you going to cry again?"

Elizabeth shook her head fiercely, but the tears began to roll as she spoke. "It is simply that I cannot believe I brought this dilemma on myself. Mr. Darcy does not want to marry me any more than I want to marry him. And it is entirely my fault!"

"I would place some of the blame on Mr. Lucas," Madeline Gardiner declared, pulling a handkerchief from her pocket. She began to dab at Elizabeth's wet cheeks. "He made promises he did not intend to keep."

"I should never have taken his promises seriously. Moreover, I never cared for him as anything other than a brother, so how can I blame him for falling in love with someone who will love him in return?"

"That is all in the past. You are about to be married, so I suggest you start thinking of how to please your intended."

Elizabeth frowned, believing her aunt was speaking of the marriage bed again. "Is there more you have not told me?"

"I am not speaking of your marital duties. I am speaking of getting to know his heart. There are those who will tell you to avoid his bed as much as possible."

"Like Mama?"

"Yes. In my opinion, fulfilling love comes only with familiarity, and the only way to truly know a man is to sleep in his bed. It has been my experience that if you try to fulfil his desires, he will do all in his power to make you happy."

When Lizzy did not reply, she continued. "Now that you are to be married, there is something I must say, though it pains me." Mrs. Gardiner took a deep breath and let it go. "You are too apt to find fault. I blame your father. Ever since you were old enough to make complete sentences, he taught you to ridicule other people."

"But Papa only makes light of their foibles."

"Once you begin to look for the worst in a person, you will find it. We all have our foibles." She patted her niece's hand. "Even you."

Elizabeth lifted both shoulders in a shrug. "I have never claimed to be perfect. It appears, however, that the thought of having a fault never crossed Mr. Darcy's mind."

"That is not what I hoped to hear. At this point, however, all I can do is pray you will rise to the occasion and be the wife Mr. Darcy needs—the wife I know you are capable of becoming."

"I promise I will consider your advice."

"That is all I ask," Mrs. Gardiner said. She smiled. "Now, step back up on the stool. I must get this gown hemmed before I retire."

Chapter 6

The Gardiners' residence
A bedroom

The sounds of footsteps in the hallway—the number of which was a sure sign the household was already abuzz with activity—awakened Elizabeth. Recalling what was to happen today, disappointment washed over her like a summer breeze atop Oakham Mount.

Aware that her aunt would soon come to wake her, Elizabeth rose, donned her dressing gown and crossed to the window seat. Sitting down, she pulled her feet up and hid them under her robe before unlatching the window. Pushing it open, she rested her head against the wall as she watched the world slowly come to life in the park across the street. This had been a favourite activity for as long as she could remember, but today her heart was too heavy to enjoy it.

This will be the last time I begin the day in this spot.

Whilst pondering whether she might be able to see Hyde Park from her bedroom at Mr. Darcy's residence, the cough which Elizabeth continued to suffer struck again. At the same time, Madeline Gardiner, about to knock on the door, heard her coughing and entered the room without warning. When she spied her niece at the open window, she rushed forwards to close it.

"Lizzy, the chilly morning air will make you sicker." She placed a hand on her niece's forehead. "Oh, me! Your fever has returned in force. Do you feel ill?"

"I feel well enough. I do not believe my cough has gotten any worse."

"Or any better. Still, there is no time to dwell on that. We must make time for my maid's cousin to style your hair. I wish for you to be ready at least an hour before the ceremony in case Mr. Darcy arrives early and wishes to speak to you."

"Is it not bad form for the groom to see the bride before the ceremony?"

"Be that as it may, if Mr. Darcy asks to see you, we cannot refuse him."

"Why must Esther's cousin fix my hair? I would rather you style it."

"Florence was the late Lady Atherton's maid, and according to Esther, she is very accomplished with the latest styles. She is presently searching for another position and hoped you might be sufficiently pleased with her work to hire her after you are married. Frankly, I am relieved she is doing your hair. I have not the skill to do it justice."

"I had not thought of having a lady's maid. My sisters and I have shared one maid all our lives; it will feel odd to have one all to myself."

"Mark my words. Mr. Darcy will insist that you have your own maid. If you like Florence, would it not be better to hire her rather than allow your husband or the housekeeper to hire one for you?"

"I suppose."

Mrs. Gardiner patted her hand. "Of course it would. Now, Esther will bring up some tea, toast and jam shortly. Eat only enough to keep from getting faint. I imagine your stomach is filled with butterflies, as was mine the day I married, and it will not do to be sick to your stomach. It was very kind of Mr. Darcy to host the wedding breakfast and you may eat all you wish once we are there."

Her aunt walked towards the door. "I will be in the parlour helping Mrs. Olds arrange the flowers. Send for me if you need me."

As the woman turned to leave, Elizabeth called, "Aunt Madeline?" Mrs. Gardiner looked over her shoulder to see fear in her niece's eyes. "Has Uncle heard anything more about Papa?"

"I completely forgot. An express arrived late yesterday after you had retired. Once he is dressed, Edward intends to share it with you." Seeing her niece's anxious expression, she added. "Just so you do not worry excessively, I will tell you that according to the physician, your father is holding up well."

"I am so relieved to hear it. I have been so—" A sob halted Elizabeth's reply.

Rushing to embrace her, Madeline Gardiner rocked her back and forth as she had when she was a child. "Hush now, Lizzy. Your father is strong, and I believe he will recover completely. Just wait and see."

Once Elizabeth had calmed, her aunt kissed her forehead and left the room. Thankful to hear that her father was doing well, Elizabeth sank down in the window seat again.

"At least that is one thing for which to be thankful."

A little later

The carriage carrying Richard Fitzwilliam and his cousin Georgiana Darcy to Gracechurch Street was halfway there before the colonel gathered enough courage to tell his cousin where they were going and why. After he had done so, he watched Georgiana carefully, not knowing how she would react.

"Why is Brother marrying someone I have never met, or even heard of, for that matter?"

"I wondered the same thing. From what Darcy told me, he met Elizabeth Bennet at John Lucas' estate in Hertfordshire the Christmas of 1810. It was only recently they had an opportunity to meet again, and one thing led to another."

Georgiana appeared to mull over that information. "That was the Christmas after Father married Lady Henrietta and William did not come home."

"Yes, it was."

"I wish he and Rietta were not at odds. It makes it difficult, since I enjoy her company."

"Rietta?"

"Have you forgotten? That is what I call Lady Henrietta."

"I had forgotten. And as for your brother's issues with her, there are matters—grown-up matters—that you will not understand until you are older. Maybe then your brother's attitude will make sense."

"You speak in riddles, just like my brother," Georgiana said petulantly. "I am not a child!"

"As far as I know, you have not attained the age of majority yet!" Richard declared, chuckling as he patted her hand. "What say we return to the subject of your brother's marriage?"

"What else do you know about Miss Bennet?"

"Her father's estate is called Longbourn; it is just outside of Meryton in Hertfordshire. She has four sisters, one of whom is engaged to Mr. Bingley."

Georgiana's face lit up. "I really like Mr. Bingley. He is so entertaining."

Richard smiled. "Entertaining. Yes, that is a good description of Bingley."

"Why did William not pursue Miss Bennet when they first met?"

"Your brother takes his responsibilities seriously, and he would not pursue any woman until he completed university. They just happened to meet again at the right time."

"There is something else that bothers me. Why did you spirit me away from my aunt and uncle's home without telling them where we were going? Were they not invited?"

"You are very observant. You are also aware that my parents have always tried to direct your brother's life and that he does not welcome their interference."

"Still, to marry without their knowledge or approval can only heap coals on the fire and I hate to think of what Aunt Catherine will say when she hears of it. I hope I am not around when that happens. She frightens me."

"To be honest, she frightens me, too!" Richard declared, his humour coaxing a smile from his young cousin. "Now tell me, how do you feel about all of this?"

"All I want is for Brother to be happy. If Miss Bennet brings him happiness, then I shall be happy for them both."

"Me too, Poppet."

Just then the carriage came to a halt in front of the Gardiners' residence. Richard reached for Georgiana's hand. "Are you ready?"

"Promise to stay by my side, and I shall try my best to make you proud."

"I am your devoted servant. Now, let us show Miss Elizabeth and her relations that not all of Darcy's family are curmudgeons, by welcoming her into our family."

Just then a footman opened the carriage door and let the steps down. Richard stepped out and had turned to help Georgiana down when the Gardiners' front door swung open and William walked out to greet them.

Mr. Gardiner's study
Before the wedding

Expecting Elizabeth, when Mr. Gardiner entered the study instead of his intended, William was taken aback.

"Mr. Darcy, since Lizzy is not ready yet, I have seized this opportunity to ask you about a matter of great importance. Last night I received a letter from my niece, Jane Bennet, and—"

"Has Elizabeth's father taken a turn for the worse?"

"Quite the contrary! According to Jane, the new physician has been a godsend, working wonders with new medicines and procedures. She allows that her father is doing quite well, given the severity of his injury."

As he watched William relax, Mr. Gardiner continued. "It is the physician who concerns me. Dr. Graham arrived in Meryton days ago, telling the family that he was sent from London to direct my brother's care. Moreover, when asked who sent him, it seems he implied that I did."

William looked uncomfortable. "Forgive me. That was my doing. I meant to tell you before now, but with plans for the wedding and meetings with my solicitor, I completely forgot."

"That is understandable."

"Dr. Graham is my personal physician, and it was I who asked him to manage Mr. Bennet's care. It is my understanding that once Elizabeth's father shows improvement, he will leave one of his associates in charge at Longbourn and return to London. Graham will, however, stay in touch with the assistant and continue to supervise every aspect of his recovery."

"That cannot be inexpensive, so why was I given credit?"

"I do not want Elizabeth to learn of my part in it."

"Why ever not? It might change her attitude towards you."

William glanced away. "It is not gratitude that I seek from Elizabeth."

"You wish her to feel love, not obligation."

Embarrassed to be discussing something so personal, William merely nodded.

"I understand completely, but what if she learns of your intervention later?"

A pained smile crossed William's face. "Perhaps by then she will have decided that marriage to me is not a horrible sentence, after all."

Touched, Mr. Gardiner clamped a reassuring hand on the young man's shoulder. "If it means anything, you must know that Madeline and I believe you are far and away the best man for Lizzy. She is not an average woman, and we feared she would never meet a man who would appreciate her uniqueness. My brother never had a son, you see, so he taught her everything he would have taught his heir about estate management. Moreover, he passed along his passion for reading a variety of books: histories, novels, plays and poetry, some in Italian and French. It has been my experience that most men, especially those of the *ton,* are intimidated by any woman who thinks for herself. They want a beauty with no brains for a wife, and whilst Lizzy is beautiful, it is her intelligence that sets her apart. Because of her intellect, she does not suffer fools easily."

"We are alike in that."

"However, I must warn you that Lizzy does possess one glaring fault." William's brows furrowed. "She leads with her heart. This means that at times she is apt to act before thinking—ergo, the need for your hasty marriage. She is still so young that I like to believe she will outgrow that flaw."

At the anxious look on his soon-to-be nephew's face, he added, "Just remember one thing, and you shall fare well. If a marriage is to succeed, both of you must work at it. Giving, as well as taking, is the key."

That very second there was a knock on the door, and as it opened, Madeline Gardiner stuck in her head. "Elizabeth is here to speak with Mr. Darcy."

"Give us just another minute, my dear."

As the door closed again, Mr. Gardiner leaned in to whisper. "Jane warned me that her mother is still livid with Lizzy for rejecting Mr. Collins. She allows it might be best if her sister does not return to Longbourn until Fanny has calmed down. By the way, I did not inform either of Lizzy's parents of your impending marriage. I believe that is your business."

"I am relieved to know that Elizabeth's father is doing well. I cannot leave for Pemberley until I finish some business in Town and that will likely be the end of this week. Perhaps by then Mr. Bennet will be on the mend, and Mrs. Bennet's temper will have cooled."

"I pray that is so. Now, let me leave you young people alone so you may talk."

As Mr. Gardiner hurried from the room, he passed Elizabeth, who was right behind his wife. Giving her a fatherly smile, he patted her on the back before Mrs. Gardiner waved her into the study and closed the door.

Dressed in a simple blue satin gown trimmed with Chantilly lace at the bosom and the hem, Elizabeth looked stunning. A bonnet featuring a few white roses covered her dark hair. Moreover, the remedy her aunt had administered right before she came downstairs had calmed her persistent cough, so William saw no evidence that she was still sick. Unable to recall what he wished to say, he stared at her in amazement.

Self-conscious under his gaze, Elizabeth coloured and looked down. Seeing her discomfort, William came to his senses and hurried to explain.

"Elizabeth." Her head came up. "I want you to know the wedding ring I chose for you was my mother's favourite."

Pulling a small velvet box from his pocket, he opened it to reveal a delicate, gold filigree band, featuring small diamonds and rubies set in a random pattern around the circumference. He was unwilling to burden her with the fact that this, a few more of his mother's rings and a pearl necklace and matching earrings were the only jewellery not tendered as collateral against the new loan. "If it does not suit, you have only to tell me. There are several rings from which to choose, and you may discover you like another one better."

"Mr. Darcy, I assure you this ring is perfect," Elizabeth answered, giving him a fleeting smile.

"Is it not time to call me something less formal?" When Elizabeth did not reply, he ventured, "My mother called me William to distinguish between me and my cousin, Richard Fitzwilliam, who often stayed with us when I was a boy."

"William," she repeated just as a soft knock announced yet another interruption.

Mrs. Gardiner opened the door. "I hate to intrude, but the bishop is ready to proceed with the ceremony. Mr. Darcy, if you will accompany me, Edward will escort Elizabeth as soon as the music begins."

As his wife walked back to the parlour with William on her heels, Edward Gardiner slipped into the study. Seeing the trepidation in Elizabeth's face, he said, "I like your young man, Lizzy. Please give him a chance to win your heart."

She smiled wanly. "What choice do I have, Uncle?"

"You have a much better choice than you realise, my dear."

The Gardiners' parlour

As Elizabeth entered the parlour to the music provided by Aunt Gardiner, she was so focused on the figure of the imposing bishop that she failed to notice who else was in the room. Those in attendance included Mrs. Thornhill, Richard, Georgiana, all the Gardiners' children and a few of their long-time servants. William had requested a short ceremony, so the wedding concluded before she had time to be nervous. Nonetheless, the moment the bishop pronounced them man and wife, she turned to face the witnesses. Afraid to meet her new husband's eyes, Elizabeth smiled at no one in particular.

Immediately, William's sister, who had taken Richard's suggestions to heart, was standing before her.

"I am Georgiana Darcy, your new sister," she said with a shy smile. "I am so happy to welcome you into our family, Miss—I mean ..."

Startled to discover William's sister was as tall as she, Elizabeth could not help but smile at her discomposure. "If you will call me Elizabeth, I shall call you Georgiana. I am so pleased to make your acquaintance."

"Richard tells me you are from Hertfordshire and that you have four sisters." At Elizabeth's smile, Georgiana's apprehension disappeared, and she became livelier. "I have always wanted a sister, and now that I have you, I hope to become acquainted with all of them."

Seeing William frown, Richard stepped in. Taking Elizabeth's hand, he placed a kiss on the back. "Colonel Richard Fitzwilliam, Darcy's cousin. I am happy to make your acquaintance, as well."

"Colonel Fitzwilliam, Mr. Darcy has spoken to me of you."

"I plead innocent of all charges."

"On the contrary," William cut in. "I told her you were a decisive man, unafraid to speak your mind."

Richard smiled. "In that case, I cannot disagree."

Suddenly Mrs. Thornhill, who had kept her vow to attend the ceremony, interrupted enthusiastically.

"I am so pleased to have witnessed your wedding, for I feel I had a small part in your happiness." Neither Elizabeth nor William wanted to disabuse her of that notion, so both smiled without answering. "Please forgive me for not attending the wedding breakfast, but I am expected in Croydon later today."

"Of course," William said. "Mrs. Darcy and I are honoured that you took time to come."

"I would not have missed it for the world!" She beamed. "I had a small wager on whether you would marry, and I am proud to have been correct. I wish you joy."

With those few words, William's landlady disappeared out the front door just as Mrs. Gardiner, who had been speaking with the bishop, walked over to them.

"The bishop informed me he has business to attend to this afternoon, so if he is to enjoy the wedding breakfast, I am afraid we must all remove to Darcy House straightaway."

William turned to Elizabeth. "Shall we, Mrs. Darcy?"

Forcing a smile, Elizabeth replied, "Of course." Then she added, "Do ride with us, Georgiana, and you, too, Colonel Fitzwilliam."

William's sister looked to him expectantly. Though disappointed Elizabeth did not wish to be alone with him, he tried not to show it. "Yes, please do."

Georgiana threaded her arm through Elizabeth's and they began towards the front door. William's sister chatted animatedly the entire time. Richard walked over to stand next to his cousin, who was watching them leave.

"Take heart, Darcy. Georgiana is merely excited and will soon settle down. Besides, we will leave right after the breakfast, and you will have your bride all to yourself then."

"Not that it will make Elizabeth happy," William murmured under his breath.

"What did you say?" Richard asked as he donned his hat and gloves.

"Nothing of importance."

Suddenly, the Gardiners were calling for them to hurry, and William and Richard exited the house. They were the last to enter Darcy's carriage, finding Georgiana already sitting beside Elizabeth. Having no other choice, William took the seat opposite them, while Richard sat beside him.

Noting the glum faces of the bride and groom, Richard tried to lighten the mood.

"I cannot wait to see what Mrs. Colton has prepared to eat! That woman is an artist when it comes to food."

Georgiana laughed. "All you think about is food, Richard!"

"Spend a month on military exercises in His Majesty's service eating nothing but rations, and that is all you will think about, too, Poppet!"

Darcy House

Richard had been correct. Mrs. Colton had outdone herself with the variety and quality of foods prepared for the wedding breakfast. There were easily enough dishes for a roomful of guests, and she was disappointed at the small number assembled to eat them. If not for the Gardiners' children, the room might have looked empty, though the event was being held in the smallest dining room in the house.

Encouraged by Elizabeth, Georgiana took the place beside her at one round table, in a spot obviously designed for the groom. Instantly, they were surrounded by the Gardiner children, causing Madeline Gardiner to chide them to move so the bride and groom could sit together. Assuming a wan smile, William insisted they were fine seated as they were and walked to the other table and sat down. Uneasily, Madeline Gardiner took the seat on his left, whilst Richard sat on his right. Mr. Gardiner and the bishop completed the rest of their table.

Almost an hour later, after everyone had finished eating, the quiet celebration took a decidedly different turn when the door flew open. All heads turned to inspect the handsome, blonde-haired woman with sparkling, green eyes now standing in the doorway.

Although Elizabeth and the Gardiners regarded her curiously, William swore under his breath whilst Richard leaned in to hiss quietly as they both stood, "How the bloody hell did she find out?"

Lady Henrietta had staged her appearance to be bold and daring. She was wearing a red velvet riding habit with gold leather trim—one side fashioned with a split skirt that offered a view of tall, black riding boots. On her head was a red three-cornered hat and perched jauntily upon it were gold feathers and a small bird covered in crystal beads.

Never having seen anything so garish other than the costumes worn by actresses at Drury Lane, Henrietta's red lips and cheeks piqued Elizabeth's curiosity more than her manner of dress. Suddenly, realising the intruder was smiling at her husband, Elizabeth recalled having once found a novel in the park. It was about a courtesan who was known for wearing rouge. Glimpsing the shocked expressions on William's face as well as on his cousin's, Elizabeth's curiosity grew even stronger.

Lady Henrietta sauntered towards William, exaggerating the sway of her hips as she walked. "I was riding in the park with Lady Jergenson, and we met some ladies who told us the most delicious gossip, Fitzwilliam. Nothing would do but for me to rush over here to ascertain if it was true."

Instantly, Georgiana was on her feet, flying towards the interloper. "Rietta! You are just in time to celebrate Brother's wedding!"

Never taking her eyes off William, Lady Henrietta allowed Georgiana to hug her. "So, it is true, dear girl! Your reticent brother has married in secret. I would never have believed him capable of anything so...romantic."

Henrietta let go of Georgiana to approach William. She attempted to pat his arm affectionately, but he thwarted her by crossing to where Elizabeth stood. Taking his wife's hand, he brought it to his lips and placed a kiss thereon. Effectively snubbed, Henrietta turned her attention back to Georgiana.

"What have you been up to, darling girl?" she asked, though her eyes were now fixed on Elizabeth.

"I have been taking harp lessons alongside Lady Esme. She

has a master come in twice a week and her mother asked me to join them."

"It is very kind of Lady Farthingham to allow you to share her daughter's lessons."

In truth, William could not afford private lessons for Georgiana, so Lady Matlock arranged with Esme's mother to pay for half of the lessons.

As she continued to talk with Georgiana about mundane things, Elizabeth whispered to William, "Who is she?"

"My father's second wife, Lady Henrietta. Georgiana calls her Rietta."

"Whilst you wear black arm bands and your sister black ribbons to honour your father, his widow wears red?"

"In his will, Father left a letter stating that neither she nor Georgiana should mourn him by wearing black. It seems he thought his new wife too vivacious to wear bombazine. Whilst Georgiana insisted on the black ribbons, Lady Henrietta took my father's wishes to heart."

After speaking to the bishop, whom she knew socially, Henrietta walked in their direction. "Fitzwilliam, darling, will you not introduce me to your bride?"

Aware that Lady Henrietta held rank over Elizabeth, William disregarded decorum and addressed his wife.

"Dearest, may I present my late father's wife, Lady Henrietta." To his stepmother, he declared, "May I present Mrs. Darcy, the former Elizabeth Bennet of Hertfordshire."

"Where in Hertfordshire, Miss Bennet?"

"*Mrs. Darcy*," William stated dryly.

"Forgive me. I shall have to get used to there being another Mrs. Darcy."

Without missing a beat, Elizabeth said, "My father's estate is Longbourn. It is in Hertfordshire near Meryton."

"My goodness! That must be a quaint little village. I have never heard of it."

At her condescending tone, Elizabeth lifted her chin. "Indeed, a quaint little village where character weighs more than status."

Lady Henrietta studied her a little too long. "Welcome to the family, Elizabeth. May I call you that?" Without waiting for a reply, she added, "You may call me Rietta. All my dearest friends and relations do—well, with the exception of Fitzwilliam. He is too old fashioned."

Before Elizabeth or William could respond, Lady Henrietta turned to face the other occupants of the room as though awaiting an introduction.

William obliged. "It is my pleasure to introduce Elizabeth's aunt and uncle, Mr. and Mrs. Edward Gardiner of London."

Intrigued that they had no titles either, Henrietta said, "I once knew some Gardiners who lived in Birmingham. I believe their estate was called Wycliffe Park. Are you by chance related to them?"

"No," Edward Gardiner replied. "I own two warehouses in the business district, and we reside near them."

"You live in Cheapside?"

"Yes."

"I see." Realising they were of no consequence, Henrietta quit the Gardiners to address Georgiana again. "Come, dearest! I must go upstairs and change clothes. Whilst I do, you can tell me everything that has happened during your stay with Lord and Lady Matlock."

"Are you going to eat?" Georgiana asked. "Cook has prepared so much food, and it is all delicious."

"I am certain it is, sweetie. But I have already eaten, and a lady must watch her figure."

Like a summer storm that quits as rapidly as it starts, Lady Henrietta went out the door with Georgiana in tow. Suddenly remembering her new sister, Georgiana came rushing back into the room and over to Elizabeth.

"I shall not be long, Elizabeth. As soon as Rietta and I have shared our news, I shall look for you so that we may continue our conversation."

Richard interrupted. "My parents are expecting us back shortly, Poppet."

"As long as I am with you, they will not worry if we are late."

Having said that, Georgiana rushed back to Lady Henrietta,

and the sounds of their chatter grew quieter as they walked up the grand staircase.

Chapter 7

Darcy House

Immediately after Georgiana left, the cough remedy Elizabeth had taken that morning began to wear off. When she began to cough, her aunt suggested she go to her bedroom, take another spoonful of medicine and lie down to rest for a while.

"I do not want to rest, Aunt," Elizabeth complained. "I wish to spend as much time with you as possible before you have to leave."

"But, Lizzy, we cannot stay any longer," Madeline Gardiner replied. "The children are growing restless, and if George does not get his nap, he will start to whine. Tell Florence I put the bottle of cough remedy in your smallest bag, and she will have no trouble finding it."

"I agree with your aunt, Elizabeth," William interjected. "You really should rest. Mrs. Reynolds has already shown your lady's maid to your suite. Most likely she already has your things organized. If you will say your farewells, I shall escort you upstairs."

Elizabeth was not happy with William's interference. "I shall take enough syrup to keep from coughing, but I shall not lie down. If I do, I will sleep all day, and I do not wish to disappoint Georgiana."

William offered a wan smile. "My sister will occupy all your time if you allow it. You must set boundaries with her from the beginning."

"I will try to keep that in mind," Elizabeth answered tersely.

Though not happy with her niece's behaviour, Mrs. Gardiner attributed it to be the fact that she did not feel well.

Ignoring Lizzy's irritable disposition, she addressed her host. "Mr. Darcy, the breakfast was delightful; however, it is time Edward and I took our leave. Would you please have our carriage brought around?"

"Certainly," William said. He walked over to pull a cord and almost immediately a footman appeared. "Have the Gardiners' carriage brought to the front."

As the footman nodded and disappeared, Mrs. Gardiner turned to her husband. "Edward, if you will handle George, I shall get the rest of the children ready to leave."

As Elizabeth went to each of her cousins to say goodbye, Edward Gardiner walked over to William with four-year old George in his arms. "I want to thank you once more for all you have done for my niece."

"No thanks are necessary."

"Well, be that as it may, I know the sacrifice you have made to correct my headstrong niece's mistake. She should never have put you in that situation, and you were very kind to do the honourable thing. I shall forever be in your debt, and Elizabeth's father will feel the same way after he learns of it."

"I suppose at some point you may have to tell Mr. Bennet what happened, but please do not present me as a saint. I am far from it."

"Perhaps in your estimation, but not in mine."

Suddenly, Madeline Gardiner called from across the room. "We are ready, Edward."

After her relations left, Elizabeth took another spoonful of the remedy and, despite her wishes, fell asleep sitting in a chair in her new bedroom. She did not waken until Georgiana went searching for her an hour later. As for William, he had little chance to see his new bride that day, much less speak with her. His sister's decision to stay at Darcy House until the end of the week to become better acquainted with Elizabeth made being alone with her impossible.

Richard, who had returned to Matlock House to inform his parents that Georgiana was staying with Fitzwilliam until he returned to Pemberley, planned to stop by his office before returning for dinner as his cousin requested. It seemed that everyone was exhausted from the day's events, so when Georgiana and Elizabeth expressed a desire to take naps instead of coming downstairs for tea, Lady Henrietta decided to take tea in her suite. All of this resulted in William having tea in his study whilst catching up on his correspondence.

By dinner-time, all the ladies were well rested; thus, Elizabeth, Georgiana, and Lady Henrietta carried on a lively conversation at the table, whilst William conversed with Richard.

Had Richard not returned for dinner, William might have spent the hour without uttering a word. Consequently, once he and Richard separated from the ladies after dinner, the frustrations of the day came to a head. Heading straight for the liquor cabinet, William poured two fingers of brandy in a glass and tossed the contents down without serving his cousin. Grimacing, he poured another.

"Slow down, Cousin! If you keep this up, you may not feel well enough to erm... shall we say...fulfil your duties."

"Duties! What duties?" William said, slamming the glass down and throwing his hands up in frustration.

"Surely you do not need me to explain the facts of life," Richard replied, whilst pouring his own glass of brandy.

"I believe that as far as my wife is concerned, my duty is to leave her and my sister to their conversations. Frankly, at this point I do not think that would be a problem."

Richard smiled. "Even I can see that Georgiana is taking her *sisterly* responsibilities a bit far. If you like, I can speak to her privately and explain—"

"How do you propose to explain to a girl of fourteen why

men and women wish to be alone on their wedding night?" William sighed. "You know she will ask too many questions."

"You have a point. If only your mother were alive to handle such things."

"But she is not, and Lady Henrietta only encourages Georgiana's domination of Elizabeth's attention. You saw that at dinner."

"Yes, I did. So, what do you plan to do about it?"

"Nothing. If my wife wishes to ignore me, so be it."

Swirling the contents of his glass, Richard said sombrely, "That does not bode well for your future."

"One plays the cards one is dealt, and at present, I do not have the energy to deal with Elizabeth's attitude in addition to Pemberley's problems. And those problems are why I asked you to dinner. It seems the bankers are reluctant to consolidate my loans unless someone signs with me."

"I would be happy to, but I have so little funds in their bank they would laugh at the offer."

"I appreciate the gesture. No doubt your father will not be of a mind to oblige me, since I married Elizabeth without his approval."

"I agree."

"I am certain that Lady Henrietta told your parents the minute she learned of my marriage. It surprises me that your father has not yet appeared to voice his disapproval."

"I could tell the second I entered the house that they had heard, and they let me know in no uncertain terms what they thought of my part in the deception."

"I am very sorry to have brought this down on you."

"No need to apologise. I know why you could not invite them."

"Why do you think my uncle has not yet come?"

"I believe Father would have, if not for Mother's intervention. She believes you will come to your senses when you realise what a grave mistake you have made. She convinced Father to wait until you ask for his assistance."

"Assistance? With what?"

"Apparently, Lady Henrietta knows more about your wife

than she let on. She told Mother that Mrs. Darcy is under the age of majority. You do know that marriage contracts are null and void if those involved have not reached their majority and marry without the consent of their father or guardian."

"I am aware of that, but Elizabeth's uncle had her father's permission to act in his stead."

"But if Mr. Bennet were to swear he never gave his permission, and Mr. Gardiner went along with—"

"Why would they do such a thing when it would ruin Elizabeth's reputation?"

"One guess."

"Money." William threw down his pen and stood up. "A man might rise above such a thing, but not a woman. I would never agree to degrade my wife in that manner, and I have not the time to dwell on your parents' fantasies. I must find someone to sign the loan, or Pemberley could be lost. Do you suppose Leighton would?"

"I like to think my brother would; however, according to Father, after my parents insisted Leighton wed Lady Susan, he returned to gambling full force."

"I can believe that. Your father thought that woman a good match for me before he foisted her on Leighton. I knew she was a fortune hunter the first time we met."

"I am not surprised. My understanding is he and Father have had several arguments about his spending of late. Therefore, I fear that Leighton's funds may not impress the bankers either. What about your godfather, Lord Appleby?"

"I considered Appleby, but we have not spoken since he tried to coerce me into marrying his granddaughter."

"Good Lord! How old was she? Fourteen?"

"Thereabouts. As it turned out, she was with child. I understand she has since married the father—a duke old enough to be her grandfather."

"A duke? Then old Appleby should be happy you refused. Perhaps it is time you called on him to see if he is over his disappointment. I think I would ask him before I asked Leighton."

"Thank you for your insight. I had no idea Leighton was gambling again."

"Yes. It is a shame," Richard said solemnly. Then suddenly his affable manner returned. "I should be glad to accompany you when you call on Lord Appleby, if you so desire."

"I think it best that I go alone."

"As you wish. Now, if you are going to have any time tonight alone with your bride, I suggest we join the ladies in the parlour."

William rolled his eyes.

"What do you say to this? After half an hour, I shall yawn and say it has been a long day, and I need to return to my quarters. My departure will provide an opening so that you may suggest that everyone retire."

"I doubt anything I suggest will carry any weight."

Richard reached out to pat his cousin's shoulder sympathetically. "I am more convinced than ever that I was right all along. There are more advantages to remaining a bachelor than becoming a husband."

Elizabeth's bedroom
Later

Even after Richard had departed, the party continued until Georgiana grew so sleepy she could not keep her eyes open. Consequently, after she and Lady Henrietta announced that they were retiring, William escorted Elizabeth to the sitting room situated between his bedroom and hers.

Once there, he kissed her hand gently. "Will a half-hour be enough time for you to prepare?" Not having any idea, Elizabeth nodded. "I shall return then."

She watched William disappear through the door she had been told led to his bedroom. Given no choice, Elizabeth turned to enter the door that led to her own bedroom. Inside, she found Florence waiting.

"I am sorry. I should have told you not to wait for me. You may go to bed."

"But...but, Mistress, do you not wish for me to unbutton your gown and help you into your nightgown?" As she spoke, Florence motioned towards a beautiful, pink silk creation her aunt had slipped into her bag the day before. Lying on the bed next to it was a matching robe.

"I have decided to wear my usual nightgown."

Though Florence looked puzzled, she began to put away the silk gown and robe and replaced them with Elizabeth's plain muslin ones. After she had made the exchange, she found her mistress waiting.

"If you will unbutton me, I can manage the rest."

Florence did as she was instructed and left the room immediately. In no time at all, Elizabeth had donned the plain, white nightgown. Since William had not returned, she went into the adjoining dressing room and sat down at the elegant white dresser, trimmed in gold. The matching mirror hung on the wall above it, and as she stared at her image, she remembered her aunt's admonition: *Let your hair down. Men love to see their wife's hair unbound.*

Dutifully, she began to remove the pins from her hair. When she began to brush it, she caught a glimpse of William in the mirror. He was propped against the door frame, watching her. He looked so very handsome clad in nothing save a black banyan loosely tied at the waist that Elizabeth found herself enthralled. And, as her eyes drifted to his hard, muscular chest, covered in dark hair, the hairbrush she was holding was left suspended in mid-air. When a devastatingly handsome smile crossed his face, she immediately knew why and began to brush her hair more vigorously. As though on cue, her cough returned.

At once William was beside her, placing a hand on her forehead. She recoiled at his touch, but William carried on as though he had noticed nothing. "You are still feverish. Why did you not say something earlier?"

Rushing back into her bedroom, he soon reappeared with a glass of water. "You need to drink plenty of water." As she drank, he continued. "This will not do. Tomorrow I will send for the physician."

"I do not think that will be necessary, Mr. Darcy," Elizabeth answered sharply. Seeing him flinch, she began anew. "William, rather than staying here and seeing the physician again, I would like to see my father tomorrow."

"I am afraid we cannot leave London that quickly. However, just as soon as my business is finished, which should be in the next day or so, we will visit Meryton on our way home."

"But what if my father dies?"

"Elizabeth, your uncle assures me the physician attending your father thinks he is doing very well. It is his belief that waiting a few more days will make no difference."

Too angry to speak, Elizabeth rolled her eyes. Contemplating what he wished to say next, William took no notice.

"I will be out of the house early tomorrow, so I want you to know that I scheduled Georgiana's modiste to come at nine to take your measurements. I took the liberty of ordering several gowns, cloaks and coats for you, as well as two muffs and two pairs of fur-lined boots. The winters are much colder in Derbyshire than Hertfordshire, and you will need those items. Once Madame Dupré has your measurements, she has pledged to work with the bootmaker to have everything finished and shipped to Pemberley as quickly as possible. You may order whatever else you may need once we are in Derbyshire."

"You chose the styles, colours and materials for my clothes?"

"I have always done so for Georgiana."

"I see," Elizabeth said through clenched teeth.

His wife looked so beautiful with her dark hair down that William reached to touch one long silky strand. Elizabeth recoiled, and his expression became unreadable.

"Goodnight, Elizabeth," he said, turning to leave.

"Are you not...I mean...should I expect you to return tonight?"

William turned to face her. "I would never force myself on you, especially not when you are ill. Given the circumstances, perhaps it would be best if you came to me when you feel that you are completely well."

Suddenly, he was gone. Exceedingly puzzled, Elizabeth went back into her bedroom. After she was convinced he was not going to return, she took another spoonful of the cough remedy and walked over to the tall bed that now belonged to her. Climbing a small set of stairs useful for one as petite as she, Elizabeth slipped between the silk sheets and pulled the satin counterpane over herself. She was so exhausted that sleep came quickly.

The next day

If Florence was surprised to find Elizabeth alone in a clearly unruffled bed, she was too discreet to say as much. Still, she was almost certain from the state of the bed and the room that Mr. Darcy had not visited his wife last night. This caused her to ponder the circumstances in which she found herself.

Florence was a handsome woman of seven and twenty with a thin frame, auburn hair and hazel eyes. Though her father was a gentleman, he was the third son. He had taken orders and was now a vicar in Sussex, though he had very little means to help any of his children. Thus, when she reached the age of majority, she went in search of employment. Being talented with a needle and thread and in styling hair, she sought work as a lady's maid and was hired by Lady Atherton. However, that woman's marriage was an unhappy one, and Florence had suffered the husband's inappropriate advances. Not wishing to work in a similar situation, she now wondered if she should continue serving Mrs. Darcy.

Elizabeth roused and stretched when Florence opened the drapes to let in the sunlight. "The modiste will be here at nine, ma'am, and it is already eight. I thought you might wish to eat before she comes."

"I do. I am famished."

Florence smiled. "Perhaps, then, whatever has been ailing you is losing its grip."

"I hope so," Elizabeth said. Then she recalled what she had decided last night. "Florence, after the modiste leaves, I want you to accompany me to Gracechurch Street."

"You do remember that Mr. Darcy has arranged for a physician to see you this afternoon."

"We will return before then."

"I should be glad to see my cousin again," Florence replied with a smile.

In another bedroom

"Where have you been?" Lady Henrietta hissed as Sarah walked into her bedroom.

"Unlike you," the maid said, "I was up most of the night spying. I was too tired to rise earlier."

"Pray tell, what did you learn?"

Sarah smiled conspiratorially. "I know Mr. Darcy did not spend the night with his new wife. In fact, if she was a virgin when they married, she still is."

"Do tell!"

"I was watching Mrs. Darcy when Mr. Darcy came into her dressing room. I could not hear all they said, but from the look on both their faces, they seemed to be at odds."

"How marvellous! What else did you notice?"

"As I watched, he abruptly turned on his heel and went back to his bedroom. I had to rush down to the servants' hall in order to watch him undress."

"I take it that he still sleeps in the nude?"

"Yes!" Sarah exclaimed. "He is the handsomest man I have ever—"

"Never mind the superlatives! Are you certain Fitzwilliam did not return to his wife's bedroom last night?"

"Why do you think I was up so late? He did not go straight to bed. Instead, he paced the room for hours, like a caged animal, only stopping occasionally to sip his brandy."

"And you stayed awake to watch that?"

"He was naked the entire time."

Lady Henrietta laughed. "I see your point." Then, taking a

deep breath, she let it go. "Their marriage is a farce, and I mean to find out why Fitzwilliam went through with it."

"I will do whatever I can to assist you."

"I want you to sneak into Elizabeth's rooms whenever she is out. Perhaps she will pen some letters to her family that will shed light on the situation."

"Getting into her room will be easy but finding letters may be difficult. What lady leaves her correspondence lying about for anyone to read?"

"But you forget, dear Sarah, Elizabeth is no lady."

Lady Henrietta's cleverness made both women laugh.

"One thing puzzles me, though," Henrietta added.

"What is that?"

"I told the Earl and Countess of Matlock of the wedding in time for them to ruin the breakfast, but they have yet to confront Fitzwilliam."

"Perhaps they are planning to exact revenge on Mr. Darcy in some other manner?"

"You have a point. They can be vindictive. In any case, I will wait with bated breath to see how they respond."

The Gardiners' residence

The moment the Gardiners' front door opened, Elizabeth raced in, followed by Florence. Madeline Gardiner was coming down the stairs, and seeing her niece, she imagined the worst.

"Lizzy, what brings you here so early?"

Elizabeth turned to Florence. "Please visit with your cousin whilst I speak to my aunt." As Florence complied, Elizabeth addressed Mrs. Gardiner. "May we use Uncle's study to speak privately?"

"Of course we may. Edward has already left for the warehouse."

Once they were inside with the door closed, Elizabeth's aunt directed her to a settee, where they sat down. She placed one hand on her niece's forehead. "You still have a slight fever. Did you come for more of my draughts?"

Elizabeth shook her head. "Mr. Darcy is having the physician examine me again today, so that is not why I am here."

Hearing the distress in her niece's voice, she smoothed Elizabeth's hair as she would one of her own children. "My dear, is this about last night? Did Mr. Darcy hurt you?"

Elizabeth coloured. "It has nothing to do with...with that. He did not—" Beginning to cough, Elizabeth pulled a handkerchief from her pocket to cover her mouth. Once she was able to speak, she continued. "He did not lie with me. He said he would never impose on someone who is ill, and he would wait until I was ready to come to him."

Her confession made Madeline Gardiner more concerned. "If he is that considerate, why are you here?"

Elizabeth put forth all the things she found irritating about her new husband.

"If these are your only complaints, I cannot understand why you are upset."

"I am upset because it never occurs to him to ask what I want or to consider my feelings. What if the styles of the clothes, the colours, or the fabrics are not to my liking?"

"Lizzy, be fair. Poor Mr. Darcy has helped rear a much younger sister for many years. Most likely, he is used to making those decisions without giving it a thought."

"Poor Mr. Darcy? Is that all you can say? What about the fact that he will not take me to see Papa straightaway?"

"Mr. Darcy told Edward he will be travelling to Derbyshire at the end of the week, and he would stop by Longbourn on the way to Pemberley."

"But—"

"We went through this before your wedding, Lizzy. You were saved by a decent man from a circumstance *you* created, yet you insist on acting as though you are the injured party."

Elizabeth did not answer. Instead, she kept nervously threading her handkerchief through her fingers. She looked so helpless that Mrs. Gardiner was reminded that her niece was barely eighteen, and her annoyance diminished somewhat.

"Lizzy, I suspect one reason you are finding fault with your husband is that you are afraid of being intimate with him. Am I right?"

She watched Elizabeth's eyes fill with tears. "I do not love him. How can I pretend that I do?"

"Look at me." Mrs. Gardiner waited until she had Elizabeth's attention. "If you listen to nothing else I have said, heed this. People have joined in marriages of convenience for centuries. For the most part, the difference between those marriages that turned out well for the woman and those that did not, was simply kindness. Just because you accept that Mr. Darcy is your husband and allow him his rights, does not mean you are madly in love with him. Conversely, just because he exercises his rights, does not mean he is in love with you. Love develops when kindness is reciprocated. He meets your needs, and you meet his. That is what leads to a harmonious marriage and to love."

Elizabeth dabbed at her eyes. "I am finding all of this very difficult."

"I have learned that nothing worth having comes easily. Now, if you need to talk before you leave London, I am here. Once you are at Pemberley, you may write to me as often as you need, and I will respond swiftly."

Elizabeth threw herself into her aunt's arms. "I fear I am not cut out to be anyone's wife, much less someone like Mr. Darcy. Pray for me."

Mrs. Gardiner framed her niece's face with her hands. "I pray for you every day. Now, go home and wait for the physician to come. One cannot think straight when one does not feel well."

"I shall."

Chapter 8

Darcy House
The same day

Upon returning from Lord Appleby's townhouse, William enquired after his wife. Mrs. Barnes informed him that Mrs. Darcy and her maid had taken a carriage to the Gardiners' residence immediately after the modiste departed.

"Did you send for Dr. Graham's associate?"

"He will be here this afternoon."

"Then let us hope Mrs. Darcy returns before then."

Troubled that Elizabeth felt the need to see her relations again, William took solace in the fact that once they were settled at Pemberley, it would be impossible for her to flee to her family every day. Brushing his irritation aside, he walked to his study and had barely seated himself when shouting in the foyer garnered his attention. Rushing in that direction, when he turned the corner, he was surprised to see John Lucas confronting Mr. Barnes and waving his arms in the air like a madman.

"I do not care if the knocker is not on the door. I know Darcy is here! I *will* speak to him this instant!"

Perplexed at his behaviour, William called out, "Lucas?"

The unruly visitor whirled about, the fierce look on his face growing even fiercer once he spied the man he had come to challenge.

"There you are, you blackguard!" Lucas shouted, stumbling towards William.

Two burly footmen moved to stand beside their master, though Lucas was too inebriated to be intimidated. "How dare you marry *my* Lizzy under false pretences!" he bellowed.

From his dishevelled appearance, slurred words and untruthful accusations, it was obvious to William that John Lucas had had too much to drink. Seeing servants peeking around corners, William motioned towards the library.

"Follow me into the library, and we will discuss your accusations in private."

"I will not!" Lucas declared. "I wish for all your servants to know how much of a cad you are! You knew I would not abandon Lizzy should her mother force a match with Collins, yet you never tried to contact me."

"How could I contact you? Cambridge was surrounded by water."

"And once you got to London, you arranged a secret wedding right under my nose without attempting to locate me."

"Explain why I would think marriage to you a viable solution when you dismissed your promise to marry Elizabeth as childish? And by your own admission, you left Cambridge to offer for Lady Aileen."

"You should know me well enough to know that Lady Aileen was merely an acquaintance. It is Lizzy I have always loved, and she loves me."

"Really? You once said she refused you because you were too much like a brother."

"Do not twist my words. Lizzy may not be *in love* with me, but she does love me, which is more than I can say for you. How cruel of you to marry her, knowing how much she despises you."

"Be sensible. You have no idea what happened at Cambridge after you left. Why I—"

"I know enough! I received a letter from my sister informing me that Mr. Bennet had been injured and that Lizzy went to Cambridge to look for me after her mother threatened to make her marry Collins. I believe when Lizzy arrived, you saw your chance to have her whilst hiding behind the guise of an honourable man keeping her from ruin. You thought Lord Matlock might not fault you for that."

"If I was so eager to marry Elizabeth, why did I avoid going to Meryton after that Christmas of 1810?"

"Because you could not handle rejection from someone you thought so far beneath you! Oh, you wanted Lizzy; you have from the minute you laid eyes on her. You were just too ashamed to admit it; you knew she hated you."

Unknowingly, Lucas had hit close to the truth, and William did not reply.

"I did not come here to argue, Darcy. I came to tell you that I intend to remain Lizzy's friend, which is closer to her than you will ever be."

"If you feel so strongly that I wronged you or Elizabeth, I shall be happy to answer your challenge."

"I would not stand a chance. You hold the title in fencing at Cambridge and are unequalled with a pistol. No, I shall bide my time and pray you die whilst Elizabeth is still young enough to marry someone whom she loves."

"Someone like you, I suppose?"

"At least I know her well. For instance, she is very close to her father, and I would have spirited her straight to Meryton from Cambridge to allow her to see him."

"I plan to take her there when we leave for Derbyshire. Meanwhile, I have been assured Mr. Bennet's condition is improving."

"My sister would not lie, and her letter to me stated that Mr. Bennet was gravely ill and near to death!"

William's hands formed into fists as he stepped forward. "When you sober up, Lucas, I pray you will recall the truth—not these lies you have concocted to soothe your conscience. Now, I warn you, leave my wife alone and do not darken my door again until you can accept our marriage."

"I will go, but know this! I intend to make a point of calling on Lizzy whenever she is in Meryton, or we are both in Town. You cannot prevent our friendship from continuing. She will not stand for it."

"If you were not drunk, I would—" Realising he was at the

point of losing control, William addressed the footmen. "Show Mr. Lucas to the pavement."

As each footman grabbed an arm, Lucas shrugged them off. "I can find my own way out!"

Mr. Barnes held the door open, but the instant Lucas crossed the threshold, he closed it and made a point of securing the latch.

"He is never to set foot in this house again until I say so," William declared. Then he stalked back to his study in a huff.

In the music room

When John Lucas had arrived at Darcy House, Lady Henrietta was half-listening to Georgiana play a selection that she had recently learned on the harp. The loud voices coming from the foyer frightened Georgiana, so Henrietta instructed her to remain in the music room whilst she investigated. Tiptoeing to the end of the hall on the opposite side of the foyer from the hall leading to William's study, she peered around a large potted plant. As the drama unfolded, she listened with delight to every cruel word spoken.

So, I was correct! Fitzwilliam was compromised by that little tart! Now, how can I use this information to ruin his marriage?

"Rietta?"

Lady Henrietta whirled around. "I told you to wait in the music room," she hissed at Georgiana.

By then the confrontation had ended, and Henrietta feared one of the servants would catch her eavesdropping. Putting an arm around Georgiana's shoulder, she guided her back to the music room.

"We must hurry so your brother does not learn that we were listening. You know how private he is."

"But I am worried. Mr. Lucas sounded so angry."

"You know that man?"

"Yes. He shared a house at Cambridge with Brother."

"I see."

"Did you learn what their argument was about?"

Quickly realising Georgiana could be used to spill the news to Elizabeth, she said, "Mr. Lucas was angry that your brother has not already escorted his wife to Meryton to see her father. It seems Mr. Bennet is gravely ill and could die."

Georgiana's hands flew to her mouth. "Oh, no! Poor Elizabeth! I must tell Brother to take her home right away."

"Oh, no, my dear. No man appreciates his sibling telling him how to handle his wife, especially someone as young as you. Besides, as soon as Elizabeth hears her father has taken a turn for the worse, I am certain she will insist on seeing him. And that will be that, unless—"

"Unless?"

"Well, your brother was angry enough to ban Mr. Lucas from Darcy House. I wonder if he will even tell Elizabeth he was here. And if he does not, how will she hear about her father's worsening condition?" Georgiana looked concerned, so Lady Henrietta continued laying her trap. "I could tell Elizabeth, but should Fitzwilliam find out, he might banish me to the dower's house as he wanted to do before. But were you to tell Elizabeth, we both know your brother would not stay angry with you for long, if at all."

"It is settled then. I shall tell her the minute she returns," Georgiana declared.

"Good for you. Elizabeth deserves to know the truth."

William's study

It was a short while later that Richard stuck his head in the study, receiving a scowl for his trouble. "Did I just see John Lucas leaving?"

"You did."

"From the look on Barnes' face and now yours, I assume his visit was not a pleasant one."

"That is an accurate assumption."

"Do you wish to tell me what happened?"

Putting down his pen, William described his confrontation

with John Lucas in detail, including Lucas' contradiction to his former opinion on marrying Elizabeth. When he finished, Richard let go a low whistle, as was his wont.

"I cannot believe the nerve of that arse! Why would he think you are to blame?"

"Apparently in his world I am."

"I am flabbergasted. What can I say, other than his beliefs are outlandish? I thought you were good friends."

"I thought we were, too, though now I wonder if I ever knew the man."

"I apologise, too, that it is my lot to deliver even more bad news."

William propped his elbows on his desk and dropped his head into his hands. For a moment, he rubbed his forehead with his fingers, as though trying to forestall a headache. When at last he leaned back in his chair, Richard continued.

"Lady Catherine knows you are married."

William groaned. "How did she learn of it so quickly?"

"Alas, she happened to have business in Town and arrived today to stay with my parents. Knowing she would soon learn of it, Father broke the news. I walked in on her rant about your lack of responsibility to Anne and the fact that you married far beneath your station and in secret. I did my best to explain the circumstances and to paint you in the best possible light—an honourable man doing his duty and all that. I fear, however, I was not successful."

"Why am I not surprised?"

"Brace yourself. I fear she is planning some form of retaliation."

"Let her. I no longer care. By the way, Appleby agreed to sign the consolidation loan."

"Thank God for that. What did he ask in return?"

"My firstborn."

"That does not surprise me."

"In truth, he has always admired Zeus and—"

"Surely you did not give Zeus to Appleby?"

"No. I promised him Zeus' offspring—a colt who is almost a year old."

"That is a relief. Still, I worry Father may join with Lady Catherine to punish you in some form."

William stood and walked over to his favourite spot in front of the windows. As he admired the gardens, he said, "If I am no longer considered a part of the family, I shall go it alone."

Richard joined him, placing an arm over his cousin's shoulder. "You will never be alone so long as I am alive."

William smiled. "I feel the same way about you."

"Musketeers[5] forever!" Richard declared, slashing an imaginary sword in the air and chuckling. "That was our rallying cry when we were boys, was it not?"

"It was. But that was before everything French was banned," William said, smiling. "If only we had known then what the future held. Life was so much simpler when we thought our parents were always right and invincible."

"Yes. It was a big disappointment to find out neither was true."

Unbeknownst to William, whilst he and Richard were talking, the carriage bearing Elizabeth and Florence returned through the alley. And, as it happened, when they entered the rear of the house, they encountered Georgiana and Lady Henrietta, who were about to ascend the staircase there. Seeing Elizabeth, Georgiana rushed to her.

"Oh, Elizabeth! There is something I must tell you. Hurry! Let us go upstairs before Brother learns you are back. We can speak freely once we are in your sitting room."

Elizabeth's first inclination was to worry; however, recalling how secretive her younger sisters acted whenever they had a surprise to share, she allowed Georgiana to lead her up the stair-

5 **Musketeers** – The Three Musketeers, a historical novel by Alexandre Dumas set in 1625-1628. For the purposes of this story, the book has been published much earlier than its true publication date of 1844.

case. Once in her sitting room, she dismissed Florence and she, Georgiana and Lady Henrietta sat down.

Feigning ignorance of what Georgiana was about to share, Lady Henrietta said, "Georgiana, whatever you wish to tell Elizabeth, you must hurry. It is almost time to leave if you are to join Lady Esme for your harp lesson."

"I am ready to go, but I must tell Elizabeth how sorry I am that her father is gravely ill."

Elizabeth paled. "Gravely ill? Fitzwilliam said he was doing very well."

"That is not what Mr. Lucas said only minutes ago."

Elizabeth's expression darkened. "John Lucas was here?"

"Yes, he and Brother had an awful argument just before you returned. That is when I heard Mr. Lucas say that your father was gravely ill."

Lady Henrietta broke in, "Georgiana, dear, you should have let Fitzwilliam break the news to Elizabeth."

"But...but, you said—"

"Go to your room and wait for me."

Confused, Georgiana hurried from the sitting room.

"I apologise you heard that from Georgiana. I feel certain Fitzwilliam will tell you that your father has apparently grown worse as soon as he hears you have returned."

"How could John Lucas have possibly known about Papa?"

"What do you mean?"

Elizabeth dropped her gaze. "John, a friend and neighbour of longstanding, has been attending Cambridge. He shared a house with Fitzwilliam. I travelled there to speak to him, but when I arrived, Fitzwilliam explained he had left for Richmond. How could he have known about my father's injury?"

"Unfortunately, along with Georgiana, I heard the entire argument. Mr. Lucas mentioned a letter from his sister, informing him about your father. After he told Fitzwilliam what was said, things grew tense."

"What do you mean?"

"Fitzwilliam brought up someone named Lady Aileen, and Mr. Lucas shouted that your husband should know him well enough to realise he would never abandon you. He accused Fitzwilliam of ..." Lady Henrietta feigned unwillingness to continue.

"Please. I need to know the truth."

"He accused Fitzwilliam of marrying you under false pretences."

"I...I find it hard to believe Mr. Darcy would do something so dishonourable."

Henrietta made a show of patting Elizabeth's arm sympathetically. "My dear, I hesitate to put you off when it comes to husbands and truth, but I would be remiss if I did not share my experience with that grand institution. I learned in my first marriage that most men will say or do anything to get their way. And nothing changed when I married George Darcy." She sighed. "It is a fact of life with which women must deal. Still, perhaps if you explained to Fitzwilliam that you really must see your father—"

"I have, and he refuses to travel until his business is finished." Teary-eyed, Lizzy stood to her feet. "I must speak to John today!"

"I understand the physician is to be here at any minute."

"I forgot. Then as soon as he leaves, I shall speak to John."

"I heard Fitzwilliam order Barnes to bar Mr. Lucas from this house. Were he to learn you plan to speak to Mr. Lucas, he may try to prevent you from leaving the house. Fitzwilliam can be very stubborn when he believes he is right."

"How well I know. I shall wait until the physician has left and find an opportunity to leave the house undetected. I will not need a carriage for it is only a few blocks to John's townhouse. I can walk that far effortlessly."

"My dear, no lady walks the streets of London, especially not alone."

"They do if they wish to leave unhindered."

"Well, at the least take your maid."

"No. If I do, the servants will realise it is me and alert Fitzwilliam. I had rather go dressed as my maid and slip in and out of the house undetected."

Lady Henrietta smiled. "Brilliant!"

Elizabeth's bedroom

After the physician had examined her and left, Elizabeth feigned exhaustion when William entered her bedroom.

"I am sorry I missed the physician. Richard was here, and I became involved in a conversation with him. What did he have to say?"

"He said I am doing well and to continue taking my aunt's remedy."

"Did you enjoy your visit with the Gardiners?"

"I always do."

"I trust your family is well."

"They are."

"Will you be down for tea?"

Elizabeth made a show of removing her slippers and lying down on a chaise lounge. "If I feel well enough, I will."

Seeing he could prod no further conversation from his wife, William crossed to the door. He paused before exiting. "I shall look forward to seeing you at dinner, then."

Elizabeth did not reply. More perplexed than ever about how to reach his wife, William left the room.

As soon as he was gone, Florence stepped out of the closet where Elizabeth had motioned for her to hide at his knock.

Wringing her hands nervously, she said, "I do not think this is good idea, ma'am. A lady traipsing about London by herself—not to mention a married woman calling on a gentleman alone. It is just not done."

"It is not as though John Lucas is a stranger. We have been neighbours all my life and are the best of friends. I only wish to speak to him a few minutes privately. Then I shall hurry back here. No one will be the wiser."

"The best laid plan of mice—"[6]

"I do not want to hear it. Now, help me into the gown you brought for me. With the gown and your bonnet, anyone who sees me will think I sent you on an errand."

Florence did as she was asked, and Elizabeth was pleased with the results. "Hand me your shopping basket, and I shall be on my way."

Carrying Florence's wicker basket, Elizabeth left through the door used by the servants and walked unnoticed past the men at the stables. Upon entering the alley, she made the trek to the Lucases' townhouse in good time.

When the Lucases' long-time butler answered her knock, he seemed indifferent. "You will need to go around to the side door, miss. The housekeeper's office is just inside. Ask for Mrs. Penrod."

"Do you not recognise me, Mr. Walsh?" Elisabeth teased, smiling as she pushed the bonnet up so he could see her face.

"Miss Bennet! I did not recognise you."

He stepped aside to let her enter and then walked out onto the portico and looked in both directions.

"I am alone."

Walsh's voice sounded higher than usual as he repeated "Alone? Then how on earth did you get here?"

"I walked from Grosvenor Square."

If the butler was shocked, he was too polite to show it. "Well, I fear you have arrived at an inopportune time. The Master is leaving for Meryton shortly, and he is busily engaged in supervising the packing."

"Where is he at present?"

"In the study...alone." The last word was said as a warning. "The rest of the family is still in Meryton, you see. Do you wish for me to summon him?"

---

6 From **To A Mouse** by Robert Burns, 1785

"No, thank you. I know where the study is."

The butler looked stunned as she walked towards the hall that led to Mr. Lucas' study.

Chapter 9

Lucas House
The study

Having spent the hours since his return from Darcy House consuming strong coffee, John Lucas was almost completely sober, howbeit with a wearisome headache. Though deep down he knew everything Darcy had said was true, he had yet to admit it to himself. Instead, he was still wallowing in undeserved pity because his foolish decision to offer for Lady Aileen, something he now regretted, had given Darcy a chance to marry the girl he had always coveted.

Whilst these thoughts ran through his mind, he busily packed files into a satchel to take with him to Lucas Lodge. He had been away from Meryton far too long after graduation and did not wish to raise his parents' ire more than he had already. Occupied as he was, he did not see Elizabeth walk in through the open door.

Hearing the creak of a floorboard, Lucas' head snapped up. "Lizzy? What in the world!"

Dropping the file he held onto the desk, he hastened forwards to grasp her hands and plant a kiss on her forehead, just as he had always done when they had been apart for any length of time. Then recalling Darcy's warning, he looked past her to the open door.

"Are you—that is to say—did anyone accompany you?"

"No, I came alone."

Relieved, Lucas guided her to a chair. "Why are you here?"

"I came because I understand you were at Darcy House earlier today," she replied, sitting down. "And, I was told you had an awful argument with Fitzwilliam."

As he sat down beside her, Lucas bristled. "I can only imagine what lies Darcy told you. In fact, I got the impression he would dearly love to keep you from ever speaking to me again. In that way, he could keep the truth from you."

"He told me nothing. I learned of the argument from my new sister and was determined to hear the details from you."

Fully aware he had lied about the seriousness of his interest in Lady Aileen when he confronted Darcy, Lucas became defensive. "We talked of many things. To what are you referring?"

"Georgiana said you told Fitzwilliam my father is gravely ill, whilst he tells me my uncle said that Papa is improving. At least that is the reason he gives for refusing to leave for Meryton until the end of this week."

"I only know what Maria said in the letter that awaited me upon my return to London. I prefer to believe someone who is actually *in* Meryton over those who are not."

Elizabeth looked down as if pondering his explanation. Eventually, she raised her head, locking eyes with him. "You accused Fitzwilliam of marrying me under false pretences. What did you mean by that?"

Swallowing hard, John Lucas made a conscious decision to do something he had never done in all the years he and Elizabeth had been friends. He lied to her.

"Darcy knows how much I have always loved you, Lizzy. It was no secret. And he knew I was prepared to step in and marry you if your parents ever tried to force you to marry Mr. Collins, or anyone else, for that matter. Marrying you was not his only option. All he had to do was get in touch with me."

"But...but why would he want to marry me?"

"I believe he secretly admired you, though he was too cowardly to go against his relations when it came to selecting a bride. He probably thought this was his chance to do as he pleased and play the honourable man whilst doing it."

"When we were in Cambridge, Fitzwilliam told me you had left for Richmond to offer for another woman—a Lady Aileen."

Sighing loudly, Lucas shook his head. Then he stood because he could not look Elizabeth in the eye whilst he continued to spin his tale. "Lord Dunbar was one of my classmates at Cambridge, and I happened to meet his sister, Lady Aileen, on several occasions. I told Darcy I was going to Richmond to arrange a deal with Dunbar concerning some livestock Father wished to sell. Darcy teased me about going to see Lady Aileen, but I never dreamed he would tell anyone I went there to offer for her."

Her ire rising, Elizabeth's demeanour changed entirely. "Why, that horrible—" Huffing, she stood. "Please take me with you when you leave. I simply must see Papa."

"If I do, Darcy may do something rash. You are aware he has an awful temper?"

"I do not care. I want to see Papa, and I shall. If you will not take me, I will take a post coach. I have enough funds in my reticule for a ticket."

"If you insist on going, you shall ride with me. I just received a note from Charles Bingley stating that he has business to complete and cannot accompany me, so I am travelling alone. I shall have Mrs. Penrod fetch a maid to accompany us as a chaperone. At least Darcy will not be able to accuse you of travelling without one."

Elizabeth reached for his hand. "You have always been truthful with me, even when I did not wish to hear it. Thank you, my friend."

Ashamed, Lucas looked away. "Lizzy, I must say again that you may face grave consequences for defying Darcy. Are you certain you want to do this?"

"I am."

He glanced back to her. "Always remember that everything I have ever done is for your benefit."

Elizabeth smiled. "I have never doubted that."

Darcy House

William walked through the library and onto the terrace to find Georgiana and Lady Henrietta seated but Elizabeth nowhere in sight. Addressing a maid who had just poured each of them a cup of tea, he said, "Go upstairs and check on Mrs. Darcy. Please tell her that tea is being served."

"Yes, sir."

Not long afterwards, whilst the three of them were waiting for Elizabeth before partaking of refreshments, the maid reappeared and whispered something to William.

Throwing down his serviette, he pushed back his chair and stood. "There is no need to wait any longer. Please begin whilst your tea is still hot."

As her brother exited the terrace, Georgiana leaned across the table to whisper, "Do you think Elizabeth's absence is the result of knowing about Mr. Lucas?"

"I have no idea, but even if it was, you did the right thing. Now, let us do as your brother said and enjoy our tea."

Elizabeth's sitting room

When William opened the door to the sitting room separating the mistress' suite from his, he found Florence pacing the floor. She stopped abruptly upon seeing him, her hand flying to her mouth as though to keep from crying out.

"Where is Mrs. Darcy?"

"I...I am not at liberty to say, sir."

"I appreciate that you are trying to be loyal to my wife, but I want to know right this minute where she is. If I cannot locate her in the house, I plan to scour London until I find her."

Florence's eyes dropped to the floor, her wringing hands an indication of her anxiety. "She said she was going to speak to Mr. Lucas."

William's expression darkened. "How in the world did she leave Darcy House without anyone being aware of it?"

"She left on foot wearing my clothes," Florence replied, glancing up at her employer's now livid expression.

"On foot! Good Lord!"

"I...I tried to persuade her not to, but—"

William raised a hand to silence her. "Return to your rooms."

"Yes, sir."

As William hurried down the grand staircase, he was not surprised to find Mr. Barnes and his wife in the foyer. Without skipping a beat, he barked an order. "Barnes, send a footman to the stables to have my carriage brought round."

Instead of responding immediately, Mr. Barnes glanced at his wife nervously. The housekeeper held out a letter. "This was delivered whilst you were upstairs. We felt perhaps you would want to read it at once."

William took the missive, promptly broke the seal and began to read.

Fitzwilliam,

After hearing that you and John Lucas had an argument and that some of it concerned my father's health, I went straight to John's house to determine what he knows that I do not. He believes my father is close to death; therefore, I have decided I can wait no longer to return to Longbourn.

Since John is returning to Lucas Lodge today, I have asked him to escort me. If you still plan to stop at Meryton on your way back to Derbyshire, you will find me at Longbourn.

Elizabeth

After taking a deep breath and letting it go slowly, William addressed the butler and housekeeper quietly so no one else could hear.

"Never mind the carriage, Barnes. It seems my wife decided she could not wait until Friday to return to Meryton. As we speak, she is already on her way."

Mrs. Barnes was stunned. "I had no idea Mrs. Darcy was not in residence."

"You could not have known. Now, I plan to speak to Lady Henrietta and then go directly to my study to handle some business matters. It is still my plan to leave for Pemberley on Friday."

With motherly concern the housekeeper said, "Sir, you have not eaten anything. Would you like me to fix a tray of tea and biscuits for you?"

"No. I have lost my appetite. However, I will likely be up late tonight, so a pot of coffee would be appreciated."

Mr. and Mrs. Barnes watched with anxious eyes as the master walked through the library and back towards the terrace.

"What in the world could have possessed Mrs. Darcy to do something so foolish?" Barnes whispered.

"Immaturity," his wife whispered in return. "Pure childishness, if you ask me. That young lady has a lot of growing up to do, if it is not too late already."

"Aye," her husband said. "If it is not too late."

Upon reaching the terrace, William walked straight to the one he believed had revealed his argument with Lucas to Elizabeth.

"Lady Henrietta, explain to me how it was your business to inform my wife of Mr. Lucas' visit?"

Immediately, Georgiana broke in. "It...it was not Rietta, Brother. I was the one who told Elizabeth...but only because I thought she had the right to know her father was gravely ill."

William's expression changed from one of anger to hurt as he confronted his sister. "And you thought me incapable of caring enough about my wife to tell her what Lucas said?"

"But...but you forbade Mr. Lucas from setting foot in this house again."

"What I did or did not do regarding Lucas has no bearing on my wife. I would have told Elizabeth everything, most especially since Lucas was spouting lies. I would have wanted her to know the truth."

Georgiana began weeping. "Oh, William, I am so sorry. Forgive me. I shall apologise to Elizabeth the next time I—"

"You have done enough already!" William declared a bit too frostily. "After tea, you will return to Matlock House where you will reside until your harp lessons have concluded." He then addressed Henrietta. "And you, madam, will impose on someone else's hospitality until the time comes to escort Georgiana back to Pemberley."

Without uttering another word, he stalked back into the library. The sounds of Georgiana's sobs followed his retreat, yet he was too busy mulling over his present circumstances to notice. He kept walking until he cleared the library and turned down the hall that led to his study.

Once in there, he closed the door and walked over to sit behind his desk. Dropping his head into his hands, it took all his strength not to weep in despair. He had not felt this despondent since Mr. Sturgis revealed the extent of his father's betrayal of him, Georgiana and all those whose livelihoods depended on Pemberley.

At length, William steeled himself to do what he must. Taking paper from a drawer, he began to pen a letter to his solicitor. Once finished, he rang for a footman.

"Yes, Mr. Darcy."

"I want this letter delivered to Mr. Cranston on Bond Street straightaway."

William held out the note and the footman came forwards to take it. "Yes, sir."

After the footman exited the room, William looked at the documents lying on his desk. There was no time to mourn his short-lived marriage, for there was work to be done before he could think of going home. And, until Cranston sent a reply, he was unsure what his next step would be.

That evening

To William's great relief, his copy of the executed bank loan was delivered soon after he had secluded himself in his study. Lowering his payments to the bank substantially, this loan would free enough capital to move forwards with his plan to upgrade Willowbend Hall, his great-grandmother's estate in Weymouth, which he could then sell to get out of debt. Thoughts of that estate brought back memories of a large white-washed stone manor situated on a cliff overlooking the bay, its proximity to the sea a large part of its attraction. Fondly recalling summers spent there with his mother before Georgiana was born, he was melancholy at the thought of selling it. Still, he knew it had to be done.

Long neglected by his father, what tenants were left at Willowbend brought in just enough income to pay the few servants who remained. By building additional tenant housing, William was certain he could attract more, which would appeal to prospective buyers. Satisfied with his decision, William decided that when he returned to Pemberley he would charge Mr. Sturgis with evaluating how many tenant houses ought to be built and what repairs would be most needed to the manor itself. Sturgis, a genius at picturing the whole project, was one of the few people William trusted with those kinds of decisions. And, since there would be a finite amount of money to spend, it had to be handled efficiently.

A knock on the door disturbed his concentration. "Come!"

William was stunned when Barnes announced Mr. Cranston, and he stood when the elderly solicitor appeared in the doorway. As that gentleman hobbled into the room with his ever-present cane, he continued until he stood directly in front of William's desk.

"Fitzwilliam," he said, not waiting for pleasantries, "what is the meaning of this letter?" As he spoke, he pulled William's letter from his pocket and thrust it towards him. "You cannot be serious."

"Sit down, Mr. Cranston, and I shall explain."

Cranston did as he was asked, though his expression displayed his displeasure at not being answered immediately. The second William sat down again, Cranston said, "Well?"

"First, I do not want anyone, not even a clerk, to know what we are about to discuss."

"I will make certain of that."

"Excellent. To answer your question, my note meant exactly what it said. I wish to know the law concerning incompetence as it applies to marriage."

The solicitor glared at him. "If the newspapers are to be believed, you have just married. Surely you are not—"

"Mr. Cranston, my wife has left me. Without my knowledge, she returned to her family home. I received a note after she was already on the road. It informed me that she was travelling with a neighbour from her home village."

"Was this neighbour a man or a woman?"

"A man. Hence, I feel obligated to consider all my options. As my solicitor, I expect you to explain what the law is without argument. Can I rely on you to do that, or should I engage another solicitor?"

Cranston's grey eyes turned steely. "Hear this, Fitzwilliam Darcy. I was your father's solicitor for over thirty years and have been yours since you reached your majority. I may at times speak to you as though you were one of my sons, but I am too old to change now. If you wish to consult someone else, then so be it. But, should you decide to keep me on, you will always hear the truth as I see it."

William sighed. "I am sorry if I spoke too severely. It is just that I am at my wit's end, and I feel I must decide soon what action to take."

The old man's eyes softened. "I shall try to be of help. Tell me what brought on this situation."

After William explained the circumstances leading up to his marriage and what had happened since, Mr. Cranston said, "This is grave indeed." Pulling a paper from his satchel, he began to read. "One is incompetent under the law and cannot be held to a contract if one is underage or insane."

"My wife may be insanely irritating, but she is certainly of sound mind."

Mr. Cranston had stopped reading at the interruption and began anew when William said no more. "Contracts are null and void if either party has not reached their majority, and they marry without a father or guardian's consent."

William nodded matter-of-factly. "That was what I thought. I just wanted to make certain I was correct."

"May I ask if this is truly something you wish to pursue? Are you so angry with your wife that you cannot work out a compromise?"

William's eyes dropped to the floor. "I am not angry. But in truth, I never thought that marrying me would make Elizabeth so unhappy. However, if she would rather not be wed, then perhaps her father should claim he did not give his consent and let the marriage be dissolved."

"It may well free her from the marriage, but it could affect her future. Your position in society will insulate you from too much controversy—well, that and your connections—but her prospects for an advantageous marriage would be impacted."

"I will keep that in mind." William stood. "Thank you for responding so quickly. I did not expect to hear from you until tomorrow at the earliest."

Cranston took the measure of the young man. "When I read the note, I felt I must come right away." He stood and propped on his cane once more. "Would you consider taking advice from an old man who has been happily married for three and thirty years?"

A long sigh escaped William. "I suppose it could not hurt, though you do know that in my circle such marriages are the exception, not the rule."

"Perhaps they are the exception precisely because of what I am about to say." When William did not answer, he continued. "Give each other the benefit of the doubt, and never make judgements in haste. Oft times when you do, you will regret your actions. If you love this woman, give her time to adjust. She is still young, and you cannot fault her for loving her father, now can you?"

"No. I cannot fault her for that."

"I am glad you see my point. Now, if you need me, I shall be in

Town until the end of next week. However, you can always contact me by post. My office forwards my correspondence to wherever I am at the time. Rest assured I shall respond immediately."

"Thank you for your expertise and for the advice."

"You are welcome."

Longbourn
Late that same day

John Lucas' coach had not yet disappeared through the front gate when Jane rushed out of the house to greet her sister.

"Lizzy!" Pulling her into an embrace, Jane declared, "I am so relieved to see you! I have been so worried."

"I am just as relieved to see you," Elizabeth murmured into her sister's hair as they twisted side to side in a hug.

Suddenly, Jane's brow furrowed, and she began to pull her sister behind one of the large trees that lined the walkway.

"Did you not get my message? I told Uncle Edward you should stay away for as long as possible. Mama is still livid that you ran away, and Mr. Collins could not be persuaded to return to Longbourn." She glanced to where a coach was barely visible in the distance. "Why did John not come inside to greet us since he is family now?"

Avoiding the subject of marriage, Elizabeth replied, "I asked him to go on to Lucas Lodge, for I hoped to see Papa before anyone knows I am here." With Jane's nod, she added, "Tell me the truth, how is he faring?"

Jane could not prevent a smile. "Papa is so much better since the physician, Dr. Graham, arrived. In only one day, I saw great improvement."

Elizabeth looked perplexed. "But according to a letter received from Maria, John thought that Papa was near death."

"I do not know why Maria would have written such a thing unless she wrote it when Papa was first injured."

"Tell me about Dr. Graham."

"Our uncle commissioned him, and he has been a godsend.

Mama's nerves are so much better since he took over Papa's care from the local apothecary. You just missed meeting him. He returned to his room at the inn at Meryton only minutes ago."

"That is peculiar. Neither Aunt Maddie nor Uncle Edward mentioned having sent a physician."

"Perhaps, in all the confusion, they simply failed to think of it."

"Jane, there is so much I need to tell you, but first I must see Papa."

"Since you wish to see him unhindered, I suggest you go in the side door and up the back staircase. Mrs. Hill is sitting with him at present. Once Mama learns you are back, no doubt she will have another fit of nerves."

"Where are Lydia, Mary and Kitty?"

"They are with Mama in the parlour. Whilst you go in the back door, I shall go in the front and distract them."

Elizabeth gave her sister a kiss on the cheek. "Thank you. After I see Papa, I shall wait in our bedroom. If I can manage it, I may not tell the rest of our family I am home until tomorrow."

"Just be quick about it. I do not know how long I can keep them occupied."

Chapter 10

London
The Gardiners' residence

Madeline Gardiner waited patiently whilst her husband read the missive that had just arrived from Mr. Darcy. Even so, her patience was wearing thin when he began to read it through again.

"Well?" she asked at length.

"Mr. Darcy wishes to see me as soon as possible."

"That is all he said?"

"He said he is leaving for Pemberley later today and desires to discuss something with me before he does."

"Did he mention Lizzy?"

"No."

She closed her eyes. "This cannot be good. I had hoped all would be well after our last talk."

Edward, who had already rung for a servant, was busily pulling on his coat. "Now, Madeline, we do not know that. Let us keep a positive outlook until we learn what this is about."

A maid appeared in the open study door. "Tell Mr. Shelby to bring the carriage around to the front," he ordered. Then, to his wife he added, "I shall go to Darcy House straightaway. Send a servant to my office to inform them that I shall be in later than usual."

Darcy House

Since Lady Henrietta and William's sister were no longer in residence, the house was devoid of feminine chatter and Georgiana's music. Instead, a steady activity of a different sort filled the silence—the sound of footmen carrying trunks down the grand staircase to join those already stacked in the marble foyer. There, they would wait until it was time to load the Darcy coach, which was being readied for the trip to Pemberley.

Watching everything with fretful eyes, Mrs. Barnes shivered the instant their absent mistress' trunks began to join those in the foyer. Fitzwilliam Darcy had acted oddly unruffled after learning his wife had left London with another man, and his expression had been particularly frosty when he ordered all of Mrs. Darcy's clothes and personal items packed.

"How many more are there?" Startled from her reverie, Mrs. Barnes turned to see her husband eyeing the increasing mound. "I do not see how they will get them all on one coach," he added.

"These four are not going on the coach," Mrs. Barnes said. "They contain Mrs. Darcy's clothes."

"Oh? Then why were they packed?"

"I was told the master is sending them to Hertfordshire."

Glancing around to see no one about, the butler whispered, "Do you suppose we have seen the last of our new mistress?"

Before his wife could reply, there was a loud rapping on the front door. Motioning for the footman there to open it, both butler and housekeeper were shocked when Lady Catherine de Bourgh walked through the door the instant it was opened.

"I wish to see my nephew immediately!" she exclaimed, casting a disdainful look at the pile of trunks in the foyer.

Mr. Barnes, who had been walking towards the door, stopped in his tracks. "I will inform him that you are here, my lady."

"Never mind!" the haughty woman exclaimed, walking past him. "I shall tell Fitzwilliam myself."

As she proceeded down the hall that led to the study, the steady tap of her cane competed with Mr. Barnes' pleadings, "My lady! My lady, if you will allow me to—"

William was busily packing files to take to Pemberley when he heard his aunt's shrill voice in the foyer and Mr. Barnes' entreaties. Pausing to take a deep breath as the sounds of her cane grew closer, he had gathered his wits and courage by the time Lady Catherine walked into his study.

"Fitzwilliam, you can be at no loss to understand the reason for my visit. Your own heart, your own conscience, must tell you why I had to come."

William feigned complete ignorance. "Indeed, you are mistaken, madam. I am not able to account for the honour of seeing you today, especially since I had no idea you were in Town."

"Nephew," she replied in a biting tone, "you ought to know I am not to be trifled with. But, however insincere *you* may choose to be, you shall not find *me* so. My character has always been celebrated for its sincerity and frankness, and I shall certainly not depart from it today. When I was informed you had married a woman of no consequence, no connections and no dowry to speak of in a hastily arranged ceremony, I instantly resolved to make my sentiments known to you."

"I wonder you took the trouble to come when you know I always follow my own counsel with respect to my life."

"And the result of following your own counsel is a disastrous marriage that will not benefit Pemberley's coffers one iota!"

Though William could not argue with that fact, he refused to flinch. Instead, he kept a steely gaze fixed on his aunt as she continued her rant.

"If you had followed my advice, you would have had Anne's fortune! But you always fancied yourself too good for my daughter."

"Anne does not want to marry me any more than I want to marry her. Her health prevents her from ever bearing children, and she wishes never to marry anyone."

"Had you truly wished to do what is *right*, you could have had a child by another woman and passed it off as Anne's!"

"You have not the faintest idea what the word right means!"

"And you do? You are just like your father. George never listened to me, either! After Anne died, he married that hussy and paid off her debts, not caring that it would bankrupt Pemberley." Seeing William's look of surprise, she cried, "Do you think I do not know everything about your financial position? I have many well-placed friends who keep me informed. I know that if you do not reverse your fortunes soon, you will lose everything." She sniffed in disdain. "Perhaps that would be a good thing. Only *after* you have lost your inheritance will you understand that family counsel is not to be treated so meanly. Sadly, Georgiana will suffer for your stubbornness."

"I do not intend to lose Pemberley."

"Oh, no? Well, be advised I have instructed my solicitors to withdraw all of Rosings' investments in the stocks and bonds we share jointly, and I have asked my brother to follow suit. Matlock and Rosings have been carrying you. Once we withdraw our capital, the funds will collapse because Pemberley has not had the money to pay her fair share for some time."

William lifted his chin defiantly. "Do what you wish, Aunt! If it must, Pemberley will survive without your help or that of my uncle."

Lady Catherine huffed. "We shall see about that!" As she stalked out of the room, she stopped in the doorway. "Love flies out the window when money is in short supply. I hope your wife is prepared to do her own cooking and cleaning in the future."

"Fortuitously, my wife is not a slave to the trappings of society. And I hope you enjoyed your visit, Aunt, for it is time for you to leave!"

Mumbling to herself, the pompous woman stalked down the hall and out the front door of Darcy House without stopping. As she waited on the pavement for the footman to open the door to her coach, Mr. Gardiner's carriage pulled up behind her vehicle. Stepping out of the carriage, Elizabeth's uncle smiled and tipped his hat in her direction, only to be challenged.

"Who might you be?"

"Edward Gardiner, my lady."

"Humph! From the look of you, I assume you are one of my nephew's new relations."

Having said that, Lady Catherine entered her coach and tapped the ceiling with her cane, urging the driver on. Upon hearing her insult, Mr. Gardiner wondered if that woman had anything to do with Mr. Darcy's summons. However, before he had time to dwell on the subject, the butler appeared on the portico, prompting him to start up the steps.

"Mr. Gardiner, sir. Mr. Darcy is expecting you." As he entered the house, the butler hurried to take his coat and hat. "If you will wait here, I shall be pleased to tell my master you have arrived."

William's study

By the time Mr. Gardiner was announced, William was once more seated behind his desk. Standing to shake hands, he motioned to a chair. "Please, be seated."

Mr. Gardiner gave William a wan smile that vanished as soon as he sat down and began to speak. "I was surprised to read that you are leaving today."

"My business concluded earlier than I thought possible," William replied. Then he continued, "I should like to get straight to the point and not waste your time or mine. Are you aware that your niece left London with John Lucas late yesterday afternoon, Mr. Gardiner?"

The gentleman looked stunned. "I ... I had no idea!"

"I received this," William slid the letter across the desk, "after Elizabeth had left for Hertfordshire. I thought perhaps she might have written one to you as well."

He picked it up. "She did not." After reading the missive, Gardiner said, "May I be so bold as to ask if you and she had an argument?"

"I can truthfully say that since we have been married, I have not been around my wife long enough to engage in an argument."

"It appears Elizabeth believes her father is close to death."

"That would be John Lucas' doing."

William began to explain all that had happened, including Lucas' drunken accusations that he had deliberately kept Elizabeth from her father and had married her under false pretences. When he finished, Mr. Gardiner looked confused. "I find it hard to believe John would lie outright to Lizzy. They have been the best of friends since they were children." Glancing to see William's expression grow darker, he quickly added, "Please do not mistake my meaning. I know that you married my niece to protect her from the gossip Mrs. Thornhill was so eager to spread. For John to accuse you of taking advantage of the situation is asinine."

"I appreciate your faith in my character, for all the accusations Lucas made were lies. I swear when he left for Richmond, it was to offer for Lady Aileen. By the time Elizabeth knocked on my door at Cambridge, I took for granted that if he was not already engaged, he soon would be. Even if we had not been surrounded by flood waters, I would never have thought to send for him."

"Your willingness to marry my niece tells me all I need to know about your character. It would certainly have made no sense to send for Lucas under those circumstances, and once Mrs. Thornhill discovered you, both your fates were sealed."

"Since Lucas was drunk when he made the accusations, I believed his tirade was simply that of a man unable to face the consequences of his actions. I hoped once he was sober, he would admit what had actually transpired."

"Lizzy would never have left London with Lucas had he been drunk, so evidently sobriety did not improve his memory."

"Whatever the reason, she chose to leave with him."

"I will not take my niece's side. What she did was wrong. However, in her defence, may I remind you that Lizzy is very young and—"

A hand went up to silence him. "I did not ask you here to argue why she left. I asked you here because my solicitor, Mr. Cranston, assures me there is a way to end the marriage. It is my belief that is something Elizabeth would welcome."

"Wha...what are you saying? The marriage has already been consummated. My niece could already be with child."

"Because my wife was ill when we married, our union was never consummated," William stated irritably. "There is nothing to worry about in that regard." When Mr. Gardiner did not reply, he continued, "In your opinion, is Mr. Bennet's health stable? Would he be able to discuss this solution?"

"I believe so. Dr. Graham says he is doing remarkably well."

"I am glad to hear it, for Mr. Cranston advised me the law states that anyone not over the age of majority cannot marry without the consent of their father or guardian. Since Elizabeth is underage, she can have her father testify he was unaware of the marriage and did not give his consent."

"But Thomas did give his consent. I have his letter granting me authority to sign a marriage contract in his stead."

"Mr. Gardiner, if you want to help your niece, you have only to destroy the letter and agree with Mr. Bennet's version of the event."

Gardiner stood and began to pace with his hands locked behind his back. "This would cause a scandal. My niece's prospects for another marriage would greatly diminish, and your reputation would suffer as well."

"Let me worry about my reputation. Can we not agree Elizabeth's happiness is more important than her reputation? And as far as prospects are concerned, she would be free to marry John Lucas, which is evidently what she wants."

Gardiner stopped to observe William. "When we spoke at Cambridge, you admitted you have cared for my niece since the Christmas of 1810, howbeit in secret. Today you speak as though you no longer have any feelings for her."

"I no longer believe a one-sided admiration is enough to preserve our union. I am offering Elizabeth something she wants very badly—a way out."

"I am not convinced she wants that. I think her judgement was clouded by her love for her father. They have always been very close, and if she feared he was going to die before she could see him again—"

"I understand her concern for her father, but I do not share your opinion regarding our marriage. I would rather part now than spend my life married to someone who is in love with another man. Moreover, I intend to settle a thousand pounds on Elizabeth for her trouble. In truth, I would give her more, but my present circumstances prevent me from doing so."

"Oh?" From the sceptical expression on Mr. Gardiner's face, William knew he would have to trust that gentleman with his secret.

"May I count on your discretion? If what I am about to say becomes common knowledge, it could hurt my family and Pemberley's future."

"Of course, you may."

"After my father died, I learned Pemberley was on the brink of ruin. This very week I was in London to negotiate a loan that will allow me to improve a property left to the estate by my great-grandmother. I hope to sell it and pay off most of Pemberley's debt."

"I had no idea of the burdens you were carrying. Allow me to apologise that marriage to my niece has only added to them. Still, I ask you not to act in haste."

"In my opinion, the sooner our marriage is dissolved, the sooner the gossip will die down. May I count on you to at least present my plan to Mr. Bennet? As I remember, that gentleman never cared for my company, either, so I imagine he will be agreeable."

"I will do as you ask, though I disagree with the plan."

"That is all I ask. Elizabeth left town in such a hurry that she left everything behind. I had her clothes and personal items packed so that you may take them to Longbourn with you. My servants will deliver the trunks to your home shortly." William stood. "Now, if you will excuse me, I must see to the packing of the last few items. I leave for Pemberley in less than an hour."

"Can I not persuade you to stop by Longbourn on your way north? If you and Thomas would only take the time to discuss the state of your marriage, it would afford him the opportunity to discover your character."

"I am afraid I must be in Derbyshire as soon as possible. Besides, I had rather Elizabeth not feel pressured by my presence at Longbourn."

Defeated, Mr. Gardiner sighed. "Yes, of course."

"Getting to know you and Mrs. Gardiner has been a pleasure. I am sorry the marriage did not work out as you and I hoped it might."

"May I hold out hope that circumstances will improve for you and my niece?"

William stared at him solemnly before saying, "You may, so long as the definition of improve includes the possibility of living separate lives."

Longbourn
Lizzy's bedroom
The next morning

When sunlight finally broke through the gaps in the muslin curtains, it fell upon a sleepless Elizabeth. Her father had been sound asleep yesterday when she entered his bedroom, and after talking quietly with Mrs. Hill, she had been relieved to discover that he was doing extremely well under the circumstances. Asking the housekeeper not to reveal her presence and promising to present herself in the morning, she had sneaked out of his bedroom and into the one she shared with Jane. When her sister eventually joined her, Elizabeth was able to calm Jane's fears that their mother might learn she was home, and she had remained hidden in the bedroom all night.

She was not looking forward to seeing her father's reaction to the news that she had married Mr. Darcy. Having despised that gentleman since meeting him that Christmas of 1810, her father often used him as an example of the type of person who, though highly educated, lacked common sense. Moreover, a niggling suspicion that her marriage may have been irreparably harmed by her decision to leave London with John Lucas made her uneasy about revealing the marriage to her mother as well, because she was just as certain her mother would be euphoric about the match.

Glancing at her sleeping sister, Elizabeth decided she had best start by enlightening the one she could always count on to be on her side. "Jane," she whispered, "Are you asleep?"

Jane stirred, scratched her nose and then pulled the covers over her head. Elizabeth tried again. "Jane, I have something very important to tell you."

Eventually the covers came down, and Jane squinted at her, murmuring sleepily, "What is so important that you must tell me now?"

Elizabeth took a deep breath and said hurriedly, "I am married to Fitzwilliam Darcy."

Her sister rolled over and pulled the covers back over her head. An instant later, she bolted upright. "What did you just say?"

"I said I am married to Fitzwilliam Darcy."

"That is preposterous, Lizzy! You do not even like him."

"It…it is a bit complicated, but we are definitely married."

Jane moved to sit on the side of the bed, her expression anxious. "I see no wedding ring."

Reaching for the thin gold chain around her neck, Elizabeth pulled the wedding ring from her décolletage. Jane eyed the ring suspiciously as Elizabeth slipped it back on her finger.

"Please tell me how something so absurd could have happened," she urged.

Elizabeth detailed all that had occurred since she had left for Cambridge, up to and including her marriage, conveniently stopping before telling her sister what had brought her back to Longbourn.

"Then that was Mr. Darcy's coach I saw in the distance?"

"No, it was the Lucases' coach."

"But if Mr. Darcy did not bring you—"

Elizabeth interrupted. "The truth is I left London without… without telling my husband. I sent a note informing him of what I had done to be delivered after I was already on the road."

"Lizzy, you did not!"

"I did! But allow me to explain."

Elizabeth related what Georgiana and Lady Henrietta had said about Lucas' argument with William and her decision to go to his house to learn the truth.

"When he mentioned Maria wrote that Papa was dying, I knew I had to come straightaway."

"But that was not true. Papa is not dying."

"I know that now. I suppose Maria's letter was written when Papa was first injured."

"Or perhaps John overstated Papa's condition simply to make Mr. Darcy look unkind in your eyes for lingering in town. Lizzy. It was I who told our uncle not to let you return until Mama had calmed down. He must have passed that along to Mr. Darcy."

"Why are you taking his side?"

Jane reached for Elizabeth's hand. "I am on your side, Lizzy. But since John always wanted to marry you, naturally he would be jealous of the man who did. Even I can see how he might manipulate their argument to make Mr. Darcy appear uncaring. Consider this. Knowing you would learn the truth eventually, why would Mr. Darcy lie about John offering for another woman? It makes absolutely no sense."

"I think Fitzwilliam Darcy is used to getting his way, regardless of what he must do to accomplish it. And since John is neither engaged nor married, it is clear who told the truth."

"That is hardly proof. His offer could have been refused."

"No woman in her right mind would refuse John."

"You did!" Flustered, Jane stood and reached for her robe. "In any case, you are married to Mr. Darcy now. What will you do if he does not forgive your imprudence?"

Elizabeth lifted her chin defiantly. "He should be worried I will not forgive *his* deception!"

Jane's hands flew to her hips. "Why are you so convinced Mr. Darcy is at fault?"

"I inherited Papa's ability to sketch character. That is why I am confident John is telling the truth."

"You thought Mr. Wickham charming until he tried to elope with Mary King and that only after he learned of the large sum she recently inherited from her uncle. Moreover, after he left town, all the merchants claimed he owed them money."

Displeased, Elizabeth kept silent, so Jane tilted her head towards the door. "Are you prepared to confront Mama now? She will be livid if she suspects you arrived yesterday and did not tell her."

"I am praying she will be so astonished to see me she will not realise I did not just walk in the front door. Besides, I am certain that hearing of my marriage to Mr. Darcy will distract her." Elizabeth reached for Jane's arm as she went towards the door. "However, there are things I do not wish any of our family to know."

"Oh?"

"I want to keep John's argument with Mr. Darcy a secret. Let them think my husband approved of John's offer to escort me home because he could not leave London until he was finished with his business."

"But should they learn the truth—"

"Please, just keep silent. If afterward the truth comes out, I will swear you had no knowledge of it."

Jane sighed. "As you wish."

Chapter 11

Longbourn
The breakfast room

When Elizabeth followed Jane into the room, Mrs. Bennet jumped to her feet.

"There you are, you ungrateful child!" She glanced at the open door to the hallway. "How did you get here?"

"I…I was—"

Before Lizzy could explain further, her mother interrupted. "I have suffered heart palpitations every day since you disappeared so suddenly. Where have you been all this time?"

"I was under the impression that Uncle Edward informed you I was with him and Aunt Madeline in London."

"Do not be impertinent, Lizzy. I am in no mood to—" Suddenly, she caught sight of the ring on Elizabeth's left hand. "What is that?" Rushing forwards to grab her daughter's hand, she brought it to her face. "You are wearing a wedding ring! Edward has not mentioned a marriage."

"Uncle wanted me to have the honour of announcing it myself." Elizabeth fixed a week smile on her face. "I…I have married Fitzwilliam Darcy."

Her younger siblings began to snicker, prompting Mrs. Bennet to issue a warning. "Do not vex me by jesting about something so important, Lizzy! Now, tell me the truth. You are married to John Lucas, are you not? After all, he is the only man who has ever paid you any attention." Instantly, her mother began to flounce around the room, waving her handkerchief in celebration. "This is most advantageous, for he will inherit Lucas Lodge!"

"No, Mama, I did not marry John. As I said, I am married to Mr. Darcy."

"Mr. Darcy of Pemberley?"

"Yes."

Turning pale, Mrs. Bennet began to fan herself with the handkerchief whilst grasping the back of a nearby chair. As she sat down, she cried, "Hill! Hill! Bring me my smelling salts!"

Once Mary, Kitty and Lydia realised Elizabeth was not teasing, they all stopped laughing. "You *hate* Mr. Darcy," Lydia exclaimed. "Why would you marry that pompous—?"

"Hush," Jane commanded. "He is now our brother, and you should speak of him with respect."

"I will never respect the man who told Kitty and me we were too loud and boisterous and should act more ladylike," Lydia declared defiantly.

"Though Papa should have been the one to discipline you, not Mr. Darcy, he was correct," Jane answered.

"Humph!" Lydia said. "Papa did not think so! And if Papa was satisfied with our behaviour, Mr. Darcy had no right to say a thing."

"Stop arguing this minute!" Mrs. Bennet barked. "I do not care what Mr. Darcy said or did in the past. He is now my son, and given his wealth, we shall never be thrown into the hedgerows should your father die." She embraced her least favourite daughter. "All is forgiven, Lizzy! Now, where is the dear man?"

"Mr. Darcy has business in London and cannot come until the end of the week," Elizabeth replied, *and I have no idea if he will come then.*

"Then why are you here?"

"I wished to see Papa right away, so he allowed John Lucas to escort me to Meryton."

"You rode home with John Lucas?" Mrs. Bennet asked, her brows rising in disbelief.

"A maid accompanied us."

"You should have waited and ridden with your husband. After all, you have been away all this time, and your father is so much improved that later this week would have sufficed."

"I thought Papa was near death! That is why I insisted on coming now." Praying that would satisfy her mother, Elizabeth added quickly, "If you will excuse me, I wish to see him now."

"Why not eat first? Your father is not going anywhere."

"I shall eat once I have seen him. I will not be long."

At that moment, Mrs. Hill walked into the breakfast room with the smelling salts, and Mrs. Bennet's attention was diverted. "You took so long I do not need them now, Hill. Go put them back."

The only reaction from their beleaguered housekeeper was the slight rise of her brows before she turned and retreated. Mrs. Bennet had turned back to the business of eating and did not look at Elizabeth when she cautioned, "Do not be too long, Lizzy, or everything will be cold."

"I shall keep that in mind."

Breathing a sigh of relief, Elizabeth turned to smile conspiratorially at Jane. Then she hurriedly ran up the stairs that led to the bedrooms. Equally pleased that things had gone so smoothly, Jane joined her mother and sisters at the breakfast table.

Mr. Bennet's bedroom

Elated to find her father awake when she opened his bedroom door, Elizabeth rushed to him. Tears rolled down both their faces as they embraced. Witnessing the poignant reunion, the maid who was sitting with Mr. Bennet quietly exited the room.

Elizabeth sat on the side of the bed. "Oh, Papa! Yesterday I heard from John Lucas that Maria had written you were near death. I was so worried I could think of nothing else but to come straight home."

"As you can see, that is not the case, Lizzy. My concern was for you, until Edward wrote that he had found you at Cambridge and brought you back to London."

He attempted to sit up, so Elizabeth placed several pillows

behind his back. Once he was settled, she related all that had transpired since she left for Cambridge, with the exception of Lucas' argument with William. Upon hearing she had married Mr. Darcy, an expression of repugnance crossed her father's face, yet Elizabeth continued as though nothing was amiss.

"Fitzwilliam had business in London, so he could not leave. John was returning to Meryton at once, and when I insisted on seeing you right away, Fitzwilliam allowed him to escort me home. A maid rode with us, so everything was proper."

"Humph! No newly-married gentleman should let someone else escort his wife back to her family home. Evidently, I need to have a good talk with him. When may we expect the elusive Mr. Darcy to grace us with his presence?"

"I...I am not certain of the exact day."

Silently, Elizabeth prayed that Mr. Darcy would not come anytime soon, for once he did, her deceit would be exposed.

"Lizzy?"

From the tone of his voice, she realised her father was waiting for an answer. "I am sorry, Papa. I was woolgathering and did not hear what you said."

"I asked if Mr. Darcy has been kind to you."

"I cannot say he has been unkind. He is just so...different. His sphere is so far removed from ours that I find him hard to understand."

Mr. Bennet looked thoughtful. "I can appreciate your uneasiness, yet time and familiarity will alleviate that." He reached to cup Elizabeth's cheek. "After all, he is a man, and you have always possessed the ability to wrap any man around your little finger. Surely, Mr. Darcy will not be able to resist you."

Elizabeth's gaze dropped to her lap. "It is as I said. If Mrs. Thornhill had not found us and threatened to create a scandal, we would never have married."

"A man of Darcy's calibre would never be pressured into a marriage he did not want. He could have left you to muddle through the humiliation whilst his relations and contacts helped him to overcome it. No, he must have feelings for you, else he would not have married you."

Wishing to steer the conversation away from that subject, Elizabeth said, "I do not want to talk further about him. I want to talk about you. Tell me about Dr. Graham. Jane has nothing but praise for him. What does he say about your injury?"

"Graham has been a godsend. I do not think I would be talking to you now had he not come. I have thanked Edward several times for sending him, but your uncle is too modest to admit to being my benefactor."

"What is it you admire about Dr. Graham?"

"He uses the latest remedies and methods. For instance, his theory is that lying abed does nothing to promote healing. He insisted I sit up on the third day after the accident." Mr. Bennet smiled at the memory. "Your mother did not agree with him in the beginning, but when I started to improve, she changed her mind. Yesterday I even stood for a time."

"Was it very painful?"

"I will not lie to you; it was. Still, I felt better afterwards. Dr. Graham says I am doing so well that he plans to return to his practice in London. He is merely awaiting the arrival of the assistant who is to take his place."

"So, it seems I will get to meet this miracle worker before he leaves."

"You will. Dr. Graham is staying at the inn in Meryton. He returns once a day to assess my condition, and you will meet him then. Your mother asked him to stay with us, but he prefers the inn." Mr. Bennet smiled knowingly. "I think your mother's *nerves* got on his nerves."

Elizabeth giggled. "Surely not."

Just then the door opened, and Jane stuck her head in. "Mama is asking for you, Lizzy, and if you do not come downstairs, she will come up here."

Mr. Bennet groaned. "Pray go to her, Lizzy. We can visit again after she falls asleep on the sofa this afternoon, as she inevitably will."

Elizabeth stood and leaned over to kiss her father. "I shall return as soon as I can, Papa."

With a final glance back, Elizabeth left with her sister.

Jane whispered as soon as they were in the hallway. "I did not want to say this in front of Papa, but our uncle and aunt have arrived from London, and they asked about you the moment they alighted from their coach. If I had to guess, I would say they know everything that happened between you and Mr. Darcy."

Elizabeth straightened to her full height. "If Mr. Darcy has told them his side of the story, then it is time I told them mine."

The garden

The moment the Gardiners spied Elizabeth coming down the stairs, Edward turned to Mrs. Bennet. "Fanny, Madeline and I wish to speak to Lizzy privately, so we shall take a walk with her."

Without waiting for his sister's approval, he offered an arm to Elizabeth. "Shall we tour the garden, my dear?"

Putting on a brave face, Elizabeth took his arm. Before long, the three of them were strolling through the far end of a flower garden situated on the right side of the manor. It was far enough from the house that they could not be overheard, though Fanny and all of Elizabeth's sisters could be seen staring out the windows.

Edward Gardiner stopped between two facing concrete benches. "Let us sit down." Once he was seated next to his wife and opposite Elizabeth, he began. "You can have no doubt as to why we are here, Lizzy."

Elizabeth considered feigning ignorance but thought better of it. "I have a good idea." Defiantly, she added, "Mr. Darcy has told you that I left London without consulting him."

"And to make matters worse, you left town with John Lucas," her uncle stated.

"Lizzy, how could you?" Mrs. Gardiner added. "After everything Mr. Darcy has done for you, is this how you repay him?"

"Done for me?" Elizabeth declared, eyes flashing. "Let me tell you what he has done for me, Aunt Madeline. He lied about why John went to Richmond. John had no plans to ask for another woman's hand in marriage. Had Mr. Darcy sent him word, he would have returned to marry me."

"Do you believe Mr. Darcy would lie about something so easily proven false?" Mr. Gardiner said, his voice particularly harsh.

"I do!"

"Then you are more foolish than I ever believed possible. Furthermore, Mrs. Thornhill was eager to create a scandal, and if you had not married Mr. Darcy, she would have done just that!"

"Mrs. Thornhill would not have cared whom I married, so long as there was a ceremony!"

"Let me inform you, young lady, that you are badly mistaken. Furthermore, Mr. Darcy had no reason to atone for your mistake in coming to Cambridge alone. A man of his consequence could easily survive such a scandal, especially if your culpability was made known. But did he do that? No! Instead he agreed to marry a girl of no importance, to save her reputation."

Mrs. Gardiner reached to touch her husband's arm. "Now, Edward, pray remember Lizzy is young. She does not realise how close she came to ruining her life and the lives of her sisters."

"Being young is no excuse! Any young lady worth her salt knows not to allow herself to be in a compromising situation."

"Had he wished to do the honourable thing, Mr. Darcy had only to send for John once we arrived in London." Elizabeth stood and began to pace. "Besides, if he had agreed to bring me home when I asked, all this might have been avoided. I had resolved to make the marriage work when I learned that Papa was near death."

"That is preposterous," Mr. Gardiner exclaimed. "Dr. Graham has been in touch with me almost daily, and I passed along your father's progress to Mr. Darcy. Moreover, I told him of Jane's wish that you stay in London as long as possible to give your mother time to calm down."

"Even so, what business could be more important than my father's health?"

"I happen to know what his business entailed, and whilst I was sworn to secrecy, believe me when I say it is of the utmost importance to the future of everyone connected to Pemberley."

"So, my husband told you about his business, but did not think it important to tell me."

"I believe Mr. Darcy feels he can trust me. Do you think you have demonstrated that he can trust you?"

Elizabeth dropped her head. "It is not my wish to hurt Mr. Darcy. I only wish I could undo the past week."

"You may get your wish."

Elizabeth lifted her head. "What do you mean?"

Edward Gardiner went on to explain William's offer concerning their marriage. When he had finished, Elizabeth was smiling broadly.

"That would be wonderful. Do you think you can persuade Papa to agree?"

"I do not think it is in his best interest to agree." His wife nodded in agreement.

Elizabeth was taken aback. "Why ever not? It would solve everything!"

"We are of the opinion that Mr. Darcy is not only an honourable man, but the ideal husband for you," Madeline Gardiner replied.

"But...but others are just as honourable," Elizabeth declared. "John Lucas, for instance."

"We do not agree," Edward Gardiner replied. "However, the decision will be left to your father."

"I am certain Papa will take my side. He has always disliked Mr. Darcy."

"Be that as it may, I intend to tell him everything that has happened and my impression of your husband. If he decides afterwards to go along with this absurd scheme, so be it."

Sighing, Mr. Gardiner stood and addressed his wife. "Pray wait here with Lizzy until we send for her, my dear. I do not want Fanny asking a thousand questions whilst I speak with Thomas."

Madeline Gardiner held a hand out to Elizabeth. "Come. Sit beside me. We shall talk of other things whilst we wait."

Thomas Bennet's bedroom

Edward Gardiner was pleased his brother was seated when he entered his bedroom, for after hearing what had happened after he found Elizabeth at Cambridge, Mr. Bennet was as pale as a ghost.

"I would never have believed Lizzy could be so foolish. Lydia, perhaps, but not my Lizzy. I am shocked she left London without Mr. Darcy's knowledge and hurt that she was not truthful with me about why Lucas escorted her home. I feel as though someone has pulled this chair from beneath me."

"I felt the same way when Mr. Darcy asked if I knew she had left London with Lucas." Edward Gardiner sighed. "I would like to believe she did not tell you because she feared for your health."

"Even if that were true, she had to know I would find out eventually."

"Unfortunately, people her age rarely consider the consequences."

"Moreover, had anyone other than you sung Mr. Darcy praises, I would never have believed that dour man capable of such generosity."

"I realise Mr. Darcy did not make a good impression when he was in Meryton, but I find him to be a very kind-hearted, shy sort of fellow. Frankly, I was amazed he was more than willing to do his duty without being coerced. God knows he could have left Lizzy to fend for herself."

"Why do you think he acquiesced so quickly?"

Edward gathered his thoughts for a moment before he spoke. "At Cambridge, he admitted to having fallen in love with Lizzy at first sight. Yet, for reasons he did not express, he never acted on those feelings. However, once confronted with having to salvage her reputation, he did not hesitate."

"If this man is in love with Lizzy, why did he propose a way to end the marriage?"

"I asked him the same thing. He said he no longer believed one-sided admiration was enough to preserve their union, so he offered Elizabeth something she wanted very badly—a way out.

He also said he would rather part now than spend the rest of his life married to someone who was in love with another man."

"He thinks she is in love with John Lucas?"

"Apparently."

"That is preposterous. Lizzy likes Lucas well enough, but she is not in love with him."

"Thomas, I believe marriage to Fitzwilliam Darcy is the best thing that could have happened to Lizzy. Not because of his wealth or station, but because he is a solid young gentleman who will not only protect her but appreciate her intellect. And her liveliness will complement his shyness."

"You think very well of him."

"Madeline thinks highly of him, too. And there is one more thing that I feel you should know before you make a decision regarding the marriage. Darcy asked me not to say a thing, but since his character is being weighed, I feel I must speak up."

"What is it, Edward?"

"I did not send Dr. Graham here, nor am I paying his fees. Naturally, living in London, I had heard of the man, but I had never met him. He is Mr. Darcy's personal physician, and the minute we arrived in town from Cambridge, Darcy contacted him. Your new son is paying all his expenses and the expenses his assistant will accrue once he arrives."

"My word! From what Lizzy said, she has no idea."

"Darcy does not want her to know. He does not want her gratitude."

"That does make me think more highly of him. Not because he is paying for my physician, but because he wanted to help without her knowledge." Thomas Bennet struggled to stand. "Help me back into bed and fetch Lizzy. It is time I had a talk with her. And if you will, I would like you and Madeline to be here when I do."

"Take your time, Thomas. We will bring Lizzy to you once you are settled."

Later

When Mr. and Mrs. Gardiner finally came down the stairs, Jane rushed towards them. "Where is Lizzy?"

"I have no idea," her uncle said. "I am afraid that when she fled your father's bedroom, she was not happy that he agreed with Madeline and me that her marriage to Mr. Darcy would be to her advantage."

"Lizzy can be so stubborn when she thinks she is right," Jane exclaimed. "She must be on her way to Oakham Mount. I shall go there. Perhaps I can convince her to listen to reason."

"I pray you are more successful than we were," her aunt replied.

Oakham Mount

The moment Jane reached the pinnacle of Oakham Mount, she spied Elizabeth sitting in her favourite spot beneath the tallest tree, her back against the trunk. Though her knees were pulled up and her head was lying upon them with her eyes closed, Jane had no doubt Elizabeth was aware of her presence well before she stood in front of her.

"Lizzy, we have always been able to share a burden. Do you not wish to talk to me?"

"What good will talking do? Papa has his mind made up. They all do. I am to continue as Mr. Darcy's wife because marriage to him will benefit our family."

Jane sank down beside her. "I do not think that is why they want your marriage to continue—well, Mama may, but not the others."

"I never thought you would take their side."

"That is not fair."

Lizzy sighed. "I am sorry. I do not mean to be unkind. Yet, I thought that you, of all people, would understand why I want to annul this marriage."

"I do, but I also know you better than anyone. In fact, I probably know you better than you know yourself." When Elizabeth did not reply, she continued. "When you confided to me that you were going to Cambridge to find John Lucas and marry him, I understood why you felt you had no choice; however, I was concerned because I did not feel he was a good match for you."

"What makes you say that?"

"John cares nothing for the things that make you happy—plays, poetry and literature of every kind. In this manner, he is much like Charles. And, whilst I love him dearly, one could never accuse Charles Bingley of being an intellectual." She laughed. "And I am satisfied because I do not consider myself one, either."

"Do not disparage yourself, Jane. You enjoy reading and—"

Jane broke in. "Lizzy, do you not recall Sir Lucas telling Papa that John barely passed his courses because he frequented the pubs too often and neglected to study? And I have since heard he gambles on cards far too often."

"Who told you that?"

"Charles. I fear that if John had to take the reins of Lucas Lodge anytime soon, he would not make a success of it. He lacks a sense of duty, whereas Mr. Darcy seems the kind of man who is aware of his responsibilities and is very capable of fulfilling them."

"What he is *capable* of is thinking himself above our company."

Jane shrugged. "He *is* above our company; however, I never felt he was a snob. My impression of him is that he is a very shy man who does not perform well to strangers."

"Call it what you may, but he keeps so much hidden that I still feel as though I do not know him."

"How can you say that after—" Jane halted, turning crimson. "You know."

Elizabeth understood Jane's meaning. "It never came to that," she stated dryly, busily brushing phantom bits of leaves off her skirt.

"You never consummated your union?" Jane declared loudly enough that Elizabeth looked around to be certain no one was there to hear.

"No. You see I had a terrible cough and he ..." Elizabeth faltered. Then, her chin came up defiantly. "Fitzwilliam decided to wait until I was well before claiming his rights."

"Oh, Lizzy, that makes me hold your Mr. Darcy in even greater esteem."

"Will you stop calling him *my* Mr. Darcy!"

"Lizzy, it is time you accept the fact that you *are* married."

"You are the fourth person to tell me that today." Elizabeth stood, smoothing the back of her skirt. "I wish life could return to the way it was before Papa was hurt."

Jane embraced Elizabeth, hugging her as she said, "I know."

After a time, Elizabeth pulled back to give her sister a wan smile. "It seems I have no choice. I told Papa if he would let me stay until Sunday, I would leave for Derbyshire without another word of complaint. Our uncle is to return at that time to escort me to Lambton, so I have only a few days to say my farewells."

Jane hugged her. "I truly believe you will find marriage to Mr. Darcy makes you happy, and I shall pray every day for that happiness to come soon."

Trying not to cry, Lizzy nodded. "I fear I shall depend on your prayers more than you will ever know."

Chapter 12

Pemberley
Days later

Alerted by one of the guards at the gate who had been tasked with notifying her of the master's return, Mrs. Reynolds spotted the vehicle in the distance and by the time the coach approached Pemberley, the entire staff was prepared to greet the new Mrs. Darcy. Since the letter arrived announcing the marriage and stating that the couple would soon travel to Derbyshire, the housekeeper had ordered the house thoroughly scoured from top to bottom. All these preparations had even the lowest servants on pins and needles, for everyone was not only expected to perform their job, but to be ready to assemble at a moment's notice wearing a crisp, clean uniform.

Once the guard alerted her, Mrs. Reynolds notified the butler, Mr. Walker, and he gathered the footmen whilst she collected the maids. Now servants lined both sides of the steps to the portico like soldiers at attention. Glancing at the orderly display, the long-time housekeeper could not help but smile, despite the butterflies wreaking havoc with her stomach. Her apprehension was a result of learning that a woman she had never met before or had ever heard mentioned, was now the new mistress. As a consequence, a niggling thought crossed her mind constantly: *Has the young man I practically raised from a boy been compromised?*

Swiftly the coach entered the circle and abruptly pulled to a stop, which left no more time to speculate on the circumstances surrounding the master's marriage. Giving the butler a nod, she and Mr. Walker began down the steps in anticipation of being introduced to their new mistress. They were still several steps from the ground when a footman suddenly opened the door to the vehicle, and the master stepped out. Yet, instead of turning to help his wife from the coach, he surprised everyone by closing the door. Mrs. Reynolds could not help but glance over his shoulder at the coach windows as he began to speak.

"Mrs. Reynolds...Mr. Walker," William said, launching into the explanation for his wife's absence that he had been formulating during the entire journey. "I am sorry I did not have time to inform you that Mrs. Darcy is not with me. Her father was injured falling from a horse, and she has travelled to Hertfordshire to be with him. I should have written to you when our plans changed, but everything happened so quickly that I did not."

Recovering her equanimity, Mrs. Reynolds said, "There is no need to apologise, sir. I am certain I speak for all of us when I say it is very good to have you home, and we will all pray for a swift recovery for Mrs. Darcy's father."

"It is good to be home. And as for Mr. Bennet, it is my understanding that he is improving steadily." William's expression became more guarded. "Mr. Sturgis insisted there is a crisis concerning the tenants he needed me to handle, hence I came here directly."

"He asked me to say that he is ready to meet with you at your convenience," Mrs. Reynolds replied.

"Is Mr. Sturgis in his apartment?"

"Yes."

By then they had entered the foyer, and Mr. Walker relieved William of his hat and gloves whilst the maids and footmen slipped quietly back into the house to resume their duties.

"Give me time to wash the dust off and change clothes," William said. "Then send word that I shall meet him in my study."

"Surely you are weary after being on the road so long," Mrs. Reynolds ventured. "Would you not rather start tomorrow?"

"I am tired; nevertheless, I wish to see him directly."

Sighing, the housekeeper replied, "I will inform him."

Suddenly William's valet appeared on the landing above the grand staircase. "Mr. Darcy, it is good to see you again."

"Adams, it is fortunate that you left Cambridge when you did. You just missed being trapped by the floods along with me."

"That would have been unfortunate indeed," Adams said. "I just wanted to say that there is water boiling, should you wish a hot bath."

"That sounds wonderful. Thank you. I shall be right up."

William turned to address Mrs. Reynolds. "Please have Mrs. Lantrip prepare a tray of sandwiches and tea. She may send them to the study once Sturgis and I are settled in."

"Do not be surprised if your favourite biscuits are on the tray as well. Upon hearing of your return, she mentioned baking them."

"Oatmeal ginger?"

"Yes."

"Very thoughtful."

Giving the housekeeper a smile that quickly faded, William began to ascend the staircase. She and Mr. Walker watched until he disappeared completely from sight.

The butler leaned in. "What do you make of our new mistress not returning with the master?"

"I would say something is definitely out of kilter. However, I shall be satisfied if she is nothing like Lady Henrietta."

"My thoughts exactly."

William had dreaded this day, not because he did not wish to come home, but because he was not looking forward to all the questions his wife's absence would create. He had tried to rehearse what to say, but having no idea if Elizabeth's father would agree to his plan to dissolve the marriage, he was unsure how to proceed. In fact, until the moment he stepped out of the carriage, he had been indecisive of what to tell his most trusted employees. He felt certain that Mr. Walker was too reserved to ask many questions, but not so Mrs. Reynolds. No, eventually she would insist on knowing everything.

Moreover, he would have to inform Adams. His valet had been with him for so many years he was more of a confidant than a servant. All of this was on his mind as he entered his bedroom suite to see Adams snap to attention.

"Sir, I have laid out your favourite clothes." he said, motioning to the items hanging on a rack. "I overheard Mr. Sturgis tell Mrs. Reynolds he would like to meet with you today, and I know you prefer to wear something comfortable when you deal with estate problems."

"Thank you, Adams. Yes, I shall fare much better in those."

William began to slip out of his coat and Adams rushed to take it. Then the valet began unbuttoning his waistcoat. Having divested his employer of that item, he immediately began to untie the cravat. Whilst labouring over it, Adams pursed his lips as though trying not to smile.

"You do not approve of how I tied my cravat?"

Adams finally allowed the smile to breach his normally staid expression. "Let me just say that it looks as though you tied it."

"It may not be as intricate as when you do it, but it sufficed."

At once, Adams' smile vanished. "Mrs. Reynolds informed me you were married in London. If you do not mind my asking, how in the world did you manage to meet a proper lady and marry in so short a time?" A sigh escaped his employer, so he added, "Even now, I find it hard to believe."

Sitting in an upholstered chair whilst the valet removed his boots, William's head fell back, and he closed his eyes. "In truth, so do I." Then he added sombrely, "I married Miss Elizabeth Bennet, a gentlewoman from Meryton in Hertfordshire."

Adams grew silent for a time before speaking. "May I enquire as to why Mrs. Darcy did not accompany you to Pemberley?"

Because he never kept secrets from Adams, William proceeded to tell him all that had occurred since they parted in Cambridge, including the solution he had chosen.

"Forgive me if I am being meddlesome, but is it your wish to end the marriage?"

This same question had plagued William since he learned of Elizabeth's flight to Longbourn in John Lucas' company. "I am no longer certain how I feel. Perhaps I convinced myself that Elizabeth would be a better match than one of the debutantes my relations favoured. You know how I despise women with nothing in their heads but designs for tables, the latest fashions and a desire to be wealthier than their friends."

"I can see why you might doubt your decision to marry; however, knowing you as I do, I do not think you would have taken that step unless you believed you were in love with the lady. I would strongly suggest that you put off dissolving the marriage until you have given it more consideration."

"Oh? Of all people, I imagined you would want things to remain as they were."

"On the contrary, I have felt for quite some time that you were not meant for bachelorhood. My hope was that you would choose a woman who did not value position and fortune above all else."

"What makes you think my wife is not one of those women?"

"From what you said, Mrs. Darcy is apparently no fortune hunter. At the risk of losing your good opinion, and by extension your fortune, she went to her father because she feared he was dying. In my opinion, it would be worth the effort to win the heart of someone who loves that fervently."

William stood to remove his trousers. "You forget. It is easy to love one's own family."

"I cannot agree. Not all family is lovable," Adams replied.

Disrobed, William proceeded to go into the dressing room where a footman was emptying a last bucket of hot water into a huge copper tub. "That will be all."

The footman nodded and backed out of the room, closing the door. Stepping into the tub, William sat down and slid entirely under the water. Seconds later, his head popped up just as Adams entered the room.

"In any case, what is done is done. I expect Mr. Bennet will accept my offer—at Elizabeth's insistence, mind you—and the matter will be settled."

As Adams laid out towels, brushes and a razor, he replied, "The marriage may be settled, but seldom is love cast off as easily. I hope for your sake you can live with the results."

"I have no choice but to live with them. Now leave me. I wish to soak until the water grows cold. I shall ring for you when I am ready to get dressed."

With a nod, Adams entered his master's bedroom and closed the dressing room door. Once he was alone, William was struck by a thought from out of the blue: *What would it be like to be loved that fervently by Elizabeth?*

Immediately, he vanquished that idea from his mind. *No! Elizabeth will never love me. It is best if I forget she ever existed.*

William's study

Mr. Sturgis had only just laid his files on William's desk when there was a knock on the door. "Come!" William called.

The door opened and Mrs. Reynolds walked in carrying a tray with tea, sandwiches and biscuits. "I thought I would deliver this myself," she said, "for I thought you would want to know that Lady Emma is coming down the drive on her stallion this very minute."

William groaned, leaving the housekeeper to glance at Mr. Sturgis, who had dropped his head so the master could not see his smile.

Everyone at Pemberley was familiar with the daughter of their nearest neighbour, Lord Waterston, for Lady Emma Marshall made a point of visiting often when William was in residence. Indeed, the whole of Lambton knew the beautiful red-haired woman had her heart set on marrying the Master of Pemberley.

"How in the world did she find out so quickly I was home?"

"I fear she has spies amongst our servants," Mrs. Reynolds replied. "That is the only thing that would explain it."

"Please inform her that I am busy, and I will call at Parkleigh Manor tomorrow."

"I will be happy to do so, but you know as well as I that she will not leave until she has spoken with you."

William closed his eyes, took a deep breath and stood. "I shall return shortly, Mr. Sturgis."

"Yes sir."

By the time William walked into the foyer accompanied by Mrs. Reynolds, Lady Emma was handing her bonnet and riding crop to Mr. Walker. Spying William, she rushed to give him an impassioned hug.

"Fitzwilliam! I have missed you so!"

With a wan smile on his face, William gently set Emma at arm's length. "I cannot imagine you being so bored as to miss me, Lady Emma."

"Emma!" she insisted. "We have known each other far too long to be formal. I shall not stand for it!" she declared, her blue eyes twinkling. "I expected you home a week ago. What delayed you?"

"Business," William answered. "Some of us do have estates to run."

Instantly tears filled her eyes. "You speak as though I do not have any responsibilities now that Father can no longer function effectively because of his illness."

William regretted his choice of words. "I am sorry. I thought Lord Waterston was improving. The last time I made an enquiry, I heard his physician was pleased with his progress."

Emma began to sniffle, so William escorted her into the library, pulling a handkerchief from his pocket as he did. "Forgive me for being so insensitive," he said, handing her the cloth. "I have been concerned with the problems I must handle and gave no thought to what you must be enduring. What is the latest report?"

"Father is improving, but he is still too frail to carry out his duties, and he seems too confused to make major decisions. Moreover, just this week the physician said he could no longer ride. Since Father fired our steward, I have no idea who will instruct our tenants with regards to crop rotations this year, not to mention settle a dozen other pressing issues."

"Your father has not hired a replacement for Mr. Morgan?"

"No, and I worry that he is not sensible enough to hire anyone now. I received recommendations for several, but I wanted you to examine their references before I choose."

"You will do the choosing?"

"I will let Father think he is, but with your assistance, it shall actually be my choice. I fear being taken advantage of by another unscrupulous steward."

William nodded. "I promise to call on your father tomorrow. If nothing else, perhaps my steward can be of help until you hire another."

"Whilst I believe Mr. Sturgis a good man, I had rather talk with you about Parkleigh's situation. Surely, you understand."

"I shall do what I can, Emma. Now, if I am to come tomorrow, you must let me return to my work."

The vivacious young woman stood on her toes to kiss William's forehead.

"Emma, I have told you time and again! You cannot kiss me now that we are adults."

"If I promise to do it only when we are alone, will that make you happy?"

"No. If someone were to see us, they could interpret an innocent act as something entirely different."

"What makes you think it is innocent?" she teased, smiling beguilingly. "Would it be so awful if we were forced to marry?"

William considered revealing he was already married, but since he had not heard from Mr. Bennet, thought better of it. "Please do not speak of such things."

Emma reached for his hand and brought it to her lips. "We are not children, Fitzwilliam, and it is time we honoured our fathers' wishes to combine our estates."

"Is that all that marriage means to you? Combining estates?"

"Of course not, foolish boy. You know I love you. I always

have. Still, joining our estates would be a wise financial decision. With our resources combined, we would be unstoppable."

If you only knew how close Pemberley is to ruin, William thought. Aloud he said,

"I care for you as a friend only. We will never marry. How often do I have to say it?"

"A deeper love will follow once we are wed. It will be good for everyone concerned. You will see."

Before William could object, Emma kissed him again, but this time she did something she had never done before—she kissed his lips. Then, she hurried towards the door. "I shall look forward to seeing you tomorrow. Come early, and we shall talk before you meet with Father."

After she rushed from the room. William walked over to the window to watch her ride away. An enthusiastic equestrian, she sat a horse as though born to it.

It would have been much simpler had I fallen in love with you.

Acknowledging that there was no simplicity where love was concerned, William quit the room and headed back to his study.

After seeing Lady Emma out, Mr. Walker found Mrs. Reynolds watching their guest ride away from her favourite vantage point, the floor-to-ceiling windows in the front parlour.

"I thought I would find you here." Not acknowledging him, the housekeeper kept her eyes trained on the rider as he continued. "I do not suppose Lady Emma knows Mr. Darcy is married; otherwise she would not have come."

"Spoken like a man," Mrs. Reynolds said. "Lady Emma would still have come, if only to intimidate his new wife. However, I agree that she does not know, or she would not have been in such a good humour when she arrived."

"And she was still in a good mood when she left. What does that tell you?"

"It tells me that Mr. Darcy did not inform her of his marriage, and I find that very strange."

"If that is true, so do I."

"I pray the master tells us what has happened soon; else I may make a blunder if someone enquires about Mrs. Darcy."

"I could not agree more. It could place both of us in awkward positions."

Lucas Lodge
The next afternoon

As Jane and Elizabeth walked the path through the woods that led to Lucas Lodge, each was silently thinking of their own concerns. However, as the manor house came into view, Jane decided to voice hers.

"Do you not think it odd that John Lucas has not come to Longbourn since he brought you home?"

"Not in light of mother's temper. He knew she was angry and most likely was afraid she would attack him the moment he arrived."

"Still, I think the least he could have done is come to see Papa and offer his support for you, if he is as honourable as you believe."

"Jane, would you please stop trying to make Mr. Darcy appear the better man?"

"I am not trying to—" Suddenly Charlotte Lucas came into view, startling Jane. "Charlotte, you frightened me!"

"I apologise. I was trying to slip through the woods quietly. John told me not to warn you that Mr. Bingley is here, for it is supposed to be a surprise. But I know you do not like surprises any more than I, Jane, so I came ahead to tell you."

Jane looked down at the well-worn gown she was wearing. "I cannot bear for Charles to see me in this old thing. It is stained on the front."

Lizzy sighed. "Mr. Bingley cannot expect you to look like a debutante constantly. How can you be expected to accomplish anything wearing your best gowns all the time?"

"I had rather he not see me like this until after we are married." Jane turned to leave. "Lizzy, you go on. I shall return to Longbourn and change clothes."

Elizabeth grabbed her sister's hand and began pulling her towards the house. "You certainly will not. Mr. Bingley will never notice the stains."

Jane had no time for further protest, for by then they had reached the lawn where they were easily seen by John Lucas and Charles Bingley from the terrace. Immediately, Bingley's hand went up in a wave, whilst his face broke into a wide smile. Without waiting for Lucas, he strode towards the woman he loved.

"Miss Bennet," he said, taking her hand and bringing it to his lips for a kiss. "I have missed you." Though she was so happy she could only manage a smile, Jane's eyes shone with love. "Miss Elizabeth, may I steal your sister for a walk in the gardens?"

"Of course you may, sir."

By then John Lucas had reached them, and he and Elizabeth watched the couple walk away.

"I shall be surprised if Bingley and your sister wait until he graduates to marry."

"I believe they have no choice," Lizzy replied.

"Have you seen Charlotte?" Lucas said, looking around. "I suspected she had gone to tattle on Bingley. He returned to Meryton much earlier than he told Miss Bennet he would in his last letter."

"Charlotte is—" looking about, Elizabeth saw no sign of her friend, "not here."

"Will wonders never cease! I owe her an apology then."

Not wishing to expose her friend, Elizabeth just smiled. "John, I am glad we are alone for a moment. I have a question."

"Ask me anything you wish."

"Why have you stayed away from Longbourn since you brought me home?"

"Why?" Lucas repeated.

To Elizabeth it appeared he was trying to put off answering until he could think of a reply.

"Surely you know that my aunt and uncle followed us to Longbourn. Everyone in Meryton knows when a coach comes through town, and if it is a familiar vehicle, they know to whom it belongs and where they are headed."

"I suppose I was worried that since my mistake left you at Darcy's mercy, my presence would only make your father angrier." Pondering his answer, Elizabeth said nothing, so he continued. "Did you think me a coward not to come?"

"I did not, but—"

"Did Darcy call me a coward?" he exclaimed crossly.

"He did not."

"Then who? Your uncle?"

She watched the muscles of Lucas' jaws twitch as he awaited an answer. "It does not matter," she said. "I did not agree with them in any case."

Lucas relaxed and reached for her hand, bringing it to his lips. "Just remember, Lizzy. No matter what Darcy tells you, I have always had your best interests at heart and will be your friend forever."

A moment later, Charlotte walked across the lawn towards them. "Lizzy, will you be joining us for dinner? Mother is sending a servant to Longbourn to tell them that Jane will be escorted home after we dine." Elizabeth hesitated, so Charlotte added, "We are going to play croquet on the back lawn now. Please say that you will stay and join us."

"Of course, you must stay, Lizzy," John Lucas said.

Feeling as though she had no choice, she consented.

Whilst walking in the gardens with Mr. Bingley, Jane felt it her responsibility to inform her fiancé that Lizzy was now married to Mr. Darcy. Clearly surprised at the news, Charles' reaction prompted Jane to confide that Elizabeth had returned to Longbourn with John Lucas and without Mr. Darcy's knowledge.

"I hate to hear they are having conflict," Charles said. "Darcy is a good friend to me, and I am confident he is an excellent match for your sister." He sighed heavily. "Are all of my friends destined to fail at love? Only days ago, Lucas was despondent over being rejected by a woman to whom he had made an offer in Richmond."

"Wha...what did you say?"

Charles repeated what John Lucas had told him when they met outside Hoby's in London.

"Are you certain that it was John Lucas who told you he had offered for a woman and been turned down? Could it not have been another of your friends?"

"No. It was definitely Lucas. Why do you ask?"

Stunned, Jane said, "I am merely surprised, that is all."

She kept silent about this new version of Lucas' trip to Richmond, deciding instead to speak to Elizabeth privately before confiding in Charles. During the rest of the day at Lucas Lodge, she wrestled with the knowledge that Bingley's slip of the tongue could not only cause a break between her sister and John, but an end to his friendship with her fiancé. Even so, she felt Mr. Darcy deserved to be exonerated, and her sister needed to hear the truth.

The moment that Lizzy climbed into bed that night, Jane raised the subject, "Lizzy, there is something that I must tell you."

The reluctance in Jane's voice made Elizabeth uneasy. Now wide awake, she turned over to face her sister. "What is it?"

Jane swallowed hard. "I knew Charles would hear about it at some point, so whilst we were walking in the gardens at Lucas Lodge, I told him of your marriage to Mr. Darcy."

"That is understandable."

"I also told him that you returned to Longbourn with John Lucas without Mr. Darcy's knowledge."

"Why did you have to mention that?"

"Lizzy, we have no secrets between us. When he heard about it, and eventually he would, he would have wondered why I did not tell him first."

"What was his reaction?"

"Charles said that he hated to hear you were having conflict because Darcy is a good man and an excellent match for you."

Lizzy rolled over on her back. "I do not wish to hear one more person sing Mr. Darcy's praises."

"That is not why I brought the subject up. Charles was concerned that his friends seem to be unlucky in love because he met John Lucas in London a few days ago, and he said…he said—" Jane hesitated.

"I am not a child. Just tell me."

"John told Charles he had just returned from Richmond where a lady had refused his offer of marriage."

Elizabeth sat up. "Why would Charles contradict John's account?"

"He had no idea that he was contradicting John's account. I never revealed what John had told you."

"Surely he is mistaken. John would not lie to me."

"I questioned Charles again and he was not mistaken."

Elizabeth moved to sit on the side of the bed and for a time was silent. Jane was about to ask her what she was thinking when Lizzy dropped her head and began to cry. "It cannot be true. John told me that Lady Aileen was merely the sister of an acquaintance from university. He spoke as though he did not know her well at all."

Jane crawled across the bed to sit beside her, wrapping her arm around her sister's waist.

Elizabeth sobbed, "Why would he do such a thing?"

"If I had to guess, I would say that though John always loved you, he knew in his heart you did not love him—at least not in the way he wanted. Lady Aileen represented his chance for happiness, but with her refusal and learning that had he remained in Cambridge, you could have been his wife, he became bitter. In his heartache, he aimed that bitterness at the man you married—Mr. Darcy. Having made untrue accusations at your husband's home, when you arrived at his townhouse, John lied to protect himself."

"All of this time I was so certain that my husband was a calculating—" Elizabeth stopped to sigh heavily. "Because it fit my prejudice to believe he was at fault, I acted like a fool."

"Do not be so hard on yourself. You believed a lifelong friend and I dare say that anyone in your place would have done the same."

"No. Anyone in my place would not have dismissed Mr. Darcy's benevolence so casually. After hearing his opinion of our family at Lucas Lodge, I was so angry that I pledged to despise him forever." She took a shaky breath. "What I have done is ensure that he will hate me forever as well."

"I do not believe that," Jane declared more confidently than she felt.

"How can I face him again?" Elizabeth stood, slowly shaking her head as tears ran down her cheeks. "The truth is, I have not the courage."

"You will, because you must. You owe Mr. Darcy that much."

"Perhaps he will refuse to see me. If so, it will be nothing more than I deserve."

Lizzy crossed to the window and watched whilst a silvery moon played hide and seek with the clouds before she added, "To think that I once fancied myself an excellent judge of character. How little I knew."

Left speechless, all Jane could think to do was to embrace her sister. They stood that way until the clouds covered the moon entirely, and the room became black as pitch.

As rain began pounding the window, Elizabeth murmured, "It is fitting that the weather now mirrors the tumult in my soul. I deserve to be miserable."

"Come to bed, Lizzy. Each new day is another chance to set things right."

As she followed Jane to the bed, Lizzy whispered a prayer. *Please, Lord, just let Fitzwilliam see me long enough that I may apologise. That is all I ask.*

Chapter 13

Pemberley
The next day

Though William and Mr. Sturgis had still not attended to most of the steward's concerns, William put off further meetings with him until he could speak with Mr. Kendal, a tenant embroiled in a quarrel that had erupted in violence. Since he had promised Lady Emma he would visit her father, he planned to stop by that tenant's home on his way to Parkleigh Manor.

Jedidiah Kendal had been a tenant at Pemberley since before William was born. A hard-working man, he farmed twice the acreage as other tenants because he needed the income due to his large family. He could manage the job due to the fact that he and his wife had nine children ranging in age from six to twenty, and as they grew older, each helped work the land. The trouble began after the eldest child, Masie, married a scoundrel named Toby Harvey. She had begged her father to allow the marriage and permit her and her husband to occupy the empty house on the additional tenant parcel, promising that Toby would work the land alongside her family.

Unfortunately, after the wedding, Harvey proved unsuited to the life of a farmer. As a result, Masie's father and brothers continued to work both parcels whilst he did little to nothing. Consequently, when Mr. Kendal harvested the crops, he gave his daughter and her husband only enough of the profits to live on. This made Harvey angry, and his disagreement with her father came to a head during William's last semester at Cambridge. During an argument, Harvey struck Masie and hurled a knife at her father. Fortuitously, the knife caused no serious injury, and Kendal's neighbours responded in time to help rout Harvey, who swiftly fled.

Mr. Sturgis had notified the local constable, who was still searching for the scoundrel. In addition, Kendal's oldest son moved in with Masie as protection for her and her son, Caleb who was almost a year old. Neighbouring tenants were on edge, fearful that Harvey would make good on his promise to exact revenge by burning their homes; thus, William's mission today was to inform them that he planned to post several sentries to watch the area until that blackguard was captured.

Preoccupied with these thoughts, William was totally oblivious to his surroundings as he neared the turn that led to the tenants' cabins; thus, when a carriage came around the bend in the road directly towards him, he had little time to react. Zeus reared in protest, whilst the driver of the carriage pulled his horse sharply to the right, the vehicle coming to a stop in the tall grass on the side of the road.

The driver, the vicar William had appointed at Kympton after Wickham refused the living, began apologising immediately. "Fitzwilliam, please forgive me," James Green said. "I was wool-gathering and not paying attention. I should not have been riding in the middle of the road."

Now one and fifty, Green had first met William when he served as a curate under the vicar of Hunsford when the heir of Pemberley was still a boy. He had vacated that position when the vicar died, and they had lost touch until William entered Cambridge. As luck would have it, Green's nephew was a classmate of William's, and he happened to mention his uncle was the vicar of a parish near Epperson, just north of Cambridge. Consequently, William often travelled to Epperson on Sundays to hear his sermons, resulting in Mr. Green being offered the living at Kympton when it became available.

Struggling to control Zeus, William's stomach formed a knot the moment he recognized the carriage driver's voice. He had hoped he would not encounter the vicar until the disposition of his marriage to Elizabeth was settled. Wearing a thin smile, he said, "No apologies are necessary, Mr. Green. Neither was I paying attention, so we were both at fault."

The vicar's grey eyes softened with fondness. "I was on my way to Pemberley. You know how fond Judith and I are of you, and as soon as she heard you had returned, she insisted I call. She has her heart set on meeting your new wife right away. I tried to explain that both of you are undoubtedly very busy getting settled in, but she insisted we welcome you sooner rather than later."

Fondly recalling afternoons spent with the Greens at their parsonage in Epperson, William was torn. Whilst he longed for the familiarity of their company, he was certain they would never agree with his plan to dissolve his marriage. In any case, he realised he could not keep it from them.

"I regret to say that my wife did not accompany me to Pemberley. Her father was injured falling from a horse, and she is attending him in Hertfordshire. Business dictated that I come on ahead."

"I am sorry to hear about Mrs. Darcy's father. How is he faring?"

"He is doing well under the circumstances."

"That is good to hear. Judith and I shall remember him when we pray."

William nodded absently. "I am on my way to call on a tenant, and then I must handle some business at Parkleigh Manor. I shall be pleased to stop by the parsonage on my way home."

"That is very gracious of you," Mr. Green said. Then his expression grew troubled. "It is a shame about Lord Waterston. I was there yesterday, and he is still not himself. Moreover, Lady Emma seems overwhelmed by the idea of running the estate in the event he does not recover completely."

"The purpose of my visit is to advise Lady Emma."

"How good of you to step in to help. It is my belief that kindness never goes unrewarded."

Remembering his unrewarded kindness to Elizabeth, William

did not agree. Instead, he replied, "If I am to fulfil my commitment to Lady Emma, I must be on my way."

"Do not let me hinder you. I shall return to the parsonage and inform Judith to expect you later."

William tipped his hat. "Until then."

A tenant's cabin

As William approached the Harveys' cabin, a young man came out of the house holding a rifle pointed in his direction. Once he recognised the master, he quickly let the barrel drop.

"I am sorry, Mr. Darcy. Masie's husband has us all on edge."

"And you are?"

"Hal Kendal, sir."

"Tell me, has anyone reported seeing Harvey since he and your father argued?"

"Not that I have heard; however, I do not think we have seen the last of that ne'er-do-well."

All of a sudden, a pretty woman with dark hair and coal black eyes pushed open the door and walked onto the porch, balancing a child who looked about a year old on her hip. "Mr. Darcy," she said. "We were not expecting you, sir."

Dismounting, William's hand went to the brim of his hat. Tipping it slightly, he said, "Good day."

"You do not recognise me? I am Masie Kendal, or I was before I married."

William's last recollection of the eldest Kendal was that of a skinny girl with skinned knees. "Pray inform your father that I would like to speak to him and the tenants on either side of his land as soon as they can gather here."

"As you wish." To her brother, she said, "You heard the master."

Hal Kendal propped the gun against the wall and jumped off the porch. As he ran towards a field, he exclaimed, "Mind the gun, Masie. It is loaded."

As William watched Hal leave, Masie said, "Would you like to come inside, Mr. Darcy? It is hot out here."

Turning to find her smiling beguilingly, William recognised the danger. Assuming his Master of Pemberley demeanour, he replied, "No, thank you, madam." Pulling Zeus towards a nearby tree, he added, "I shall wait in the shade until Hal returns with your father."

Masie shrugged and went back inside the house.

Parkleigh Manor

Although not as large as Pemberley, Parkleigh Manor was a very impressive estate. The red brick façade of the two-storey, one hundred-room manor house featured a wide white portico across the front, supported by six Corinthian columns. Built in the twelfth century as a much smaller house, it was later enlarged, and the columns added. Its design spoke of wealth and position. As William approached the manor this day, his mind was occupied by the discussion he had just had with his tenants; consequently, he did not notice Lady Emma watching his progress from a second storey window.

A letter from London had arrived only an hour earlier, and it meant an end to her campaign to entice Fitzwilliam Darcy into marriage. In the missive, her best friend, Lady Beatrice, shared the news that had the *ton* reeling—the mysterious marriage of the heir of Pemberley to an unknown girl from Hertfordshire. The moment she had finished reading, Emma rushed to show it to her father and was dismayed that he showed no anger or surprise. Upset and unsure if she could keep a civil tongue when William arrived, Emma had sent the housekeeper to greet him, instructing the servant to say she was occupied elsewhere and that he would meet with Lord Waterston alone.

Now observing as William reined in his stallion and leapt to the ground, several thoughts swirled in Emma's head. *Why did you not tell me yesterday you were married? Why is your bride not with you? Could you be ashamed of her?*

Instantly, she determined she would find the answers to those questions.

Lord Waterston's sitting room

William was surprised when Emma did not greet him in the foyer as she usually did. He was even more surprised to be escorted directly to Lord Waterston's sitting room by the housekeeper.

The instant the servant opened the sitting room door, Lord Waterston called, "Come inside, Fitzwilliam! It has been too long since last we talked."

Shocked to see how pale his neighbour had become, William tried not to show his surprise as he took the earl's extended hand and shook it. "It has been too long, but now that I have finished university, I hope to see you more often."

"Nothing would please me more," Lord Waterston declared. He motioned to a chair. "Pray be seated."

William nodded, sinking into the upholstered chair. "Did Lady Emma tell you why I have come?"

Lord Waterston smiled. "I assumed this was merely a neighbourly call."

"It is that, but I also want to offer my services, should you feel you need them, until you can replace Mr. Morgan. Lady Emma told me you have received references for three candidates for his position, and she asked if I would examine them and give my opinion. I told her I would be glad to do so, if it pleased you."

His host sighed. "My daughter believes just because I cannot ride, I have lost my senses. If I listened to her, I would be in bed round the clock."

William smiled. "If my assistance is not needed, I will not be offended."

"Do not think I am rejecting your help, Fitzwilliam. Oh no! When that ungrateful Morgan left, he took with him the details he and I had worked out for rotating crops for the next two years. And I admit my memory is not so reliable as to allow me to recall what we had decided. Your help would be invaluable in that area."

"Consider it done."

"Also, if you could look over several tenant parcels that I hope to divide, that would be helpful. They are much larger than those most of my tenants occupy, and the excess land is given over to pasture. I am in need of the income that planting those parcels would provide. Could you possibly advise me on that?"

Realising this would delay Sturgis' trip to Willowbend Hall even longer, William still could not decline. "I shall."

Lady Emma's father smiled. "I knew I could count on you, my boy." Then suddenly his mood changed. "You do know that I had my heart set on you marrying my daughter?"

William's head dropped, and he stared at his boots.

"She read me the letter she received today from town. It seems your marriage is the talk of the *ton*."

"I am always amazed at how fast gossip travels."

"Is it gossip or the truth?"

Knowing he could not lie now that the new from London had reached Derbyshire, William's expression grew more sombre. "It is true that I am married."

"Please, do not feel that you are being called out, Fitzwilliam. I am old enough to know that just because you care for someone does not necessarily mean you wish to marry them. I am certain that you care for Emma in your own way. I told her this. I believe most men just happen to meet the right woman at the right time and fall in love. There is nothing wrong with marrying in a whirlwind of passion. Emma's mother and I did. Tell me, is that what happened?"

"You could say that."

Lord Waterston smiled. "However, I must ask. Why did you not tell Emma that you were married when you saw her yesterday?"

William stood, walked over to a window and locked his hands behind his back. "I think you know that Emma is very...excitable. As usual, she talked on and on, and I made the decision that it would be better to tell her when she was not so concerned about your health. Besides, my wife has not yet joined me here, so I saw no harm in waiting."

Lord Waterston studied William a little too long, making him nervous. "I certainly understand your reasoning, but I feel I must give you a bit of advice. Your wife will not be pleased when she learns that you have not told the world you are married—and she *will* learn of it. Women are peculiar in that way."

"I shall keep that in mind."

"If you wish to remain married, you will."

Afterwards, William and Lord Waterston ate whilst reviewing the candidates for the steward's position. In the end, William asked to take the applications home so he might study each man more fully that evening. They agreed that he would come for a portion of each day and ride the estate with a trusted employee who would point out the parcels that Lord Waterston wished to divide and allow William an opportunity to speak with each tenant. The plan was to record what crops they had planted the last two seasons and note which ones had fared best, all in preparation for the next planting.

When it was time for him to leave, Lady Emma still had not appeared. In view of her father's account of the letter from London, William was not surprised.

The parsonage

The instant William threw his leg over the saddle and leapt from Zeus, Judith Green opened the parsonage door and rushed out to greet him. She looked just as he remembered—tall and handsome, her blonde hair now almost white, with dark blue eyes the same shade as Anne Darcy's. Seeing her never failed to remind him of his mother.

Leaning in to plant a kiss on his cheek, Mrs. Green declared excitedly, "Fitzwilliam, I am delighted to learn of your return to Pemberley, and I wish you joy in your marriage!" Taking his arm, she began to pull him towards the house. "Are you hungry? I made your favourite supper—vegetable soup, fresh bread and a gingerbread cake."

William smiled. "If you feed me as well as you did during my days at Cambridge, in a few short months, I shall be too great a burden for Zeus."

Judith Green kept hold of his hands as she stepped back to inspect him. "Nonsense! If you ask me, you could stand to gain some weight."

"Maybe we should let Zeus be the judge of that," William teased.

Smiling as he watched their reunion, Mr. Green interrupted. "Bring him inside, my dear. I should like to eat before everything grows cold."

William followed Mrs. Green through the door, stopping to shake Mr. Green's hand. "It is wonderful to be in company again with you and Mrs. Green, sir."

"I was thinking the same thing about you, my boy."

Unable to take another bite, William was now situated on the sofa in the Green's parlour with Mr. Green sitting beside him, whilst Mrs. Green occupied the chair across from them. William knew better than to take his leave immediately after dinner. The Greens would never allow him to go until they were certain all was well in his world. Moreover, both the vicar and his wife were blessed with extraordinary powers of observation.

Given their worried faces, William decided that he should speak first. "You must have questions about my wife."

"James explained why Mrs. Darcy had to remain with her father," Judith Green volunteered, though her expression suggested that his explanation was not convincing.

"Fitzwilliam," James Green began, "we enquire about your circumstances only because we sincerely care about you."

William's eyes dropped to his lap where his threaded fingers tightened. "I know."

Mrs. Green slid to the edge of her seat. Leaning forwards, she took William's hands in her own and waited until his eyes met hers. "Fitzwilliam, if you had rather not tell us, we will understand. However, often those who care most about you can offer a helpful perspective on what is troubling you."

"I will gladly tell you all that has transpired if you will promise me one thing." Seeing them nod, he continued. "After you hear everything, you will not try to persuade me to change my mind. It has been very difficult, but I have come to a decision regarding my marriage. In return for your silence, I promise that should I feel the need for guidance, I will ask for it."

Mr. Green looked to his wife. "Judith and I care for you as though you were our own son. And, as much as we may want to voice our opinions, we will refrain from doing so unless you ask."

Satisfied that the Greens would stand by their word, William began to tell them about his marriage, beginning with the day Elizabeth arrived in Cambridge.

That night

As Judith Green snuggled closer to her husband in their large bed, she let go a ragged sigh. It did not go unnoticed.

"Sweetheart, I know it is maddening that you cannot speak to Fitzwilliam about your misgivings. I wish I could voice mine, too. For now, however, we must share them only with each other."

"I simply find it hard to understand why he will not fight for something he obviously wants so very badly."

"I did not get that impression. In fact, I was disturbed that he acted so cavalierly about the dissolution of his marriage."

"You did not see the signs because you are a man."

James Green laughed aloud. "Then suppose you point out the signs, my love."

"They are subtle. Like the way his eyes grew soft when he described how she looked whilst she slept or the way his voice caught when he spoke of her betrayal, or even the way his hands formed fists when he recounted Mr. Lucas' accusations. Even though he believes he has overcome his regard, I am convinced that Fitzwilliam is very much in love with his wife."

"I understand why he does not trust easily—what with his father's betrayal of him and Pemberley for the sake of that woman. Consequently, he may not be willing to give Mrs. Darcy another chance to wound him. Nevertheless, you promised not to say anything. What will you do if he holds to his plan?"

Judith smiled conspiratorially in the darkness. "I never promised not to pray! And I believe that God will open our dear boy's eyes and heart if only we ask."

Chapter 14

Meryton
Oakham Mount
The next day

It was just after dawn, and Elizabeth was already at the crest of Oakham Mount. Today her uncle would return to escort her to Pemberley, so she had to visit her sanctuary one last time to retrieve her journal. Moreover, she wished to make her position clear to John Lucas before leaving for Derbyshire. To that end, she had given Charlotte, who had stopped by Longbourn the day before, a missive to deliver to her brother. That note asked John to meet her at the one place where in years past they had often tried to work out all the world's problems, real and imagined.

Upon unearthing her journal, Elizabeth sat down, took a pencil from her pocket and began to write one last entry.

Today I leave for Derbyshire. Will Fitzwilliam allow me to apologise, or will he be repulsed by the very sight of me? I cannot blame him if he should, for I have been incredibly thoughtless and cruel.

I still cannot believe I allowed remarks made two years past to blind me to his generosity. Perhaps had I followed my heart instead of my head, I would have seen his true character. Now I think it may be too late.

One thing I know for certain—I do not wish to hurt him ever again. Therefore, I will abide by his wishes concerning our marriage, even if it means returning to my family in disgrace.

Wiping a tear from her face, Elizabeth closed the book and slipped it and her pencil into a small bag she had brought for that purpose. Just as she finished, the sounds of hoofbeats caught her attention, and she stood to watch the horse and rider come up the trail.

As John Lucas came into view, he waved and kicked his horse into a trot. In mere seconds, he was beside her, tying the horse's reins to a tree.

"Lizzy, I had no idea you were leaving Meryton today."

"My uncle is on his way to escort me to Derbyshire."

"Then is it safe to say that Darcy is not angry with you?"

"I have no idea. My father is doing much better, and it is he who insists I join my husband at Pemberley."

Lucas looked down. "I will always regret that I was not there when you needed me most. Because of my negligence, you are forever bound to Darcy."

"To be honest, I no longer consider that a punishment."

His head flew up. "Why ever not?"

"Because I now know you lied."

For the longest time, Lucas stared at her in disbelief. "If...if that is the case, why are you not screaming and yelling? The Lizzy I have always known would be dressing me down, not talking rationally."

"With God's help, that Lizzy has been left behind."

"What are you saying?"

"Just as no amount of anger will change what you set in motion, no amount of regret will change how I responded. I acted as arrogantly as I accused Fitzwilliam of being."

"You are judging yourself too harshly."

"You are mistaken. I always thought myself an excellent judge of character. I felt superior to those with whom I found fault, and since I found fault with Fitzwilliam, I gave no weight to his opinions. I was so blind." Tears began to pool in her eyes. "I am so ashamed that I took your word over his without question, especially since he has been nothing but kind since I appeared on his doorstep in Cambridge."

Lucas reached for her hands. "I am so very sorry."

Pulling them back, Elizabeth said, "It is too late for apologies. Besides, that is not why I asked you here. Before I leave, I must know what prompted you to lie about Lady Aileen."

"I did not start out to lie. After I heard you had married Darcy, I tried to drown my regret in brandy, and the more I drank, the angrier I became. In my cups, I went to Darcy's townhouse and confronted him. I said that since you hated him, you and I would always be closer than he and you. However, it was only after he had the audacity to pretend he did not rush you into marriage because of his desire for you that my anger turned into rage. That was when I accused Darcy of lying about my intentions towards Lady Aileen. I do not know why I said it. I can only blame it on the drink."

"Why do you keep insisting that Fitzwilliam rushed me into marriage? When we were alone at Cambridge, he did not act as though he wished to marry me. In fact, it was completely the opposite."

"Oh, Darcy would never admit it, but that dour man fell in love with you at first sight. I saw the signs. Here was someone who never said a word about any woman, yet once we were back at Cambridge, he talked incessantly about you."

"Sadly, when I thought of him, it was only to despise him more."

"He insulted you and your family, Lizzy. You had every right to despise him."

"No. I should have been grateful for his care at Cambridge and for offering me his protection afterwards. Instead, I chose to find fault with everything he said or did. And the second I heard that you and he had argued, I struck out to find you in hopes of proving my reasons for disdaining him."

"I should have been truthful when you found me, but I was afraid of losing our friendship."

"Yet, by lying you have ruined it forever. Worst of all, I may have destroyed my marriage. I will do my best to forgive you, John, but our friendship is over."

Watching the one who had once been his closest friend walk

away, Lucas could not hold back his tears. There was no one to blame but himself.

Longbourn

As the maid began to close the last of the trunks Mr. Darcy had sent to Elizabeth from London, Jane rushed into the room holding two pairs of slippers, a silk chemise and a beautiful white shawl.

"Wait!" she cried. "I found these in Kitty and Lydia's bedroom. I should have known they would go through your things, Lizzy."

The stray items were added to the trunk; it was closed, and the maid left the room to attend to other duties. Having just said farewell to her father, Elizabeth was melancholy.

"I would not mind if they kept them."

"You must consider Mr. Darcy's feelings. He selected these things expressly for you, and he will expect to see you wearing them. Even if they are not to your liking, you should pretend they are."

"You are right," Elizabeth admitted. "I must begin to see things from his point of view."

"Forgive me for asking, and you certainly do not have to answer, but do you not care for Mr. Darcy even a little? After all, one cannot deny he is a handsome man."

"Appearances have always carried little weight with me in that respect. And, frankly, I spent so much time resenting Fitzwilliam that I gave little thought as to whether he was handsome."

"I am certain you will find more to admire now that you know he is not the ogre you once believed him to be."

"I was the ogre, not he. And now my husband is fully aware of just how cruel I can be."

"Please do not say such things. I choose to believe that Mr. Darcy still cares for you and that he will forgive you."

"He may forgive, but I fear he will never think well of me

again. I once heard him say, 'My good opinion, once lost, is lost forever.'"

"And you once said, 'Mr. Darcy is the last man in the world whom I could ever be prevailed on to marry.' We all say things we do not mean when we are upset. The key is to admit when we are mistaken and to change our course."

"That is something I am striving to do," Elizabeth said. Then she framed Jane's face with her hands. "Do you know what I shall miss most about you?"

Smiling sweetly, Jane shook her head.

"Your outlook. If only I could see things through your eyes, I would be a much better person."

"Just be yourself, dearest."

Tears filled Elizabeth's eyes. "Oh, Jane, what if we can never recover any semblance of trust? What if my marriage is beyond repair?"

"Just concentrate on being the wife Mr. Darcy needs, and things will resolve themselves. You shall see."

"I will do my best."

The sounds of carriage wheels on the gravel drive drew Elizabeth to the open window. She watched her uncle Gardiner's coach come to a halt in front of the house.

Jane, who had joined her sister, said, "I do not understand why Uncle Edward will not spend the night and begin your journey tomorrow."

"My guess is that he does not wish to listen to Mama lamenting about the state of my marriage," Elizabeth replied. "He wrote that he planned to stay only long enough to look in on Papa."

Suddenly there was a knock on the door. Jane opened it to find Mr. Hill and another servant standing without. "They are ready," she said, motioning to Elizabeth's trunks.

Whilst the men were removing the first trunk, Jane gave her sister a kiss on the cheek. "We are connected by more than blood, you and I. No matter how far apart we may find ourselves, we are connected heart to heart. You have only to think of me, and I shall be right there with you in spirit."

"Oh, Jane! How will I ever manage without you?"

"You will write to me every day, silly goose. And I shall come to visit you once you are settled in."

"I shall count on it."

Derbyshire
Parkleigh Manor
The same day

As he departed, William reflected on Lady Emma's change of behaviour. Whereas she had hidden from him the day before, today she met him in the foyer straightaway and escorted him to her father's sitting room as though nothing had changed. He had been anxious all the while he and Lord Waterston discussed candidates to fill the steward's position, for she had stayed in the room.

In the end, he and Waterston agreed that a Mr. Stockham was the most suitable, even though he could not fill the position for at least another month. William offered to continue providing advice until Stockham's arrival, which had suited both father and daughter. Afterwards, as Emma walked back to the foyer with him, she stopped at the open door to a drawing room and, grasping his hand, drew him inside. Closing the door, she fell into his arms and began to cry.

"Pray forgive me, Fitzwilliam," she said, pulling back to look in his eyes. "Only after I had time to study your situation did I come to the realisation that you must have been compromised. Given a choice, you would never have married someone so far beneath your station. Now I understand why your wife is not at Pemberley and why you did not tell me you were married. You must still be in disbelief."

Whilst Emma was speaking, William carefully extricated himself from her grasp and gently pushed her to arm's length. Fearing if she knew of his plans to dissolve the marriage, she might conclude he was positioning himself to marry her, he tried to quell her suspicions delicately.

"I fear your assumption is wrong."

As William tried to explain, Lady Emma stomped her foot, exclaiming, "I do not believe a word of it! A friend related the rumours circulating in London, and it is her opinion, as well as mine, that you were forced to marry that woman! Why else would you not have told me straight away that you were married?"

"I believe that I am the best judge of what happened. And, as for why I did not tell you, you were so emotional that I decided it was best to wait for a more opportune time."

"Humph!" Emma said, raising her chin defiantly. "I will be surprised if your wife ever shows her face in Derbyshire, much less at Pemberley."

Irritated because her remarks hit close to the truth, William replied, "I suggest you concentrate on the problems you face at Parkleigh Manor and quit trying to scrutinize my marriage. It will give you no satisfaction."

"Spoken like a man who is hiding something."

Unwilling to engage in a war of words with Lady Emma, William quickly departed Parkleigh Manor without comment.

His marriage and Lord Waterston's plight were churning through William's mind as he returned to Pemberley, and thus occupied, he was nearly to the manor before he looked up to see footmen removing luggage from a coach stopped at the portico. Instantly realising it was one of his own coaches, his heart sank. He had hoped Lady Henrietta and Georgiana would stay in London at least another fortnight, giving him more time to settle the uncertainty of his marriage. Apparently, that was not to be.

He reined Zeus to a halt beside the coach, and a groom rushed forwards to take the horse's reins. "Mr. Darcy, sir, Miss Darcy has just returned from Town."

"So I see, Crabtree." Throwing a leg over the saddle, William slid to the ground. "Make certain Zeus is rubbed down and given some oats."

"Yes, sir."

Following the procession of footmen carrying trunks up the steps, William entered the foyer just as Georgiana came rushing down the grand staircase with a small white terrier on her heels—the dog, a birthday present from Colonel Fitzwilliam last year.

"Brother, I saw you coming from my window."

As she rushed into his arms, William picked her up and whirled her in a circle. "One would think you missed me," he teased, setting her on her feet again.

"One would be correct!" Georgiana replied with a giggle. "I believe I missed you as much as Clancy missed me."

William glanced at the furry ball of white now whining and dancing on its hind legs in an attempt to gain Georgiana's attention. He smiled. "Then you must have missed me a great deal!"

"I did. I also missed Elizabeth. Where is she? I searched her suite, but it looks as though she has never been in there."

"My wife is still in Hertfordshire with her family."

Instantly Georgiana paled. "Is her father worse?"

"I understand he is doing better."

Georgiana let go the breath she had been holding. "I am so pleased to hear it, and I hope he improves quickly so that my sister will be able to join us soon. I am so anxious to know her better."

Before he could reply, Lady Henrietta appeared on the landing dressed in one of her usual vulgar gowns—this one fashioned of lime green damask. Beside her stood a man William had met only once after his father's marriage to Lady Henrietta. William's face lost all expression as the two began to descend the stairs.

"Lord Hartford, what brings you to Pemberley?" he asked, his voice noticeably unwelcoming.

"He is teaching me to draw," Georgiana interjected excitedly. "When it came time for us to return to Pemberley, I insisted that he come with us, so I might continue the lessons."

Lady Henrietta felt compelled to explain. "My cousin called on me in London, and once Georgiana learned of his skills as an artist, she begged him to teach her to draw. It was Georgiana's idea that he visit Pemberley."

William studied the man in question. At White's, Lord Hartford had quite the reputation as a ladies' man, likely because he had a different woman on his arm every time he appeared in public. Though not as tall as Darcy himself, there was no doubt Hartford's dark blond hair and brown eyes appealed to the fairer sex, and William was convinced he was an opportunist when it came to women.

"May I ask how you became an artist?"

"My father was a patron of the arts, and since I was the second son, he insisted I learn to draw at an early age. I believe he thought I might become a great portraitist."

"I had no idea you were not always the heir."

"My older brother died when I was fourteen, and I succeeded my father as the Earl of Hartford after he passed."

"I see."

"In any case, I was never fond of paints. I found drawing with charcoals more challenging. Once I saw how talented Georgiana was, I was persuaded to pass along my knowledge to her."

Feeling guilty that he could not afford masters for his sister, William said, "If Georgiana can benefit from your tutelage, I have no objection to your company for a *few* weeks."

The emphasis on *few* went unnoticed only by Georgiana, who exclaimed, "I told you Brother would not mind, Rietta!"

"Yes, you did," she replied woodenly.

Not in a mood to converse with his stepmother or her cousin, William turned his full attention back to Georgiana. "In addition to my duties here, I have agreed to help Lord Waterston with Parkleigh until his new steward arrives. All this has put me behind, and I am afraid work awaits me in my study as we speak. May I suggest that you rest from your journey until time for tea? We shall talk then."

"Of course," Georgiana said. Then she called, "Come, Clancy!"

A flash of white fur followed his mistress back up the stairs. After Georgiana had disappeared from sight, Lady Henrietta declared, "I think a rest is a marvellous idea. What say you, David?"

"I agree."

Instead of acknowledging their remarks, William turned and walked away.

On the road to Pemberley

Edward Gardiner had nodded off to sleep in the coach immediately upon leaving Longbourn. It was not until they neared their first stop, an inn near Kettering, that he roused to find his niece staring dolefully out the window.

"Have you been awake the entire time?"

Elizabeth nodded.

"Try not be too discouraged, my dear. Mr. Darcy is a kind-hearted fellow. I feel certain he will give me a chance to make your case."

"I fear there is no case to be made."

"What do you mean?"

Elizabeth studied her hands. "After you returned to London, I learned something that makes my flight to Meryton even more irresponsible." Watching her uncle's expression grow more concerned, she added, "Charles Bingley returned to Meryton just after I did. By chance, he mentioned to Jane that John *had* gone to Richmond to offer for another woman. He told Mr. Bingley that she refused him."

Mr. Gardiner slowly shook his head. "I am not surprised to hear that your husband was telling the truth."

"What can I say in my defence? I was foolish to take John's word over Fitzwilliam's?"

"I do not rejoice in saying this, but Madeline and I tried to warn you, Lizzy. You have always been too headstrong. I blame your father. He encouraged you to find fault with others and question their motives before you were old enough to form a sentence."

Tears pooled in Elizabeth's eyes. "Do not blame Papa. I am no longer a child. I should have been more discerning and given credence to both sides instead of faulting my husband simply because I despised the idea of being married to him."

"Taking responsibility is the first step to solving any dilemma."

"It is just—I cannot fathom why Fitzwilliam agreed to marry me. In his own words, I was not handsome enough to tempt him."

"The night Mrs. Thornhill and I discovered you, Mr. Darcy told me he had cared for you since the first time you met."

"He never said a word."

"Lizzy, I was sworn to secrecy by Mr. Darcy and even asked your father not to say anything to you, but with all the grievances you hold against the man, I have changed my mind. I now feel it necessary to break my word, so you may know what an exemplary person you married. Dr. Graham is tending your father only because Mr. Darcy sent for him. All of his expenses and those of the assistant who is to take his place are being paid for by Darcy."

"Why?" Elizabeth asked, taking a shaky breath. "Why was I kept uninformed?"

"Mr. Darcy did not want your gratitude."

Tears rolled slowly down her cheeks. "This makes it perfectly clear why he wants to be rid of me."

"If I believed that, I would not waste my time escorting you to Pemberley. Mr. Darcy is convinced you are in love with John Lucas, and it is *your* desire to be free of your marriage."

"But I am not in love with John!"

"Your husband does not know that. His words were: 'I no longer believe a one-sided admiration is enough to preserve our union.'"

"I do not believe I truly knew myself until I learned that John had lied. It was then I realised how I had ignored his flaws along with Fitzwilliam's merits. That is why I want my husband to take me back *only* if he is convinced I am sincerely sorry for my actions and that I am capable of being the wife he deserves. Otherwise, it will never work."

"That is a noble aim, Lizzy, but I insist you let me handle your reconciliation. A man can speak more frankly to another man. Besides, regardless of whether you made mistakes, Mr. Darcy is obligated to—"

"Just as he did not want my gratitude, I do not want him to feel obligated!"

"You are being foolish, and I have no intention of going over this again. I will not let you face him alone."

Knowing that arguing would only make her uncle more determined, Elizabeth said a silent prayer.

Lord let my uncle see my point. My only hope is to show William that I am a contrite woman wishing to return to her husband—not a child being forced to join him.

Chapter 15

Lambton
Four days later

Because of heavy rain, it had taken the better part of four days for Elizabeth and her uncle to reach Lambton. She had often visited that small village as a guest of the Gardiners because her aunt's parents, Duncan and Sophie Gavin, had lived there for many years and owned the local confectionary shop. Having been raised in Lambton, Aunt Madeline was quite fond of her childhood home and eagerly sang its praises to anyone who would listen. Elizabeth felt certain that had the reason for their current trip been a more pleasant one, her aunt would have accompanied them.

Fortuitously, they arrived in the early afternoon just as one of the wheels on the coach began making an awful noise. Edward Gardiner was hopeful the blacksmith would be able to determine the problem and repair it quickly; thus, upon entering Lambton, he ordered the driver to take the coach directly to the smithy. However, whilst her uncle and the blacksmith discussed a solution to the problem, the shop's stifling atmosphere sent Elizabeth scurrying outside.

As she exited the shop, she noted the paddock on one side of the structure held a cow and several horses. As was the local custom, farmers often brought their livestock to town on designated days in hopes of selling them, and already a crowd was gathering to inspect what was available. Scrutinising those assembled,

Elizabeth saw no one she knew and quickly turned her attention back to finding a pleasant place to wait. Across the yard a small concrete bench was conveniently situated beneath a large oak tree, so she headed in that direction.

After months of indecision, the reverend James Green had come to the conclusion that he required another horse. The old mare they presently owned was not used to being ridden and was no longer able to pull their carriage at a decent pace. A younger animal would make shorter work of his errands, and if it could also be ridden, he could forego the carriage altogether if his wife, Judith, was not with him. That would mean less wear on their aging vehicle. All told, he felt compelled to inspect the animals in Lambton today.

Judith Green was not averse to the notion of purchasing another horse, and since she needed a few items from the grocer, she was pleased to accompany her husband. As it happened, when they approached the blacksmith's shop in their carriage, they found the yard full of people with a similar purpose.

"James, tether the horse in the shade beside that large tree, and I shall wait in the carriage. I am certainly no judge of horseflesh and would rather rest whilst you inspect them. I am in no hurry, so take your time and do not worry about me."

"You are so agreeable, my dear, that I believe I shall escort you to the inn for a custard tart and a cup of tea once I am finished."

"What an excellent idea! A tart will be just the thing to fortify you."

"Fortify me?" he said, laughing. "For what?"

"To accompany me and carry my packages."

"How many shops do you plan to patronise today?"

"You shall find that out in due time," she replied playfully.

By then they had reached the tree. The vicar pulled the carriage to a halt, leapt to the ground and secured the reins to a limb. "I should not be long."

As he strode towards the crowd, feminine heads turned to

follow his progress. Watching, Judith's heart swelled with pride, for James was still a very handsome man. Barely twenty when they met, he was a year older than she the night he requested her first dance at a local assembly and she had instantly fallen in love. Even after all these years she could not believe that Providence had blessed her with such a man.

After he disappeared into the crowd, she closed her eyes and leaned into the corner of the vehicle. Weary from sitting with a sick parishioner the night before, she fell fast asleep. Sometime later, she was awakened by the sound of raised voices, and sat up straight. Regardless of how she repositioned herself, she could not see who was speaking because the wide trunk of the tree hid the participants from view. Still, she heard clearly what was being said.

"Please, Uncle. Tomorrow is soon enough to decide on a course of action." Obviously, this was a young lady speaking.

"Stop pleading, Lizzy! You have gotten your wish." This voice belonged to an older gentleman, perhaps the aforementioned uncle. "The smithy cannot get to the wheel until later today. We have no choice but to stay with your aunt's parents tonight. Do not think for a moment, though, that I have changed my mind. The wheel is supposed to be ready in the morning. After we retrieve the coach, we shall confront Mr. Darcy."

"Will you not try to see my point?" the lady continued. "I know it will embarrass Fitzwilliam to discuss our situation under the curious eyes of his servants. Pray do not carry the conflict to Pemberley. Instead, let us keep our discussion private. Perhaps we could talk with him at the Gavins' home or let a room at the inn."

"The whole point of speaking to Mr. Darcy at his estate is to make the matter public," the man retorted. "Matters handled in public are harder to disavow."

"Allow me to apologise and leave, I pray you. I shall make it clear that I will be in Lambton for a sennight. That will give him time to decide what he wishes to do."

"And should he decide he will not have you back?"

“That is his prerogative. I do not intend to impose myself on him if he does not wish it.”

“Your head-strong attitude is what got you into this dilemma in the first place, young lady. I will not let you ruin, perhaps forever, your life and the lives of your sisters. Now, if you will excuse me, I shall arrange lodging for my servants and try to find someone to take us to the farm.”

“The smithy does not have a carriage to rent?”

“No. And I do not relish the idea of staying at the inn. Beyond the exorbitant prices, the last time I stayed there the mattress was too thin and hard for me to get any rest. At least Madeline’s parents have decent beds.”

The instant the young lady mentioned Fitzwilliam’s name, Judith Green realised that she had been eavesdropping on his new bride. Whilst trying to decide how best to introduce herself, she overheard the man declare his intention to seek a ride and watched him march back to the shop. Exiting the vehicle, she was surprised to see James coming towards her.

“I must have been wrong about God’s promptings,” he said. “All of the horses here today are far too old to suit my purpose.”

Craning her neck to follow the older man’s route, Judith murmured, “Perhaps you did not mistake Him after all.”

“Whatever do you mean?”

“I do not have time to explain. Just trust me. Do you see that older man in the green jacket, the one speaking to the young man in dark blue?”

“I do.”

“I heard him say he and the young lady sitting on the other side of this tree need a ride to a nearby farm. Go and offer our services.”

Having learned to trust his wife’s instincts, the vicar was soon introducing himself to Edward Gardiner.

The Greens' carriage could only accommodate three people, so upon spying a couple from his parish, James asked if they would transport Mr. Gardiner to the farm. Mr. and Mrs. Smith agreed straightaway, leaving the young lady to ride with him and Judith. Mr. Gardiner followed the vicar back to the bench to inform his niece of the arrangements and to introduce her to the Greens.

Judith prayed her husband would not react upon hearing the woman's name. Still, James was astonished enough to stammer, "Did—did you say *Mrs. Darcy*?"

Unsettled by the look on his face, Elizabeth glanced to her uncle.

"Yes, my niece was recently married to Fitzwilliam Darcy of Pemberley."

Recovering his composure, Reverend Green said, "Judith and I are well acquainted with Mr. Darcy. He granted me the living at Kympton not long after his father died, but I have known him since he was a boy."

"What is your opinion of him?" Mr. Gardiner asked.

"I have found him to be honest and kind-hearted. He is benevolent towards his family, those under his authority and those less fortunate."

"That is reassuring to hear," Mr. Gardiner replied. He turned and began to help Elizabeth into the Greens' carriage. "Lizzy, you know the way to the farm. Direct the vicar and I shall be right behind you."

The Gavins' farm

After selling the confectionary, the Gavins had moved to a white-stone farmhouse on the outskirts of town. That farm was now Elizabeth's destination.

Life-long members of the Kympton parish, the Gavins were

familiar with the new vicar and his wife and were pleased the Greens had brought Elizabeth from town. Whilst they were welcoming everyone inside for tea and refreshments, the Smiths' carriage pulled up, and Mr. Gardiner alighted. Though invited to stay as well, the Smiths insisted they had to get home, and with promises to call again, they promptly departed. Everyone else entered the house, and before long, tea and biscuits were being served in the parlour.

After seeing to her guests, Mrs. Gavin crossed the room to sit beside her husband on the sofa. As she sat down, Edward Gardiner was telling Duncan Gavin about the broken wheel. Not being privy to the troubles surrounding Elizabeth's marriage, the elderly Gavins were unaware of his mission in escorting her to Derbyshire and upon hearing what had kept them from reaching their destination, Mrs. Gavin declared, "We could send a servant to alert Mr. Darcy. No doubt he would be glad to retrieve his wife."

Hoping to end that discussion, Mr. Gardiner replied, "There is no need. My driver and footman are lodging at the blacksmith shop tonight. If you take us there in the morning, the coach will be ready and we shall be on our way."

"It would not be an imposition," Mrs. Gavin continued, giving Elizabeth a motherly smile. "Lizzy must be eager to see her husband again."

"In truth, I am very tired," Elizabeth replied a little too hastily. "I would rather get a good night's rest and see my husband when I am in better spirits."

Mrs. Green noticed Elizabeth's lack of enthusiasm. "That is understandable. Any new bride would want her husband to see her at her best. I can only imagine how draining your father's injury must have been for you, not to mention the journey here."

At Elizabeth's puzzled expression, she added, "When last we spoke to Fitzwilliam, we enquired after you, and he explained about your father. James and I have been praying for his recovery and have looked forward to meeting you."

"Has your father's health improved?" James Green asked.

"My father is doing well under the circumstances."

"That is such a relief," Sophie Gavin declared, fanning herself with her hand. "In Madeline's letter informing us of the tragedy, she mentioned that many believed Mr. Bennet was close to death."

"At first, we were all fearful he might not survive," Edward Gardiner explained. "However, God graciously spared him."

"God is faithful," James Green said. Then finishing his cup of tea, he set it down on a table and stood. "Pray forgive us, but Judith and I must be on our way. We have several items to purchase before we go home, and at the rate our mare can manage these days, it may be midnight before we get back to the parsonage!"

Whilst everyone else laughed, Judith Green studied Fitzwilliam's wife. With no intention of leaving until she had reassured that young woman, she walked over to Elizabeth and gently took her hands.

"Mrs. Darcy, believe it or not, I was once a young bride, just as you are now." She smiled warmly. "And should you ever feel you need to speak to someone who understands the challenges you face, I would be so pleased if you would consider talking to me. James and I regard Fitzwilliam as a member of our family, and we would love to include you, too."

Involuntarily, tears filled Elizabeth's eyes. "I would feel blessed to be counted as family."

"Then, so be it," Judith Green exclaimed, giving Elizabeth's hands a soft squeeze before letting them go. Addressing the Gavins, she said, "We will see you both on Sunday. Do not forget that you are to stay after services and share a meal with us."

"We would not miss it for the world," Mr. Gavin replied.

Pemberley

Having arisen at dawn and spent a difficult morning with Lady Emma going over a list of what needed to be done at Parkleigh Manor, by the time William slid off Zeus at Pemberley, he was exhausted. So weary was he, that had a footman not pointed it out, he would have missed seeing his cousin coming down the drive in the distance on his red stallion, Titan. William handed Zeus' reins to a groom and waited for Richard.

Richard pulled his stallion to a stop and leapt to the ground. "I swear I am getting too old for this." Making a display of rubbing his backside with both hands, he added, "If General Lassiter does not assign me a coach soon, I will be forced to retire earlier than he expects."

William could not help but smile at his cousin's proclamation. "You have been making that same threat for the past year. Why do I feel you will not follow through?"

"Go ahead, Darcy, make sport of me!" Richard tossed Titan's reins to a groom. "You do not have to worry. You have excellent coaches waiting to transport you from one end of the country to the other."

William glanced to be certain no servants were near enough to hear, saying quietly, "And if I do not sell great-grandmother's estate soon, I may be forced to part with them."

"Forgive me. Given the circumstances, my jest was out of line."

"No need. It is I who should apologise. I left London in such a hurry that I did not take the time to say farewell."

"After reading your note, I understood why."

"Still—"

"I am not angry at you, so stop upbraiding yourself. There are enough people willing to do that, and they do a much better job." Proud to have coaxed a smile from his cousin, Richard added, "Have you heard from Mr. Bennet? Has he accepted your offer?"

"I have yet to hear anything from Elizabeth's family."

"That woman has no earthly idea what a treasure she is throwing away, and I am not speaking of your wealth—all for the likes of that arse Lucas, for heaven's sake! Mark my words, Darcy. Once he inherits Lucas Lodge, that simpleton will bankrupt the estate in less than a year."

"If you do not mind, I had rather not talk about him or Elizabeth," William said as he began to climb the steps. In only a few steps, it was as though another person had taken his place.

Smiling, he turned to say, "I am so pleased that you are here. How long can you stay?"

Richard hurried to catch up. "Only long enough to enjoy a soft bed and some delicious food. I leave the day after tomorrow for Sheffield."

"I take it, then, that my lively conversation was not a factor in your decision to stop here?"

Richard grabbed William's arm, halting his progress. "It is good to hear you tease me, Cousin. I have been worried about you."

"No need for that," William replied. In a rare glimpse of vulnerability, sadness encompassed him as he added, "If I survived Mother's passing and Father's betrayal, I can survive this."

All of a sudden, Mr. Walker called from the front door, "Welcome back, Colonel Fitzwilliam!"

Richard watched the Master of Pemberley facade settle on William again before he answered. "It is good to be back, Walker."

As they entered the foyer, William said, "In less than an hour, we can have tea either in my study or, should you prefer, we can join Georgiana, Lady Henrietta and her cousin on the terrace. Most likely they are already there enjoying the beautiful weather."

"Lady *Harlot* has a cousin? Is she pretty?"

William lowered his voice. "She is a *he*—Lord Hartford."

Richard's smile vanished. "Hartford? Of Spelling Park?"

"The same."

"Though I have heard talk of him, we have never met."

"You have not suffered by the lack of acquaintance."

Richard stifled a laugh. "I think I would rather join you in the study. I will catch up with Georgiana at dinner."

"Do you wish to wash the dust off first and change clothes?"

"Yes. Then, I will slip down the back stairs to avoid being seen by the others. I shall meet you in the study in half an hour or less."

"As you wish."

William turned to Mrs. Reynolds who appeared at his side. "See that hot water is delivered to Colonel Fitzwilliam's room.

I shall be in my study, and he will join me there for tea. By the way, he wishes his presence here to remain unknown until he decides to declare it."

"Yes, sir." Smiling at Richard, she added quietly, "We are delighted to have you with us again, Colonel."

"It is good to be back," he replied. "Now, let me hurry to my room, lest I be discovered!"

As his cousin raced up the grand staircase, William headed to his study.

William's study

After pouring another cup of tea, Richard picked an apple tart from the tray on the edge of William's desk. Taking a bite, he returned to his chair and sat down.

"So, you have not told Mr. Sturgis what you have in mind for Willowbend Hall?"

"Until I can place all my attention on Pemberley, I need him here. Sturgis is aware that I plan to sell my great-grandmother's estate, but until he is free to leave, there is no point in telling him I plan to put him in charge of repairs and improvements. He will begin to worry long before he leaves for Weymouth. That is his nature."

"Even if he could not influence Uncle George, that man certainly seems to be of help to you."

"It was not his fault that my father would not listen to his advice. In my opinion, Sturgis did, and continues to do, an excellent job under trying circumstances."

Richard decided he should get right to the point. "Forgive me. I know you do not wish to dwell on the subject, but—"

"But you intend to make me."

"Yes, I do," Richard retorted. "Now, tell me. Are you certain you want to dissolve your marriage? I ask because I have never seen you enamoured of any woman before Mrs. Darcy, and I fear this fiasco has soured you on the whole idea of marriage. If I say so myself, I believe you are not formed for bachelorhood. You should think hard about what Fitzwilliam Darcy desires before making a decision you may regret."

William slowly took a sip of tea, then set his cup down. "Were I to dwell on what I desire, I would go mad."

Standing, he crossed to the windows and looked out. Richard walked over to grasp his cousin's shoulder, giving it a brotherly squeeze.

"Which is precisely why I feel obligated to make certain you see all sides."

William's shoulders rose and fell in a shrug. "I am grateful for your concern; however—"

"Pray hear what I have to say."

As his cousin silently nodded, Richard began to pace the room whilst he put forth his argument. "Have you considered that if you had married any of the debutantes my parents promoted, you would have had a marriage of convenience? Would it be possible to stay married to Elizabeth under the same type of arrangement? At least she is more palatable than the women you have already rejected."

"In truth, it would be far better if I felt nothing for her. Joined forever to someone I love, knowing there is no hope of that love being returned—" Unable to continue, William returned to his desk and sat down. "That is my idea of Hades."

Richard slammed his hand down on the desk. "I should have tried harder to convince you not to marry her."

"This is not your fault!" William declared. "I would have done my duty regardless of your advice. Still, I have learned a valuable lesson."

"And what is that?"

"After Elizabeth left London with Lucas, I vowed that my heart would no longer rule my life. Henceforth, only facts will sway me." After a brief silence, William added, "I believe that dissolving the marriage is for the best. Were Elizabeth forced to stay, she would grow to hate me even more than she does now, and in truth, I would resent her for forcing me into a loveless union."

"Have you spoken to the vicar about this? If the dissolution goes forward, he could be forced to take sides. I know that you hold Mr. Green in high regard, but will he support you?"

"Being a man of God, naturally he would advise me to forgive and forget. However, as you well know, my good opinion once lost is lost forever. Even if I took Elizabeth back, I could never trust her again."

"Distrust is a hard burden to bear, Cousin."

"Nevertheless, it has been part and parcel of my life."

"That is true." Suddenly Richard smiled. "What would Athos[7] do in a circumstance such as this?"

"I believe he would run his enemy through with a sword."

"Too bad you cannot do the same to John Lucas."

"Unfortunately, Lucas is not my enemy. My heart is."

---

7 ***Athos** - one of the Three Musketeers.

Chapter 16

Kympton parsonage
The next morning

In the bedroom of the small parsonage, James Green paced in what little space was available between the bed and the dresser. "I have a bad feeling about this, Judith. Once Fitzwilliam learns his wife is here, he will think we have gone against our word."

"He may at first. However, once he knows the facts, he will understand that Elizabeth sought *us* out and not the other way around. Besides, since she agreed to be a part of our family, how can we refuse? And frankly, I believe it is better that they meet here than at Pemberley."

"I agree entirely; however, that does not negate the fact that you and I promised to allow him to make his own decisions regarding his marriage. He is like my own son, and I do not wish him to think I betrayed him."

Mrs. Green stepped forward, grasping his hands to stop his pacing. "I feel the same way, James, but we cannot refuse to help Elizabeth."

"I pray he does not bolt for the door as soon as he sees Mrs. Darcy. He may, you know."

"I have been praying that God will soften Fitzwilliam's heart towards his wife." She gave his hands a squeeze. "Now, let us return to the parlour before Elizabeth concludes that her request has created a problem and decides to leave."

Reverend Green leaned down and placed a soft kiss on his

wife's forehead. "I thank God that we never had to deal with what these young people are facing."

"God has truly blessed us, which is why we must help them."

In total agreement, the Greens squared their shoulders and returned to the parlour to address their visitors.

The parlour

Elizabeth was thankful that Mrs. Gavin had overheard her arguing with her uncle this morning before leaving for Lambton. As a result, she had deduced why Edward Gardiner had escorted his niece home, and the elderly woman had taken it upon herself to enter the fray, successfully convincing her uncle not to confront Fitzwilliam at Pemberley.

She could still hear Mrs. Gavin's argument.

Edward, Lizzy is right! It is best to deal with Mr. Darcy somewhere other than Pemberley. I suggest you meet him here or, better yet, go to the Greens and ask them to send for him. The parsonage will serve as a reminder of his wedding vows, and the Greens may influence him to make the right decision.

Though she was not in favour of coercing Fitzwilliam in any manner, Elizabeth was pleased with the results of Mrs. Gavin's support. They had arrived at the parsonage not long after daylight, and the Greens had invited them in. After listening to their request, the couple excused themselves to talk over the matter, leaving her and her uncle alone in the parlour. Not a quarter-hour later, the door opened again, and the Greens walked in with sombre faces.

Seeing their expressions, Edward Gardiner rose to his feet. "I pray we have not asked too much of you. If we—"

The vicar interrupted. "Judith and I agree that meeting Fitzwilliam here is for the best. Hence, we will send a servant to Pemberley with a letter requesting he come as soon as possible."

Edward Gardiner visibly relaxed. "You are very kind."

"Not at all," Reverend Green replied. "We are only doing our Christian duty."

"Still, I must thank you," Elizabeth said. "You will never know how much this means to me."

"We care for you, my dear," Judith Green reminded her. "We could do no less."

Pemberley

By the time the sun was up, William was already dressed for another trip to Parkleigh Manor. Growing weary of being at that estate a substantial portion of each day, he was pleased that he had now met with most of its tenants. Seeing their dwellings allowed him to note any repairs that might be needed, as well as to enquire about the crops they had planted over the last few seasons. He could now begin to recreate the plan for crop rotations which Lord Waterston has asked of him. Unfortunately, Lady Emma always insisted on accompanying him, slowing his progress considerably. As he walked out of his bedroom today, that fact played on his mind, making him more irritable than usual.

When he reached the landing halfway down the grand staircase, he was not surprised to spy Mrs. Reynolds and Mr. Walker in the foyer below. Before he could continue, however, Georgiana called out, asking him to wait for her. She came running down the stairs behind him, Clancy in her arms.

As she reached William, she asked, "Will you be home in time to take me fishing? I asked Richard last night, and he said that he would, but I fear he has forgotten. He is still asleep."

In the past, William often took Georgiana fishing this time of year, but he felt so overburdened at present, he wanted to tell her he did not have the time. Nonetheless, seeing the anticipation in her eyes, he indulged her.

"Your cousin is exhausted. I suggest you let him sleep. If you will promise to be ready, I shall take you fishing when I get home. I should return soon, and if we are lucky, we may be able to convince Mrs. Lantrip to pack us a picnic with tea and refreshments."

"You are the best brother!" Georgiana exclaimed, standing on tiptoes and kissing his cheek. "Clancy and I will be ready and waiting."

As she turned to go back up the stairs, William called, "If you bring Clancy, he will scare the fish away."

"I shall make certain he knows to be quiet," Georgiana replied, quickly vanishing from sight.

William smiled at her naivete before turning to continue down the stairs. When he reached the bottom, Mrs. Reynolds held out a letter.

"This was just delivered, sir. A local lad brought it."

William took the missive and turned it over. "I cannot tell who sent it." He broke the seal, his expression changing to puzzlement as he read. "The Greens wish me to come by the parsonage as soon as possible."

The housekeeper and butler exchanged curious glances whilst William merely shrugged. "I shall stop by the parsonage on my way to Parkleigh Manor."

"Are you not going to eat before you leave?"

"Lady Emma brings a basket of food and drink when we ride out. She insists that we stop at the bridge to eat before inspecting the tenant holdings. There is no need to eat now."

As they watched, a footman opened the front door, and William departed. Both butler and housekeeper walked onto the portico to observe their master as he rode away.

"I imagine the whole village is abuzz by now with rumours of the master's marriage, so why would Lady Emma act as though he is available?" Mr. Walker asked.

"Perhaps Lady Emma is emboldened because Mrs. Darcy still exists mainly in our imaginations."

"I wonder what would happen if she were to suddenly appear," Walker mused.

"One thing we know for sure —it would hinder a certain neighbour's plans for the master."

By then William was almost out of sight, and the two servants resumed their duties.

The parsonage

William had just dismounted when he noticed an unmarked coach in the shade of a tree near the rear of the parsonage. Eying the vehicle, he tied Zeus to a limb and walked towards the house. Startled when the front door opened before he could knock, he was relieved to see the vicar. William's smile of relief grew even wider when Judith Green stepped into view.

"Thank goodness," William exclaimed. "From your note, I feared one of you had taken ill."

As the Greens beckoned him inside, they apologised profusely for having worried him.

"If neither of you is ill, why did you summon me to come so quickly?" The Greens exchanged worried glances, and he immediately became uneasy.

"To be honest," James Green said, "there is someone here who wishes to speak to you."

Immediately William knew what the summons was about. Bristling, he said, "You promised to stay out of my business unless I asked for your opinion."

"And we have, Fitzwilliam," the vicar argued. "Mrs. Darcy came to us this morning, asking to use our home for—"

"And you thought that by agreeing to let her have her way, you were not breaking your word?" William snapped. "I expected more of you."

He turned to leave, prompting Judith Green to cry, "Wait! You are here. Will you not at least hear what she has to say?"

Suddenly Elizabeth stood in the door to the parlour, her uncle right behind her. "Please, Fitzwilliam, do not blame them!"

William could not help examining Elizabeth. She looked lovelier than he had remembered in a sky-blue muslin gown, her mahogany locks gathered at the back of her head and tied with ribbons of the same colour, leaving most of it to cascade down her back and shoulders. Her coal-black eyes appeared to be filled with remorse, though he no longer gave credence to his ability to distinguish true sentiment.

"Your trust in the Greens was not misplaced."

Her second declaration brought him out of his introspection, and he steeled himself against the conflicting emotions washing over him. "That is for me to decide!"

"All I ask is for a few minutes of your time," Elizabeth pleaded. He did not reply. "Surely you cannot be afraid to speak to me alone."

"Lizzy, I do not like—" Edward Gardiner began, only to be cut off.

"Please, Uncle. This is my marriage. Let me speak to my husband alone." Never taking her eyes from William, Elizabeth found herself holding her breath as she awaited his reply.

William's eyes narrowed. "Follow me."

William stalked towards the door, and it took a moment for Elizabeth to realise he

had agreed. Hurrying after him, she went through the door as he held it open for her. As she did, she prayed he could not hear her heart drumming, for that traitorous organ was pounding so hard she feared she might faint. Continuing towards the garden, she took deep breaths in hopes of calming it.

Pemberley
Lady Henrietta's sitting room

"I have no idea why you insisted I accompany you to Pemberley," Lord Hartford said, taking a sip of his brandy. "Mrs. Darcy is not even here."

"I was not certain when she would arrive," Lady Henrietta replied. "However, whilst Elizabeth may be a dullard, I am convinced at least one member of her family will realise that marriage to the Master of Pemberley has its advantages. Once that happens, she will be forced to join Fitzwilliam."

"I have to ask—why would a woman with no fortune and no connections be so foolish as to spurn Fitzwilliam Darcy? Lord knows I do not like the man, but something about his appearance appeals to the ladies, not to mention his wealth."

"Apparently the new Mrs. Darcy is a little spitfire who does not like being ordered about by her husband."

"Well I, for one, cannot wait to meet this spitfire," Lord Hartford said, smiling wryly. "I have a fondness for women with spirit."

"Which is precisely why you are here. She is evidently not in love with Fitzwilliam, which will make her an easy mark. I expect you to catch her eye."

"Have I told you lately that you have a devious mind, Rietta?"

"My mind works exactly like yours."

"So it does, Cousin," he said, holding his glass up in a toast. "So it does."

The parsonage garden

Whilst Elizabeth occupied the bench in the garden, William stood stiffly in front of it with a blank expression on his face. Once she had finished speaking, however, he continued to regard her with the same indecipherable expression.

Waiting for his response, Elizabeth was astounded by how blind she had been concerning his appearance. Even with a scowl on his face, he was easily the most handsome man of her acquaintance. Lost in that revelation, she was startled when he spoke.

"Let me see if I understand correctly. You expect me to forgive you because you recently learned it was Lucas who lied about Lady Aileen, and not I?"

"No. I—you have it all wrong."

"Do I? In your own words, you thought me a liar until Bingley revealed that Lucas had offered for Lady Aileen."

Elizabeth blinked steadily in hopes of not crying. "I meant to say that I do not *expect* your forgiveness. I wish only for the opportunity to earn it."

William did not reply, so she took a shaky breath and continued. "All I ask is for a chance to begin again. Let me prove I can be the wife you deserve."

"Frankly, I thought you would welcome a way out of our marriage."

"I will not lie. At first, I was in favour of the dissolution; however, that was before I realised I had never given you a chance."

She watched his expression harden even more. Had she been too candid?

"Do you care to explain?"

Elizabeth's eyes dropped to study her hands, which busily twisted a handkerchief into knots. "When first we met, I overheard you tell John you would not choose me for a wife, even if you were looking for one decidedly inferior in rank."

Throwing up his hands, William looked to the sky. "That was not mean for you to hear. My comment was meant to silence Lucas, nothing more."

"Still, it was obvious you were angry at Mr. Bingley for showing interest in Jane."

"I was worried he would raise expectations he could not fulfil, given his circumstances at the time."

"In any case, your words were like a dagger to my heart, and I let them fester until, by the time we met again at Cambridge, nothing you could have said or done would have changed my opinion of you."

William sat down on the bench across from her. "No wonder you hated me." He ran a hand through his hair as he considered all she had said. "What of your father? I felt certain he would favour my plan to dissolve our marriage?"

As he looked to her for an answer, she implored him with her eyes to understand that though she did not want to hurt him, she felt she must be candid.

"Truthfully, he never liked you, either. He was in favour of the dissolution until my aunt and uncle convinced him that our marriage is the best thing that could have happened to me."

"No doubt because of my station," William retorted. Almost as soon as the words left his lips, his insolent expression vanished, and he looked away.

Elizabeth bristled. "That was not their motive, and neither is it mine. Even if my family objects, if you no longer wish me to be your wife, I will return to Longbourn. I will leave without taking a farthing from you."

"If your father and I sign the dissolution agreement, the money spoken of in the document belongs to you, whether you want it or not."

"Then you may place it in an account for my younger sisters' dowries. My ruin will affect them more than anyone." Elizabeth stood. "I shall remain in Lambton a sennight. Should you care to find me, the Greens know where I am staying. If I do not hear from you by Saturday next, I shall assume you want me to leave."

William watched as the woman who still haunted his dreams walked away. Once she disappeared inside the parsonage, he mounted Zeus and turned towards Pemberley, too spent to deal with Lady Emma today.

Upon entering the house, Elizabeth's face reflected the pain in her heart as she began her explanation. "I have given him the rest of this week to decide whether he wants me to stay. If he should not—" Her voice broke, and she hurried into the parlour and shut the door.

"I must go to her," Judith Green murmured.

After his wife disappeared into the parlour as well, Mr. Green said, "I think I could use a brandy. May I pour one for you, Mr. Gardiner?" More affected by his niece's tears than he let on, Edward Gardiner merely nodded. "If you will follow me."

The vicar walked straight to the kitchen where he opened a cabinet and began moving items about. At length, he drew forth a bottle of brandy. It was nearly empty, but there was still enough to fill two small glasses. Handing one to Elizabeth's uncle, he took a sip of the other.

Before bringing the glass of brandy to his lips, Edward Gardiner said, "I hope I did the right thing by letting her speak to Mr. Darcy alone."

"Knowing Fitzwilliam as I do, I believe it was for the best."

"You are more familiar with him than I. In your opinion, does he care for my niece still?"

"My wife is certain he does, and Judith is rarely wrong where matters of the heart are concerned."

"I pray she is right, for lately I have seen a drastic change in Lizzy—a maturing, if you will. There is a world of difference between the young girl who ran home to Longbourn and the one who accompanied me here. She has her heart set on making amends for her actions."

"I must be honest. My worry is that Fitzwilliam may be too proud to take her back, even if that is his desire."

"He would not be the first man—or woman—too proud to forgive and forget. In my opinion, that is why there are so many unhappy people in miserable marriages."

Reverend Green smiled. "You are very astute. Perhaps you should have taken orders."

Gardiner grinned. "That would have been a disaster! No, I am merely a merchant who happened to marry a very wise woman. I have learned so much from my Madeline over the years."

Mr. Green lifted his glass. "To our wives. Where would we be without them?"

Edward Gardiner lifted his in response. "Only the good Lord knows."

Judith Green crossed to where Elizabeth sat sobbing on the sofa. Sitting beside her, she patted her back. "Go right ahead and cry, my dear. Tears touch the heart of God." As Elizabeth's tears began to wane, Mrs. Green said, "Just remember that once you have no tears left, you must begin to exercise faith. Believe that God will answer your prayers and change Fitzwilliam's heart."

"I have tried, but the agony in his eyes when I—" Another sob escaped.

"You are fortunate."

"How can you say that?"

"Men are complicated creatures. Most think it unmanly to show their feelings. Even if their hearts are breaking, they suffer stoically. Though Fitzwilliam *is* such a man, he has never quite mastered the art of concealing his emotions entirely. If you study his eyes, you will see straight through to his heart."

"Given the agony I saw in his eyes today, he must truly hate me."

"I do not believe that. And you must remember that agony looks akin to hate, but then so does remorse…and regret."

"You do not understand!" Elizabeth protested. "You have no idea how cruel I was to him. If I were Fitzwilliam, I would never forgive me."

"Be that as it may, I am confident that, in time, he will."

Retrieving a handkerchief from her pocket, the vicar's wife handed it to Elizabeth, who began wiping her eyes. Willing herself not to cry again, she made a show of smoothing her skirts. "My uncle and I should go. The Gavins will worry if they do not hear from us soon." Standing, she added, "I am sorry, though, that Fitzwilliam is angry with you for my sake."

Pulling Elizabeth into an embrace, Judith Green gave her a hug. "The Fitzwilliam I know and love never stays angry long."

"One day I hope to know him as well as you."

Moving Fitzwilliam's young wife to arm's length, Mrs. Green's eyes met Elizabeth's teary ones. "I have faith that you will."

All Elizabeth could manage was a nod.

Pemberley

When he arrived at Pemberley, William was surprised to learn Colonel Fitzwilliam had not forgotten his promise to take Georgiana fishing, and they were already at the lake. After changing into more comfortable clothes, he took the gravel trail which circled that body of water. His sister, Richard and Clancy were seated on a covered bench at the end of a pier that extended thirty yards into the lake. The bench had been constructed for his mother, who loved to fish without being bothered by the sun. It had also proven an excellent place to enjoy the magnificence that was Pemberley; thus, William had often watched the sun rise from that very spot.

Upon seeing William circling the lake, Richard took note of the slump of his shoulders and as he drew closer, the look on his face. Worried, he left Georgiana watching the cork on her line bob up and down and walked to the shore to greet his cousin.

"So, have you come to join us at last?" he ventured. "We have plenty of poles."

"No," William answered. "I have no patience for fishing today."

"That is just as well. They are not biting." Suddenly Richard recalled what William said he must do that morning. "Given the hour, I thought you would still be catering to Lady Emma."

"I had to call at the parsonage first, and I could not find the stomach to deal with Lady Emma after that. I sent her a note not to expect me until tomorrow."

"What happened?"

William glanced to Georgiana. Seeing that she was still occupied, he began to tell Richard everything.

Once he had finished, Richard let go a low whistle. "Had you not told me, I would never have believed it."

"What do you mean?"

"I find it unbelievable that someone as young as Mrs. Darcy would have had the courage to speak to you without her uncle present. Not only that, to hear that she apologised and threw herself on your mercy is astonishing."

"I do not comprehend your admiration."

"See here, Darcy! If your wife was a member of the *ton* or a mercenary, she would have had her uncle remind you of your duty and negotiate the terms of her return without ever showing her face."

"Perhaps speaking to me alone was merely a clever ploy."

"Not very clever if you ask me—leaving the final decision to you and refusing any compensation."

"She agreed the monies would go to her sisters' dowries."

"You are splitting hairs. Mrs. Darcy has refused to take a farthing from you."

"You make her sound like a saint," William retorted irritably.

"Compared to most of the women I know, she is." When William did not reply, Richard added, "I take it your mind is made up. The marriage is over."

William studied the ground. Softly he said, "She will never own my heart again."

Just then, Clancy began barking because Georgiana had pulled a fish no bigger than her hand from the lake and was trying to keep it from him. As William walked towards his sister, Richard shook his head.

I fear it is already too late for that, my friend.

Chapter 17

Pemberley
William's study

Tomorrow is Saturday. Elizabeth leaves Lambton tomorrow.

Unable to purge this thought from his mind, William tossed the report he had been attempting to read onto his desk. Crossing the room, he stopped before a bank of windows to stare into a distant pasture where, inspired by the brisk morning air, several young colts were playing. That bucolic scene, visible from this vantage point, had often been a balm to his tortured soul. This day it proved inadequate for the task.

In the days since Elizabeth's apology, he had avoided thinking about her by keeping busy, a strategy that proved ineffective at night when she invaded his dreams. Furthermore, having concentrated on completing his visits to the tenants at Parkleigh Manor and compiling a report for the incoming steward, he was behind on issues of concern regarding his own tenants. For that reason, he had promised to read Mr. Sturgis' report and discuss it with him this afternoon. Only now he was uncertain if he could keep that appointment.

Where his marriage was concerned, William's feelings fluctuated from hour to hour and, at times, minute to minute. Sometimes he was convinced Elizabeth regretted her behaviour and might become a suitable wife. Other times, he thought her willing to say anything to get back in his good graces.

Would that Richard was still here!

His cousin had always been more than a relation. He was William's confidant and often his conscience. If anyone could force him to weigh both sides of an issue, it was the colonel. Moreover, without his presence at Pemberley to keep conversations light, it was becoming more difficult to stomach Lord Hartford, who suffered under the delusion that his views mattered. To avoid running into that buffoon this morning, William had eaten earlier than normal and retired to his study directly after.

A knock on the door interrupted his thoughts. Closing his eyes in frustration, he called out, "Come!"

Mr. Walker opened the door but did not enter. "Mr. Green is here to see you, sir."

"Tell him I am indisposed!" William roared. Instantly, he thought better of his response. "Wait!" Confused, Mr. Walker halted. "Send him in."

The butler closed the door, and not long after it opened again. The vicar stepped inside, but instead of advancing, he appeared to be assessing the situation.

Once he decided to move closer, William motioned to a chair in front of his desk, saying dryly, "How may I be of service, Mr. Green?"

Ignoring William's formality and the question, the vicar sat down. "You look exhausted."

"As you well know, I have been helping Lord Waterston with his estate. Adding those responsibilities to my duties here has kept me rather occupied."

"Before I get to the purpose of my visit, let me say that I not only admire your willingness to help your neighbour, but I admire how you have handled Pemberley since George's death. With so many lives dependent upon this estate, you have risen to that responsibility admirably."

"Be that as it may, you have come to take me to task," William said cynically.

"Surely, you cannot expect me to express similar pride in how you are handling your marriage. You cannot be serious about sending your wife back to her family."

William bristled. "Did Elizabeth send you here to plead with me?"

"I think you know her better than that. She has no idea I am here."

"So tell me. Why would I not send her back? Elizabeth was completely serious when she left me."

"How old is Georgiana?"

"I do not see how that has anything—"

"Humour me."

"Almost fifteen," William replied curtly.

"Do you realise that Elizabeth is barely three years older? Yes, what your wife did was foolish, and it was wrong, but she regrets her behaviour exceedingly. Will you not give her the chance to make amends?"

"She is old enough to know what leaving London with Lucas would mean. She made it clear that she trusted him, not me."

"Is that what prevents your forgiveness? Jealousy?" William would not meet his gaze. "I thought you a bigger man than that."

"I am sorry to be a disappointment to you," William answered, tossing a pen down on the desk.

James Green's attitude softened. "Forgive me. I should not have said that. And if you believe nothing else, believe me when I say that I am not here for Elizabeth's sake; I am here for yours. Judith and I love you, and we believe you are making a grave mistake."

"Mistakes are a part of life."

"I am not speaking of buying the wrong horse, Fitzwilliam. I am speaking of spending the rest of your life regretting the woman you love."

"At this point, I am not certain how I feel about Elizabeth."

"Are you not? Judith is convinced that you still love her. Can you say with certainty that she is mistaken?"

When William looked away, the vicar continued. "If you still do, it would be foolish not to forgive your wife and get on with your lives. We all make mistakes, and I dare say at some point you may need to ask Elizabeth for forgiveness."

Mr. Green stood. "I have said what I came to say, so I will

leave you with this: If that coach leaves Lambton tomorrow morning with Elizabeth on it, it will carry her away from you forever. Once set in motion, the pain it will cause will likely never be overcome. If you have any misgivings about letting her go, you would be wise to head straight to the Gavin's farm after I leave."

The vicar walked out of William's study, closing the door behind him. William reflected for some time on Reverend Green's advice before going upstairs to change clothes.

The Gavin's farm

Ultimately, what persuaded William to give Elizabeth another chance were the lessons instilled at his mother's knee. Whilst he pondered all Mr. Green had said, a miniature portrait of Lady Anne in his desk beckoned, and he opened the drawer to retrieve it. Studying the face that he loved so well, he could hear her say, "No gentleman would ever do harm to a lady."

Trusting that his mother was watching over him still, William could not bear the thought of disappointing her. Therefore, it was her advice that compelled him to act, for whilst Elizabeth might be too young to realise how cruelly the dissolution of their marriage would affect her, he knew full well. No, he simply had to give her one last chance.

The carriage was nearly to the Gavin's farm before he had decided how he would approach her. With his proposal, he hoped to have fewer expectations of Elizabeth and, theoretically, a less engaged heart. Moreover, should she reject his offer, at least he could rest knowing he had done his part as a gentleman. Satisfied at last, his wildly fluctuating feelings began to calm as the carriage turned into the drive that led to the Gavin's home. Not long after, the vehicle came to a stop, then swayed under the weight of a footman climbing down to open the door. The moment it opened, William was surprised to see Mr. and Mrs. Gavin walking towards the carriage.

Once he gained his feet, William tipped his hat. "Mr. Gavin, Mrs. Gavin, it is a pleasure to see you again."

"And you, Mr. Darcy," the lady of the house said.

"How long has it been?" Mr. Gavin asked.

"I believe we have not met since you sold the shop. As you may know, I left for university about that time. I have met the new owner, but I only frequent the place now when Georgiana is with me. I try not to eat as many sweets as I did in my youth."

"What a pity," Mrs. Gavin said, flashing a broad smile. "You loved my fudge when you were a boy, and I gave Mr. Strong all my recipes when he purchased the shop."

"How fortunate for him," William said, attempting to smile.

There was an awkward silence before Mrs. Gavin said, "Mrs. Darcy is in the vegetable garden which lies behind our stable. I should be glad to send a servant to fetch her."

"If you do not mind," William said, "I would rather go to her. Please excuse me."

The Gavins watched William walk around the side of the house. Once he was completely out of sight, Mr. Gavin whispered to his wife, "I had given up hope he would come."

"As had I."

William was surprised at the scene that greeted him when he approached the stable. Less than a hundred feet ahead, in a newly tilled plot, Elizabeth was on her knees with her back to him. As he watched, she reached into a bucket and brought out a plant, placed it in a prepared hole and raked dirt around it with her gloved hands. In his lifetime, he had seen only one other gentlewoman do such a thing, and that was his mother. Anne Darcy loved her gardens, and when spring plantings began, she would often be found on her knees beside the gardeners. Whilst it bothered his father immensely, and he chided her that no gentlewoman should ever be seen in such a position, his mother's reply was to laugh and say that she was only giving the gardeners instructions.

Shaking off the recollection, William walked on, though as he drew closer to Elizabeth, he began to hear soft crying and stopped abruptly. He watched her remove a glove and wipe her face with the back of her hand. It touched him more than he was willing to admit, but steeling himself, he pressed on. The crack of a twig underneath his feet garnered Elizabeth's attention. She glanced over her shoulder, and the gloves fell to the ground as she came to her feet. After frantically wiping her face, she turned to him with red and swollen eyes.

"Fitz...Fitzwilliam," she stammered, forcing a wan smile. "You frightened me."

William could not stop his eyes from drifting to the front of her gown, which was covered in dirt. She crimsoned. "I apologise for my appearance. I had given up all hope that you would—" She went silent.

"It appears you like to work with your hands," he replied awkwardly.

Elizabeth swallowed hard before replying. "It helps to calm me when I am...when I need peace of mind."

There was another awkward silence before he said, "Surely you know why I am here."

Though Elizabeth's ebony eyes grew wider, she said nothing.

"I came to make you a proposition, that is, should you still wish to be married."

In the carriage

Resplendent in fresh clothes and newly styled hair, Elizabeth sat in Fitzwilliam's luxurious carriage on her way to Pemberley. All the while, she concentrated on the scenery outside rather than risk meeting the indecipherable gaze of the man across from her. She was still unsure why she had agreed to Fitzwilliam's offer, but as she had been preparing to turn him down, a voice prompted her to say yes.

Was it Providence? Having prayed unceasingly since realising she was the one in the wrong, she did not wish to miss God's guidance; thus, she had murmured her consent. Even so, the fear that had almost prompted her to decline had since returned with a vengeance, and she worried that he would see the misery in her eyes and enquire about her wellbeing.

And what would I say? I am disappointed you no longer wish for a marriage based on respect and devotion? Suddenly, a voice whispered, *You should be grateful he is willing to take you back under any terms.*

And she was...except. After realising how cruelly she had misjudged him and having listened to glowing reports of his character from not only her uncle, but the Greens and the Gavins as well, an unexpected admiration for him had blossomed. Consequently, she had begun to believe that, given the chance, she could prove her remorse and win his respect, if not his heart. But the offer he made her crushed that notion. She had been afraid to share it even with her uncle, who had left Lambton thinking she was returning to her husband just as though nothing had happened.

A marriage of convenience. How can I win his admiration if we spend so little time together? The thought made Elizabeth unbearably sad.

Nonetheless, the proviso for resuming her position as his wife was to accept that they would live separate lives, except for the begetting and rearing of children or when social obligations required they appear in public together. Making it plain he expected her to fulfil her marital duty, he stipulated that he needed the obligatory heir, and expected her to provide four children in total.

Even so, it had been his last dictate that had pierced her heart: Until their last child was five years of age, neither would be allowed a *close friend* of the opposite sex. When she questioned what he meant, he had explained that this was to assure any children born during their marriage were his issue.

Did Fitzwilliam really think I would seek comfort in another man? Or could it be that he was warning me not to be surprised when he took a mistress?

In truth, whilst he was explaining how their marriage would function, all Elizabeth could think of was her fervent desire when she and Jane had dreamed of marriage in the past: Only the deepest love will persuade me to marry.

She took a ragged breath. *How far from that goal you have fallen.*

Suddenly, William interrupted her thoughts. "So that you are not caught unawares, I must tell you my sister has returned to Pemberley with Lady Henrietta and her cousin, Lord Hartford." Cynically, he added, "Lady Henrietta touts Hartford as a great artist who has deigned to instruct Georgiana in charcoals. Personally, I believe he seeks a place to lodge at someone else's expense."

"I look forward to seeing your sister again," Elizabeth volunteered. If William noticed she did not mention his stepmother, he hid it well. "May I ask what I should say if anyone enquires about where I have been?"

"Those who matter have already been informed that you were attending your father in Hertfordshire because of his injury. If someone should pry, remember you are the Mistress of Pemberley. You do not owe anyone an explanation."

As the carriage approached the huge, wrought-iron gates that signified they had reached the estate, guards in the attached, imposing watch towers on either side waved them on. Before long they crested a hill where the woods ceased, and the eye was instantly drawn to the manor house beyond the valley. Pemberley was a magnificent, grey-stone building backed by rolling hills and a stream that meandered from one side of the property to the other. The sight took Elizabeth's breath away. Never had she seen a place for which nature had done more or where natural beauty had been so little offset by tasteless displays. In that moment, she felt that to be Mistress of Pemberley was the highest honour imaginable.

Glancing at William, she found him studying her, though he abruptly looked away. Too self-conscious to comment, she turned back to the view.

Not certain if Elizabeth would accept his proposal, William had not informed his servants of his plan to speak with her today. Therefore, when the carriage stopped in front of the manor, there were no servants lining the drive and steps to welcome their new mistress.

After helping Elizabeth from the vehicle, he had begun to escort her up the steps when Mr. Walker suddenly appeared in the front door. Watching his butler's face, it was obvious the second the old servant realised who was on his arm. A panicked look and a jerk of his head sent the nearest footman after Mrs. Reynolds.

"Mrs. Darcy," William said upon reaching the servant, "may I present Mr. Walker. He has served Pemberley in one capacity or another for well over twenty years."

"Pleased to meet you, madam" the butler said, immediately performing a smart bow. "Welcome to Pemberley."

Just as Elizabeth was about to answer, a woman appeared behind Mr. Walker in the doorway. "And this is our housekeeper," William continued. "Mrs. Reynolds has served Pemberley since before I was born."

From the look in the old woman's eyes, it was evident she was upset that he had brought his wife home with no warning. Ignoring that fact, William said, "Mrs. Reynolds, may I present my wife."

The housekeeper curtseyed. "I am pleased to meet you. Welcome to your new home, Mrs. Darcy."

"I am delighted to be here and pleased to meet you both," Elizabeth replied.

By way of an apology, as they entered the foyer William said, "Forgive me for not alerting you and Mr. Walker. I was not certain if my wife would be joining us."

Though Elizabeth's cheeks flamed, she managed not to frown.

Suddenly Georgiana appeared at the top of the grand staircase. "Elizabeth!" Running down the stairs so fast that William cautioned her not to fall, she was soon rushing across the marble foyer towards her new sister. "I am so happy you are here!" After twisting Elizabeth side to side in a hug, she pulled back. "How is your father's health?"

"He is doing much better. Thank you for asking."

"I am so relieved to hear it."

In a flash, Georgiana's dog appeared beside her. Barking excitedly, he danced across the marble floor, his toenails clicking with each hop.

"Who is this?" Elizabeth asked, stooping to pet the white bundle of energy.

"This is Clancy," Georgiana replied proudly. As she watched her pet rise on his hind legs to lick Elizabeth's face, she marvelled, "He likes you! I cannot believe it! He usually does not take to strangers."

Elizabeth scratched Clancy's ears. "I get on well with animals…except for horses. I once broke my arm falling off a horse; thus, I am not very fond of riding. I much prefer to walk."

"Oh, but you simply must ride, Elizabeth. Otherwise, you will never see all of Pemberley. I am an excellent rider. If you wish, I shall be glad to help you."

"We shall see," Elizabeth said, giving her new sister a wink. "But I make no promises."

Their reunion was interrupted by a familiar voice. "How wonderful that you have finally joined us, Elizabeth!"

That declaration drew everyone's eyes to the landing above where William's stepmother stood next to a man Elizabeth assumed was Lord Hartford. As the two descended the stairs, the gentleman's scrutiny of her person made Elizabeth uneasy.

Once in the foyer, Lady Henrietta began introductions, and the blond stranger reached for Elizabeth's hand. Bringing it to his lips for a kiss, his brown eyes lit up as he smiled, exposing even, white teeth. "Rietta's account did not do you justice." Eyes still locked on hers, he added, "Darcy, you are a very lucky man."

Grasping Elizabeth's arm, William began to guide her towards the stairs. "If you will excuse us, I intend to show my wife to her suite." To Georgiana he said, "Give Elizabeth time to settle in, Georgie. You will have plenty of time to talk when she comes down for tea."

"Of course, Brother."

As they took the first stair, Mrs. Reynolds spoke up. "I sent a maid to unpack Mrs. Darcy's trunks, sir. If you had rather she put the task off until later, send her back to me."

After a nod from William, they began again to ascend the stairs. The others in the foyer did not move. Instead, they watched the couple leave with varied emotions—the servants with genuine concern, Georgiana with unbridled affection and Lady Henrietta and her cousin with disquiet, for they knew what Elizabeth's arrival had set in motion.

If Elizabeth had thought Darcy House was exquisite, she was at a loss for words to describe Pemberley. Whilst ascending the grand staircase, it had taken great determination not to crane her neck to view the fresco that graced the ceiling two floors above. Not only was Fitzwilliam's home stunningly beautiful, but from what she had seen, it was tastefully furnished, unlike some of the homes she had toured with the Gardiners. Though obviously the house held years of furnishings, portraits and other artwork belonging to residents of past generations, it felt more like a home than a museum, and she was eager to see it all.

When at last William opened a door halfway down a long hall, she was directed in to a sitting room easily larger than the parlour at Longbourn. It featured fern green carpets and drapes, whilst the sofa and chair upholstery, as well as numerous cushions, were in a pattern utilising that same green, a pale yellow and coral. All of the furniture and woodwork were white. A large window at the rear, with a charming window seat, showcased the balcony beyond.

As she took in the view, William explained that his bedroom was through a door on the left, whilst hers was beyond an identical door on the right. Crossing to that door, he opened it and motioned for her to go ahead. Taking a deep breath, Elizabeth stepped inside the room and was instantly disappointed at what she saw.

"My mother had decorated this room in muted shades of green, much like the sitting room. This," William said, waving a hand dismissively at the vivid red, dark purple and gold furnishings, "was by Lady Henrietta's design. You may change it however you please."

"I should certainly like to change the colours."

"I had hoped you would." William walked over to a set of French doors and threw them open. "I think you will enjoy the balcony; I do." As she followed him onto it, he pointed to a matching set of doors some thirty feet away. "Those doors open into my bedroom."

Unsure what to say, she was spared the trouble when William continued. "There is more."

As they re-entered her bedroom, he went straight to a door on the opposite side. "In here is your dressing room." He turned the knob and opened it to find a young maid busily hanging Elizabeth's gowns on a rack. The servant instantly froze, then remembered to curtsey.

"What is your name?" William asked.

"Daisy, sir."

"Finish what you are doing after your mistress goes downstairs for tea, Daisy."

As the woman nodded nervously, Elizabeth said, "If you do not mind, I should like to change clothes before taking tea, and Daisy's assistance would be helpful."

"As you wish," William said woodenly.

He started back into her bedroom, and she followed. "I will give you a proper tour of Pemberley later. At present, there are things that require my attention." He glanced to a clock on the mantel above the hearth. "Tea will be served in less than an hour on the terrace."

He turned to leave, and Elizabeth ventured, "Would it be possible for Florence to return as my maid?"

"I am not certain if she is still at Darcy House. I shall write Mrs. Barnes, and if she is, have her brought here."

"Thank you."

Without another word, he disappeared through the door that led into the sitting room.

Once in his bedroom, William leaned back against the door and closed his eyes against the agony. Upon opening them, he crossed to a dresser where a bottle of brandy and several glasses occupied a tray. Pouring himself two fingers of the liquor, he tossed the contents down, grimacing as it burned his throat. After repeating the procedure, he went into his dressing room and poured water from a pitcher into a basin. He splashed his face in hopes of triumphing over the emotions threatening to engulf him, then dried his face and studied his image in the mirror.

How could doing my duty as a gentleman bring such misery?

Showing Elizabeth the mistress' suite had been a harsh disappointment. Having defied Lord Matlock and Lady Catherine in hopes of marrying someone he loved and who would return his love, the taste of defeat was bitter. He had borne many setbacks, but this one was like no other. This would haunt him for the rest of his life.

Once more closing his eyes against the heartache, he was startled to find Adams watching from the doorway when he opened them again.

"Are you going to change your clothes before taking tea, sir?" the valet asked.

"No," William said curtly. "You may take your leave and return when it is time to dress for dinner."

"May I say that you look like Hades, sir."

"You overstep your bounds, Adams."

"That is nothing new." The valet began to move around the room, pretending to set things in order. "From the look of you, I would say that Mrs. Darcy's return has not set things to right."

"How do you know she is here?"

"The moment you alighted from the carriage, all of Pemberley knew."

"I pay my servants well not to gossip."

"In my opinion, the majority of Pemberley's servants are discreet. However, it is unrealistic to expect us not to talk amongst ourselves."

"A poor excuse for disobeying the rules for employment."

"Perhaps you are right." Adams made a show of brushing invisible lint from a coat hanging on the back of the door. "By the way, I believe there is still time to repair your marriage if you act quickly."

"What makes you an expert on the subject?"

"My parents were happily married for over thirty years. Moreover, I know you well enough to know you have not yet forgiven her; therefore, Mrs. Darcy must have agreed to return under certain conditions. That kind of manipulation can destroy all possibility for happiness."

"Adams, if you wish to remain in my employ, from this day forward you will keep your opinions to yourself," William said, tossing down the towel. "Now, if you will excuse me, I have matters to attend to in my study."

William stalked through the door leading into the hall, leaving Adams to meditate on his outburst. *And to think, there was a time when I envied you.*

Chapter 18

Pemberley
Later that day

Elizabeth was dressed and waiting by the time a maid knocked on her door to inform her that tea was being served. "If you will follow me, ma'am, I will show you to the terrace."

The servant walked towards the rear of the house where another staircase led to the main floor. Once there, she navigated two halls, the last ending abruptly at two enormous, intricately carved doors which stood open. Glimpsing the magnificent library beyond, Elizabeth was so spellbound that when the servant stepped inside and stopped abruptly, she almost walked into her.

"The terrace is just through there, ma'am," the maid said, motioning to a set of French doors across the room.

She thanked the maid, and after she curtseyed and walked away, Elizabeth could not help but examine the impressive room. Mahogany bookshelves rose two storeys high, whilst two spiral staircases led to a walk that circled the entire space. As she was admiring the grandeur, raised voices from behind caught her attention. Certain one voice belonged to her husband, Elizabeth crept to the library door and surreptitiously peeked into the hallway. Seeing no one, she tiptoed towards the room next door. Fortuitously, a grand arrangement of urns, topiaries, and small tree stood beside the entrance, and she slipped behind the foliage to listen.

"I have done all I said I would!" William declared testily. "I just now finished compiling the report detailing the tenants' needs and which crops were last planted."

"Still, your promise was to spend a part of each day at Parkleigh until our new steward arrived," a woman argued. "And you have begged off several times already, including yesterday and today."

"I also said I would devote certain days to Pemberley's concerns."

"You have done that numerous times already, but you have yet to survey the land Father wants to convert to tenant tracts or to estimate the amount of lumber needed to construct the houses. Am I to conclude that you are too busy to honour your promises?"

"Lady Emma, I—"

"Stop using my title! As I said before, you and I are far too close to maintain such formality," came a forceful reply. "Now, tell me. What is your excuse for today?"

"My circumstances have changed."

"Whatever do you mean?" There was a brief pause before she exclaimed, "Oh, my heavens! Do not tell me that your wife decided to come home!"

"She arrived today."

"So, I am finally going to meet the elusive Mrs. Darcy!"

"Emma—" William drew the name out like a warning.

"Oh, do not have an apoplexy. I am well-versed in feigning civility. Where is she?"

"Tea is being served on the terrace. I imagine she is already there."

"Come, then! I simply must meet this paragon of feminine virtue."

Hearing that, Elizabeth held her breath and stood as still as possible whilst a whirlwind dressed in burgundy exited the drawing room, followed closely by William. Whether it was the fact that her green gown blended with the foliage or the swiftness with which the two hurried down the hall, neither noticed her. After they entered the library, Elizabeth followed at a more dignified pace.

Upon reaching the open French doors, she paused in hopes of ascertaining what awaited her on the terrace. From her vantage point, she could see William standing beside a wrought-iron table where Georgiana, Lady Henrietta and Lord Hartford were seated. As William conversed with his sister, a slender woman with glossy red hair, sides held back with pearl combs whilst the rest cascaded down her back, stood with one arm threaded through his. Clad in a beautiful burgundy riding habit with black leather trim, the mystery woman's dark-blue eyes were full of unconcealed adoration as she looked up at William.

Suddenly, Lord Hartford spied her. "Ah, Mrs. Darcy! There you are!"

As Elizabeth walked onto the terrace, Lady Henrietta declared, "We were just discussing where you might be."

"Forgive me if I am late," Elizabeth said, offering a fleeting smile to no one in particular.

Georgiana motioned to the seat beside her, and since Lady Emma refused to let go of William's arm, Lord Hartford jumped to his feet to pull out her chair. Elizabeth nodded her thanks and sat down.

"How fortunate to have so many lovely ladies in one place," Lord Hartford stated, resuming his seat. As William freed his arm from Lady Emma, Lord Hartford addressed her. "Did you come all this way just to have tea with us, Lady Emma?"

Eyes locked on Elizabeth, that woman replied, "No, I came specifically to see Fitzwilliam. He happened to mention that his wife was here, so I insisted upon meeting her. Truthfully, I was beginning to wonder if she actually existed."

From the look on William's face, it was obvious that Lady Emma's taunt angered him. Still, he sounded unruffled as he said, "Elizabeth, may I present Lady Emma Marshall. Her father, the Earl of Waterston, owns Parkleigh Manor. Their estate borders Pemberley on the north." Turning to his guest, he said, "Lady Emma, may I introduce my wife, the former Elizabeth Bennet of Longbourn in Hertfordshire."

Elizabeth pasted on a smile. "I am pleased to meet you."

"Likewise," Lady Emma answered, though her eyes belied her

sincerity. "My family and Fitzwilliam's go back centuries, and your husband and I have been very close since we were children."

"How fortunate," Elizabeth said.

"Has anyone hosted a dinner party to celebrate your marriage?" Lady Emma asked.

Lady Henrietta's eyes danced with mirth. "Until now, they have not been in the same place long enough to celebrate."

"Well, you must allow me to be the first, then," Lady Emma replied. "I am certain our neighbours are dying to meet the woman who persuaded Fitzwilliam Darcy to renounce bachelorhood. I know I was."

"That will not be necessary," William said dryly. "You know how I despise soirées."

"Nonsense!" Lady Henrietta retorted. "How else will your wife meet Derbyshire society?"

"Then it is settled," Lady Emma exclaimed. "Now, I should be on my way. I have a party to host, and there is much to do."

Lady Henrietta stood. "I shall escort you to the door, my dear. It has been far too long since we had a chance to talk."

Lord Hartford stood when his cousin did, and after she and Lady Emma left through the library, he sat in the chair beside Elizabeth. Leaning closer, he said, "At least Georgiana and I still have your lively conversation to entertain us, Mrs. Darcy."

His quip served to encourage Georgiana, who had been listening raptly to everyone else. Instantly, she began peppering Elizabeth with questions. Curious to see how his wife would handle Lord Hartford, rather than sitting down, William took his cup of tea and propped himself against one of the pillars supporting the roof to observe.

Since his father's death, he had mastered the art of ignoring Lady Henrietta's prattle whenever they were in company in order to focus on his sister. However, Lord Hartford's arrival had made that task more difficult, for that gentleman talked over everyone else, just as he was doing now. He quickly tired of watching him compete with Georgiana for Elizabeth's attention and announced he had work to do and quit the terrace.

Georgiana was the only one to reply to his pronouncement,

and William believed his departure had gone unnoticed by Elizabeth. He was mistaken. Aware of how gauche Lord Hartford's attentions were, she was struggling to be civil whilst wondering why her husband did not seem to care that his guest was openly flirting with her. Disappointed when William left her at Lord Hartford's mercy, she begged to be excused shortly after that to rest before dinner and returned to her room.

Once on the portico, Lady Henrietta took hold of Lady Emma's arm to keep her from continuing down the steps. There was only one servant about, and he was holding the reins to Lady Emma's stallion.

"Wait! We can speak here without being overheard." Lady Emma stopped and turned to face Lady Henrietta, who continued, "I know you and I have never been the best of friends, but I believe we both are of the same mind when it comes to Fitzwilliam's wife."

"Oh?" Lady Emma said, taking a measure of William's stepmother, who, as usual, was clad in a gown cut far too low for daywear. "And what *mind* might that be?"

"I know you are in love with Fitzwilliam—you always have been. And I imagine you would not grieve if his marriage was voided because of a technicality."

"I would not, but why should you care?"

Not willing to reveal her true motivation, Lady Henrietta lied. "If I help you to rid Pemberley of Elizabeth, I trust you will act kindly towards me when you are the next Mrs. Darcy. After all, my living is now dependent upon Fitzwilliam's mercy."

"I see."

"So tell me. What is your plan? Surely you did not offer to host a dinner party out of the goodness of your heart,"

"I aim to show Elizabeth Bennet that she will never fit into polite society."

"How will you do that?"

"I have not worked out the details yet."

"It is my belief that Fitzwilliam married her because they were compromised; this is not a love match. That leaves Elizabeth vulnerable and attractive to other men. Even Lord Hartford is enamoured of her, but thus far she has showed him no preference. Perhaps another man would have more luck."

"I shall make certain to invite many unattached gentlemen to the party and spread the rumour that Mrs. Darcy is not in love with her husband and, therefore, open to seduction."

Lady Henrietta smiled. "You are more devious than I thought."

"I can be when it comes to the man I love."

"So are we all."

At dinner

If tea had been a tortuous affair for William, dinner was not much better. On the terrace, Lord Hartford's strategy had been to regale Elizabeth with witty anecdotes of his life in Liverpool, and he persisted in that practice during dinner. William told himself he was not jealous, but it galled him to see how assiduously Lord Hartford pursued his wife's approbation right under his nose. When at length he deigned to glance at Elizabeth, however, William was puzzled to find her studying her plate and not Lord Hartford. Since she seemed to welcome distractions in the past, he pondered why that gentleman was having so little luck amusing her. Then, an explanation struck him. *She must be pining for John Lucas.*

After dinner, Georgiana insisted that everyone gather in the music room to listen to a duet she and Lady Henrietta had been practising. William escorted Elizabeth to the sofa nearest the pianoforte and took the seat beside her, whilst Lord Hartford commandeered the chair nearest his wife. During the performance, Hartford attempted several times to engage Elizabeth in conversation, but she kept her eyes fixed on the performers and said little in return.

Once the duet was over, Georgiana and Lady Henrietta each performed several solo selections. Lady Henrietta was the last to perform, and once she rose from the instrument, she said, "Now it is your turn, Elizabeth."

"Alas, I do not play. I am told that my only talent lies in singing, though I fear I am not of a mood to sing tonight," Elizabeth said. "My throat is sore."

"Should I send for the physician?" William asked, brows furrowing.

"No. Rest normally restores my throat, so I believe it best that I retire. Would you be so kind as to escort me to my room?"

William stood and offered her his arm. "I have much to do tomorrow. I believe I shall retire as well. If you will excuse us."

Once they entered their sitting room, Elizabeth said, "I hope you do not think I am feigning a sore throat to—" her eyes dropped to the carpet, "to escape my marital duties."

Secretly, William was relieved. He was determined to reach a certain detachment before consummating his marriage, one in which marital relations meant nothing more than a means of procreation, and he was by no means to that point yet.

"I thought no such thing." There was an awkward silence before he added, "Mrs. Reynolds makes a honey and lemon concoction that works wonders for a sore throat. I shall ring for a footman and request that she send Daisy up with a bottle of her special syrup."

"That is most thoughtful. I would like that."

"You may direct the maid to sit with you tonight if you wish… just in case your health should deteriorate."

His concern was touching, and a small smile refused to be suppressed. "I do not think that will be necessary."

"I leave that up to you. However, should you feel worse during the night, you have only to knock on my door."

With Elizabeth's nod, William walked to the door leading into his bedroom. Stopping with his hand on the knob, he said, "I bid you goodnight."

"Goodnight."

Once in her bedroom, Elizabeth pulled the bag containing her journal and a pencil from underneath her bed where she had secreted it. Taking the chair nearest the candle, she began recording her thoughts.

For better or worse, I am here. Whether my husband has noticed I have changed, I cannot say. Nevertheless, I intend to do my best by word and deed to show him how much I regret my mistakes and how hopeful I am that our marriage will exceed his expectations.

Satisfied, she closed the book and placed it back under the bed.

A week later

As one day faded into the next, Elizabeth found herself not only sleeping alone, but breaking her fast each morning without her husband's company. It appeared that though she and William were the only early risers at Pemberley, no matter how early she awoke and enquired of Mrs. Reynolds as to William's whereabouts, she was informed that he was already on his way to Parkleigh Manor.

With the exception of William, Elizabeth had plenty of company. Georgiana was determined to know her better, so when they were not reading, discussing books, plays and poetry, or sitting in the music room whilst she played, Georgiana conducted tours of the house and the grounds. Though William had promised to show her his home, he had not followed through, and Elizabeth was pleased when her new sister assumed the task. Fortuitously, Georgiana knew all the history regarding the portraits in the gallery and many paintings elsewhere in the manor, all of which fascinated Elizabeth.

During the time Georgiana was occupied with her lessons, Lady Henrietta often sought her out, though Elizabeth had no idea why. Whilst she had no firm reason to dislike William's stepmother, they had absolutely nothing in common, and she felt awkward feigning interest in fashion, which was Lady Henrietta's subject of choice. As for Lord Hartford, when he was not instructing Georgiana, he seemed to appear wherever Elizabeth was, which was becoming insufferable.

Resigned to seeing very little of her husband, Elizabeth had resolved to use the solitude of her morning walks to contemplate how she might conquer her husband's indifference, and the time following to consult with Mrs. Reynolds regarding the household accounts. The housekeeper appeared taken aback when she first enquired about them, something Elizabeth attributed to misgivings about her age and abilities. Whilst she dressed this day, she recalled their initial conversation and smiled.

"I would like to go over the household accounts and the menus directly after my morning walk today, Mrs. Reynolds. That has proved a quiet time for me, and I hope it is for you as well. If so, we may continue at that hour in the future."

"My job is to serve whenever it suits you."

"Still, I wish for us to accommodate each other's schedules whenever possible."

"Yes, madam. I believe my office would be a good place to discuss such things because, at present, the household ledgers are stored there. You will find it on the same hall as the dining room, third door on the right."

"Excellent. I shall meet you there upon my return. Oh, and there is one more thing. Is there a room where you store items for the tenants? My sister Jane and I always kept a ready supply of baby clothes, blankets and food available for distribution to needy tenants."

"I am afraid that we have not had such a room since Lady Anne passed away," Mrs. Reynolds said. "No one has visited the tenants regularly since her death, though I have tried to see to their needs whenever they are brought to my attention. One of the kitchen maids has a sister who is married to a tenant. She keeps me abreast of matters that affect them and has delivered items when necessary."

"Perhaps she will accompany me until I am familiar with all the families."

"Of course, Mrs. Darcy."

"By the way, if we have no material in stock, I will use my pin money to purchase some materials to make blankets and clothes. I brought my sewing box and the patterns we used for baby gowns and caps."

"It will not be necessary. The Master will pay for it."

"No. Pray do not mention this to him. Unless he asks, I had rather this be our secret."

Mrs. Reynolds brows knit. "May I ask why?"

"The Bible instructs us not to do our alms before men, to be seen of them. Consequently, I prefer to keep my small contributions private. Now, if you will, begin thinking of an extra room, or even a large closet, that I might use for the storehouse. My intention is to begin visiting the tenants as soon as I have sufficient provisions."

If some things were awry in her world, Elizabeth could not say the same about her new home. Pemberley's grounds were exquisite, and they drew her like a moth to a flame. There were eight gardens, each with a different family of plants, and all criss-crossed by gravel paths. A few paths included small fish ponds graced with benches, whilst others led to gazebos or canopied swings. Moreover, the longest path, the one around the lake, had quickly become her favourite place to exercise each morning. Several footpaths veered off that trail into the woods behind the lake and they beckoned to her. Elizabeth intended to see where each led as soon as she devised a way to elude the footman who followed her wherever she went.

This morning she had been sitting on the bench at the end of the pier for several minutes when a voice broke though the morning stillness startling her. "It is refreshing to know that someone else enjoys this hour of the morning as much as I do."

Elizabeth turned to see Lord Hartford approaching, his brown eyes twinkling as though he knew something she did not. "There is something sacred about seeing the dew still on the plants and flowers, is there not?" Reaching the bench, he made a show of taking a deep breath of fresh air. "I relish this."

"Indeed?" Elizabeth said somewhat cynically. "I do not recall seeing you at this hour before."

"I fell into the habit of sleeping late when I came to Pemberley. Then, this morning I walked onto the balcony and saw you in the distance. You inspired me to return to my routine of walking before breaking my fast. If you do not mind, I should like to join you on your morning walks."

His charming banter brought to mind George Wickham and Elizabeth stiffened. "I believe it would be inappropriate for just the two of us to walk out every morning."

Lord Hartford's voice rose indignantly. "Inappropriate?" He motioned to a footman resting against a tree beside the path. "Your security is not a hundred feet away. Is he not chaperone enough?"

"You are fully aware that he is not a proper chaperone, and I do not intend to ignore propriety."

"How odd that you worry about propriety whilst your husband spends his days with another woman and ignores you when he deigns to come home!"

Elizabeth was immediately on her feet. "How dare you!"

As she turned to leave, Lord Hartford caught her hand. "Stay! Please…allow me to apologise." Pulling her hand from his, Elizabeth waited.

"I am sorry. What I said was completely untoward. It is just—" Lord Hartford dropped his head as if trying to regulate his emotions. "It wounds me to see Darcy treat you so meanly."

"You have no right to speculate on something you know nothing about."

"Once more, I apologise, and if you wish it, I shall leave Pemberley."

Elizabeth paused to consider what that would mean. "Georgiana would be disappointed if her lessons end prematurely. I had rather you stay—that is, if you promise never to say anything like that again or to approach me when I am alone, especially in the mornings."

"You are too kind. Rest assured that I have learned my lesson. Please sit back down and enjoy the view. I am the one who should leave."

As Lord Hartford retreated down the pier, Elizabeth pondered whether to tell William what he had said. Deciding it could create even more problems, especially if William thought she had encouraged Lord Hartford's behaviour, she waited until that gentleman was halfway around the lake before returning to the manor in the opposite direction.

Unable to contend with Lady Emma's foibles, William had sent a note earlier that morning saying he had work to do at Pemberley. Once he was ensconced in his study, however, he could not concentrate as the walls seemed to be closing in. Abruptly, he quit the room and headed upstairs to play billiards. He had excelled in that sport at Cambridge, winning numerous awards, though he appreciated the game most because it helped to relieve his tension. After practicing for a time, he laid down his cue and walked onto the balcony for some fresh air. From that vantage point, he had a clear view of the lake and instantly spied Elizabeth and Lord Hartford on the pier. By all appearances, they were enjoying each other's company and immediately his jaw clenched.

Ironically, Mrs. Reynolds chose that moment to walk in with a bottle of brandy he had enquired about earlier. "This is the last bottle of that particular brand. I found it in the rear of the cellar." She opened the liquor cabinet to place it inside. "Since you ordered it when you were in London, I have no idea where to purchase more."

William's eyes stayed locked on the pier. "Tell me. Does my wife walk out every morning?"

Thinking it odd that he changed the subject, Mrs. Reynolds studied him. "She does."

"And does Lord Hartford accompany her?"

Glancing in the same direction as her employer, she recognised the source of his questions. "I have never seen him walk with her. Rogers is assigned to follow her. Shall I ask Mr. Walker to send him up once Mrs. Darcy returns?"

Seeing his wife stand and Lord Hartford reach for her hand, immediately William turned from the window. "That will not be necessary."

Noting his tormented expression, the housekeeper was tempted to reveal how Mrs. Darcy had thwarted many advances by Lord Hartford according to more than one maid, but she knew that Mr. Darcy never put any stock in hearsay. All she could do was hope that he learned the truth soon.

"I will see to ordering the brandy, Mrs. Reynolds. That will be all."

With his dismissal, Mrs. Reynolds bit her tongue and returned to her duties.

The breakfast room

When at last Lord Hartford entered the breakfast room, the only person therein was his cousin. As he proceeded to the sideboards teeming with food and drink, Lady Henrietta asked, "Why have you returned so early? Surely Elizabeth is not done walking."

Bringing a finger to his lips to silence her, Lord Hartford proceeded to pour a cup of tea and add sugar and cream. Once finished, he took the cup and sat down next to her.

"I had rather you not speak so loudly," he whispered. "With servants going in and out, they might overhear. Where is Georgiana?"

"She was not hungry, so she took a scone and returned to her room."

"And Fitzwilliam?"

"As far as I know, he ate earlier and is in his study."

"Good." Taking a sip of the hot liquid, Lord Hartford leaned towards her. "It appears that Mrs. Darcy is not interested in hearing about her husband's neglect. She became quite indignant and asked me never to join her in the mornings again."

Lady Henrietta bristled. "You were to charm her with your caring manner, not insult her or Fitzwilliam. If she tells him, I will not be able to keep you here."

"Do not trouble yourself. I apologised. and she accepted. I even volunteered to leave Pemberley if she so desired."

"That would not have helped in the least."

"I knew she would not accept. She is too kind for her own good."

"Am I to assume you have fallen in love with her too?"

"I could...very easily. Now, if you will excuse me, circling the lake has improved my appetite, and I am famished. Should you desire to discuss what you want to try next, send a note to me later, and I shall join you in your sitting room."

As Lady Henrietta watched her cousin cross the room and begin filling a plate, she worried about her plans. *You would be just the kind of fool to fall for that little chit. Must I keep an eye on you as well as her?*

Chapter 19

The parsonage

Whilst Judith Green sat in her favourite chair working on her mending, her husband was ensconced at the small desk in their parlour preparing his next sermon. She kept glancing at him, uncertain whether to bring up the subject she knew full well occupied his mind. As time passed, however, she began to feel that she must.

"I suppose that by refusing to attend services Fitzwilliam hopes to demonstrate that he is not over his anger."

James Green laid aside his Bible. Pinching the bridge of his nose, he squinted as though he had a terrible headache. "I tell myself that he is weary from working such long hours—what with helping Lord Waterston and discharging his duties at Pemberley; however, I have no idea why Miss Darcy or Elizabeth have not come."

"Perhaps they do not wish to anger him, or perhaps because it would be fodder for the gossips if they attended without him."

"Perhaps." The vicar stood and stretched, arching his back for relief from having sat so long. "I had hoped to postpone calling on him again so soon—give him time to calm down, if you will. However, should this continue, I feel it my duty to enquire if he would rather I vacate my living at Kympton. I would sooner he attend church, even if under another shepherd, than be forced to stay away because of my presence here."

Judith Green stood and walked to her husband to console him. "Surely it will not come to that."

Pulling her into his arms, he kissed the top of her head. "Let us pray it does not."

Suddenly there was a knock on the door. "Who could that be?" the vicar asked.

"You are tired. Sit down, and I shall see who it is."

Upon opening the front door, she was pleased to find Elizabeth on her doorstep. "My dear, how good to see you!" she declared, wrapping her arms around the young woman and giving her a hug. Upon straightening, she looked over her guest's shoulder to the gig[8] waiting in the drive. "Surely you did not come in that?"

"I did. Since I do not care for riding horses, I use it to call on Pemberley's tenants. I always have a basket or two with me, so it works well for my purposes."

"And Fitzwilliam allows you to drive it?"

"In truth, he has no idea that I do. When I began calling on the tenants, I asked the housekeeper not to mention it to him unless he should ask."

"I see. You do not wish him to think you are trying to impress him. I do not know which of you is the more principled," Mrs. Green teased. "Still, no gentlewoman should traipse about the countryside alone, even to call on tenants."

"Normally, a maid accompanies me. Mary—that is her name—has a sister who is married to a tenant, and today we visited her. She is with child again and not feeling well, so Mary asked if she might stay overnight and help with the children. When I was returning to Pemberley, I reached the road and recalled that the church was not far in this direction."

"James will be just as pleased as I am to see you." With one arm over Elizabeth's shoulder, she walked their visitor into the parlour. "Look who has come to visit."

The vicar walked forwards to take her hands. "It has been far

8 **Gig**: A light two-wheeled cart that held one or two persons and was drawn by one horse. https://allaboutromance.com/carriages-in-regency-victorian-times/

too long, young lady. We have missed you."

Elizabeth forced a smile. "As I have missed both of you."

"James, will you put on a pot of tea whilst Elizabeth and I catch up with all that has happened since last we spoke?" As he walked away, she added, "I can only imagine how difficult it has been to put your struggles behind you and come together as a couple."

Elizabeth looked around to see if the vicar had closed the door. He had, and assured that they were alone, she said, "I am so thankful to have you to confide in."

Sensing something was terribly wrong, Judith Green reached for her hand. "Come. sit down so we may talk."

As Elizabeth sank onto the sofa all attempts to appear happy crumbled, and she began to cry softly. Mrs. Green squeezed her hand reassuringly and waited until Elizabeth had collected herself before saying, "Oh, my dear, will you not tell me what is troubling you?"

"If...if not for Georgiana, my life would be unbearable. I am rarely in Fitzwilliam's company, and when I am, he completely ignores me."

Leaning over to engage Elizabeth's eyes, she said, "If you share a bed, he cannot be ignoring you completely."

"He has not—" A sob escaped and Elizabeth fought once more for control. "He has not come to me."

"I see. When he met with you about returning, did he put forth conditions?"

Elizabeth proceeded to relate William's stipulations for her to return. Once she had finished, Judith Green remained silent for a time. Then pulling a handkerchief from her pocket, she dabbed at the tears silently running down Elizabeth's face.

"James and I had no idea that you were living under such constraints."

"Lady Emma is giving a dinner party in our honour in a few days, and if things continue as they are, I fear I cannot conceal my despondency," Elizabeth replied.

Squeezing her eyes shut, she covered her mouth with both hands as though to keep another sob from escaping. Eventually, she stammered, "After how horridly I treated him, I do not blame Fitzwilliam. Nevertheless, I long for him to accept me."

Judith Green patted her back. "Give Fitzwilliam time to understand that you mean to love him. In my opinion, he is acting in this manner because he is determined not to have his heart touched again. Therefore, I believe a change of course is in order."

"What do you mean?"

"He is a man, Elizabeth, and a man can be seduced. That is what you want, is it not? To coax him into your bed so that he might fall in love with you again?"

Elizabeth crimsoned, looking away. "I…I do."

"Then you must put aside all modesty and pursue him. If you do not, there are plenty of women who will try when they learn your union is merely a marriage of convenience."

"Do you mean I should not wait for him to come to me?" Elizabeth asked shyly.

"Precisely! If he will not come to your bed, go to his."

Elizabeth let go a shaky breath. "What if after…after we…he resents me for seducing him?"

"Resentment will not eclipse desire. Once he has tasted the rewards of the marriage bed, he will not be able to resist. If you follow my advice, I promise his attitude will change. He loved you once. He will again."

Elizabeth tried to smile.

"Now, let us find James and all share a cup of tea."

"As much as I would like to stay, I really should get back to Pemberley before Fitzwilliam returns from Parkleigh Manor."

After seeing Elizabeth off, Judith Green returned to the kitchen to find her husband enjoying a cup of tea whilst sitting at the table.

"Where is Elizabeth? Has she left already?"

"She wished to return home to wait for Fitzwilliam." She sat down across from him and watched as he poured another cup of tea. He slid the cup across to her. "Did you know that before he would allow Elizabeth to come home, Fitzwilliam demanded that she agree to a marriage of convenience?"

The vicar's shoulders slumped. "I had no idea."

She began to recite all the constraints Elizabeth had shared with her. Once she was done, her husband shook his head slowly.

"If that boy could only see that he is erecting impediments to his own happiness."

"I fear that only God can change his mind now. We must pray that He does before Fitzwilliam destroys the admiration that had begun to take root in Elizabeth's heart."

He reached for her hand. "There is no time like the present."

Ere long they were kneeling beside their bed, beseeching the Lord to extend grace to the young couple they both loved.

Pemberley

The day had not begun well. One of Mr. Kendal's sons had knocked on the door at dawn to report the river bridge nearest their property had caught on fire during the night. Since there had been no storms and hence no lightning, everything pointed to the fire being deliberately set. Toby Harvey was the presumed perpetrator since he had made threats against his wife's father and rumour was that he had been seen again in Lambton.

Typically, a river serves as a boundary line between estates, but in this case, the river zigzagged through both Pemberley and Parkleigh Manor. Thus, William had spent the morning examining the damage alongside Lady Emma because some of Pemberley's tenants lived across the river near Parkleigh Manor's tenants, whereas further downstream, the opposite situation applied. The oddity of this division could have been a source of dispute, had not the owners maintained a strong friendship through the years. As it was, the Darcys and the Earls of Waterston had always shared responsibility for the road that paralleled the river and the bridges that crossed it. Unfortunately, this new complication meant William would spend even more time in Lady Emma's company until Parkleigh Manor's new steward arrived.

Therefore, it was a downhearted William who finally headed home astride Zeus. He had not gone far before he realised that his favourite stallion was favouring one of his forelegs. By the time they arrived at Pemberley, he was so worried that he walked Zeus to the stables himself instead of handing him off to a groom. As he discussed his concerns with Mr. Wilson, the head groom, William noticed a horse fastened to a gig on the side of the paddock.

"Who ordered the gig readied?"

"Mrs. Darcy, sir. She has just returned, and I have not had time to take care of it."

"My wife drives that gig?"

"Yes, sir. Every morning."

"Where does she go?"

"I do not know, Mr. Darcy."

Instead of continuing to ask questions of someone who evidently had no answers, William marched in the direction of the manor, the expression on his face and his stiff bearing an indication of his annoyance. Recognising the signs, the footman who guarded the back door was instantly on alert, and he nodded silently when the master reached him.

"Find Mrs. Reynolds and ask her to meet me in my study straightaway."

"Yes, sir!"

Instantly the man disappeared down the hall.

William's study

William had barely gone through that day's mail when his housekeeper entered his office.

"You sent for me, sir?"

"Yes, Mrs. Reynolds. Please be seated. I learned only minutes ago that my wife has been driving a gig. Did you know about this?"

"Yes, sir."

"I would ask where she goes; however, I believe this speaks for itself." He slid an envelope across his desk.

The housekeeper recognised the name of the dry goods store in Lambton on the envelope. She was about to explain when William retrieved it and began to read the bills inside aloud. After he had finished, he said sarcastically, "I ordered day gowns for Mrs. Darcy whilst we were in London, but apparently they did not suffice. Is she a seamstress or does she intend to have the modiste construct them using the muslin she purchased?"

"Neither. The cloth is not for her, sir."

If possible, William's mien darkened even more. "Pray, enlighten me then. Who is it for?"

"The tenants, Mr. Darcy. It is being used to create blankets, gowns and caps for the babies."

"If I am not mistaken, when we discussed Pemberley's financial situation, I stressed that all non-essential purchases were to be approved by me. Why was I not consulted?"

"These bills are not being paid from Pemberley's coffers."

"Then just who *is* paying them?"

"Mrs. Darcy is—from her pin money."

William appeared taken aback but ignored that issue and quickly moved on to another point. "If she is not taking the gig to Lambton, where does she go?"

"Since she does not care to ride on horseback, I suggested that she use the gig to call on the tenants."

"She is calling on them already?" At her nod, his brows knitted. "And you thought it not important enough to tell me?"

Growing frustrated, Mrs. Reynolds took a deep breath and let it go. "She asked me not to say anything unless you enquired. Had you been here more of late, you might have noticed her absence, and I would have informed you."

"And her reason for keeping it a secret?"

"She quoted a Bible verse about performing one's good deeds in secret, but I believe she simply did not wish to draw attention to the fact that she has been quietly doing her duty as Mistress of Pemberley."

His expression was unreadable as he continued to regard her. However, Mrs. Reynolds was not easily intimidated and refused to look away.

"Please send a servant to fetch my wife. I wish to speak to her."

"Yes, sir."

Elizabeth's sitting room

As Elizabeth returned to Pemberley, Georgiana spied her from a balcony and hurried to meet her new sister in her sitting room. She greeted Elizabeth with a hug and followed her into the bedroom and then into her dressing room. Georgiana chatted whilst Elizabeth changed clothes behind a dressing screen.

"I am so grateful that you call on the tenants, Elizabeth," Georgiana said. "I fear I would not know what to say, and I am useless with needle and thread. That is why I never tried to follow Mother's example...well, that and because Rietta said I should let Mrs. Reynolds handle such matters."

"If you accompanied me just once, you would see that they are merely people trying to live their lives as best they can. I often find that if I ask about their children, they begin to talk more freely. Or I may comment on something I observe, such as a well-made quilt, a crocheted shawl, or even a freshly-made pie. You will become comfortable once you begin, and the feeling of being of service to others is so rewarding that I dare say you may wish to continue."

Cocking her head, Georgiana grinned. "Perhaps I shall one day!"

Elizabeth had tossed her sewing bag on the dressing room table the night before, and it lay open. Amongst assorted threads and sewing goods, a small gown stood out, and Georgiana reached for it. It lacked only a sleeve to be complete, and she began to admire Elizabeth's neat stitches.

"I cannot boast of my skills with a needle and thread, but might I help you by cutting the pieces for the gowns?"

"So long as you do not neglect your music or your drawing lessons, I should be happy for your assistance. I do not want to take you away from things your brother may feel are most important."

"I can continue my lessons and help you."

"Well then, if that is your wish, I normally cut the pieces out after my morning meeting with Mrs. Reynolds and stitch one or two items together before I retire. If, after breaking your fast you come to the storeroom Mrs. Reynolds designated for my use, I shall show you how to proceed. And, should you wish it, I may be able to help you improve your sewing."

"I should like that."

Suddenly, there was a knock on the door. "Come," Elizabeth called.

The door opened to reveal a maid. "Mr. Darcy wishes to see you right away in his study, ma'am."

Worried that being beckoned in this manner did not bode well, Elizabeth's heart began to race. Pasting on a smile, she replied, "Please tell him I shall be right there."

After the maid curtseyed and closed the door, Georgiana mused, "Brother was supposed to be done with Parkleigh Manor's concerns today. I hope Lady Emma has not found something else he *simply must* handle." Sheepishly she added, "Forgive me if I sound too critical of her."

"To be truthful, I do not know what to make of Lady Emma's...of her attachment to Fitzwilliam."

Georgiana sighed heavily. "As long as I can remember, she has acted as though Brother was her intended. It is my opinion that she is jealous of you, and that is one reason she demands so much of his time now."

"I can understand why she would think in that manner. It would have been the logical thing for them to marry," Elizabeth replied. Taking a last look in the mirror, she pushed a stray lock of hair behind one ear and sighed. "This will have to do. I cannot keep Fitzwilliam waiting."

As she exited the room, Georgiana called, "I shall wait for you here. Hopefully, Brother will not keep you long, and we may resume our discussion of *King Lear*."

Elizabeth smiled, repeating, "Hopefully."

William was standing at a bank of windows behind his desk, hands clasped behind his back, when Elizabeth entered the study.

"You sent for me?"

Without turning, he replied, "May I ask, do you recall the terms you agreed to abide by when I allowed you to return?"

Elizabeth swallowed against the lump quickly forming in her throat. "I do."

"Then perhaps you just mean to ignore them."

"I have no idea what you are talking about."

When he turned, she almost gasped. Having never seen his Master of Pemberley mien directed at her, she found it unnerving.

"I am referring to the rule regarding no secrets between us. How can I carry on any semblance of a marriage if I cannot trust you? And if I cannot trust you in trivial matters, how can I trust you to care for my children?"

"I do not understand the basis for these questions. What have I done?"

"Merely by chance, I learned today that you have been driving a gig." She opened her mouth to reply and was immediately silenced by a raised hand. "Furthermore, upon opening the mail, I found numerous bills from the dry goods store. I questioned Mrs. Reynolds, who informed me that you have been purchasing materials to make clothes for the tenants. Not only that, but you have begun visiting them without my knowledge."

"If you will let me explain—"

"There were to be no secrets!" William declared. "Is that not clear? What about that rule is so difficult to understand?"

"I was only trying to do my duty."

"Behind my back?" he retorted. "Had you bothered to ask, I would have assigned a groom to drive you in the gig. Manoeuvring a gig is not without its dangers, and someone unused to driving one is at risk of an accident; not to mention you should not be calling on tenants alone."

"A maid who helped deliver goods to the tenants in the past accompanied me. She drove most of the time."

Ignoring her reply, William continued. "It is my place to purchase goods for the tenants, not yours. Had you asked, I would have negotiated a better price for the quantity you purchased. Moreover, had I been told of your plans to begin calling on the tenants, I would have warned you away from certain homes."

Disregarding his remark about the cloth, Elizabeth said, "The maid who accompanied me never expressed any misgivings about the families I visited."

"Not everyone at Pemberley is aware of every circumstance, Elizabeth. She had no misgivings because she is not aware of the situation. It did not concern her."

"I do not understand."

"A former tenant has been making threats since I banned him from Pemberley for battering his wife and attacking her father. Toby Harvey has no quarrel with most of the tenants; however, given opportunity he would likely harm his wife's father, Jedidiah Kendal. Just this morning the bridge nearest Mr. Kendal's house was set afire, which makes it difficult for him to access the land he cultivates on the other side of the river. I believe that Harvey is responsible."

"Surely this man would not harm me. I have done noth—"

"He threatened to kill me," William interjected. "I have no doubt he would harm you to get even with me."

"I had no idea."

"That is one of many reasons there ought not to be secrets. If our arrangement is to work, communication is crucial."

"What an odd thing to say. This is the first conversation we have had since the day I arrived."

William's expression grew sterner. "At present, my time is at a premium. With any luck, once Parkleigh Manor's new steward arrives that will change. In any case, should you have any questions or merely need to address me, just say as much."

"I do have a question."

William's chin came up as he awaited her question.

"You said that you wished us to have children, but you have never—" Her cheeks flamed, and she went silent.

Immediately, he turned his back and feigned studying the gardens below. "How ironic that you should ask. If I recall correctly, when we first married, you recoiled whenever I touched you. Naturally, I assumed you would dread consummating our marriage."

"It is obvious that I hurt you very deeply, Fitzwilliam," Elizabeth murmured, her voice full of regret. "Please, show me how I may make amends, and I will."

More than anything, William wished to say he forgave her and they could begin their marriage anew, but he could not reconcile himself to the fact that she was in love with another.

"I fear it is too late for that."

The second the words left his mouth, he regretted them. Hearing footsteps, he turned in time to see the hem of Elizabeth's skirt clear the door. Instantly, he recalled a friend's counsel. *The first rule of an arranged marriage is to keep your feelings to yourself.*

That bit of advice had been offered after an evening at White's spent drinking with Lord Corvin, who had been forced into a marriage of convenience by his father. Too drunk to care, Corvin had provided insight into coping with the pitfalls of such a union to anyone who would listen, and his chief admonition was to keep one's feelings hidden from one's wife.

Vowing to guard his tongue from here on, William quit his office and went straight to the stables. He hoped that a visit to his mother's cottage, which had become his sanctuary after her death, might provide a sense of equanimity.

Chapter 20

Pemberley
The next morning

William was already astride Zeus and well on his way to the bridge when the sun began to rise. He hoped to find that at least part of the lumber he had ordered to reconstruct it had been delivered the evening before as promised. As in the past, he and Lord Waterston were to split the labour and the cost of the lumber needed to rebuild the structure, but he feared the workers might be waiting at the bridge for materials yet to arrive.

He had much to do before attending Lady Emma's soirée that evening, an event that had transformed from a small dinner party to a ball seemingly overnight. According to Emma, once her friends in London learned of her plans, so many insisted they be invited that she felt compelled to enlarge the event. Considering the number likely to attend, he not only dreaded going himself, he was dreading exposing Elizabeth to those on the list. Whilst their marriage was unconventional, she was his wife, and he did not wish to see her attacked by the denizens of the *ton*.

Since fleeing from his study just days before, she had been avoiding him, and he feared that spending tonight trying to appear the devoted newly-married couple would be difficult, especially for someone as young and inexperienced as Elizabeth. As he neared the river, he was distracted by these thoughts and almost did not hear the shout that came from somewhere behind him. Looking over his shoulder, he was surprised to see Richard riding towards him. Reining in Zeus, he waited for his cousin to reach him.

"I swear, Darcy, you are growing deaf!" Richard exclaimed upon reaching his side. "I have been calling you for the last mile, but you would not rein in."

"I was preoccupied. Moreover, I was not expecting you. When you left, you implied it would be weeks before you would be in this area again."

"General Lassiter revised his plans. He decided he needed me in London this week."

"How long can you stay?"

"Just overnight, but I have accumulated a good deal of leave, and it pleases me to say that in a fortnight, give or take a few days, I shall be your guest again. Then I shall be able to stay for two months complete."

"Will your parents not expect you to spend part of your leave with them?"

"Father and I did not get along well even before my subterfuge with Georgiana. After I spirited her to your wedding without his knowledge, he became even more irascible."

"I apologise that doing my bidding made your situation worse; however, rest assured I shall welcome you here with open arms. It will be most agreeable to have someone at Pemberley who is not always put out with me."

"Have you managed to alienate your wife already?"

"How did you—" William paused. "Adams."

"Do not blame him. I happened to encounter him when I arrived, and I enquired if you had come to a decision regarding Mrs. Darcy."

"I must speak to him about discussing my business."

"Be reasonable, Cousin. Together, he and I have managed to steer you along the correct course for years."

"He assumes too much."

"Adams has always been more friend than servant. Now, quit stewing over something of no importance, and tell me what happened. Adams said you offered her a marriage of convenience. Did my brilliant argument steer you in that direction?"

"Your contentions were logical, but it was my mother's teaching that persuaded me to make Elizabeth another offer. If she had not agreed to my terms, at least my conscience would have been clear."

"I still recall much of what Aunt Anne taught me about being a gentleman," Richard said. "She had a bigger influence on me than Father." William's expression had grown melancholy, so Richard changed the subject. "I hear we are invited to a soirée tonight."

William could not hold back a smile. "I do not think Lady Emma is expecting you."

"Perhaps not. Still, had she known I would be at Pemberley, she would have invited me. Naturally, I plan to attend so that I may watch Lady *Harlot* make a fool of herself with the men."

"Naturally."

"Likewise, I enjoy watching Lady Emma make a fool of herself over you."

"Now that I am married, I am of no consequence to her."

Richard laughed. "Do you actually believe that?"

"Lady Emma has changed since meeting Elizabeth. I think she has realised I would never have married her in any case."

"Believe what you will, Cousin. Personally, it is my opinion that a clever spider is more than willing to lie in wait for its prey!"

"Enough of your imaginings," William declared. "I must be on my way. Are you riding to the bridge with me?"

"Why else would I have come?" As William kicked Zeus into a trot, Richard followed suit. "Darcy, I must ask. Why not put Mr. Sturgis in charge of rebuilding the bridge? Surely, he is capable of handling it."

"I am certain he could. Unfortunately, Sturgis is halfway to Weymouth. Having finished Lord Waterston's business, I felt free to concentrate on selling my great-grandmother's estate; thus, I sent him on his way two days ago."

"It is a shame that someone added to your burdens by burning the bridge." Suddenly, Richard began to laugh uncontrollably.

"What do you find so funny?"

"I would not be at all surprised if Lady Emma had it set ablaze herself, if only to keep you at her beck and call a little longer."

William frowned. "Please do not say such things, especially in front of Elizabeth."

"Surely you know that I would only tease you about such things in private."

"I merely wished to remind you. I have enough on my plate without having my wife suspicious of Lady Emma."

"I imagine she already is, Darcy," Richard teased.

"With any luck, Parkleigh's new steward will soon take over. It will be a relief to be able to concentrate my efforts on just Pemberley again."

"When is the new steward to arrive?"

"In less than a sennight."

Reaching the bridge, they found a team of men unloading a wagon stacked high with lumber.

"Looks as though those you hired have the job well in hand," Richard said.

"It would seem so. I will have a word with the foreman, and then we can return to Pemberley."

In a few minutes, William rode back to where Richard waited. "Have you eaten?"

"I pinched a scone on my way out of the house, but I would not turn down a cup of coffee and something more substantial."

"Neither would I. Let us return before all the late risers come downstairs and force us to eat in my study."

Elizabeth's dressing room
Later that day

As she studied herself in the mirror that hung over her dressing table, Elizabeth said a prayer of thanks that Florence had arrived. Adept at styling hair, she had piled Elizabeth's atop her head in an array of large curls, then entwined a ribbon that matched her gown through them. Just as Elizabeth smiled at the result, the door flew open and Florence rushed in carrying two small, white rosebuds.

"I found just what was needed. You are so fortunate to have a conservatory at your disposal. Fresh flowers are always a lovely addition to one's hair, and I hear that most men prefer them to combs or jewels."

Florence proceeded to pin the roses at the back of Elizabeth's head beneath the curls. Once finished, she stepped back. "Done!" She handed a small mirror to Elizabeth. "What do you think?"

Using the mirror to see the back of her head, Elizabeth smiled. "I am amazed that you have managed to make my unruly curls appear elegant." Then her face fell. "If only my gown was more stylish."

William had ordered day gowns for her in London but no ball gowns. And though she had brought all her clothes from Longbourn, the gowns she wore to the assemblies in Meryton were not sophisticated enough for a ball. Reluctant to broach the subject with William since being chided for buying material, she settled on the only decent gown in her closet: her blue satin wedding gown.

"I think your gown is perfect, ma'am," Florence said as Elizabeth sat back down.

Having already seen Lady Henrietta's gown—a dark-blue, off-the-shoulder silk-damask, with dropped sleeves and plunging neckline—Elizabeth opened the robe she had donned to protect her gown during her toilet. Fingering the delicate lace her aunt had added to the bodice, she said, "Do you not think it too plain?"

"You are not like those ladies who need embellishments to catch the eye."

I fear my husband may not share your opinion. Just as that thought crossed her mind, Elizabeth caught sight of William in the mirror. He was leaning against the doorframe and looked very handsome in a black suit with a stark-white linen shirt and cravat. A gold waistcoat embroidered with multi-coloured threads added just the panache needed and seeing him, her heart began to race.

Instinctively, she clasped the sides of the robe together. This announced his presence to Florence, who bobbed a curtsey and rushed from the room. Elizabeth held her breath as he stared without saying anything, and it seemed forever before he approached, stopping behind her chair. Then he reached around her to lay a black velvet box on the table in front of her.

"I wish you to wear these."

Opening the box, Elizabeth was stunned to find a pearl necklace with matching earrings and bracelet. They were a delicate shade of pink so subtle as to be taken for white at first glance. She had no way of knowing that they were the only Darcy jewels not being held by the bank as security against the loan.

"How beautiful," Elizabeth whispered.

William reached for the necklace and began to fasten it around her neck. "Not long before Mother died, she called me into her bedroom and handed me this box. The pearls were a wedding present from my father, and she said she hoped I would present them to my wife with her blessing."

William's expression was indecipherable as he watched her don the earrings; however, after fastening the bracelet, she looked up to find he had disappeared. Rushing to the dressing room door, she watched as he crossed her bedroom and stopped at the door to the hall.

"We must leave shortly," he said. "Please come downstairs as soon as you are ready."

Finding his cousin's bedroom empty, William was not surprised to hear Richard's voice as he approached the grand staircase. Hesitating at the landing, he listened as his cousin, in full dress uniform, conversed with Georgiana in the foyer.

His secrecy did not last long, however, as Georgiana spied him, exclaiming, "Brother! I was just telling Richard how handsome he looks in his red coat."

William swiftly descended the stairs. "No doubt every debutante there tonight will be vying for his attention."

"All for naught!" Richard retorted. "I have no intention of getting married. It makes one's life too complicated."

"Oh, la!" Georgiana declared. "One day a lady will catch your eye, and you shall sing another tune." Picking up Clancy, who ran into the room at that precise moment, she addressed William. "I still do not know why I cannot attend the ball. After all, it is in honour of you and Elizabeth."

"We have discussed this before, Georgiana, and I do not wish to repeat myself."

Georgiana dropped her head, pouting. Lifting her chin with two fingers, Richard said, "Cheer up, Poppet! Before long you will be out in society and breaking hearts. It shall come too soon to suit me."

Suddenly Elizabeth was at the landing. Upon spying her, Georgiana was almost speechless. "Oh, Elizabeth," she murmured reverently, "you look just as beautiful as you did on your wedding day. Does she not, Brother?"

William's disloyal mind whispered: *She looks like an angel.* Though he said nothing aloud, the look on his face gave evidence of his feelings.

Whilst Georgiana raced up the stairs to join arms with her sister and escort her, Richard leaned in to whisper, "Thank your lucky stars you did not end up with one of those hideously ugly women my parents favoured."

Instantly the spell was broken, and William's expression grew sombre. "My only worry is how the *ton* will react to Elizabeth. I pray they will be kind, if only because of her youth."

"Have you ever known the harpies of the *ton* to be kind? A beauty such as she will create a frenzy amongst the men and stir jealously in the women. Fortunately, I am here. Perhaps between the two of us, we can keep her from being crushed by their malice."

"I am obligated to dance with Elizabeth and Lady Emma; otherwise I do not intend to stand up with anyone. If you dance with Elizabeth whilst I partner Lady Emma, one of us will always be available to watch over her."

Richard sighed. "The best laid schemes of mice and men—"

As he, his cousin and Elizabeth entered Darcy's carriage for the trip to Parkleigh Manor, Richard was relieved to learn that Lady Henrietta and her cousin would be following in a separate carriage. He could barely stomach William's stepmother, much less her cousin, and the thought of riding in close quarters with either made his stomach turn.

After riding a short while, he noticed the honourees of the ball exchanged little by way of conversation, and he decided to lighten the mood.

"Mrs. Darcy—"

"Elizabeth," she interrupted.

He smiled. "If you will call me Richard."

She nodded.

"Elizabeth, will this be the first time you have stood in a receiving line at a ball?"

She dropped her head as though embarrassed. "It will."

"Just a word of warning. Receiving lines are ugly affairs, and at a soirée such as this, by the time the line winds down, your mind will likely be as numb as your feet."

Though Darcy began to tug at his cravat, as was his wont when he was worried, Elizabeth smiled. That was all the encouragement Richard needed.

"Consequently, I thought I would share with you a game your husband and I dreamt up when our parents decided we were of age and forced us to stand alongside them in receiving lines."

"Richard, must you?"

"I must, Cousin, or would you have me let your wife die of boredom?" Richard retorted. "Now, the key to surviving the scrutiny of the *ton* is to imagine that you are Noah, and it is your job to choose occupants for the ark from amongst those in line—in other words, try to picture the people as animals."

Elizabeth giggled, prompting a heavy sigh from William.

"Now, not all may remind you of animals, but you will be amazed at how many will. For simplicity, we did not require matches to be husband and wife, or even a man and a woman. A case in point is the Davenport twins, Lady Mary and Lady Martha. They talk so rapidly we were reminded of magpies; thus, we chose to include both on our ark. Another example is Lord Cummings. Given his moustache, he is the perfect walrus, whilst Lady Davenport's jowls made her the ideal match for him, not Lady Cummings."

Stifling another giggle, Elizabeth glanced to see if William was attending.

"We were children and we devised that game for amusement," William protested. "Only Richard persists in continuing it. What does that say about how much he has matured?"

"May I remind you that His Majesty found me sufficiently mature to command his troops and lead them into battle," Richard said with a smirk. "I will never be as fastidious as you when it comes to facing the *ton*."

Suddenly, the carriage began to slow as it entered the circular drive in front of Parkleigh Manor. Elizabeth pulled the curtain back and immediately a thousand butterflies began to flutter in her stomach. Along the drive and across the lawn, large torches were aflame, whilst men dressed in the finest livery stood at attention on both sides of the steps all the way to the portico. Moreover, every window in Parkleigh Manor was aglow with light, the result of numerous candles that filled hundreds of candelabra and several magnificent chandeliers. The effect was mesmerising.

In only a short while, they had ascended the steps to the house and were shown into the foyer. Elizabeth had never seen so many flowers in one place; thus, she made a complete circle to see them all. Whilst she was distracted, Lady Emma appeared and rushed towards William. Without addressing Elizabeth or Richard, she grabbed his hand.

"At last! Where have you been, Fitzwilliam? I expected you half an hour ago!" She began to tug him towards the grand staircase. "Father is not able to attend, but he wishes to speak to you before the ball begins."

Removing Lady Emma's hand, William held out his arm to Elizabeth. "Mrs. Darcy."

Gratitude flooded Elizabeth, and she hurried to take her place. Judging from the look on Lady Emma's face, William's decision to include her was not appreciated. Still, their hostess pasted a wide smile on her face when William turned around.

"Hurry! There is not much time."

Once they reached the landing, William slipped his arm around Elizabeth's waist in a bid to guide her down a hall in pursuit of Lady Emma. The feeling of being protected by her husband was almost overwhelming, and Elizabeth's heart raced. Suddenly, however, they were standing before an ornate door.

"I shall await you in the foyer," Lady Emma said. "The guests should begin to arrive soon, so please keep your conversation brief." With that, she opened the door and motioned them inside.

William led Elizabeth into the room, and she heard the door close. Few candles were lit in the space, though a fire burning in the hearth provided some light. Her eyes had just begun to adjust to the darkness when a voice boomed, "Come over here, Fitzwilliam. Did you bring your new bride? You must introduce us."

Catching sight of a man's head over the back of a chair near the hearth, she allowed William to usher her in that direction. Soon they were standing before the owner of Parkleigh Manor, who was dressed in a robe and covered by a blanket. Though obviously not in good health, he sported a broad smile on his face.

"Elizabeth, may I introduce Lord Waterston. He has graciously served as both my mentor and my confidant since I was a boy." To their host he said, "Lord Waterston, this is my wife, the former Elizabeth Bennet of Longbourn in Hertfordshire."

"The pleasure is mine, Lord Waterston," Elizabeth said, dropping a curtsey.

"No, no, my dear, it is mine," Waterston replied. To William he added, "Now I see why you married so hurriedly. Anyone with good sense would not let a beauty such as this young lady get away."

"You are too kind, sir," Elizabeth replied.

"I must tell you that I have known your husband since the

day he was born, and there is no finer man in all of Derbyshire—perhaps not in the entire country, my dear. When I heard that he had married, I was anxious to see the woman who had captured his heart. Now that we have met, I understand completely."

Heart full of emotion, Elizabeth said, "I agree with your assessment of my husband, and I wish *I* had known him all my life." She felt William stiffen.

"Fitzwilliam, I asked Emma to bring you here so that I might thank you once more for taking care of my estate. I am truly sorry that helping me has taken you away from this lovely woman far too often. It is my understanding that your steward is on his way to Weymouth."

"That is correct, my lord."

"Therefore, with your permission, when Mr. Stockham arrives, I shall put him in charge of overseeing the rest of the repairs on the bridge."

"I would welcome his participation."

"Good! Then it is settled. The music is beginning, so you had best hurry downstairs before my Emma comes to fetch you. She can be a tyrant when it comes to having things her way."

After saying their farewells, William escorted Elizabeth back to the foyer, though this time, rather than holding her hand or putting his arm around her waist, he offered her an arm. Though disheartened, she prayed that the rest of the evening would improve.

Richard was at the door to the ballroom, listening to the musicians tune their instruments when Lady Emma spied him. "There you are! Come with me. I need you to stand in the receiving line since Father is feeling poorly."

"Before I agree," he said, "are my parents expected to attend?"

"Lady Matlock declined my invitation. She said they had no plans to leave London." As they continued to the foyer, Lady Emma said, "I understand your parents do not approve of Fitzwilliam's wife."

"Darcy is a grown man, and as such, he does not depend upon my parents for direction or approval."

"A pity. Elizabeth will need the support of people such as your parents if she is to be accepted by our circle."

Rolling his eyes, Richard followed her to where Elizabeth and William were now standing. He placed himself at the end of the line on Elizabeth's left; William stood on her right, whilst Lady Emma positioned herself at the head of the line on William's other side. As she began to bend his cousin's ear, as was her wont, Richard noted that a large group of guests were arriving.

Leaning closer to Elizabeth, he whispered, "I do believe I see a giraffe who would work splendidly for your ark."

Elizabeth, who had been trying to overhear Lady Emma's conversation with her husband, looked towards the front entrance. One of the men in the party coming in their direction was several inches taller than William.

Restraining a smile, she whispered back, "One down; now we need only find his mate."

Chapter 21

Parkleigh Manor
The ball continues

After being inspected by what seemed like most of England, Elizabeth was relieved when the ball finally began and William escorted her to the dance floor. As they went through the steps, he said very little, and her attention drifted to those around them. As it did, something became clear. An inordinate number of women, dancing or not, were apparently spellbound by her husband, because their eyes followed his every move. The irony of the situation struck Elizabeth as funny, and she stifled a laugh.

William's interest was piqued. "May I ask what you find so amusing? Another secret?"

Reminded of his lecture, Elizabeth's temper flared. "Am I not allowed any private thoughts?"

The rest of the set was performed in silence, making her wonder what their audience thought about their lack of conversation. She was relieved when the music ended and William escorted her to Colonel Fitzwilliam, who had requested the next set.

Amongst the last to arrive for the ball, it did not take long for Lady Henrietta to create a stir, given her attire. Her dance card filled rapidly, though not with the young viscounts and lords she wished to attract, for they were busy vying for Elizabeth's attention. Since she was aware of the reason for their enthusiasm, her jealousy was somewhat curtailed.

After the fourth set ended, Lady Henrietta crossed the ballroom to stand next to her cousin. A deep furrow creased Lord Hartford's forehead, and she followed his eyes to where Elizabeth was dancing.

"Why so downhearted?"

"I asked Mrs. Darcy for a set, but her card was already full."

"I am not surprised...given the circumstances."

Hartford turned to study her. "What do you know that I do not?"

"Suffice it to say, Mrs. Darcy will soon learn that those competing for her attention are not longing for friendship."

Having gone to fetch a glass of punch, Richard returned to the ballroom, intending to watch over his cousin's wife. Glancing about the room, he spotted her near the open French doors and instantly recognised her dance partner, Lord Osborne. All that he knew of that gentleman was that Darcy thought him a braggart because of his habit of boasting at White's when he was in his cups. Another sweep of the floor revealed that his cousin was standing up with the Countess of Armistead, one of Lady Emma's friends.

What happened to dancing with only Lady Emma and your wife, Darcy?

After taking a sip of the punch, a group of young men nearby laughed a little too loudly, drawing Richard's attention. Though half-hidden by a cluster of palms in an alcove, the ones he could see were staring in Elizabeth's direction. Intrigued, he slipped closer to them in hopes of hearing what they were saying.

"Who has her next set?" one asked.

"I have," came the reply.

"Do you intend to allude to a tryst or ask for one outright?" said another.

"Why wait? If her marriage lacks passion, she should have no reason to object."

Suddenly, their conversation grew urgent.

"My word! She left Osborne and rushed from the room!"

"Did she look upset? Or do you suppose she meant to spur him into following her?"

"She looked as though she was upset, but if I know Osborne, that will not matter." There was a pause. *"There! Just as I predicted; he followed her!"*

Vexed that he had missed seeing what happened, Richard knew he had to find William. Fortuitously, the set was coming to an end, so he turned to a woman standing nearby—Lady Cornwall, a recent widow—and offered her the glass of punch.

"For you, madam," he said, employing his most charming smile. "I thought you might enjoy some refreshment."

If her smile was any indication, she was pleased with the attention. She took the cup, but before she could reply, Richard disappeared into the crowd. Locating William, he grabbed his arm. "Come with me!"

Pulling his cousin through the French doors and onto the terrace, he declared, "Elizabeth is somewhere in the gardens, and I have reason to believe that Lord Osborne is pursuing her."

"You search the left side!" William ordered as he ran down the gravel path to the right.

Somewhere along the way, raised voices caught Richard's attention and he followed them. They led him to a gazebo where Elizabeth was standing with her back pressed against the rear wall of the structure, whilst Osborne blocked the only exit. It was clear the blackguard had been drinking, for he had no idea Richard was nearby, and when he spoke he slurred his words.

"Be reasonable, Mrs. Darcy. Your husband despises you because you forced him into this marriage, but you do not have to live without affection. More than likely he has a mistress—perhaps two—so why not take a lover? I have an apartment in Town and we could meet there whenever—"

Though she was clearly frightened, Elizabeth declared vehemently, "Everything you have said is a lie. I am a happily married woman, and I have no intention of meeting you or anyone else."

"Perhaps I can change your mind," Osborne said, taking an unsteady step towards her.

Richard flew into the gazebo, grabbed Lord Osborne by one shoulder, and spun him around. A solid blow to the chin knocked him on his arse, but Richard pulled the blackguard back to his feet and tightened the cravat around Osbourne's neck as though it were a noose. "How dare you speak to my cousin in such a vulgar manner? Darcy will be here at any second, and he will kill you unless I stop him. Convince me why I should!"

Osborne began to tremble. "I was told that she...that he—" Struggling to breathe, he fought to continue. "I was assured Mrs. Darcy would welcome my attentions since Darcy despises her for compromising him. Furthermore, I was told he would look the other way since they had struck a bargain."

"Osborne, I always suspected you were a dullard, but this proves it. Tell me, who dared to foster such lies."

"I swore I would not—" Richard tightened the cravat. "Please! I cannot breathe!" Instantly, the cravat loosened. "It was Lady Emma," he croaked.

"Why, that conniving—" Letting go of the cravat, Richard grasped the lapels of Osborne's coat, raising him on tiptoes, "And you thought it clever to insult Fitzwilliam Darcy's wife on the word of a jealous woman?"

Suddenly, William appeared out of the darkness, breathless from having run so far. One glance at Elizabeth's wide, frightened eyes, and he snatched Osborne from Richard's grasp and felled him with one blow. Pulling him back to his feet, William struck him again. This time, he grabbed Osborne's cravat to keep him from going all the way to the floor, and as he drew his fist back a third time, Richard stayed his hand.

"Wait, Cousin! I fear he may prove more valuable if he is conscious."

William let the villain hit the floor. Standing over the addled man, his angry eyes flicked to Elizabeth. "Why are you out here?"

"I will explain that later," Richard interjected. "Suffice it to say that Lord Osborne is here because he believed the rumours being circulated tonight about your marriage—lies meant to bring about an embarrassing set down for Mrs. Darcy."

"What lies?"

"That you are both unhappy in your marriage and open to liaisons," Richard replied.

"Who would dare spread such nonsense?"

"We had better discuss that later. For now, it is imperative that we not react how the perpetrator expects. In view of all the members of the *ton* in attendance, to cause a scene would not be wise. I believe we should return to the ball as though nothing has happened."

Having regained his senses, Lord Osborne mumbled, "He is right, Darcy."

"If you have any sense, you will keep your mouth shut," William hissed.

Osborne struggled to stand, groaning as he did. "As much as I do not wish to anger you further, please allow me to speak."

"Choose your words carefully," William warned.

Osborne swallowed hard. "My conduct has been inexcusable. I would like to blame the liquor, but I cannot. The fault lies with me. Pray allow me to apologise and to make amends."

Aware that bringing attention to the episode would result in more harm done to Elizabeth's reputation, William said, "Just how do you propose to *make amends*?"

"I was played a fool by someone I trusted. Granted, I should never have taken the bait and believed the lies, but I did." Pulling a handkerchief from his pocket, Osborne dabbed at his bleeding lips. "I cannot return to the ball in this state, but if you will allow it, I shall quietly withdraw. Furthermore, I pledge to spread the word amongst all of my associates that Mrs. Darcy is a respectable lady, and that you and she have an enviable marriage."

Despite the urge to retaliate, William conceded. "Apologise to my wife. It is she you have slandered. Furthermore, should I ever hear that you have tarnished her good name or our marriage, I will hunt you down and call you out. Is that understood?"

Lord Osborne breathed a sigh of relief. "It is, and I appreciate your forbearance, Darcy." Turning to Elizabeth, he said, "Mrs. Darcy, you did nothing to deserve my abuse. I shall forever recall my conduct tonight with shame and remorse. Please accept my apology."

Still too upset to speak, Elizabeth merely nodded.

"Leave us!" William barked.

As Osborne hurried away, William crossed to where his trembling wife stood. Every fibre in his body ached to embrace her, to offer what comfort he could, but he steeled himself to resist. Offering her his arm, he was surprised when she ignored the gesture and fell into him, crying. Patting her back lightly, in due course he pushed her to arm's length.

Making certain to keep his voice devoid of any emotion, he said, "Try to compose yourself." Pulling a handkerchief from his pocket, he held it out. "If our ruse is to succeed, we must return to the ballroom straightaway. I think the others on your dance card will not object if I claim the next set and Richard takes the one following. Afterward, you will plead a headache, which will give us a reason to leave."

Drying her tears with the handkerchief, Elizabeth sniffled and then straightened her spine. "I am ready."

William addressed Richard. "I think it best if Elizabeth and I go back inside first."

"I agree," Richard replied. "I shall wait here a while longer."

The trip home began quieter than the ride over—at least until the carriage was clear of the drive to Parkleigh Manor. Once that magnificent estate was no longer in view, William said, "I think it time for that discussion, Richard. What did you learn?"

Richard glanced to Elizabeth, whose head was bowed, briefly wondering what she would think of what he had to say. Still, having no choice, he began. "I had walked out of the ballroom to fetch a glass of punch. When I returned, a group of young men were loitering in an alcove nearby, and I heard them laugh loudly. I moved nearer to hear what they were saying."

"And?"

Richard revealed all that he had heard. "And when they said that Elizabeth had fled the room with Osborne close behind her, I immediately went to find you."

William considered Richard's report. "And the man who fabricated the lies?"

"It was not a man." A puzzled expression crossed William's face. "Brace yourself, Darcy. It was Lady Emma."

Elizabeth gasped. "I hardly know her. Why would she—"

"Emma has had her heart set on Darcy since they were children," Richard explained. "She is jealous of you."

It was a long while before William spoke. Despite learning that Lady Emma was behind the lies, he said nothing about her. Instead, he questioned Elizabeth's motives. "Why did you flee into the gardens? Why not come to me?"

"Some of the men I danced with made remarks that I found baffling, but Lord Osborne's innuendoes were intolerable. I feared if I quit the dance and wandered about the room looking for you, it might create more of a scene than disappearing onto the terrace, so I chose to do that. My hope was that anyone who noticed would assume that I just needed a breath of fresh air."

"Did it not occur to you that being at his mercy in the garden would be worse than creating a scene in a room full of people?" William continued.

"I acted impulsively. I never thought he would follow." When William did not reply, she added, "I swear I did nothing to encourage him."

"From what little Darcy and I know of Osborne," Richard said, "he needs no encouragement to act like a fool."

By his silence, it was obvious that William was not placated, and the rest of the trip home was spent in silence. Once they reached Pemberley and began exiting the vehicle, he said to Richard, "If you will wait in the library, I will join you after I escort Elizabeth to her room."

"Fitzwilliam, please tell me why you are so angry," Elizabeth said once they reached the sitting room.

He kept walking until he stood at her bedroom door. Turning the knob, he opened it. "I am not angry. I am disappointed."

"Did *I* disappoint you?"

"Elizabeth, Richard has to leave early tomorrow. If he and I are to talk, we must do it now. You and I shall discuss this in the morning."

Frustrated, Elizabeth walked into her bedroom. Hearing the door close behind her, she went straight to her dressing room, where she paused to examine herself in the mirror. No longer able to hold back her tears, she let them slide down her face. Within a short time, she heard her bedroom door open and close again. Realising that it must be Florence, she quickly dried her eyes.

"I apologise for not being here when you arrived, madam," Florence said, as she approached her.

As the maid began unbuttoning her gown, Elizabeth replied, "You had no way of knowing we would return early. I developed a headache, so Mr. Darcy insisted upon it."

"May I get you something? A draught? Some tea, perhaps?"

"No, thank you. Now that I am home, I feel much better." The maid looked as though she wished to say more, so Elizabeth asked, "Is there something else?"

"I could not help but notice that you were crying when I came in. Have I done anything to make you unhappy?"

"Not at all. In truth, I was upset with my husband." Seeing worry cross Florence's face, she tried to reassure her. "There is no need for concern. I wanted to discuss something now, and he insisted on waiting until tomorrow."

"I passed Mr. Darcy in the hallway," Florence offered. "He looked very serious, but then he always does."

"Since coming to Derbyshire, I have had opportunity to talk to those who know him best. From them I learned that Fitzwilliam is tender-hearted and feels very deeply, but when he is uncertain or feels misjudged, he hides behind that mask of solemnity." She tried to laugh. "Moreover, he can be very stubborn, especially when he believes he is right—like tonight, for instance."

"The servants here say that he is kind and fair."

"I once thought him insensitive. I have misjudged him so many times," Elizabeth said. After silently gathering her thoughts, she continued. "Do you recall when I donned your clothes to visit Mr. Lucas, and you tried to dissuade me?"

"I do."

"Would that I had listened. Do you know that when I left London with my neighbour, I was so pitiless that I sent Fitzwilliam a note to be delivered only after we were on our way?"

Florence nodded. "It was the talk of the downstairs servants."

Elizabeth relived everything in her thoughts. "Little did I know how my cruelty would come back to haunt me. Only days after my return to Meryton, I learned that Mr. Darcy had all the honesty, whilst the man in whom I had placed my trust merely had the appearance of it."

"What do you mean?"

"It was John Lucas who lied to me, not Mr. Darcy. Once the truth was revealed, I longed for a chance to make amends—a chance to prove I could be the wife he deserves. To his credit, Fitzwilliam let me come home."

"I had no idea."

"Still, I have a cross to bear. You see, he struggles to forgive me. It is my hope to earn his trust again and, if I am fortunate, his heart," Elizabeth offered a wan smile. "Now, help me out of this gown."

After Florence left, Elizabeth slipped between the soft sheets on the huge four-poster bed, said her prayers, and closed her eyes. Nonetheless, sleep was not to be had. After tossing fitfully for more than an hour, she slid off the bed and crossed to the French doors. In the distance, flashes of lightning lit the dark countryside followed by rumbles of thunder. Opening the doors, she walked to the stone wall that ran the length of the balcony and leaned against it to watch the display of nature's fury.

Suddenly the wind picked up, drawing bits of leaves across the stone floor in a spiral pattern. Wrapping her arms around herself, Elizabeth ran her hands up and down them against a sudden chill.

A fitting tribute to the storm that is raging in my heart.

The library

"Confound it, Darcy! Why do you persist in questioning Elizabeth's motives whilst ignoring Lady Emma's perfidy?"

William slammed his glass down on a table, and what little brandy was left inside splashed over the polished mahogany. "I am not ignoring what Emma did! I will address her conduct, and I will speak with Lord Waterston when his health allows. In any case, Emma is not my wife; Elizabeth is!"

Standing, he walked to the liquor cabinet, removed the top from a decanter and poured another glass of the amber liquid. Quickly tossing it down his throat, he grimaced as it burned.

"Have you not had enough to drink?"

"I have only begun to drink!" William retorted. "And if you must know, I question Elizabeth's motives because it was she who made me look like a fool by running away with John Lucas. Not to mention that only days ago I saw her and Lord Hartford on the pier early one morning."

"Had you bothered to ask Mr. Adams, you would know that your wife has been rebuffing that arse's advances since the day she came to Pemberley. More than one maid or footman can testify to that. On that particular day, Hartford followed her to the pier, and Elizabeth put him in his place for suggesting they walk out together every morning."

"From where I stood, they were holding hands."

"Were they? The footman who follows her told Adams that Hartford grabbed Elizabeth's hand to keep her from leaving. He was about to intervene when Hartford released her."

"And if that is true, what does it prove? Only that she does not care for Hartford because she is still enamoured of John Lucas."

"Listen to yourself, Darcy. If Elizabeth was not tempted by

Lord Hartford, whom the ladies find a handsome rogue, because she cares for Lucas, why would she agree to meet an ugly rake like Osborne in the garden?"

"To be truthful, I have no idea why Elizabeth acts as she does, but what else explains her bolting into the darkness, where she could easily be accosted, instead of finding me? It makes no sense."

"She is young and simply acted on impulse."

"Using her youth as an excuse is growing tiresome."

"Let me pose another question. You once told me that Lucas said Elizabeth thought of him only as a brother. Why do you persist in saying she is in love with him?"

"She was sixteen when she told Lucas that. Evidently, her opinion of him changed in the next two years since she travelled to Cambridge to marry him."

"It is obvious to me that you and Elizabeth must learn to talk to one another if your marriage is to survive."

Sullenly, William sank into the chair he had previously occupied. "We do not talk; we argue."

"Have you asked yourself why?"

"Please give me room to breathe, Richard," William said, beginning to massage his forehead with his fingertips. "I have found it difficult straddling the line between caring about Elizabeth's welfare but not caring to the extent that my heart becomes engaged again."

Richard walked over to give his cousin's shoulder a sympathetic squeeze. "Perhaps you should start by admitting that your heart was never *disengaged*."

William dropped his head. "Each morning, when I open my eyes, I pray that this will be the last day that she owns my heart."

"This is my fault for suggesting that your marriage could continue as one of convenience. Looking back, you would have been better off in such an arrangement with someone you cared nothing about."

"Retrospection makes fools of us all," William murmured.

Chapter 22

Pemberley

Not long after Richard retired, William decided to follow suit; however, by the time he reached the grand staircase he was feeling quite unsteady. Realising he was not as sober as he had thought, he contemplated how awful he would feel in the morning if he went to bed inebriated. The only effective remedy was a cold bath, and he wondered if the water employed before the ball was still in the tub. Though the thought of using it a second time was unpleasant, he hoped it was still there. Inside his dressing room, he was dismayed to discover the tub was empty.

As he entered his bedroom, a package wrapped in brown paper lying atop the chest of drawers caught his eye. He picked up the package, read the return address, and instantly knew what it contained. Ripping open the end, he pulled out a blue velvet box, and reverently ran a finger over the name embossed in gold thereon: *Elizabeth Darcy.*

Lifting the lid, he studied the silver-plated brush and comb he had ordered the day after their wedding. He had instructed the silversmith to send it to Pemberley once it was finished, and apparently it had arrived that day. Picking up the brush, he turned it over to inspect the initials intertwined on back: E and D. Placing the brush back in the box, he snapped the lid shut and stared at the painful reminder of what might have been, before abruptly tossing it across the room. It hit a wall and fell to the floor at the same time a deafening clap of thunder shook the house.

Drawn by the sound to the French doors, William pulled back the curtains and instantly recognised the solution to his problem. He began removing his clothes and once down to his breeches, walked out into the rain. Standing at the wall that surrounded the balcony, he closed his eyes and willed the water to do its job. Little did he realise how the steady beat of the rain on his head and shoulders would conspire with the liquor to lower his celebrated self-discipline. In this vulnerable state, the weight he had borne since his father's death suddenly became too much to bear. Powerless to stop them, William's tears joined the droplets of rain rolling down his face.

Once the rain began to fall, Elizabeth had hurried inside. She stayed at the open French doors, however, because she found it exhilarating to be so near the storm, yet protected from it. Caught up in observing nature's fury, she might never have noticed William on the other end of balcony had not a small branch been swept by the wind to that side. The tall figure of her nearly naked husband stood out in the downpour, and the captivating sight of his wide shoulders, firm abdomen, lean hips and sinewy arms triggered a childhood memory.

She had been but a girl of twelve when she accompanied her uncle to deliver an order to 13 Bond Street in London, where Henry Angelo and John "*Gentleman*" Jackson shared a building, instructing men in the art of fencing and boxing, respectively. Despite a warning to stay seated in the wagon, the sights in the windows—sights meant to entice the populace inside—bade her enter. Slipping in with several patrons, she went unnoticed amongst the crowd eagerly cheering on a fencing match between two men who possessed similarly awe-inspiring bodies. Spellbound, she had watched for half an hour before being discovered by her uncle.

Whilst this memory raced through her head, William glanced to the right, affording her a clear view of the torment on his face. Deeply moved, she ran to him, stopping just short of contact. William suddenly turned around. His hair easily fell below his collar now, and the wind was whipping it in every direction. This, and his lack of clothing, reminded Elizabeth of a portrait she had once seen of a Viking standing on the bow of a longboat during a storm.

Shivering with the recollection, she stammered, "Fitzwilliam, what possessed you to stand out in—"

She was suddenly pulled into an embrace so fervent that she feared for her next breath. Once William's mouth captured hers, she was spellbound. His lips were firm and demanding, and when his tongue coaxed her mouth open and plunged inside hungrily, she lost all ability to think. Instinctively, as she began returning his kisses, her hands slid up the hard planes of his abdomen and chest to his shoulders, which she gripped in a bid not to faint.

A groan escaped William's throat, hanging in the air like an oath, and suddenly Elizabeth found herself being lifted and carried into her bedroom where a single candle still glowed. Setting her on her feet, his eyes fell to the front of her wet gown, now clinging to her breasts like a second skin. Impatiently, he untied the ribbons holding it closed and pushed the garment to the floor. Stepping back, his eyes drifted slowly down her naked body and back. Then, he gently picked her up and laid her on the bed.

When he started removing his breeches, Elizabeth looked away. Feeling the bed sink under his weight, she closed her eyes, and her breath became shallow as he slid next to her. He began placing kisses along her neck and shoulders and an ache such as she had never felt before began somewhere deep inside; however, it was when his hands began to explore previously forbidden places that the ache became a fire. As he captured first one soft mound and then the other in his mouth, suckling each before grazing its tip with his teeth, an unexpected moan escaped her throat.

Encouraged by her response, William captured her mouth again, and with this kiss, Elizabeth felt herself floating between heaven and earth. Carried to a place where consciousness no longer existed, each succeeding kiss plunged her further under his spell, and when he rolled atop her, she welcomed the weight of him. William's hands grasping her hips, and the sharp pain that followed, brought her back to the present, and with words drenched in passion, he began to guide her in how to respond. No relief was to be found for the longing he had created within her, however, for suddenly he groaned her name and collapsed in her arms, his head coming to rest in the crook of her neck. His heart continued to pound so fiercely that she felt every beat in her body, and whilst she waited for his breathing to return to normal, she noticed that a faint smell of the sandalwood cologne he preferred still lingered on his chest.

At some point, Elizabeth recalled what her Aunt Madeline had said: *If you are truly blessed, your husband will whisper words of adoration afterward.* Too sensible to believe William would shower her with words of that kind, she still longed to hear him say that he had forgiven her. She began to run her fingers lightly over his shoulders when he abruptly rolled onto his back and lay deathly still. Then, he murmured awkwardly, "Forgive me if I hurt you."

Immediately he slid out of the bed and walked towards the door. Stunned by how rapidly the passion of minutes before had been supplanted by detachment, Elizabeth almost burst into tears when the door closed behind him. Only a single niggling thought kept that from happening: *Fitzwilliam could have consummated our union without any signs of affection, but instead, he was passionate and tender.*

With renewed hope that they might still have a loving relationship, Elizabeth suddenly became aware that she was lying on a damp bed with wet hair. Sliding off the bed, she hurried into her dressing room where she dried her hair with a small towel before pouring water into a basin and washing. After drying herself, she returned to her bedroom and opened the wardrobe to retrieve a clean nightgown. Pulling it over her head, she went to close the French doors and then turned to survey the room. *I shall never be able to fall sleep in my bed tonight.*

Taking a pillow from the bed, she crossed to the settee, picked up the blanket that was always placed across its back, and lay down. Once comfortable, she reflected on the fact that, though this might not be the wedding night she had dreamt of, her prayers had been answered.

At least I am now truly his wife. And should Fitzwilliam's heart never soften towards me, I have the hope of children to fill my days with purpose and joy.

After saying her prayers, Elizabeth fell into an exhausted sleep.

William's bedroom

As William entered his bedroom, the enormity of what he had done washed over him. The events of the ball paled in comparison to the problems he had created by consummating their marriage tonight, instead of waiting until he had separated his heart from his duty. Ashamed to recall just how far afield his conduct had exceeded the perfunctory act he had envisioned their first joining would be, his conscience taunted him.

What were you thinking, letting passion overrule common sense? If you cannot isolate your feelings, how are you to survive in this marriage?

With self-disgust, William recalled a rule he created whilst explaining to Elizabeth how their marriage would work. It was solely designed to exemplify his indifference, and he cringed to recall how brazenly he had claimed no interest in her bed except to sire children, and that once she became pregnant, she would be free of his company until he decided it was time for another child.

How poetic that I will be penalised by the rules I created to punish her. Only a fool is hoisted with his own petard!

Self-loathing sent him to the chest and the decanter of brandy. Picking it up, he tried to fill a glass, but his hands shook so violently that brandy splashed over the tray. Pausing to decide whether self-respect or pity would triumph, at length he set the decanter down. Tossing the glass at the hearth, he watched as it splintered against the stone.

Pemberley
The next morning

Immediately upon entering his employer's bedroom, Adams was confronted by two things: the smell of alcohol and the sight of William still lying in bed. He could not remember the last time the master had slept so late, and the fact alarmed him. Walking to the bed, he watched for a moment to ascertain that William was breathing. When satisfied that he was, he looked about the room. A glance at the hearth revealed shards of glass. Then his eyes fell on the chest where a tray held a decanter of brandy and several glasses. The decanter, which was full yesterday, looked half empty. Noting that the stopper had not been replaced, he crossed the room and discovered the tray was filled with brandy. *That explains the smell!*

Grabbing a serviette from beside the tray, he mopped up the liquid, replaced the stopper and then took the cloth into the dressing room where he laid it out to dry. Going back into the bedroom, his eyes were drawn to a pair of boots and some clothes on the floor near the French doors. Normally William put his clothes on a chair when he undressed himself, but as Adams picked up the suit his master had worn to the ball, he discovered the breeches were missing.

After another glance around the room, he decided to check both sides of the bed more closely. One side rendered nothing at all, but on the other he spied a box lying on the floor below a fresh mark on the wall. Picking it up and reading the name engraved thereon, he instantly recognised that this may have triggered his master's present state.

Placing the box on the chest, he went to the sitting room door. Though likely pointless, he felt obligated to look in there as well. The moment he opened the door, however, he found Florence facing him. She was holding something rolled into a ball and from the look on her face—a look that declared she would not discuss the matter—Adams knew exactly what it was. Taking the item, he closed the door without saying a word and held the still damp breeches up to examine them.

How in the world did—

Not wishing to dwell on the image that popped into his head, Adams quickly dismissed the thought and began to concentrate on salvaging the breeches. He tugged on the legs, hoping to smooth out the wrinkles before they dried completely, but had no luck. Heading back to the dressing room, he laid them over a rack on the back of the door. Whilst thus occupied, a loud groan announced that William was waking.

Taking a deep breath to quell his exasperation, Adams assumed a neutral expression and went to greet his employer. He found William sitting on the side of his bed, holding his head in his hands. "Good morning, sir."

"Pour me a glass of brandy," William snapped.

"Given your present state and the condition of your room this morning, you drank too much last night, sir. I shall not be a party to helping you become intoxicated again today."

"Do not test me, Adams. You can be replaced."

"Sometimes I believe that would be a blessing. Nonetheless, we both know you will not replace me today because I am right. Your coffee should be up soon, and by the look of you, I intend to have food sent up as well."

"You know I cannot abide eating this early," William exclaimed. "The thought of food turns my stomach."

"Toast and jam cannot hurt," Adams replied. Then he cocked his head. "Do you wish to tell me what brought on your present state?"

After some silence, William confessed, "I drank too much, but it was not with the intent of getting inebriated."

"I take it the ball did not go well."

"I do not wish to discuss it."

"Well, should you ever want to discuss it, I am ready to listen."

A knock on the door announced that the coffee had arrived, and Adams went to open it. As he took the tray from the maid, he directed her to bring a light meal. Closing the door, he set the tray on the chest of drawers.

"Do you wish to have a cup now, or would you rather wait until after you are dressed?"

"Find my robe. I should like to have the coffee now. Perhaps it will help to clear my head."

"Only God can help what ails you," Adams muttered under his breath.

"What did you say?"

"I said the coffee should help."

Lady Henrietta's sitting room

As she sat with her cousin at the small table in her sitting room partaking of the tea and scones brought up earlier, Lady Henrietta's temper got the better of her after Lord Hartford mentioned the ball.

"I mean to know what happened after Lord Osborne followed Elizabeth out of the ballroom!" she snapped. "It must have been something horrid to make Osborne disappear like a scalded dog and Fitzwilliam leave so early, yet Lady Emma claims to have no knowledge of it."

"I spoke with several acquaintances after Darcy and his wife returned to the ballroom, and not a one brought up the subject," Lord Hartford said, taking another bite of a scone. "In my opinion, no one noticed."

"That is ridiculous! If I saw what happened, others must have."

"Yes, but you were watching Mrs. Darcy like a hawk; they were not. If you want my opinion, I think Darcy left early because he had all he could take of being on display. You know what an unsociable creature he is."

Suddenly, a panel in the wall slid open, and Lady Henrietta's maid stepped into the room. "Forgive me," Sarah said, turning the second she spied Lord Hartford. "I will return later."

Lord Hartford stood. "There is no need. I was just leaving."

"No!" Lady Henrietta exclaimed. "Anything you have to say, you may say in front of my cousin. He and I have no secrets."

Glancing distrustfully at Hartford, Sarah began. "I thought you might want to know that the Darcys consummated their marriage last night."

Lord Hartford's mouth fell open. "How in the world would you know that?"

"Sarah has her ways," Lady Henrietta interjected before turning back to the maid. "Did you witness it for yourself, or are you repeating the gossip downstairs?"

"I saw everything."

"Good Lord!" Lord Hartford exclaimed. "If Darcy ever so much as suspects you are spying on him, you will pay dearly."

"Sarah knows how to eavesdrop without being caught."

"Invading the privacy of their bedroom goes far beyond eavesdropping, my dear."

Dismissing her cousin's reaction, Henrietta continued to question Sarah. "Did he stay the entire night?"

"No. He left right after they—" She shrugged.

"Good! That is a sign he is not yet over his anger with her," Lady Henrietta murmured to herself. To Sarah, she said, "You may go now."

As Lord Hartford watched Sarah disappear back into the servants' corridor, Lady Henrietta declared, "Perhaps now that Fitzwilliam has satisfied his desire for her, he will visit her bed only until she is pregnant with his heir."

"You cannot be serious. Darcy is a man and the availability of a woman as beautiful as Elizabeth—" Hartford chuckled. "Trust me. He will want more."

Throwing down her serviette, Lady Henrietta stood. "Why must men act like animals in heat?"

"As I recall, when it suits your purpose, you like men in heat."

"Sometimes I wonder why I tolerate you, David."

"Because I am your closest relation and the only person you can trust with any certainty."

Lady Henrietta sighed. "Unfortunately, you are correct."

Dressed in his riding clothes, William downed a last cup of coffee whilst standing at one of the tall windows in his bedroom. Despite the pounding in his head that was sure to be compounded by riding, he resolved that he would rather confront Lady Emma than face Elizabeth. Having made that decision, he departed by taking the rear stairs out to the stables.

Chapter 23

Elizabeth's bedroom
That same day

Florence thought it odd that her mistress' bedroom was dark. Normally, Elizabeth had the curtains open and was in her dressing room by the time she arrived. Puzzled, she walked over to pull back the curtains, and turned to discover Elizabeth asleep on the settee. Instinctively, her eyes flicked to the bed. The counterpane had been thrown back, and curiosity piqued, she walked in that direction. Tripping over something on the floor, she stooped to pick it up. It was a pair of men's breeches—soaking wet men's breeches. Whilst struggling to make sense of it, another item on the floor caught her eye. It was one of Mrs. Darcy's nightgowns, and it proved to be equally wet. A quick touch of the damp sheets and a small blood stain substantiated her suspicions.

As her face crimsoned, Florence tried to compose herself. Praying her expression would not betray her mortification, she hurried to the dressing room and hung the nightgown up to dry. Rushing back to the bedroom, she rolled the breeches into a ball and headed into the sitting room. She was about to knock on the door to Mr. Darcy's bedroom when it suddenly opened. Relieved to see Mr. Adams, she thrust the breeches into his hands. Thankfully, he took them and closed the door without saying a word.

Once back in Elizabeth's bedroom, Florence began removing the sheets instead of waiting for the maid who normally performed that task. Rumours about the state of the Darcys' marriage already abounded below stairs, and she feared that if the maid noticed the blood, that bit of information would be on many servants' lips by day's end. Not willing for that to happen, Florence was certain that Mrs. Reynolds would take charge of the sheets if she solicited her help.

"What are you doing?"

The question came just as Florence had gathered up the sheets. Steeling herself, she turned with a smile. "I noticed that your sheets were damp, madam, so I thought I would take them downstairs without waiting for the maid." Seeing Elizabeth's blush, she continued, "The maid might not notice they are damp and toss them in with the rest of the sheets to be washed; they could mildew before washday."

Immediately, Elizabeth understood that Florence knew. Unable to meet the maid's eyes, she replied, "I was on the balcony when a downpour began." Offering no excuse for how the bed got wet, she added, "Thank you for taking care of the bedding."

Suddenly, Florence reached into her pocket. Retrieving a letter, she held it out. "This was delivered early this morning, ma'am."

Elizabeth sat up to take the letter. Seeing the return address, she smiled. "It is from Jane."

Though her favourite sibling had kept up a steady stream of correspondence since Elizabeth had reached Pemberley, her own responses had been cursory. She had found it difficult to lie about the state of her marriage and had feared telling Jane the truth, lest she share it with their father. After what happened last night, however, she felt that a better relationship with Fitzwilliam was possible and was confident that Jane would be more satisfied with her next reply.

Wrapping the blanket about her shoulders, Elizabeth stood. "The weather is so beautiful this morning. I think I shall read this on the balcony."

"Whilst you are occupied, I shall take the sheets downstairs."

After Florence exited the room, Elizabeth walked out and opened the letter.

Dearest Lizzy,

I cannot pretend I have not been worried because you write so seldom and say so little; still, I recognise you have many duties now that you are the mistress of such a grand estate.

First, let me say that, other than Papa, we are all in good health and, Papa is doing so well that the physician's assistant has returned to London. He plans to visit every fortnight until he is certain Papa has completely healed. By the way, our uncle confessed that Mr. Darcy has been paying the physicians, which makes me think even more highly of that gentleman. Oh, Lizzy, I pray that by now you have discovered the tender side of your complex husband and are pleased with your marriage.

Now, I simply must share a secret, or I shall burst. Charles' father has decided that since he has been so diligent in his studies at Cambridge, he will receive a third of his inheritance in January, instead of waiting until he graduates to acquire it all. This means he and I may marry sooner than we ever imagined. We have been discussing a February wedding, though I live in fear that Mama will learn of it and parade us all over the neighbourhood whenever he is here from now until the ceremony.

In addition, Charles will soon call at Pemberley to ask Mr. Darcy to stand up with him and to repay the five hundred pounds he loaned Charles when we became engaged. I had no knowledge of the loan until now, and I dare say you did not know, either, else your opinion of Mr. Darcy would have changed much sooner. Pray do not say a word to your husband. Charles wishes to surprise him.

There is nothing else of import to say, so I will just add that I miss you terribly. Please answer soon, if only to say that you will stand up with me.

Your loving sister,
Jane

Fitzwilliam loaned Mr. Bingley money to court Jane? Is there no end to the secrets he keeps?

Suddenly, Elizabeth looked up to see the tall figure of her husband striding towards the stables. Her heart sank when she realised that the talk he had promised for this morning would be delayed.

Unable to turn away, she watched as he mounted effortlessly and turned Zeus down the lane that led to the main road. By the time he was completely out of sight, a familiar ache had begun.

Will I always be the least of your concerns, Fitzwilliam?

The breakfast room

When Elizabeth entered the breakfast room, Georgiana put down her fork and ran to greet her.

"Oh, Elizabeth! Will you ride with me and Rietta today? I promise to have the stable master pick out a gentle horse."

Thinking of how uncomfortable it would be to ride today of all days, Elizabeth quickly rebuffed the idea. "I promised Mrs. Jenkins—one of our tenants—that I would bring some clothes and blankets for her new baby. I would be pleased, however, if you and Lady Henrietta would accompany me."

"I travel to Waltham Park just after noon to share a harp lesson with Lady Esme who has returned to Derbyshire, but I have plenty of time this morning," Georgiana said. Glancing to her stepmother, she said, "Will you come with us, Rietta?"

"I had rather not. You go with Elizabeth. I will ask David to ride with me."

"Are you certain?" Georgiana asked.

"I am," Lady Henrietta said, offering her a quick smile. "Visiting tenants is not my strong suit."

"Let me finish my scone then, and we shall be on our way," Elizabeth said.

One result of William's protective nature was that the maid who once accompanied Elizabeth to visit the tenants had been replaced by a footman. Since the gig held only two people, today he would be forced to ride alongside on horseback and relinquish the reins to Elizabeth.

When they began down the lane, a giggle escaped Georgiana. "I cannot believe that Brother lets you drive. I do not know how to drive a gig; he would never teach me."

"Normally, Rogers drives, but today I must. I pray he says nothing to Fitzwilliam, or I shall never hear the end of it."

Georgiana's expression grew concerned. "I do not recall Brother treating you unkindly."

Instantly, Elizabeth regretted her choice of words. "I was being flippant. Your brother is merely overly cautious about my safety."

Georgiana's smile returned. "That is his nature. He takes his duty to protect those he loves seriously."

When they got to the end of the lane, instead of turning left to the road, Elizabeth turned the gig to the right, went through a gate and headed across a great expanse of open land.

"Why are we going this way?" Georgiana asked.

"Since the bridge burned, Fitzwilliam does not want me in that area. For several days now, I have been visiting tenants by this route. 'Tis a small compromise to keep your brother happy."

Just after they passed a birch copse, a small stone cottage came into view on a distant hillside. It appeared so well kept that Elizabeth had believed it to be occupied, though she later learned it was vacant.

"Georgiana, that cottage catches my attention each time I pass it. It seems completely out of place where it is."

"That was my mother's cottage," Georgiana answered wistfully. "I remember that she would disappear at times and Brother would assure me that she was only at her cottage. She never stayed away from us for long."

"Might we go inside?"

"Oh, no! Since Brother claimed it for his personal use, no one is allowed in. It has become his sanctuary now—a place to find respite when he feels beleaguered. That is how he described it to me."

Instantly, the agony Elizabeth had seen in Fitzwilliam's face last night came to mind. Before then, it had never occurred to her that a man of his wealth and position might be overwhelmed by anything. Hesitantly, she began to question her new sister.

"Does your brother escape there often?"

As she recalled the past, Georgiana became solemn. "After Father married Rietta, when he was home from Cambridge on holiday, he spent more time at the cottage than at Pemberley. And when he returned from London alone after you and he had married, he spent a good deal of time there."

"I...I confess I never thought of your brother needing respite. He seems strong-willed and sure of himself."

"He can be firm when he knows he is right; yet, he is so sensitive that his heart is easily wounded. Few can meet the measure of my brother when it comes to compassion. Someday you will learn how blessed you are that he chose to marry you."

At that point they crossed over a grassy knoll and the Jenkins farm was before them. Thomas Jenkins and his wife, Fanny, were the parents of four children—three boys and an infant girl. As soon as the Jenkins' door opened, and the family walked onto the porch, Georgiana's shy nature resurfaced. Nevertheless, she followed Elizabeth's example and climbed down from the gig to follow the family into their home.

As Elizabeth was introducing her sister, the footman was busy setting baskets of baked goods, pickles and jam on a sturdy wooden table. Glancing at the wide-eyed boys who appeared to range from three to nine years of age, Elizabeth addressed them.

"Mrs. Lantrip prepared honey cakes and molasses biscuits especially for you."

She handed a bag of the biscuits to Mrs. Jenkins, who offered one to each of her sons. "Please thank her for us."

Then Elizabeth began pulling baby gowns, caps and socks, decorated with pink embroidery, from a laundry bag. "Miss Darcy helped me make these gowns and caps, and it was she who crocheted the socks."

As Mrs. Jenkins complimented Georgiana's workmanship, Elizabeth's sister blushed.

"I am pleased that you like them."

Suddenly, Mr. Jenkins, who had disappeared into the other room, returned with a child in his arms. His daughter was wrapped in a well-worn piece of cloth, so Elizabeth placed a new blanket in Mrs. Jenkins arms, and he laid the baby there.

"There is another blanket in the bag for when this one needs to be washed," Elizabeth said.

"I...we," Mr. Jenkins began, glancing at his wife. "We have decided on a name for our daughter. With your permission, Mrs. Darcy, we should like to call her Elizabeth."

"Oh, how wonderful! I am honoured."

Mrs. Jenkins held the baby out and Elizabeth took her. Peering into the child's innocent face, another child came to mind—the one she hoped to give Fitzwilliam. Tears filled her eyes, but she willed them not to fall. Instead, she said, "I look forward to watching you grow into a lovely young woman, Miss Elizabeth."

"I made an apple pie and put some tea on," Fanny Jenkins ventured. "Would you honour us by sharing our table?"

"I had a slice of your berry pie the last time I visited, and it was delicious," Elizabeth replied. "You will not have to ask twice!"

Mrs. Jenkins began to clear the baskets Elizabeth had brought from the table. "And you, Miss Darcy?" she asked.

"If my sister has complimented your pie, that is good enough for me," Georgiana declared. There was laughter all around.

After they had eaten, Georgiana was persuaded to hold the little girl and found that she had a talent for calming her when she started to cry.

"You must have a good deal of experience with babies, Miss Darcy," Mrs. Jenkins observed. "You have just the right touch."

"To be truthful, I have never been this close to a baby before."

"Well, your skills will come in handy once Mrs. Darcy delivers Mr. Darcy's heir," Mr. Jenkins declared. "What a happy day that will be!"

Despite willing herself not to blush, Elizabeth's face reddened. "I think we had best be on our way. Otherwise, Miss Darcy may miss her harp lesson."

As they exited the cabin, a young woman with dark hair met

them on the steps. In her arms was a child approximately a year old. He had the same dark hair as his mother, though his eyes were blue instead of coal black.

At the sight of her, Mrs. Jenkins' smile disappeared. "Mrs. Darcy, Miss Darcy, this is Masie Harvey," Mrs. Jenkins said. "Her farm borders ours on the north."

"I am pleased to meet you," Elizabeth replied.

"Likewise," Masie replied offering a small curtsey.

The baby laughed, and Elizabeth asked, "And who might you be?"

"I call him Will, after his father."

Immediately, Mrs. Jenkins bristled. "That boy's father is Toby Harvey, and he was christened Caleb."

Masie Harvey shrugged. "I wanted to call him Will, but Toby objected."

"And rightly so," Mrs. Jenkins replied.

Masie ignored Mrs. Jenkins' reproach. "I hope that you and Miss Darcy plan to call on me as well. Will loves company."

Before Elizabeth could reply, Mrs. Jenkins stepped in front of Masie. "Do not let us delay you. Miss Darcy may miss her lesson."

Though the coldness between Masie and Mrs. Jenkins seemed odd, Elizabeth knew that tenants often squabbled. Having no intention of getting involved, she led the way to the gig.

Once she and Georgiana were seated, she said to Masie, "We shall try to call on you next week."

Masie's only reply was a slight smile.

Ere long they were once more crossing the long expanse of pasture, each lost in thought. As they neared the manor, however, Georgiana could no longer keep silent.

"I never knew that seeing the tenants' response to our donations could be so satisfying. I have always contributed to those in need, but this has been an experience I shall never forget. Thank you for asking me to come. I hope to accompany you again in the future as time permits."

Elizabeth smiled. "I knew that once you took that first step, you would love it."

Exiting the gig at the front entrance, Elizabeth and Georgiana were chatting like magpies when they walked into the foyer. Lady Henrietta, who was coming down the grand staircase, stopped to watch. The longer she watched the more irritated she became.

"There you are! I was beginning to wonder if you would be back in time for your lesson, Georgiana. I have sent for the carriage. Please fetch your books from the music room."

"We had such a wonderful time I almost forgot," Georgiana answered as she rushed towards the hall on the right. "Let me retrieve my books, and I shall be right back."

As Georgiana disappeared in the direction of the music room, Lady Henrietta watched as Elizabeth gave orders to a maid regarding the baskets and laundry bags a footman had retrieved from the gig. Once she had finished, Henrietta said, "I was on the balcony when you left and happened to notice that you headed across the pasture."

"We did. Fitzwilliam wants me to take that route until he decides it is once again safe to travel on the road."

"That sounds like him," Henrietta replied. "Cautious to a fault."

Though she thought William too cautious as well, Elizabeth had no intention of agreeing with his stepmother. "I find it comforting that he takes his duties so seriously."

Once Elizabeth disappeared down the opposite hallway, Lady Henrietta immediately began to plot anew how to damage Fitzwilliam's relationship with his wife. Unfortunately, her stepdaughter's return interrupted her thoughts; thus, as she and Georgiana exited the front door she resolved to think on it later.

Parkleigh Manor
A drawing room

Whilst William waited for Lady Emma, he walked around the drawing room inspecting the portraits on the wall. One, in particular, caught his eye and he crossed in that direction. Standing in front of a portrait of Lady Waterston on her wedding day, he was fascinated by how much Lady Emma favoured her mother. He concluded that, had people not known the difference, they might think the portrait was of Lady Emma. Lady Waterston had been a considerable source of comfort to him when his mother died, and he had felt a great loss upon her death the year before he entered Cambridge.

It is a shame that Emma did not inherit your kindness. That thought had barely crossed his mind when the woman in question entered the room. If she was nervous, William could not tell.

"Fitzwilliam, what brings you here today? After last night, I thought you would sleep late."

"I believe you know why I am here."

Emma's expression became guarded, and her posture stiffened. "I have no idea what you mean."

"Before the ball, you spread lies about my marriage to anyone who would listen. Your intention was to humiliate Elizabeth and embarrass us both."

"Who told you such a thing?"

"Emma, now is not the time to act indignant."

"Would you have me admit to something I did not do?"

"I would have you tell the truth for once in your life!"

"You will not speak to me in that manner in my own home! And you will keep your voice down; I will not have you disturbing Father."

"I intend to tell your father about what you did as soon as his health permits. He needs to know why you and I no longer speak."

Emma looked as though she had been slapped. "Surely, you would not upset Father or end our friendship over something so trivial as unfounded rumours."

"Unfounded rumours? You deliberately fabricated the lie that Elizabeth and I were amenable to other relationships, and then you spread it remorselessly! Lord Osborne will testify to that."

All colour drained from her face, and she sank into a chair. "My mistake was in trying to save you from a country bumpkin who cared so little about you that she ran back home to her father the first chance she got." At William's stunned expression, she added, "Did you think the truth would not come out eventually?"

William took a deep breath, trying to calm himself. "Like any couple, Elizabeth and I have our differences; however, it was not your place to interfere in our lives."

"Not my place? Since we were old enough to dance, other than your own family, I was the only woman you stood up with. What did you expect me to think? I am two and twenty and still unmarried because I believed we would marry after you finished university."

"I have always maintained that we were only friends; still, I am very sorry that you misinterpreted my actions and dismissed everything I said."

"Save your apologies!" Lady Emma exclaimed, standing. "They sound as hollow as your heart."

"I am sorry you feel that way. However, because of your unkindness to Elizabeth we can no longer remain friends."

"You have much to learn about love, Fitzwilliam, and seeing how cruelly your wife has treated you thus far, she is just the one to teach you."

Though Emma continued to hurl insults as he walked away, William did not stop until he was at the bottom of the front steps, where he mounted Zeus and swiftly rode away.

Too perturbed to think of what he should say to Elizabeth, William went directly to the bridge to check on the progress being made to rebuild it. He had not been there long when a man was trapped by a section of the bridge that shifted and fell as it was being lifted into place. Immediately he removed his coat and worked alongside the crew to free him. Mercifully, the man survived, with the local physician declaring that, though he suffered from severe contusions, he had only one broken bone in his foot.

Having stayed until he was certain of the man's condition, at length an unkempt William, wearing a ripped shirt, dirty breeches and muddy boots, mounted Zeus for the ride home. By the time he reached the manor, it was completely dark.

Mrs. Reynolds was waiting when he arrived at the back entrance, her eyes widening after she noticed the abrasion on his cheek, bloody scratches on his hands and the state of his clothes. "What in the world?"

"There was an accident at the bridge." He went on to explain what happened.

"I am relieved that the workman was not injured more seriously; however, you look as though you could use some attention as well."

"That will not be necessary."

"Dinner was more than an hour ago. Would you like a tray sent to your room?"

"After what happened, I have no appetite. Where is everyone?"

"They all retired early tonight, Mr. Darcy. Still, I think you will find that Miss Darcy and your wife are awake. They were very worried about you."

"Please inform my sister that I am home, safe and sound," William said. "I shall inform my wife. By the way, I would dearly love a hot bath before I retire. Can that be arranged?"

"Mr. Adams must have read your mind, for when you did not return for dinner, he ordered water heated. Mr. Walker was informed the moment you reached the stables, and he is organising the footmen to bring it up now."

"Adams knows me too well."

Opening the door to his bedroom, William found his valet pacing. The minute Adams caught sight of him, he exclaimed, "Good heavens! You look as though you just settled an argument with fisticuffs."

Once again William was forced to explain; however, this time the valet helped him to disrobe whilst he did. Welcoming the sound of water being emptied into the huge copper tub in his dressing room, William settled into the bath the moment he was undressed. Closing his eyes as the heat began to soothe his aching muscles, he did not see Adams roll his eyes as he busily brushed dirt from the knees of William's breeches.

"I do not know how I will *ever* make these presentable," Adams murmured under his breath.

"What are you complaining about now?"

"I said I do not know how I will get the dirt out of your breeches."

"Go to bed. You will be able to think more clearly in the morning."

"But—"

"I can don my own nightshirt; you are dismissed. And thank you, Adams."

Sighing, Adams headed towards the door. With one hand on the knob, he said, "I think you should know that Mrs. Darcy has twice sent her maid to enquire if you had returned."

"I intend to talk to my wife before I retire."

After hearing the door open and close, William laid his head back on the towel placed over the rim of the tub and closed his eyes. Suddenly, Emma's harsh words came back to him, and he wondered if he had been wrong not to deal with her infatuation years ago. He assumed that once he had married, Emma would move on to someone else. Never once had it occurred to him that she would feel betrayed.

Suddenly, her taunt flashed through his mind: "You have much to learn about love, Fitzwilliam, and seeing how cruelly your wife has treated you thus far, she is just the one to teach you."

Annoyed at the thought, William stood, reached for a towel and began vigorously drying off.

Since I no longer allow emotions to rule my life, that will never happen again.

Chapter 24

Pemberley

After his bath, William donned a black silk robe that Adams had hung on the back of the dressing room door and walked towards the sitting room. Having resolved not to visit Elizabeth's bed again until he could control his emotions, his plan was to let her know he was home and immediately return to his own rooms.

As he approached the sitting room door, however, a soft knock bade him halt. Steeling himself, he opened it only to have Elizabeth rush past him, the scent of lavender following in her wake. She looked stunning in a pale-blue silk nightgown that clung to her curves; moreover, a shiny profusion of dark curls fell over her shoulders, just as he had often seen in his dreams. The sight triggered an immediate reaction in his traitorous body, and he had to struggle against taking her into his arms.

"I have been sick with worry! The least you could have done was—" The instant Elizabeth noticed the wound on his face she stopped speaking, and one hand came up to gently cup his cheek. "What happened?"

"There was an accident at the bridge."

"Was anyone seriously hurt?"

"One man suffered contusions and a broken foot, but mercifully no one was killed."

She took his hand and began leading him. "Come. I have a salve in my dressing room that will help."

"I appreciate your concern," William protested, "but that is not necessary."

"Please, allow me this small gesture," Elizabeth replied, never slowing.

Once in her bedroom, she directed William to the settee and rushed to her dressing room. Promptly returning, she gently began to apply an ointment to his face. Her nearness and the fact that concern hovered in her gaze was too much to bear, and William could not resist pulling her onto his lap. Years of loneliness and longing were poured into a kiss so fervent that Elizabeth responded with equal passion, and before long, he rose to carry her to the bed.

Her gown swiftly joined his robe on the floor. No longer bound by his restraint or her innocence, they fell back on the bed and quickly joined. Moans of satisfaction filled the air as William began a slow and deliberate conquest. Determined not to repeat his hurried performance of the night before, he continued the slow, steady pace until Elizabeth's body quivered, and she cried out his name. Only then did he give free rein to his own gratification.

Spent, for a long time they lay where they were. Eventually, William stood and helped Elizabeth to her feet; he threw back the counterpane and gently placed her on the silk sheets. Resigned that he could no more fight the desire to have Elizabeth than he could his next breath, he climbed into bed beside her, pulling her once more into his arms. He would have her again before morning, but for now they would both rest.

The break of day saw William return to his bedroom whilst Elizabeth was still sound asleep.

Lady Henrietta's sitting room
The next morning

"I do not think Darcy will agree to your scheme, Rietta. He is very protective of his sister, and I am not one of his favourite people," Lord Hartford said as he took his cup of tea over to the windows to admire Pemberley's gardens. "Why should he take my advice and let Georgiana go to Ramsgate for more art lessons?"

"Because you are an artist, and if I say so myself, you did an excellent job of instructing Georgiana in charcoals. All I ask of you is to insist that she has the talent to benefit from Monsieur Dupuy's instructions in oil painting when I bring up the subject."

"But you said that Fitzwilliam has eschewed any extraneous expenses, so who will pay for these lessons?"

"I have it all worked out. Georgiana's friend, Lady Esme, is quite the shy, little thing. She would never attend classes without her friend to accompany her. Why do you think Georgiana goes to their estate to share harp lessons? Whilst waiting for them to finish their lessons, I have been touting Mrs. Younge's Art Academy in Ramsgate to Lady Esme's mother, stressing that Monsieur Dupuy, an expert in oils, resides in Europe and only teaches at the academy once every two years as a favour to his old friend. Lady Farthingham is so keen on having her daughter attend classes that she wishes to pay for Georgiana's lessons if she will agree to go."

"Is any of that true?"

"Only the part about his being a friend of Mrs. Younge. According to George, he is a fair portrait painter with a contrived French accent."

Lord Hartford guffawed. "Might I ask how you heard of this academy?"

"George Wickham was acquainted with Mrs. Younge's brother for years before he died. Once he learned of her good fortune, he began calling, in expectation of separating her and her money."

"Her good fortune?"

"Her husband died and left her enough to start the school. George insists that she is under his spell and will do anything to please him."

"Ah, the infamous Mr. Wickham. I had no idea that you and he were still—what shall I call it? *Friends*?"

Lady Henrietta shrugged. "What can I say? George is very

good at certain things. Besides, at times I need a man who can be paid to ignore his conscience."

"From what I have heard, Wickham has no conscience."

"Be that as it may, I shared with George that it would be useful if Georgiana were away from Pemberley for a few weeks, which would allow me to concentrate on ruining Fitzwilliam's marriage. He suggested that I send her there."

"Have you considered that George merely wants Georgiana in his clutches? After all, you said yourself that he covets her dowry."

"George knows better than to thwart me, and I have not agreed to an elopement to Gretna Green. Should I be unsuccessful in destroying Fitzwilliam's happiness, I will rethink my position on Georgiana's dowry."

"Let me be frank, Rietta," Lord Hartford said, setting his cup down on a tray of tea and biscuits. "The instant that Darcy bedded his wife, your plan to separate them was doomed. Any sensible person would see that. I suggest that you put aside your feud against the Darcys and enjoy the privileges you have as George Darcy's widow whilst they last."

"I shall never give up until I have ruined the Darcys' lives. And if you expect me to continue helping you pay your debts, you will do as I ask without further advice."

Lord Hartford bowed. "As you say, madam."

William was astride Zeus, halfway between Pemberley and the road that led to the bridge, when he happened upon the delivery wagon of Lambton's grocer. It sat in the middle of the road, and goods lay on the ground on either side. Mr. Green was assisting a tall, thin, young boy to pick up everything that had spilled. Though he did not relish encountering the vicar today, William had no choice but to stop as well.

"I was on my way to Pemberley to drop off an order for Mrs. Reynolds, when the load shifted and everything tumbled," the boy declared, setting the last basket in the wagon. "I should have distributed it more evenly after I stopped at Parkleigh Manor. If I had not been in such a hurry, this would never have happened. Thank you, gentlemen, for helping me."

"I am just pleased that I happened along in time to be of service," Mr. Green replied.

William expressed similar sentiments and soon the wagon and its driver were on their way again. After he and the vicar watched the wagon disappear around a curve in the road, an awkward silence fell.

"Fitzwilliam, this is fortuitous. I have wanted to speak to you. Do you have a few minutes?" When William hesitated, he added, "What I have to say will not take long."

Though he had been preparing to remount, William began to pull Zeus towards a tall shade tree. "If we are to talk, let it be out of the sun."

Mr. Green led his recently purchased stallion in the same direction, and once he had secured the animal, he began. "Elizabeth came to see Judith a few days ago."

"To complain about me, I suppose."

"Actually, Judith said that Elizabeth is desperate to please you. She hoped that my wife might advise her on how to accomplish that."

William was unable to look the vicar in the eye. "Am I such an ogre that my wife must have help to deal with me?"

"You are not an ogre...at least not yet. But in my profession, I have dealt with many men and women who became ogres. I learned long ago that being unwilling to forgive poisons the heart, and if not excised like a cancer, it will result in a heartless soul."

Though William did not reply, he appeared to be listening, so the vicar continued.

"I assume that you wish to have children with Elizabeth. Do you realise that even a small child can recognise when there is discord between his parents? At some point, he will side with one parent over the other, believing that the one he has not chosen is to blame. Your conflict will become theirs, whether you wish it or not. Is that the legacy you want to leave your children?"

"Elizabeth will always be treated fairly, as befits her status as Mrs. Darcy."

"You are missing the point, my boy. Elizabeth wants to love you and have you love her in return."

"We agreed to a marriage of convenience. I see no reason to change it."

"Do you believe in your heart that your mother would approve of your arrangement? I knew Lady Anne well, and she did not have a vengeful bone in her body."

"And I do?" William said sharply.

"That is for you to decide."

William untied Zeus. "I appreciate your concern, but it is my life and my marriage."

As he stepped into the stirrup and swung a leg over the stallion, Mr. Green called his name. William stopped to regard the man he had once considered as a father.

"Judith and I have faith that you will do the right thing."

Tipping his hat, William rode off in the direction of Parkleigh Manor.

Watching him leave, Mr. Green sighed. *If only you understood that what your heart longs for is already in your hands.*

London

Having received a note from Darcy's godfather early that morning, Richard was well on his way to that gentleman's townhouse as the noon hour approached. He had been in his office at army headquarters, distracted by plans for his upcoming stay at Pemberley, when the summons, vague as it was, was delivered by a footman. Though acquainted with Lord Appleby, Richard felt it did not bode well for Darcy that his godfather would beckon him. And by the time he dismounted in front of Appleby's residence, he was anxious. Squaring his shoulders, he handed the reins to a groom and marched up the steps.

As he approached the front door, it opened, and a butler

walked out. "Come in, Colonel Fitzwilliam. Lord Appleby is expecting you."

He was shown into a library where his host was seated at a writing table. Appleby stood to greet him. Not having seen the man in some time, Richard was surprised at how much older he appeared; still, he pasted on a smile and reached out to shake the offered hand.

"Lord Appleby! It has been far too long."

"Yes, it has, Colonel Fitzwilliam. I asked Fitzwilliam about you the last time he was here, and he said you were still in His Majesty's service. I hope the army is treating you well."

"Indeed, it is."

"Excellent! We need men like you to keep England strong." Seeing Richard smile, he added, "I know you must wonder why I sent for you, so please be seated, and I will get straight to the point."

He motioned to a chair beside the desk, and Richard sat down. Lord Appleby resumed his seat and began to explain. "This morning I had a visit from my personal banker, Mr. Roth. It was in regard to the loan I co-signed for Fitzwilliam."

Richard's change of expression signified his surprise.

"I would not discuss this with you had Fitzwilliam not given me permission to contact you if something important came up and he was not in Town."

"I see."

"The bank has been appraising the Darcy jewels being held as collateral on the loan. During the process, they discovered that several less noticeable pieces had diamonds, emeralds and rubies missing. They have been replaced with paste." Lord Appleby slid a small bag across his desk. "Excellent forgeries, but paste nonetheless. Here are the ones in question."

As Richard poured the contents onto the desk, he began shaking his head. "This cannot be. Darcy would never—"

"I am not accusing my godson of any deception, nor did I get the impression that the bank thinks him culpable. They are upset, as you can imagine, but Mr. Roth told me in strictest confidence that the genuine jewels and my support are sufficient to keep the loan afloat. They merely want Fitzwilliam to be aware of the subterfuge."

"I know of only one person who would do such a thing."

"I imagine you and I have the same person in mind. I tried to warn George off that fortune hunter, but he would not listen."

"Uncle George was blind when it came to Lady Henrietta, but even he would not have agreed to replace the Darcy jewels with paste."

"For what it is worth, I agree. Fitzwilliam must be told, but I thought it best done in person. That boy has had his share of disappointments since George married the merry widow, and I felt a letter would be too cruel. That is my purpose in asking you here. My health precludes me making the trip to Pemberley, and I was hoping that you would inform him."

"I have plans to travel to Pemberley at the end of next week. I will tell him."

"I knew I could count on you."

Richard began to put the jewels back in the bag. "May I take these with me?"

"Of course."

As Richard rode back to his office, his mind was swirling with plans. He would have Sergeant Brantley, recently retired, canvass all the jewellery shops, pawn shops and dens of thieves in London. Perhaps for the right incentive, whoever replaced the Darcy jewels with fakes could be persuaded to reveal who hired them. After all, replacing jewels with paste was often done amongst the *ton* to save face, and if the rightful owner was the initiator, no laws were broken. One could even argue that Lady Henrietta had the right to replace the jewels before George Darcy's death.

With any luck, someone will point the finger at you, Lady Harlot!

Pemberley

A week later, Elizabeth found herself adjusting to a new routine. Georgiana had been allowed to go to Ramsgate with Lady Esme and had left in the Farthinghams' coach two days earlier. Missing her sister more than she had ever imagined she would, Elizabeth filled her days by creating even more clothes for the tenants and packing baskets for future visits. William was still inundated by responsibilities, which now included schooling Parkleigh Manor's new steward in proper bridge construction. That the steward had little knowledge of construction had come as an unwelcome surprise, for it required William's continued involvement in the project.

Each night when she and William met at the dinner table, he was as silent and taciturn as ever in front of Lady Henrietta and Lord Hartford. It was not until after they were in the privacy of her bedroom that a completely different man emerged—a passionate and insatiable lover. She treasured the nights spent in his arms as proof that the indifferent façade he wore most of the time did not define his true feelings for her, even as she worried that if she became pregnant, he would honour his resolve to abandon her bed until the child was born.

All of this weighed heavily on her mind the day that Mr. Bingley arrived at Pemberley. Appearing just as dinner had begun, Charles joined them at the table, his easy smile and frequent laughter cheering even William.

Lady Henrietta seemed especially eager to charm their guest and persisted in trying to engage him in conversation. Oblivious to her ploy, Charles gave short shrift to her questions and always returned to his conversation with William at the first opportunity, much to that woman's chagrin.

Elizabeth could have kissed Bingley for not succumbing to Lady Henrietta's flirtations; however, even as she revelled in Lady Henrietta's defeat, she was shocked by William's next pronouncement.

"Charles, you mentioned you wished to speak privately. After we have finished eating, I shall escort Elizabeth to her bedroom, and you and I shall remove to my study."

With a heavy heart, Elizabeth wore a tremulous smile as Lady Henrietta directed a smug look her way. Not willing that anyone should see her disappointment, Elizabeth retained the smile until after William said goodnight in their sitting room and left to meet Charles.

William's study

After pouring a brandy for himself and one for Bingley, William walked over to hand his friend a glass before seating himself in the chair behind his desk. "I am pleased your father recognised how hard you have worked to make high marks at Cambridge. With as much time as you spend on the road to Meryton, it could not have been easy."

Bingley laughed. "It certainly was not! Still, it was a surprise to get a third of my inheritance now." Taking the chair in front of William's desk, he took a sip of the brandy and set the glass down. Reaching into his coat pocket, he brought out a piece of paper. With a wide grin, he slid it across the polished mahogany desktop. "Thank you for helping me when I desperately needed support."

William took the paper, which proved to be a bank cheque, and read it aloud, "Pay to Fitzwilliam Darcy, five hundred pounds." He looked at Bingley. "Our agreement was that you repay the loan *after* you graduate."

"I am well aware that you were facing a deficit of your own when you loaned me the money," Charles answered. "Since I have the funds, I wish to repay your kindness now."

"I cannot pretend it is not needed," William replied sombrely, placing the cheque in his top drawer.

"My father's munificence also means that Jane and I may marry sooner rather than later. We are planning a wedding for after the first of the year, and I would be honoured if you stood up with me. Jane will ask Lizzy, and I am certain she will agree."

"Where will you marry? At their uncle's home in London?"

"No. Jane wishes to marry at her parish in Meryton." William's expression grew more sombre, so Charles asked, "Are you worried that John Lucas may attend?"

"Knowing that Elizabeth wanted to marry him, it would be awkward if he came."

"I have it on good authority that marrying Lucas was merely a 'last resort' should Lizzy be forced to marry Mr. Collins."

"Even if that were true, they are still the best of friends."

"You are wrong there. Lizzy broke off their friendship before she left for Lambton. Did she not tell you?"

"No."

"According to Jane, she confronted Lucas about his lies and told him it would be unfair to you if they were to remain friends." William seemed to be considering what he had said, so Bingley continued, "What say you? Will you stand up with me?"

"I will."

"Excellent!"

Charles then proceeded to talk for another half hour about Jane Bennet. The ease with which he described their relationship not only made William envious, it brought to mind Mr. Green's warning about children being affected by their parents' relationship.

The vicar's counsel troubled him greatly, for William vividly recalled the first time he noticed his mother's distress at his father's frequent solitary trips to London. It had been the summer of his eighth birthday, and he had tried to alleviate her despondency by being especially attentive. His stratagem worked but never for long. Seeing her misery was one of the reasons he had hoped to marry someone he loved.

Suddenly, Bingley stood to leave. "It has been great seeing you again, Darcy; however, I am weary from the journey. If I am to get a very early start tomorrow, I must retire now."

"Why must you leave so soon?"

"Once classes resume, I will not be able to see Jane as often as I do now—at least, not until we are married, and she returns to Cambridge with me."

"I see," William said, standing. "You are a very fortunate man.

To find a woman you love and who returns that love is not something to take lightly."

"How well I know," Bingley said, holding out a hand. "It is unlikely that I shall see you again until my wedding, so I will say farewell until then, my friend."

William took the hand and shook it. "Until then."

A full hour after Bingley had retired, William was still at his desk. Learning that Elizabeth had broken off her friendship with John Lucas before coming to him had destroyed completely the wall he had erected around his conscience. Faced with his own culpability, he could no longer deny that he had played a part in the failure of their marriage.

If truth be told, upon reading the letter Elizabeth wrote to him when she left London, he knew that had he been more open with her regarding Mr. Bennet's health, she would have had no reason to go to John Lucas for answers. It was his jealously over her relationship with Lucas and the knowledge that Elizabeth was not in love with him that rendered him incapable of admitting the truth.

Unbidden, a small voice whispered: *You were taught what was right as a child, but you were not taught to correct your temper. You were given good principles, but left to follow them in pride and conceit. You have many faults—one being that you act and speak without regard to the feelings of others. Why else would Elizabeth say that your opinion of her family was like a dagger to her heart?*

William dropped his head in his hands. "Oh, Elizabeth, you did everything possible to make amends, and how did I repay you? By forcing you to accept a loveless marriage whilst I took advantage of you every night."

Standing he looked towards heaven. "Forgive me. With Your help, I vow to spend the rest of my life making it up to her."

Taking the chamber candlestick, William exited the study. His intentions were to go to Elizabeth and confess everything, but after locking the door, he turned to see Mr. Walker rushing down the hall towards him.

Chapter 25

Pemberley

"Sir, the constable is at the door," Mr. Walker said. "He insists upon speaking to you right away."

William followed the butler to the foyer, where the gentleman stood fidgeting with his cap.

"Has there been some trouble, Mr. Claridge?" William asked.

"A man was killed in a fight tonight at a pub between here and Sheffield. Some say the dead man is Toby Harvey, but not all the witnesses agree. Since Mr. Kendal swore out a warrant for Harvey's arrest, I would like him to identify the body. If it is Harvey, I will take jurisdiction since I have an outstanding warrant for the man. If it is not Harvey, the constable at Sheffield can deal with whoever it turns out to be, since it is nearest his district. I need you to show me where Mr. Kendal lives."

"Give me time to have my horse saddled."

Elizabeth's bedroom

Disappointed that William had not come to her bed after meeting with Mr. Bingley, Elizabeth was even more disheartened the next morning when Florence informed her that her husband had been called away last night and had not yet returned. Moreover, Mr. Bingley had left already. After consulting with Mrs. Reynolds, who knew nothing other than that Fitzwilliam had accompanied the constable, Elizabeth decided the best way to keep worry at bay was to stay occupied. Skipping her usual morning walk, she sent Florence in search of Rogers.

When the footman entered the sitting room, he found Elizabeth dressed and waiting. "Mrs. Darcy," he greeted her, performing a slight bow.

"Rogers, I wish to get an early start calling on tenants today. Will you please see that the gig is readied whilst I gather the items I plan to take? You will find me in the supply room once the vehicle is ready."

"Yes, ma'am."

After Rogers left, Florence asked, "Do you think you should leave without knowing why Mr. Darcy was called out?"

"If I put off all my duties until I knew what my husband was doing, I would get nothing done. I hope to have all the baskets delivered by noon, so most likely I will be back when he returns."

Florence knew that it was pointless to argue with her mistress when her mind was made up, so she said nothing more.

As Elizabeth and Rogers drew near the farm occupied by Masie Harvey, her brother came running towards them over a hill. The footman reined in the horse, and by the time Hal Kendal reached them, he was so out of breath that he could scarcely speak.

"It...it is Caleb!" he managed to stammer at last. "He fell and hit his head. Neither Masie nor I can get him to respond. I need to fetch the physician."

Elizabeth climbed down from the gig. "On foot, it will take too long. Bring Dr. Camryn immediately!" she ordered the footman.

"But, Mrs. Darcy, the master made me swear that I would stay with you whenever you leave the house."

"Hal will be with me; there is nothing to fear."

Reluctantly, Rogers turned the gig around and hurried in the direction of Lambton.

"Have you caught your breath sufficiently to show me the way?" Elizabeth asked.

"I have, ma'am," the young man replied. "Follow me."

On the road to Lambton

Because William and the constable had to awaken Jedidiah Kendal before heading north to Sheffield and then had to rouse another tenant to lend him a horse, it had taken all night to determine that the corpse lying on a table in the pub's storeroom was not Toby Harvey. Consequently, three extremely weary men returned to Lambton the next morning, each disappointed that the man in question was not the blackguard they sought.

Taking leave of Lambton's constable in the village, William and Mr. Kendal were travelling the road between Parkleigh Manor and Pemberley when they were nearly run down by Rogers and Dr. Camryn barrelling along a converging path. William's heart clenched when he realised they were occupying Elizabeth's gig.

"Where is my wife, Rogers?"

"There was an accident, sir…a child was hurt…Mrs. Darcy ordered me to fetch Dr. Camryn."

"I ask again," William said curtly. "Where is my wife?"

"When I left her, she was on her way to Masie Harvey's farm with that woman's brother."

Instantly, the idea that the killing in Sheffield might have been a diversion struck him. "Follow me!" William declared, kicking Zeus into a gallop.

The second she stepped inside the small cabin, Elizabeth realised she had been duped. A large man with filthy clothes and greasy, blond hair pointed a pistol at her whilst a battered and bleeding Masie lay on the floor at his feet. In one corner, Caleb sat crying.

"I...I am sorry, Mrs. Darcy," Hal Kendal began. "Toby said he would kill my sister and nephew if I did not—"

"Shut your mouth and sit down!" the miscreant hollered, motioning with the pistol to where Masie sat on the floor. It was obvious he was drunk, for Elizabeth could not only smell the liquor on his breath, but when he spoke, he slurred his words.

Hal instantly went silent, taking a seat on the floor beside his sister. Harvey grabbed several pieces of rope from the table and threw them into Masie's lap. "Tie his hands and feet, and do it right, or else you will get another beating."

Whilst Masie tied up her brother, Harvey leered at Elizabeth. Afraid, but unwilling for him to know it, she willed her voice not to quiver. "My husband is on his way. If you value your life, you will leave now."

A loud guffaw filled the air. "Is that so? I happen to know that Mr. Darcy is on a pointless mission to bring my lifeless body back from Sheffield! He will not save you."

"Leave Mrs. Darcy alone," Hal pleaded. "She has done nothing unkind to anyone."

"Maybe not, but she will suffer for what her man did."

"What grievance do you hold against my husband?" Elizabeth asked.

A deep scowl crossed Harvey's face. "My wife has been telling all who will listen that he fathered that boy over there." With this assertion, he tilted his head towards Caleb.

"Surely you do not believe that!"

"You have not even given the boy a proper study!" Harvey hissed. "Look at him! He has light eyes."

"So does grandfather!" Hal Kendal shouted.

"All rich men take advantage of the women beneath them," Harvey huffed, ignoring Masie's brother. "They feel they are entitled."

"You are mistaken!" Elizabeth replied even more forcefully. "Fitzwilliam is an honourable man; he would never do such a thing." She looked at Masie. "Tell your husband the truth!"

Masie dropped her head. "Mrs. Darcy is right, Toby. I pretended that Caleb was the master's son because I thought everyone would think I was special to have captured his attention."

Harvey slammed a fist against the wall. "You are lying! Fitzwilliam Darcy took you from me, and I aim to take what is his!" He motioned for Elizabeth to come forward, but she did not move. Aiming the gun at Caleb, he said, "You will tie Masie up, or I will kill Darcy's bastard right now."

Elizabeth did as he ordered. Once Masie was secured, Harvey grabbed her arm and pulled Elizabeth to her feet. Keeping a tight grip, he shoved the pistol into his waistband, growling, "If you resist, you will get a beating, too."

Elizabeth fought courageously as Harvey dragged her towards a bed. She kicked him again and again, and he had just brought a hand up to strike her when a voice boomed across the room.

"Take your hands off my wife!"

Though Rogers tried, the gig could not keep pace with the horses, so William and Mr. Kendal reached Masie's farm ahead of them. William wondered where the sentries he had posted were but had no time to dwell on that. Hearing loud voices through the partially open front door, he and Mr. Kendal stopped a safe distance away to remain out of view. Dismounting, William pulled a golden-handled, over-and-under pistol from the satchel he had carried to Sheffield. Then, not willing to put the elderly man in danger, he ordered Mr. Kendal to go for help.

"But, sir, I cannot leave you to face—"

"Go," William whispered. "The others will be here at any minute."

Just as Mr. Kendal kicked his horse into a trot several yards away, the gig appeared on the horizon. When it slowed to a stop beside William, he ordered, "Both of you take the back door. I shall take the front. Do not enter until I call your name, or you hear shots fired."

Rogers and Dr. Camryn circled the house, whilst William

slipped stealthily towards the front door. He paused beside the entrance just in time to hear Elizabeth defending him. His heart immediately swelled to hear her words of admiration, but fear overruled that emotion when Harvey declared, "If you resist, you will get a beating, too."

Pushing the door wide open, William stepped inside and ordered Harvey to release Elizabeth.

Seeing the fancy pistol pointed at him, Harvey pulled Elizabeth close as a shield. Quickly drawing his own weapon, he placed the muzzle against her temple. "If you love your wife, it is you who will do the obeying. Now, lay that pistol on the floor and kick it to me."

"No! Fitzwilliam, do not—" Instantly, a burly hand clamped over Elizabeth's mouth.

Trying to recall if he had the small pistol he usually carried in his coat pocket, William hesitated only a second before complying. Once he had, Harvey shoved Elizabeth to the side. She hit the floor hard but began scrambling to get back on her feet.

"I was going to show you how it feels to be cuckolded but killing you will be much more satisfying."

Harvey raised the gun and took aim. At that moment William shouted for Rogers, and simultaneously Elizabeth ran between him and Harvey, crying, "No!"

Harvey's pistol discharged, striking Elizabeth in the shoulder. She fell, her head striking the edge of a large rock doorstop with an ominous thud. Instantly, the back door flew open, and the footman and physician rushed in just as Harvey squatted to retrieve William's pistol. When he rose with the weapon, Rogers shot the wastrel, and he fell, mortally wounded. Immediately, the footman began to untie Hal and Masie.

As soon as Elizabeth fell, William retrieved the pistol and dropped to his knees, covering her with his body. Once Harvey had collapsed to the floor, he returned the gun to his coat and began gathering her in his arms. Not only was she unresponsive, but a large bloodstain was rapidly spreading across the shoulder of her gown. Calling her name repeatedly with no answer, his panic grew until an unearthly sob escaped him. "Please, God! Do not take her from me!"

The outburst was so out of character for the master of Pemberley that everyone watching the scene froze. First to recover from his astonishment was Dr. Camryn, who rushed forwards and dropped to his knees beside William. "Please lay your wife down, Mr. Darcy. Let me examine her."

Although in a daze, William complied. For the first time in his adult life, he found himself unable to think clearly or to take charge; thus, he watched helplessly as the physician first inspected the wound to her shoulder and then the growing knot on her forehead. Running repeatedly through his mind was the fact he had never told Elizabeth that he loved her.

Please, Lord, give me another chance to tell her.

"Untie your cravat and press it against the wound to staunch the blood." William immediately complied with the physician's order. "We must remove Mrs. Darcy to Pemberley as quickly as possible. Stay right beside her and try to keep her from being jostled about more than necessary."

Dr. Camryn stood. "I believe a wagon would be less jarring than the gig. Is there one available and hay to fill it?"

Mr. Kendal, who had already returned with several tenants, was standing in the door watching in complete shock as the spectacle unfolded. He was the first to respond. "There is a wagon and plenty of hay in the barn. Hal, unhitch the horse from the gig; he will do to pull the wagon."

Pemberley

The house was as quiet as a mausoleum when Mrs. Reynolds made yet another trip up the grand staircase to Elizabeth's bedroom with more supplies. Since Mrs. Darcy had returned to Pemberley in such a perilous state, footmen and maids alike had been tiptoeing about as though making any sound might hinder their mistress' recovery. Moreover, the usually staid and self-assured housekeeper was perplexed over what she should do to be of help. Going through her mind were the numerous draughts and potions she knew would help the gunshot wound, but the injury to her mistress' head was an entirely different matter. In fact, the long-time servant was afraid to give voice to what she knew: this type of injury often proved fatal.

As she entered the sitting room, the occupants immediately went silent, and Mrs. Reynolds encountered the fretful eyes of the master. She immediately looked away. It had been difficult to get Mr. Darcy to leave Elizabeth's bedroom, at the physician's insistence, and only the calm, reassuring presence of the Reverend and Mrs. Green kept him at bay.

Mrs. Reynolds did not want to break into tears, something she had done in the privacy of her own rooms, for fear that would reveal just how dire she judged the circumstances. Crossing to the bedroom door with an armful of towels, she paused to say a quick prayer before stepping inside and closing the door.

The instant the door to Elizabeth's bedroom closed, William stood. "It is my fault! If only I had posted more sentries or...or warned her not to visit the tenants before I left with the constable."

"You had no way of knowing she would go out so early and it was certainly not your fault that Harvey disabled the sentries. It is a wonder he did not kill them instead of leaving them unconscious."

"Still, had I been kinder, more—"

"Fitzwilliam, what happened was not your fault," Judith Green said. "Your relationship with Elizabeth had nothing to do with that blackguard's evil intentions."

"God is punishing me for being cruel when I should have shown mercy," William said, swallowing hard to keep from crying. "I do not deserve Elizabeth. He knows that."

Mr. Green put an arm around William's shoulder. "Just minutes ago, you confessed to having repented last night of your disrespectful attitude towards Elizabeth. Even if God was behind this evil—and He is not—what reason would He have to take her from you now that you are on the right path?"

"I…I had no opportunity to tell Elizabeth I am sorry or to ask her forgiveness. I have not even told her that I love—" William's voice broke, and as he dropped his head in his hands, his shoulders shook with muffled tears.

Judith Green rushed to him. "You will have plenty of chances to tell her once she awakens."

"If…if she awakens," William stammered.

"We have to have faith that she will.".

The door to the bedroom opened, and an exhausted Dr. Camryn joined them in the sitting room. Panic threatened to engulf William once more when he saw the amount of blood covering the physician's clothes.

"Is…is she—" was all he managed to say.

"Your wife is doing well under the circumstance," the physician replied. "I was able to find and remove the ball. Thankfully, it did not hit a bone. If it does not get infected, it should not present too great an obstacle. However, I am concerned with the blood lost and that she remains unconscious. The knot on her forehead has swelled considerably and is turning dark."

"What can I do?" William asked, his eyes pleading.

"For now, all any of us can do is pray," Dr. Camryn replied. "The next twenty-four hours will be critical."

"Then let us join in prayer," Reverend Green said.

Dr. Camryn placed a hand on William's shoulder as the vicar and his wife prayed for healing for Elizabeth and for reassurance for those who loved her.

In another sitting room

Thinking of what must be happening a few doors down the hall, Lord Hartford tossed down another large measure of brandy. "Do you think Elizabeth will survive?"

"If there is any justice in the world, she will not," Lady Henrietta replied, "but I have always found justice in short supply."

Hartford studied his cousin before replying, "You know, Rietta, Mrs. Darcy has never been unkind to you. One would think you would not wish her to die."

"She is a Darcy, which makes her my enemy. Besides, should she live, Fitzwilliam will have a family, which will make him happy."

"I have been thinking it might please you if you were to leave Pemberley and live in London. You are still a beauty, and there are plenty of rich men looking for a pretty woman to grace their arms at social functions."

"And their beds afterwards," she said wryly. "I am not in the mood to be another man's toy. I had rather wreak vengeance on the whole lot of them."

"Does that include me? After all, I am a man."

"You are my cousin, which exempts you."

"That is good to know." Lord Hartford eyed the brandy decanter again. "Have you heard from Georgiana?"

"No, but I expect to hear from her shortly."

"I think she will demand to return as soon as she hears about Elizabeth."

"I am glad you thought of that. I shall tell Sarah to be certain that any letters addressed to Georgiana are never placed in the post."

"I confess I grieve for Elizabeth and Georgiana. In my own way I have learned to care for them."

"If you wish to stay in my good graces, you will renounce all concern for the Darcys. Else, when your finances dwindle again, and they will, you will be begging them for help instead of me. How do you think Fitzwilliam would respond to that?"

"As usual, I am forced to see your point."

"I thought you would."

Chapter 26

Pemberley

The night seemed interminably long for William as he sat on the edge of the bed watching Elizabeth by the light of several candles. On the floor, Clancy watched him with equally anxious eyes. Having taken up with Elizabeth after Georgiana left for Ramsgate, the little dog had begun sneaking into her bedroom at night to curl up on the floor near her bed, and tonight was no exception. Though William had eschewed offers by Mrs. Reynolds, Florence and Mrs. Green to sit with her, wanting the first face Elizabeth saw when she opened her eyes to be his, he was content with Clancy's company. He would find no rest until he was certain Elizabeth would recover, and apparently Clancy felt the same way.

Even in Elizabeth's present condition, she looked so beautiful that he longed to touch her. Recalling the time at Cambridge when he had observed her similarly unaware, he began to gently trace her upturned nose once again. Her freckles were more pronounced now, and he could not suppress a faint smile before moving to her lips. Thoughts of how sweet they had tasted the last time he was in her bed made a well-entrenched ache in his chest intensify. *Oh, Elizabeth, will I ever feel your kiss again?*

Suddenly, the door opened, and he glanced up to see Mrs. Reynolds enter the room with a tray. By the time she set it down on a chest, he had already turned back to Elizabeth. However, when the elderly housekeeper reached out to give his shoulder a gentle squeeze, he recalled the few times she had stepped out of her role as a servant in the past—once when he was seven and his favourite dog had died, and again upon the deaths of his mother and father. William closed his eyes at the troubling image that gesture brought to mind.

"Are you certain I cannot relieve you from your watch? You really should get some rest, and I shall fetch you the moment there is any change."

"I will not leave her."

"I thought as much, so I made a pot of fresh coffee. May I pour you a cup?"

Though William enjoyed coffee, at present he had no taste for anything. Still, he knew Mrs. Reynolds needed to feel useful.

"Certainly. Just set the cup on the tray, and I shall drink it shortly."

Not long afterwards, he heard the door open and close. Once more alone with his thoughts, his mind wandered to a paper that his London physician, Dr. Graham, had presented to the Royal Society[9] shortly before William had left Town. Graham, with whom he liked to discuss the latest scientific advances, had provided him a copy of the paper, which theorised that unconscious people could hear everything happening around them. The presentation had stirred a firestorm of arguments for and against the notion, but due to his marital woes, William had given it little thought at the time. Now, every line sprung to the forefront of his memory.

Taking a deep breath to keep from trembling, William took Elizabeth's free hand in his and brought it to his lips. Placing soft kisses on each knuckle, he began to tell her everything he had held inside since the first day they met: how he had fallen in love with her at first sight, but quickly realised she could not

---

9 The President, Council and Fellows of the Royal Society of London for Improving Natural Knowledge, commonly known as **the Royal Society**, is a learned society for science and is possibly the oldest such society still in existence. Founded in November 1660, it was granted a royal charter by King Charles II as "The Royal Society." https://en.wikipedia.org/wiki/Royal_Society

possibly meet the requirements for his wife as put forth by his relations. He continued, apologising for all his faults and mistakes, including the day at the Gavins' farm when he had offered her a marriage of convenience.

"I was so wounded when you left for Longbourn with John that I could not admit the truth, even to myself. I wanted you to come back, but pride forced me to hide it. That was why I acted as though I was doing you a service by letting you return. I will never know why you agreed to return to me, or why you tried so hard to make amends when I criticised everything you said and did. Nor do I know how you tolerated my apathy towards you during the day, whilst exercising my rights as your husband at night. Despite my best efforts not to care, I fell more deeply in love with you each passing day." He gently brushed a curl behind her ear. "Do you wish to know the worst part? I know now just how little I deserve a woman like you. And I would understand if you told me you no longer wished to be—"

A sob shortened his declaration, and he lay his head beside her and wept. A soft touch on his hair brought his head up. Elizabeth smiled faintly, whispering, "I love you."

Instantly, he began kissing every inch of her face, save the bump on her forehead. Pulling back, he cried, "Thank God! He sent you back to me."

Elizabeth tried to rise but gasped with the pain instead.

"You must lie still," William insisted, "else your shoulder will bleed again." At her confused expression, he added, "You were shot in the shoulder. Dr. Camryn removed the ball and strapped that arm to your body to keep it from moving."

"I...I am so...befuddled," she murmured. Then her brows furrowed. "Were you hurt?"

"No. Because of your bravery, I was uninjured." He kissed her brow. "Rest now. When you feel better, I shall gladly explain everything." He stood as though to leave. "Dr. Camryn wished to be informed the minute you were awake."

"Pray, let him rest," Elizabeth said. "Lie down and hold me. That is all I need."

Unable to refuse, William removed his waistcoat and boots

before climbing into the bed and sliding next to his wife. Once he was as close as he dared, he whispered, "Oh, my darling, there is so much for which I need to ask your forgiveness. I hardly know where to begin."

"I heard everything you said, dearest, and you are already forgiven."

Burying his head in her silky hair, William whispered words of love until Elizabeth's breaths took on a steady rhythm. After he was certain she was asleep, he allowed himself to relax and soon joined her. Even Clancy fell asleep, and none woke until Dr. Camryn entered the room in the early morning hours.

Ramsgate
Younge's Art Academy

Whilst George Wickham observed, Martha Younge nervously glanced inside the classroom where her pupils were listening raptly to Monsieur Dupuy's instructions. The plain, stout woman held no attraction for him, but she was somewhat prosperous and foolish enough to help him carry out his plan to elope with Georgiana Darcy. Though Lady Henrietta thought him under her command where Georgiana was concerned, he had no intention of giving up the chance to become wealthy in his own right.

"Are you certain Miss Darcy will not recognise you?"

"Georgiana has not seen me since she was nine years of age, and I doubt she remembers seeing me then. She came into her father's study to say goodnight, and I just happened to be there. In fact, I do not think George Darcy even mentioned me. Besides," Wickham said, admiring himself in a mirror on the wall, "this moustache makes me look like an entirely different man and with a new name, she will be none the wiser."

"I pray you are right. They are soon to be dismissed for luncheon, and I thought to introduce you to Miss Darcy when they go through to the dining room. Just a casual meeting will do to begin with, I think."

"I agree," Wickham said. "Oh, look! They are standing to leave."

Mrs. Younge smiled vacuously at the girls as they filed past her out of the classroom. As it happened, Lady Esme and Georgiana, who were talking animatedly, were the last to leave the classroom, which created the perfect opportunity.

"Miss Darcy, may I have a minute of your time?" Mrs. Younge asked.

Glancing at Lady Esme, who shrugged, Georgiana walked cautiously towards her host and the strange gentleman whilst her best friend hurried on to the dining room.

"I would like to introduce you to my cousin, Lord Worley of Worley Hall in Birmingham." Georgiana curtseyed as Mrs. Younge continued, "Worley, this is Miss Darcy of Pemberley in Derbyshire."

The tall man, whom Georgiana thought very handsome, bowed. "A pleasure to meet you, Miss Darcy."

"Lord Worley is a patron of the arts and believes in placing his support behind aspiring young artists, such as yourself, who show enormous potential. Upon seeing your painting of the sea, he asked to meet you."

Wickham took up the lie from there. "I especially admire the way you conveyed so much emotion in your painting. The fury of the sea in contrast to the seagull hidden in peaceful slumber beneath the pier was very moving."

"I...I am pleased you liked it."

"Like it?" Wickham exclaimed. "I thought your execution brilliant!"

Georgiana was puzzled. Clever enough to know that some of the paintings done by other students in her class were much better, she was wary of his praise. In fact, the painting done by Lady Esme of a sand dollar and star-fish on the shore after a storm put her efforts to shame.

"I cannot fathom why you chose my painting," Georgiana replied. "There are more talented students in my class."

"I disagree," Wickham immediately interjected. "I have an eye for the details only an expert would notice. If you were to allow me to advise you, I could use my influence to have you tutored by the greatest artists in the world."

"I am not interested in pursuing art beyond this class; besides, my brother would never allow me to take advice from anyone but him. Now, if you will excuse me, Lord Worley."

Georgiana rushed towards the dining room, leaving Wickham and Mrs. Younge staring after her open-mouthed. At length, he said, "At least she did not recognise me. Now, I have only to make her fall in love with me and agree to elope to Gretna Green."

"You do not have much time. This school runs only a few weeks."

"In the end, if Georgiana values the lives of her family, she will marry me whether she likes it or not."

Martha Younge recoiled. "George! You assured me Fitzwilliam Darcy would do nothing once he learns you were married because Georgiana would plead your case. If you take her against her will, her brother will see you hang. Moreover, he would leave no stone unturned to prosecute those who assisted you."

"You are not going to hang, and neither am I. Just keep to our plan, and after I am in possession of Georgiana's dowry, we shall set sail for Canada."

"I am counting on you to win her heart just as you promised."

"Do you doubt me, Martha?" Wickham asked. Then, pulling Mrs. Younge into the now empty classroom, he added, "You and I will be together as soon as this is over. You believe that, do you not?"

"I believe in you, George." Martha Younge was rewarded with a kiss.

"Now, I am off to the inn to rest. I plan to be here early tomorrow and stay all day. Please devise an excuse for us to share luncheon on the terrace with Georgiana. Afterwards, the three of us shall take a walk about the grounds, and you will recall something you forgot in order to leave us alone. I shall gain her trust quickly. You shall see."

Having said that, Wickham kissed Mrs. Younge again and departed. The inn was within walking distance, and as he made his way down the pavement, he began to wonder if Miss Suzette still ran the brothel two streets over. By the time he reached the inn, he was in the mood to find out.

Pemberley
Elizabeth's bedroom
The next morning

Upon entering Elizabeth's bedroom, Florence found Mrs. Reynolds, Dr. Camryn and Mr. Darcy standing by the bed. It was obvious from Mr. Darcy's appearance that he had spent the entire night with his wife, for his clothes were wrinkled, his hair uncombed, and he needed a shave. Not daring to stare at that usually well-kept gentleman, she kept her eyes focused on Dr. Camryn, who was speaking to her mistress. When at length he passed her to exit the room, she got a glimpse of a very pale Elizabeth lying in bed and smiling up at her husband, who was holding her hand.

Having been unable to sleep for fear that Mrs. Darcy might not survive, Florence took her first peaceful breath since her mistress was brought home in a wagon the day before. Shoulders relaxing in relief, she continued to the dressing room with the towels and cloths she had brought upstairs. After placing them in a cabinet, she returned to the bedroom in time to see Mr. Darcy kiss his wife and leave the room. Mrs. Reynolds continued talking to Elizabeth, though shortly afterwards her mistress fell asleep again. Turning, the housekeeper caught sight of Florence watching and motioned for her to follow as she headed into the sitting room. Once the door was shut, the long-time servant addressed her.

"I know you will be pleased to hear that Dr. Camryn thinks Mrs. Darcy is doing well. Of course, he insists she stay in bed until such a time as he decides she is strong enough to be on her feet. Mr. Darcy has made it clear that he intends to be at her side until she has fully recovered, so you may not have much to keep you busy. Might I suggest that you check with Mr. or Mrs. Darcy often to see if there is anything they may want or need; otherwise, allow them their privacy."

"Yes, ma'am."

As William rushed to bathe, shave and change clothes so he could return to Elizabeth, he was completely unaware that his face had settled into a permanent scowl.

Adams waited until he had removed the last bit of whiskers with a newly sharpened razor before teasing, "Did your mother never warn you not to make a face for it might remain that way? I fear your expression might frighten Mrs. Darcy, not to mention that it is creating an ugly crease between your brows."

William stopped to observe himself in the mirror. "I was unaware that I was frowning," he replied. "However, after my wife nearly died in my arms, I am finding it hard to smile."

"According to Florence, the physician said Mrs. Darcy is doing remarkably well."

William's brows knit in question, so Adams quickly added, "I was worried about Mrs. Darcy's progress, but you were not available to ask. When I saw Florence leave the bedroom, I enquired of her."

"Camryn says that Mrs. Darcy is much improved; however, there is still such a great deal that could go wrong, so I am unable to rid myself of the dread that gripped my heart when she was injured."

Adams was touched by his confession. "Many prayers have been said for Mrs. Darcy. Trust that her improvement is a sign that God has granted your petition, as well as our own."

"Thank you, Adams," William said. "Your advice has always served me well."

"I try, sir."

When at last William was released from Adams' ministrations, he turned back to the mirror. "Does my hair need a trim?"

"Since Mrs. Darcy prefers your hair long, I would say wait another week."

William looked puzzled. "How do you know my wife's preference?"

Adams looked off. "Florence may have told me once when I mentioned giving you a haircut."

Shaking his head in astonishment, William walked into his bedroom to find his clothes waiting. As Adams began to help him dress, he said, "I wish to be there when the tray arrives from the kitchen. Elizabeth says she does not have an appetite, but I intend to coax her into eating something."

Adams smiled. "If anyone can coax her, I am certain it is you. Florence said—" The valet stopped when he realised he was gossiping.

William struggled not to smile. "What did Florence say?"

Sheepishly, Adams dropped his head. "That Mrs. Darcy is very much in love with you; however, that is obvious to anyone from the way she looks at you."

"God has given me another chance, Adams, and I am determined that from this day forward, it will be just as obvious that I am very much in love with her."

"I am certain it will be, sir."

Not even waiting until the valet could brush imaginary lint from his jacket, William rushed from the room. Adams watched him leave with a mixture of pride and satisfaction before turning to straighten up the room.

"Just as I told you, happiness was right under your nose all along."

Lady Henrietta's sitting room

As soon as Sarah left the room through the servants' corridor, Lady Henrietta declared, "Blast! Will nothing go in my favour?"

Lord Hartford rolled his eyes but did not reply to his cousin's outburst. Instead, he walked over to refill his glass with brandy.

His attitude caused her to turn on him. "I suppose the news makes you deliriously happy."

"I will not lie. I am relieved Elizabeth is alive."

"So, you do not care that her present condition has ruined my scheme to have her discover evidence that Fitzwilliam is having liaisons with one of the maids at Lady Anne's cottage."

"That is the most absurd allegation I have ever heard. Even I know that Darcy would never do such a thing."

"Elizabeth is young and impressionable. Who is to say that if presented with credible evidence that he had been meeting a woman in the cabin, she would dismiss it so readily? I even had a servant ready and willing to play the jilted mistress."

"My guess is the fictitious mistress is Sarah."

"Sarah is loyal. She would bear the blame, even knowing that if she made such allegations she would instantly be banished from Pemberley."

"It would also prevent her from getting future employment. Why would she agree?"

"Because she knows that if she is loyal to me, I will take care of her. I have only a brief opportunity to wreak havoc whilst Georgiana is away, and I do not have time to wait for Elizabeth to heal sufficiently to stumble upon Sarah waiting for Fitzwilliam at the cottage."

"Do you wish to know what I think?"

"No!"

"Well, I will tell you nonetheless. You are suffering under a mistaken notion that you can separate a couple who love one another."

"Before she was injured, Fitzwilliam did not act very much in love."

"Be that as it may, it is certainly evident now. And trust me: Elizabeth has always been in love with him."

"If I cannot separate their hearts, then I will separate them physically."

"What have you dreamed up now?"

"Mr. Sturgis is in Weymouth. Should something happen to him, Fitzwilliam would be obliged to seek him out. With him away, it would be easy to arrange for Elizabeth to suffer a fatal fall and blame it on unsteadiness caused by the blow to her head."

"Your ability to concoct wicked ideas astounds me."

"I do not know why. Was it not you who paid a band of gypsies[10] to take a servant girl you made pregnant from Liverpool, never to be seen or heard from again?"

"That was my father's idea, and it was before I reached the age of majority."

"Still, you were old enough to see it carried out."

Lord Hartford sighed. "To my discredit, I did. However, I made the leader of the band swear not to kill her. He said she would fetch a good price at the next gathering of their council, where he planned to use her to bargain for things he needed."

"Which makes it all well and good," Lady Henrietta said sarcastically.

He shrugged. "It was the best I could negotiate at the time. Had my father learned she was not going to die, he would have beaten me within an inch of my life."

Lady Henrietta reached out to pat his arm. "I well remember how cruel your father could be, which if memory serves, is how we became best friends in the first place. I made Mother intervene on your behalf when you were being beaten."

"I remember."

"You and I have come a long way since we escaped our fathers."

Lord Hartford tossed the rest of his brandy down his throat. "That we have."

---

10 The British spelling is gipsy or gipsies. For this book I have chosen to use the American spelling: gypsy or gypsies.

Chapter 27

Weymouth
Ten days later

Horace and Constance Keagan had proudly served as butler and housekeeper of Willowbend Hall for the past twenty years. Now in their late fifties, they had once played a vital role in the lives of the Darcys, including hosting a lengthy stay for Lady Anne and Fitzwilliam every summer and a visit by the entire family each January. However, after Georgiana's birth further weakened Lady Anne's delicate constitution, those visits had come to an end, replaced by occasional letters from the mistress and gifts on Boxing Day. After Lady Anne died, though the gifts continued, the correspondence ceased.

Willowbend's condition had largely been ignored by George Darcy after his wife's death, but the Keagans had been hopeful that when Fitzwilliam inherited the estate, he would do what was necessary to preserve the property or sell it. They were of a mind that anything was preferable to letting it decline; thus, when Mr. Sturgis arrived to examine the estate with the news that their new master intended to put it on the market, they were pleased.

Having served as Pemberley's steward for many years, Mr. Sturgis proved knowledgeable about spending wisely in order to obtain the best results. In fact, upon his arrival just two weeks past, he had commissioned repairs to the front steps, which had improved Willowbend's appearance immediately. Moreover, he was keeping a list of more costly repairs that he planned to present to Mr. Darcy, who had the final say in how best to spend the money allocated for the estate.

The Keagans were not only impressed with Sturgis' skill and intellect, they were very pleased with his company. Consequently, when he did not return one evening after a trip into Weymouth to meet with a prospective buyer, they grew concerned.

"What should we do?" Mrs. Keagan asked. "I do not wish to alarm the constable needlessly, but he has never stayed out past dark before."

"Perhaps he had a reason to stay in town tonight. If we do not hear from him by morning, I will inform the constable he is missing," her husband answered.

"I cannot stop feeling something awful has happened to him."

The butler reached to take his wife's hands. "Now, Mrs. Keagan, do not go borrowing trouble. Surely there is a rational reason for—"

A loud rapping on the front door halted his pronouncement.

"I knew it! Something is amiss," Mrs. Keagan cried.

Following her husband to the door, her worst fears were confirmed when she saw the local vicar standing on the portico, and her hands flew up to cover her mouth. Not as easily perturbed, Mr. Keagan stepped back and waved the reverend inside the house.

"Mr. Carnes! What brings you out at this hour?"

"It falls to me to be the bearer of sad news," he replied. "I was in Weymouth when someone brought a man into the inn who was found lying injured on the side of the road. Several people said he had been staying at Willowbend Hall; thus, to be of help to the constable, who had just returned from a long trip, I set out to inform you."

"I was afraid something had happened!" slipped from Mrs. Keagan's mouth before she quickly hushed under her husband's admonition to keep calm.

Addressing the vicar, he said, "We were just speaking of the fact that Mr. Sturgis, who is Mr. Darcy's steward at Pemberley, had not returned from a trip into town. May I assume that since you used the word injured, he is still alive?"

"He is. Though unconscious when he was brought in, he has since awakened; nonetheless, he made no sense when he tried to speak. Dr. Parker allows that the man suffered a hard lick to the back of his head and a broken arm, likely from falling off his horse. Parker put five stitches in the wound to his head and set his arm. He believes his mind will improve over time."

"Surely, foul play must be responsible," Mrs. Keagan stated.

"That is not clear yet; he could also have sustained the injury to his head when he fell. Most likely only Mr. Sturgis can say, but the constable thinks it odd that his pockets were not disturbed. His identity and papers were untouched."

"It appears he is fortunate to be alive!" Mr. Keagan declared. "We need to have him transported here."

"He is spending the night at the inn under the care of Dr. Parker," Mr. Carnes replied. "Tomorrow, when you check on his welfare, you may ask him about that."

"Thank you for coming all this way after dark to inform us," Mr. Keagan said.

"If I were Mr. Sturgis, I would want someone to do the same for me," the vicar replied. Replacing his hat and giving it a tap, he offered a wan smile. "Now let me get home before Mrs. Carnes sends a party out to look for me."

Waiting until the vicar was halfway down the front drive before they closed the door, Mrs. Keagan said, "What will you do?"

"I will send an express first thing in the morning," her husband replied. "Mr. Darcy will want to know immediately in the event—" Left unsaid was the prospect of Mr. Sturgis succumbing to his injuries.

"We must prepare the house, for the master will come as soon as he gets the news."

"I agree," Mr. Keagan said. "Let us retire and try to sleep. I fear tonight may be the last chance we have to rest for some time to come."

Pemberley

The days following Elizabeth's injury found William letting business go unattended whilst he saw to her recovery. He spent so much time in her bedroom, even taking his meals there, that he had a small desk brought up from the library and installed in place of the settee, thus allowing him to read his correspondence whilst keeping an eye on her as she slept. The moment she opened her eyes, however, he would rush to her side to ascertain if she felt well and begin where he left off—reading from one of many books of poetry from Pemberley's library. That, and encouraging her to eat the sumptuous food prepared by the kitchen, left little time for anything else. Hence, he had been having Florence sit with Elizabeth for a brief period at dawn so that he could bathe, shave and change clothes with Adams' help.

As the lump on her head shrank and Elizabeth's shoulder began to heal, Dr. Camryn agreed to her request to sit propped up with pillows. At that point, William knew it was only a matter of time until she would begin insisting on going out of doors, and that occurred on the fourth day of her confinement. Unable to refuse her anything, William promised that he would ask the physician. As it turned out, Dr. Camryn would not allow it, but promised to revisit the request as she improved. Several days later, in light of her despondency, he granted permission to have the chaise in her bedroom moved to the balcony, and from that day on, weather permitting, Elizabeth spent a short span of each day there. Occupying the chair next to the chaise, William would read whatever she chose, or they would hold hands, content merely to be together.

Everything changed, however, with the arrival of Colonel Fitzwilliam late one evening. Richard had received a letter from William just before leaving Town, informing him of what had happened, yet he was unprepared for how ill Elizabeth appeared upon his arrival. After paying his respects to his cousin's wife, he waited in the sitting room so that he and William could talk privately.

When at last his cousin walked out of the bedroom, he said what was on his heart without thinking. "Even though your letter painted a dire picture, I had no idea that Mrs. Darcy was so unwell."

Unconsciously, William ran a hand through his hair. "Dr. Camryn said I am blessed to still have her, since the amount of blood lost was significant for a person of her size, and, that does not take into account the seriousness of the injury to her head."

"She was always so...vibrant, I suppose is the word I am searching for," Richard said. "So tan and healthy, and now she looks so pale." Seeing the anguish in his cousin's face, he quickly realised he had said too much. "Forgive me for speaking so openly."

"You said nothing I have not already thought. It breaks my heart to see her this way."

Richard reached out to squeeze his cousin's shoulder. "I know." Then, trying to raise William's spirits, he smiled mischievously. "Let me take one worry off your mind. Rest assured that your old cousin will be fine seeing to himself whilst you go about the business of caring for your wife. Should I need anything, I know whom to ask, and if I require entertainment, I have to look no further than Lady Harlot and her minion."

William could not suppress a grin. "Should you choose that course, it will confirm my suspicion that you are a glutton for punishment."

"Or merely a man who enjoys watching a whore and a simpleton try to act the part of a lady and a gentleman."

William's smile broadened more. "You will never know how having you here has raised my spirits. Though I may be occupied caring for Elizabeth, never think I do not appreciate your presence."

Though greatly affected by this pronouncement, Richard tried not to show it with his reply. "I am always at your disposal, Cousin; you know that. Now, as for me, a long soak in hot water will be just what I need to cure my aching back."

As Richard began to walk away, William called, "Mrs. Reynolds has a draught that can help with that."

"Where do you think I am going, Cousin?" Richard called on his shoulder.

After Richard quit the room, William returned to check on Elizabeth.

Later that day

As it happened, William spent another brief period of time before dinner with Richard whilst Elizabeth slept; however, the second Mr. Walker announced that dinner was served, he returned to his wife, leaving his cousin to dine with Lady Henrietta and Lord Hartford or to request a tray be sent to his room. Tired from his trip, Richard chose the latter.

Upon entering Elizabeth's bedroom, William was shocked to find her on her feet, holding onto a bedpost for support. Rushing towards her, he stopped when she held up a hand.

"Please, Fitzwilliam. If I keep putting off walking, it will take forever to regain my strength."

Though he did not reply, his eyes reflected his anxiety. Letting go of the post, she gingerly walked towards him, eventually falling into his waiting arms. Relieved, he kissed the top of her head.

"I think it fortuitous that Colonel Fitzwilliam has arrived," Elizabeth began, "and I pray that his company will take your mind off—"

"Nothing can take my mind off you, Elizabeth," William declared fervently, placing an even firmer kiss in her hair.

"I did not mean to offend, dearest," she answered, gently smiling at the intensity of his pronouncement. "I only meant to say that, since my health is improving, perhaps you should return to your normal routine. After all, Pemberley has so many people counting on you to make wise decisions, and it would upset me to know that I might be a hindrance to—"

"You could never be a hindrance," William declared even more emphatically, tightening his arms around her. "Without you, nothing else matters."

Elizabeth kissed his chest through his linen shirt. "Oh, William, nothing makes me happier than knowing your feelings reflect my own, but no matter how much we both wish it, we simply cannot hide away and let the world go by. You have duties to perform, and I need to resume mine as well. I know how much you love to ride early in the morning, and it would please me greatly if you would resume that habit since Richard is here to ride with you."

Gladdened to hear her use William instead of Fitzwilliam, he said, "These last few days have spoilt me. I do not wish to give up one minute of the time I spend with you."

She leaned back to look in his eyes. Finding them full of love, she stood on tiptoes to brush her lips across his. "I know, my love, but just think how rewarding it will be when we reunite each evening."

A passionate kiss followed, and once it ended, William looked down at her, smiling. "Only you could make me believe that being parted from you could have a silver lining."

"What time we spend together will be so much sweeter—just you wait and see."

They were engaged in another fervent kiss when Mrs. Reynolds, followed by two maids carrying trays of food, opened the bedroom door. Quickly closing the door, the housekeeper rapped upon it and this time waited until summoned to enter.

The next morning

Though dawn was breaking, a knee-deep mist still lingered over the earth as William and Richard atop Zeus and Titan departed the stables. Galloping across the pastures as they had since they were boys, they reached the treeline of the highest point on the estate just as the sun was visible on the horizon. William reined Zeus to a stop, threw his leg over the saddle and slid to the ground. From this vantage point, the manor house appeared small in the distance, and he walked over to a fallen tree and sat down to take in the scene coming to life in the valley below.

Having noted his cousin's solemnity all morning, as Richard

dismounted he said, "I do not recall ever having seen you quite like this, Darcy."

"What do you mean?"

"Normally you are very much in charge of your faculties; however, though you are here today, your mind is elsewhere. Dare I suggest that you left it, along with your heart, at Pemberley?"

William offered him a wan smile. "I will not deny my heart is with Elizabeth."

"I am glad. The more thought I gave to your marriage, the more I was convinced that Mrs. Darcy was the perfect woman for you. As I recall, I tried to tell you that."

"Would that I had listened to you sooner."

"Now, that is something I never thought to hear! Can I trouble you to write it down? Then I can show it to you the next time you ignore my advice."

"Watch your tongue. You could be on the way back to London sooner than you expect."

Richard guffawed. "Your threats no longer scare me. A man as deeply in love as you cannot be bothered to make others miserable."

"I do love Elizabeth with all my heart; what is more, I have since the day we met, which makes my behaviour towards her even more incomprehensible. Since her arrival at Pemberley, I assumed she was communicating with Lucas through her sister. It was only after Bingley informed me that Elizabeth had broken off their friendship before she came to me that my eyes were opened."

"Jealousy makes fools of us all."

"I was acting like a fool, but no one could have convinced me of it. I am embarrassed to remember that upon our first meeting, I thought her an unsuitable match." He shook his head. "All the time it was I who was not worthy of her."

"Do not blame yourself. You and I are the result of our upbringing. Separation of the classes has been drummed into our heads from infancy."

"Yet, at some point, should a man not learn to think for himself...to not be afraid to trust his own instincts? She was nearly killed protecting me, Richard. What kind of woman would do such a thing?"

"One who loves you more than she loves herself," Richard said, sitting down beside William.

"When Elizabeth was shot, I vowed that if God would only let her live, I would spend the rest of my life showing her that kind of devotion."

For a time, they watched in silence as a group of foals played in a nearby field. At length, Richard spoke. "I have dreaded telling you this, Darcy. God knows you have your hands full as it is; however, Lord Appleby asked me to inform you of a development regarding the loan he co-signed."

As Richard repeated what his godfather had said, William's expression grew even more sombre. When he had finished, Richard pulled a small bag from his pocket and emptied the fake jewels into his cousin's hand. "These are the jewels in question."

Stunned, William reached for a brooch and held it up. "This is one of the pieces our mother left Georgiana." Taking a deep breath, he let it go. "Do not say a word to my sister about this. Once I sell the estate in Weymouth, I will restore the brooch, and hopefully, she will never notice."

"I think that an excellent idea. It is admirable that no one believes you had any part in the deception, and since Lord Appleby's signature, along with the other jewels, is enough to keep the loan afloat, you will not have that worry hanging over your head." William remained silent, so Richard ventured, "What are you thinking?"

"That surely Father did not have—" William stopped and shook his head. "No! After almost bankrupting Pemberley, I cannot eliminate his participation in this violation of Georgiana's trust or my own."

"For what it is worth, Lord Appleby and I think Lady Harlot was the perpetrator."

"She may well have been, but Father had to have given her unfettered access to the Darcy jewels. They are only for the use of the current mistress and are supposed to be locked in the safe when not being worn."

"What will you do now?"

"For now, nothing. Elizabeth's health is the most important thing at present. I will not concentrate on anything save her complete recovery. Besides, if my stepmother had the jewels altered, it would be difficult to prove she acted without Father's permission."

"This is true. Still, there is the outside chance that someone else was the culprit. Knowing you would not mind, I contacted some associates in London, and they are presently trying to determine who was responsible for replacing the jewels with fakes."

"Thank you."

A whinny brought both men's eyes to the pasture, where a stallion had stretched his head over a fence in order to touch noses with a mare in the next enclosure.

Richard laughed. "It seems love is in the air."

"Speaking of love, I would like to return to my wife in time to break my fast with her."

Richard stood. "Say no more! I could use a plate of eggs and ham, as well as some of Mrs. Lantrip's famous bread. Oh, and a goodly portion of freshly-churned butter and plum jam to go on it!"

William smiled. "Perhaps I need to tell Mrs. Reynolds to double the amount of jam put up this year."

"What a great idea! That would allow me to take some when I return to London. Heaven knows the jam Mother's cook puts up is horrendous."

Richard kept up a steady conversation the entire trip back to the manor. All that was left for William to do was to occasionally nod his head in agreement or say, "hmmm" from time to time. If truth be known, his mind was not on what his cousin was saying, but with Elizabeth and what she could be doing that very second.

Ramsgate
Younge's Art Academy

As Georgiana and Lady Esme made their way down the garden path behind the academy, they teased one another about a mutual classmate. Mr. Pettigrew, one year older than Georgiana, was a handsome lad with light blond hair and blue eyes. Though the boys had their lessons in another room, he was easily the most popular male amongst the girls whenever they joined classes in the dining room.

"I think him the most handsome man of my acquaintance," Lady Esme, all of twelve years of age, proclaimed.

Georgiana tried not to smile too broadly at her use of the term *man*. "Not wishing her friend to know that she found Mr. Pettigrew handsome as well, she said, "He is tolerable, I dare say, but too young for my taste."

"Too young!" Lady Esme exclaimed, halting. "How old does a man have to be to catch your eye?"

"At least eighteen," Georgiana declared decidedly. "Anyone younger is far too immature to carry on a decent conversation."

Lady Esme resumed walking. "Oh, I could never think of anything to say to someone that old."

"As you grow older, you will learn there is not much difference between a person Mr. Pettigrew's age and one who is eighteen."

Suddenly George Wickham, in the guise of Lord Worley, was standing in front of them, blocking the path. Removing his hat, he swept it across his body as he bowed. "Good morning, Miss Darcy, Lady Esme. What a lovely day for a walk."

Neither girl being fond of the man, they curtseyed but did not speak.

"Lady Esme, Mrs. Younge asked me to tell you that she is waiting in the parlour to speak with you." As the young girl's brows knit with worry, he added, "I think it concerns the upcoming art sale."

"Thank you, Lord Worley," Lady Esme replied, casting an anxious glance towards her friend. "Will you go with me, Georgiana?"

"Why not stay and walk with me?" Wickham asked.

Recalling when she was left alone with Mr. Wickham after sharing luncheon with him and Mrs. Younge, Georgiana replied, "As I explained once before, it is not proper for us to be left unchaperoned."

"Nonsense! If Mrs. Younge has no reservations about our being left alone, why should you?"

Georgiana's chin came up. "I was taught that a young woman's reputation was of the utmost importance, and I do not intend to have mine sullied." She grabbed Lady Esme's hand. "Come! We had better not keep Mrs. Younge waiting."

Once they were far enough away that Wickham could not hear, Lady Esme whispered, "You are brilliant, Georgiana. I would never have thought fast enough to avoid being left alone with him."

"Brother taught me to stand up for myself, and I advise you to learn to do the same. Prepare ahead of time what you will say and practice saying it aloud with firmness. Brother had me practice as he and I walked the trails on our estate when there was no one close enough to hear. It makes it much easier to say it again when you feel you must."

"I wish I had a brother like yours."

Georgiana stopped, pulling her to a halt. "I wish you did, too; however, if I tell you all the things my brother taught me, and you follow his advice, it will be almost like having a brother of your own."

Lady Esme smiled. "I had not thought of that."

Georgiana began walking again, taking Lady Esme with her. "Just listen to me, and you will keep your reputation."

As Wickham watched Georgiana escape, he hissed under his breath, "You little prig! You will either warm to me and go to Gretna Green willingly, or I shall drag you every step of the way."

Chapter 28

Pemberley
One week later

Colonel Fitzwilliam was thoroughly enjoying his stay at Pemberley, due in no small part to Mrs. Lantrip. He always made a point of going to the kitchen to compliment the cook whenever she served something he especially enjoyed. Therefore, whenever he was in residence, she made certain to prepare the meals he favoured: roast pheasant or lamb, baked ham, potatoes, turnips and carrots with parsley, molasses biscuits, and apple cake.

Noticing that he needed a little extra tug to button his coat, Richard decided it might be best if he started exercising more vigorously whilst he was eating so sumptuously. Hoping that William might join him in a fencing match, he headed towards his cousin's dressing room door. He was about to knock, when it opened and a maid carrying a basket of laundry walked out.

Mr. Adams was in the dressing room and caught sight of him. "May I be of service, Colonel?"

Richard entered the room, looking about curiously. "I wondered if Darcy might be late rising this morning. Given the rain last evening, we decided not to ride this morning, and I was seduced into sleeping late. I thought perhaps he was, too."

William's valet smiled. "I am afraid he is not here; however, if you will follow me—"

Richard followed Adams onto the balcony and toward the stone railing that surrounded it. At the far end, Adams leaned over and looked sharply to the right. "Ah, just as I thought. He is still in the garden with Mrs. Darcy."

Mimicking Adams' actions, Richard caught sight of William just as he leaned down to kiss Elizabeth, who was sitting in a white swing underneath a huge tree.

"I see that he is agreeably engaged," Richard said, "so I shall busy myself in the billiards room. That is one exercise I can do alone."

"I am afraid you may need to entertain yourself even more now that Mr. Darcy has finally realised Mrs. Darcy is his perfect match," Adams replied, smiling broadly.

"I have always told Darcy there are two people he can count on for the best advice—you and me!" Richard said, laughing. "I realise that everything will change now that my cousin has fallen in love, but I would not have it any other way. He deserves every happiness."

"I could not agree more."

Richard was still in the billiards room when William entered an hour later. "There you are! I was wondering why you had not come to find me."

"I did look for you, Cousin," Richard said, sinking the next-to-last ball remaining on the table. "But you were in the garden with Mrs. Darcy, and I did not wish to intrude."

"You would not have been intruding."

"Do not be so obliging. You almost lost your wife; naturally you want to be with her. Believe me when I say that I could not be more pleased to see you so content. Where is Mrs. Darcy now?"

"She felt the need to rest, so I escorted her back to her bedroom."

Richard sank the last ball on the table, then straightened. "Did Dr. Camryn say anything more about her continued dizziness?"

"No. He is still hopeful that once the lump on her head subsides, she will no longer be unsteady."

"I know that is your hope, too, for it is also mine."

William placed a hand on Richard's shoulder. "Thank you for caring so much about Elizabeth." Then he smiled mischievously. "Would playing a round for our usual sixpence interest you?"

"Suppose we make it more interesting?" Richard asked. "Say, a shilling?"

"A shilling it is!"

Almost two hours later, Mr. Walker appeared at the open door. Neither gentleman noticed him, for they were well into another match; thus, he knocked on the doorframe.

"Yes, Walker?"

"This express just arrived from Mr. Keagan at Willowbend Hall. I thought you might want to read it straightaway."

William set his cue stick against the wall and took the letter from the butler. "Thank you. That will be all."

After Mr. Walker left, Richard said, "I find it odd that it is from the butler and not Mr. Sturgis."

"My thoughts exactly."

Sliding a finger under the seal, William opened the missive and began to read. As he did, his expression darkened.

"Darcy?" was all Richard managed to say before William began to speak.

"Mr. Sturgis was found badly injured on the side of the road between Weymouth and Willowbend Hall. Mr. and Mrs. Keagan are seeing to him with the help of the local physician, but at the time of this letter they describe his health as precarious."

"Do they know what happened?"

"Mr. Keagan suspects foul play."

"What will you do?"

"Though it pains me even to think of being parted from Elizabeth, I must travel to Weymouth."

"But Mrs. Darcy is still so unwell."

"Which makes it all the more unbearable. Still, according to Dr. Camryn, Elizabeth's life is no longer in danger, and I have no choice but to see about Mr. Sturgis. Mrs. Reynolds will take excellent care of her, and I will ask Reverend and Mrs. Green to increase their visits whilst I am away."

"I am going with you."

"This is supposed to be your break from duty, a time to relax. Stay here and keep Elizabeth company."

"Whilst I enjoy her company, if Mr. Keagan suspects foul play, I can best serve Mrs. Darcy by making certain you do not come back in a box."

"We have no way of knowing this was not an accident. Until we do, let us not jump to conclusions. And, whatever you do, do not mention anything of that sort to Elizabeth. For now, I shall tell her only that he was injured falling from his horse."

"I agree that would be best."

"Can you be ready to leave tomorrow morning?"

"I am an officer in His Majesty's service. I can be ready in less than an hour."

"Tomorrow morning is soon enough. We shall leave at first light. Pray do not say anything about this at dinner. I shall tell Elizabeth after we retire."

The dining room that evening

Coinciding with Richard's arrival, Elizabeth had professed a desire to begin eating meals in the dining room again. Though William knew it was because of his cousin's presence, he could not stop smiling whenever she took her place beside him at the table. He had arranged for one chair on either side of the table to be removed, increasing the space between those seated down the length of it; thus, though Richard and Elizabeth were still seated close by, on his right and left, Lady Henrietta and Lord Hartford were now seated further away.

The first time she had come downstairs to dine, Lady Henrietta did her best to feign joy that Elizabeth had been reunited with the family at the dinner table. Of course, William was convinced of her insincerity, and his instincts proved true when she began to hold forth the possibility that Elizabeth might never regain her ability to walk unaided. Infuriated, he had tersely cut her off and changed the subject. Today Lady Henrietta once again conjectured on Elizabeth's chances of a complete recovery, this time adding that she would be glad to help Elizabeth with her duties if she so desired.

Livid at the audacity of bringing up a subject that he had closed decidedly, William did not give Elizabeth a chance to respond. Instead, he said, "Dr. Camryn assures me that Elizabeth's health is progressing agreeably, and that she will heal completely, so I do not want that issue raised again. Moreover, as I recall, you never cared for the duties of your office when you *were* the mistress of Pemberley, so I am dumbfounded as to why you would offer to assist my wife with them now."

"I was only trying to be helpful, Fitzwilliam," Lady Henrietta retorted.

"Of course. What other motive could there be?" William replied sarcastically.

He felt Elizabeth's hand on his arm and looked to see her beautiful eyes pleading with him to say no more. Giving her a loving smile, he resumed eating with renewed enthusiasm.

His stepmother was uncharacteristically silent the rest of the meal, though Lord Hartford now and again joined in the conversation maintained by William, Elizabeth and Richard. At the conclusion of dinner, Lady Henrietta stood, declaring her intention of entertaining in the music room.

"Elizabeth wishes to retire early, so naturally, I will join her," William said.

Knowing how early they planned to leave in the morning, Richard followed his cousin's lead. "I am weary; I believe I shall retire, as well."

"I would enjoy hearing you play, Rietta," Lord Hartford declared.

Seeing that the audience she most desired had vanished, Lady Henrietta stalked out of the room with her cousin right on her heels.

After escorting Elizabeth to her bedroom, William read the letter from Weymouth aloud, leaving out the part about Mr. Keagan suspecting foul play. By the time he had finished, tears were pooled in her dark eyes.

"Of course, you must go, my darling," she stammered, cupping his cheek lovingly. "Mr. Sturgis deserves our support and prayers."

Her misery mirrored his own, so William pulled her into his arms. He could feel her trembling with the struggle not to cry, and aware that it was his decision to cause this pain, his vaunted sense of duty almost shattered.

"Trust me, Elizabeth!" he declared fervently. "I will not be parted from you one second longer than is absolutely crucial."

She pulled back to look in his eyes, revealing that tears were now rolling down her face. "I believe you."

A searing kiss was interrupted when Florence knocked on the door. Leaving his wife in her maid's capable hands to get undressed, William went to his bedroom to do likewise. Following a routine begun when she was injured, Adams had been dismissed after helping him dress for dinner, leaving William free to undress himself, don whatever he wished, and return to his wife.

When he entered her bedroom next, he was surprised to find Elizabeth was not in bed. Instead, she sat on the settee, and the moment he walked in, she stood.

Instantaneously, it was as though all the air left the room. Dressed in a thin, ivory-coloured, silk robe, even with the faint light of the candles it was obvious Elizabeth wore nothing beneath it. The desire William struggled to quash every time he held her in his arms since her injury, rose with a vengeance.

His voice trembled. "You are making it very difficult for me to resist loving you as I desire, Elizabeth."

"I was hoping to make it impossible."

As though starving for each other, their lips met, and the kisses became more passionate until William drew back, breathing heavily. "Dr. Camryn has forbidden us to resume marital relations until—"

"Dr. Camryn has no idea how much I long for you."

Elizabeth's pronouncement earned another kiss so fervent that her knees began to buckle. Immediately, William untied her robe, and as it floated to the floor, he picked her up and carried her to the bed.

He hesitated. "We must not allow my weight to rest on you. Do you trust me?"

"With my life."

That declaration was rewarded with an equally passionate kiss before he laid her on the bed. "Can you lie on your right side without pain?"

Rolling on that side, Elizabeth replied, "I can."

Discarding his nightshirt and robe, William slid into the bed behind her. Pulling her silky hair away from her neck, he began tasting the satin skin there before moving across her shoulder. His hands slid around her body, cupping her breasts. Lost in ecstasy, one hand dipped lower, splaying across her flat abdomen to pull her body closer against his, and soon they were joined once more. A low moan escaped her throat as he began a rhythm they knew well, and it was not long until they knew the heights of passion.

When William went to pull away, Elizabeth pleaded. "No. Pray let us stay as we are until I fall asleep."

"If that is your desire, my love."

"Promise me."

"Anything."

"Promise you will love me again before you leave."

"I promise."

Lady Henrietta's sitting room
The next morning

"I care not that Fitzwilliam left for Weymouth, for that was my intention all along. I am only angry he left without a word to me," Lady Henrietta huffed, throwing an empty cup against the hearth and watching it shatter. "After all, I am a part of this family, not a servant to be ignored!"

Lord Hartford almost choked on his scone. "What a ludicrous

thing to say! Fitzwilliam has never considered you a part of *his* family."

Lady Henrietta was about to upbraid him, when her maid spoke. "In addition to Mr. Darcy's departure, rumours abound that Mr. Sturgis must be in some type of trouble for the master to rush off to Weymouth whilst Mrs. Darcy has not completely healed from her injury. And by taking the colonel, who is known for his ability to ferret out traitors and spies, the entire situation becomes even more suspect. Have no fear, however. I shall get the truth out of one of the footmen."

Sarah Perry's reputation as a loose woman was the talk of the male servants, according to a groom Lord Hartford overheard gossiping the last time he was at the stables.

"I have no doubt that you will." Hartford's insult went overlooked by Sarah, who was eager to do whatever it took to make her mistress happy, even if that meant raising her skirts now and again.

"I should return downstairs," Sarah said. "I want to talk to the night maids before they retire. Those who work during the day are less apt to gossip." She curtseyed and disappeared through the servants' passageway.

"Are you going to tell me what you did to Mr. Sturgis, or must I guess?" Hartford asked, pouring himself another cup of tea.

"I called on the man who sent my first husband to his eternal reward to do the same to Sturgis. Apparently, he botched the mission, since they say the steward is still alive."

"I do not recall ever hearing you say you murdered Lord Wharton."

"Murder is such a crass word! I prefer to say I arranged for him to take a spill from his horse."

"Have you no conscience, Rietta? Do you want to burn in Hades when you die?"

"I am not afraid of Hades. I lived there when my father was alive and again when I married Lord Wharton."

"Good Lord! I hope we never cross swords."

"As long as you do not betray me, you have nothing to fear." She walked over to pick up another cup from the tray and poured herself more tea. Then taking a bite from the scone on her plate, she said, "At any rate, now that Fitzwilliam is gone, I will be free to see that Elizabeth meets with an unfortunate accident."

"If you harm her, you will not get away with it. Fitzwilliam will see that you hang, if he does not strangle you himself."

"Fitzwilliam may be the master of Pemberley, but he is not above the law. I will make it appear accidental and he will not be able to do anything to me."

"I would not stake my life on that."

"That is because you have never been a gambler. I have."

On the road to Weymouth
The next day

They were nearly to their first stop for the night at Derby, and William had not said a word since passing through Pemberley's massive gates. Given what had ensued before they were out of sight of the manor, Richard could not fault him for that.

Darcy's coach had almost completed going around the circular drive when Elizabeth suddenly appeared on the portico. Fortuitously, from where William was seated, he had a view of the house, and at the sight of his wife, he ordered the driver to halt and leapt from the vehicle. Like a madman, he ran across the lawn and up the front steps two at a time until he reached Elizabeth and wrapped her in his arms.

Though he had no way of knowing what was said, Richard was greatly affected by the sight of William and Elizabeth clinging to each other. He lost sight of the couple as the coach slowly circled the drive again, and by the time it stopped, and a footman jumped down to open the door, William was there waiting. A quick glance at the portico revealed it was now empty.

It had occurred to Richard to ask if all was well, but the look on Darcy's face had dissuaded him. He had never seen his cousin so shaken, and he did not want to say anything to make the situation worse.

For his part, though it may have looked as though he was watching the landscape, in truth William was repeatedly reliving the last moments spent with his wife. Grateful to have seen Elizabeth rush from the house with Mrs. Reynolds right behind her, he tried not to dwell on what might have happened had she been too late to stop the coach. In any case, by the time he reached her, she was not only weeping, but murmuring countless apologies for both acting improperly in front of the servants and for delaying him. She had been so emotional that it had taken a kiss to quiet her.

Afterwards, he had framed her face in his hands. "Never apologise for loving me, Elizabeth. If you wish to have me return a thousand times to say farewell, that is what I shall do."

She had cried even harder then. "Oh, William, I love you so much that it is almost unbearable!"

"I feel the same about you."

Knowing he must go, he held her tightly one last time and whispered a verse from a favourite poem written by Robert Burns[11] into her ear:

And fare thee weel, my only luve!
And fare thee weel, a while!
And I will come again, my luve,
Tho' it ware ten thousand mile!

To make Elizabeth laugh, he had spoken with an exaggerated Scottish burr, poorly rendered, and it had worked. Pleased, he kissed her one last time before motioning for Mrs. Reynolds to come forwards to steady her.

His last glimpse of Elizabeth was of tears rolling down her checks as she paused at the door and mouthed "I love you" be-

---

11 **Robert Burns** (25 January 1759 – 21 July 1796), also known as the Bard of Ayrshire, Ploughman Poet and various other names and epithets, was a Scottish poet and lyricist.

fore disappearing into the manor. He recalled wondering at that moment how he could possibly live without her for the next few weeks.

Chapter 29

Pemberley
The next day

Elizabeth was enjoying the sunlight and Clancy's company on the balcony when Florence suddenly appeared. "Mrs. Green is here, ma'am."

She knew that William had asked the Greens to visit more often whilst he was away, so she was not surprised. Having been told that the Reverend and Mrs. Green were responsible for keeping her husband's emotions from spiralling out of control during the first crucial hours after she was hurt, and that they had stayed at Pemberley until her recovery was assured, Elizabeth felt even more indebted to the couple.

"Thank you, Florence. Ask her to come in, please."

Soon her friend appeared at the door and smiled widely before walking towards her across the balcony. As Elizabeth began to stand, Clancy jumped from her lap to the floor.

"Please do not rise on my behalf," Mrs. Green said.

"It does me good to be on my feet."

"How are you, my dear?" Judith Green asked, giving her a hug. "Has the dizziness finally subsided?"

"Not entirely, but I believe it has lessened. In fact, I feel quite well," Elizabeth replied, feigning a smile.

The vicar's wife pulled back to study her. "You are not very good at pretence."

Immediately, Elizabeth's countenance fell. "Whilst my health is improving, I cannot truthfully say I am well. I miss William so desperately that I ache inside. I can think of nothing but his return."

Mrs. Green sat down on the edge of the chaise and patted the spot beside her. As Elizabeth sat back down, the older woman's arm went around her waist.

"Oh, my dear, I know that feeling well. Once a man and a woman truly become one—heart, body and soul—it is painful to be parted, even for a short while. That is because you are now half of a whole."

"Novels make love sound so idyllic, but when William left for Weymouth, it was as though someone reached into my chest and pulled out my heart."

"I wish I could tell you that it gets better in time, but I found it exactly the opposite. Still, I would not trade the love that James and I share for the unremarkable existence of most married couples. You and I are blessed, Elizabeth, for it is very rare to love and to be loved in return that deeply."

Elizabeth looked down self-consciously. "I feared I was just being childish."

"From the start of our acquaintance, your attitude has impressed me. I have often told James that you are mature far beyond your years."

"If you had seen the way I acted when William left for Weymouth, you would not say that."

"Tell me."

"I embarrassed myself, and him, in front of the servants."

"I find that hard to believe."

"Because of my dizziness, William did not want me to venture downstairs to say our farewells; thus, we parted in our suite. Not long after he left the room, however, a dread washed over me. I cannot explain it, except to say I felt as though I might not see him again for a very long time. Somehow, I managed not to fall as I recklessly flew down the stairs, frightening Mrs. Reynolds when I rushed past her in the foyer. Once on the portico, I realised the coach was nearly at the end of the drive, and I could not hold back my tears. Mrs. Reynolds had just begun to console me when the coach came to an abrupt stop, the door flew open, and William leapt out, crossing the lawn towards me."

"Was he upset?"

Still in awe at her husband's actions, Elizabeth shook her head. "In truth, he was everything that is good and kind. He held me, tried to allay my fears, and even coaxed a laugh from me before he departed."

"With four sisters, surely you know women are most susceptible to childish actions when they do not feel well. Give yourself permission to be less than perfect, Elizabeth. We all are." Then, bending over to scratch Clancy behind the ears, she said, "Now, are we taking Mr. Clancy for a walk in the flower garden again today, or do you wish to blaze another path?"

Hearing his name, Clancy tilted his head to the side as though trying to decipher what was being said.

"I would dearly love to sit on the pier and feed the fish, and I imagine Clancy is eager to bark at them whilst they dart back and forth."

"If you agree to tell me the instant you feel tired, we will walk as far as you wish."

"I promise."

It was not long before both women were circling the lake, whilst the little white dog ran circles around them.

Another balcony

"I will never get close enough to Elizabeth to facilitate an accident if Mrs. Green insists on monopolising her time every day," Lady Henrietta exclaimed, angrily motioning towards the scene at the lake.

Peering in the same direction, Sarah Perry's nose crinkled with similar disdain. "It seems to me you have only one choice, ma'am."

Judgement impaired by all the liquor she had consumed, Lady Henrietta mumbled, "And what, pray tell, is that?"

"Create a situation that will keep Mrs. Green elsewhere. If

her husband was ill or injured, surely she would have to abandon Mrs. Darcy to care for him."

"True, but accomplishing that could be risky. Besides, it would take more time than I have."

"Perhaps you could make certain her carriage could not be used."

"Or the animal used to draw it," Lady Henrietta said with a wry smile. "Horses go lame every day. Most likely, Elizabeth would lend her another animal once she knew, but I need only one day to work my plan."

"There is a groom who will do a favour for me, provided I do one for him." Sarah said with no emotion.

"Then by all means, have him sneak over to the parsonage tonight and make certain the Green's horse meets with an injury. Nothing so drastic as to raise suspicions, mind you, just sufficient to render it unable to pull a carriage for a few days. That should afford me enough time." Sarah curtseyed and turned. "By the way, not a mention of this to Lord Hartford. I want him kept unaware of my plans." As Sarah went to leave again, Lady Henrietta added, "Before you head to the stables, check to see if the post has come. I still hope to intercept any letters from Georgiana."

As Sarah left, Lady Henrietta was still watching Elizabeth and Mrs. Green in the distance. After a few seconds, she held up her glass of brandy in a salute.

"Poor Elizabeth. Soon to be nothing but a memory for Fitzwilliam—a grave to grieve over. And why not? I grieve for my mother every day, thanks to George Darcy."

Longbourn
The library

Now that Mr. Bennet was able to get about, howbeit with a slight limp, he began to spend most of the day in his beloved library, just as he had in the past. Though he missed his favourite child, Jane had begun spending more time with him of late, and life seemed almost back to normal. Today, whilst he read one of his latest acquisitions, he was doing his best to ignore the sound of an argument in the parlour between his wife and youngest child, when a sudden knock on the door gained his attention. Before he could reply, Jane, who had walked into Meryton with Mary earlier, stuck her head inside.

"May I come in, Papa?"

"Of course."

She entered, closing the door behind her. "Hill said you received a letter from Lizzy whilst I was away."

"I did," Mr. Bennet replied, sliding the missive across his desk. A lump filled his throat when Jane sat down in the chair Lizzy had always occupied and began to read it.

Not wishing to upset her father, Elizabeth had purposely not yet mentioned her injury; thus, the letter was brief. It was not long before Jane looked up, smiling. "It is as though Lizzy cannot say enough good things about Mr. Darcy."

"That pleases me exceedingly. My greatest fear when Lizzy left for Derbyshire was how Mr. Darcy would react to her desire to made amends. I worried he might be too proud to forgive your sister and start anew; however, your uncle insisted that the gentleman would eventually make the right decision, and apparently Edward was right."

"I cannot lie. I was worried, too. Still, I knew Mr. Darcy would be a better match for Lizzy than John Lucas."

"I agree. Whilst I had rather she marry Lucas than Collins, he would never have earned Lizzy's respect, if only because he and books seem to be indifferent acquaintances."

Jane laughed, and he continued, "Moreover, Sir William once told me that he feared he would have to pay someone to take his son's exams in order for him to graduate."

"At least we need not worry about Mr. Darcy's intellect. Charles said he graduated at the top of his class. I have even heard him refer to Mr. Darcy as the smartest man among his acquaintances."

"I can understand Mr. Bingley's admiration," Mr. Bennet said with a wry grin. "However, your uncle said the same thing, so I am inclined to believe it."

A brief smile appeared and suddenly vanished from Jane's face. "I hesitate to ask since you are still recovering—"

"As the head of this house, I feel well enough to assert my authority. Ask what you will."

"It is just…since Charles and I became engaged, Mama has talked of nothing save having him speak to Mr. Darcy about an invitation to Pemberley for our family."

"I think it too soon to inflict your mother and sisters upon Mr. Darcy. Let him get more settled into this marriage before he witnesses their foibles first hand."

"My thoughts exactly," Jane said, "only—"

"Only?"

"Charles is beginning to dread coming here because of Mama's insistence."

"I do not believe anything could stop your fiancé from seeing you—even a zealous creature like your mother; however, I will put an end to it."

Suddenly, the door to his library flew open, and Mrs. Bennet rushed in. "There you are!" she said the minute she spied Jane. "I thought you were still in Meryton until I found Mary reading in her room. Why did you not find me when you came home? You know we are expected at Lucas Lodge this afternoon for tea."

Before Jane could answer, Mr. Bennet winked at her and turned to his wife. "Mrs. Bennet, may I have a word with you?"

Mrs. Bennet glanced nervously at her eldest daughter before saying, "Of course."

"Jane, if you would leave us."

Delighted to escape, Jane jumped to her feet. "I shall change clothes and be ready to leave for Lucas Lodge when you are, Mama."

As soon as the door closed behind Jane, Mr. Bennet spoke. "Sit down, Fanny." Reluctantly, she did as told. "It has come to my attention that because Mr. Darcy has not yet invited our family to Pemberley, you have been troubling Mr. Bingley to ask his friend about extending an invitation. Do you think him capable of twisting Mr. Darcy's arm?"

"Who told you?"

"How I know is not important, but given your answer, I assume it is true."

"I do not deny it! After all, that is what well-mannered people do—invite their new families to their homes to get better acquainted. I assumed a gentleman like Mr. Darcy had just forgotten and would welcome a reminder."

"As you well know, Lizzy returned to her husband under trying circumstances, and descending upon Pemberley now could make the situation worse."

"I do not see how visiting my beloved daughter could—"

"Please refrain from mentioning the subject again. If I hear that you have, I shall have no recourse but to take drastic measures to remind you."

"Drastic measures?"

"It will involve withholding your pin money."

"But, but—"

"Six months for the first infraction, Mrs. Bennet. I do not think you want to hear the next."

Apparently finding the library too warm, Fanny Bennet began fanning herself with her hand. "I do not consider speaking to Mr. Bingley about an invitation wrong." When Mr. Bennet began to scowl, she quickly added, "However, since you had rather I not mention the subject again, I will abide by your wishes, even though we may never be invit—"

"And you will not mention a word of this conversation to Jane or Mr. Bingley," he interjected.

She parroted, "Not a word to Jane or Mr. Bingley," before rushing from the room, leaving Thomas Bennet chuckling to himself.

Weymouth
Willowbend Hall

Four days following his injury, Mr. Sturgis was pleased to awaken in a bed at Willowbend Hall. It had been the first time he had rested well since regaining his faculties, for once he had, he discovered the walls of the inn were so thin that he could hear conversations from the adjoining rooms, as well as from the hall. That made it difficult to sleep, and Dr. Parker had given in to his pleas to allow the Keagans to transport him back to the estate using a coach the Darcys had left behind years before. That vehicle still looked new, for the head groom had little to do other than see to the animals and keep all the equipment in good repair, even if it was never used.

The Keagans saw to his every need, and Sturgis was certain he would not have been treated any better had he been at Pemberley. His only concern was that Mr. Darcy had been informed, which meant his employer would take time from his busy schedule to come to Weymouth—of that he was certain. Fitzwilliam Darcy had always depended on his help, and now that the roles were reversed, it was unsettling to the steward to say the least.

Being self-sufficient by nature, Sturgis had every intention of getting back on his feet quickly and, to this end, when Mrs. Keagan knocked and entered his room with a tray of food to break his fast, she found him sitting on the side of the bed with only his nightshirt and counterpane for cover.

Setting the tray down, she hurried to him. "What do you think you are doing?"

"I intended to stand up."

"Dr. Parker only allowed us to move you under one condition: that you stay in bed until he said otherwise. At present, he allows that you may sit up, but you may not stand."

"I do not mean to be troublesome, but I cannot abide being abed all day," Mr. Sturgis argued. "Surely moving to a chair will not be the death of me."

"Well I intend to follow Dr. Parker's orders," she declared. "Now, get back in the bed or I shall call Horace to help me see that you do."

Sturgis sighed heavily and then did as she asked.

Whilst the housekeeper proceeded to straighten the counterpane, she asked, "Do you wish to try and feed yourself?"

"I do."

"Then try to sit up." As he did, Mrs. Keagan piled several pillows behind his back before taking the tray and setting it across his lap, its legs resting on either side. "Is that high enough? I can extend the legs to make it higher."

"This is fine."

"Would you like my assistance in cutting your food?"

"First, let me see what the cook has prepared." Taking the lid off the tray, he was delighted to find a bowl of beef stew and slices of fresh bread and cheese. "I believe I can manage this with no trouble. Please thank the cook for preparing something for a one-handed man."

Mrs. Keagan laughed. "Mrs. Beatty will be delighted to know that you appreciate her efforts." Then, scrutinising the barren room, she said, "We have an excellent library. If you like, I can have some books brought up for your entertainment. What subjects do you prefer?"

"Are there any works by Shakespeare?"

She laughed. "I would never have guessed you were interested in plays and such."

Sturgis smiled. "Just because I am a steward does not mean I limit my reading to books on land drainage, crop rotation and estate management."

"So it appears."

As she turned to leave, Mr. Sturgis added, "Have you heard from Mr. Darcy?"

"I have not, but I would not be surprised to get a reply today. In any case, we both know he is already on his way."

The steward looked remorseful. "I regret I am the reason he must travel all this distance. Especially since I am being well cared for already."

"You are not responsible for what happened to you, and we both know that Mr. Darcy does as he pleases. Even if you asked him not to come, he would. I am certain that once he sees you doing so well, it will take a great weight off his mind."

"You speak as though you know him well."

"I have known him since he was a child," she said, "and there is not a finer man in all of England."

"I have never had a better employer."

"Nor have Horace and I," Mrs. Keagan replied, seeming to reminisce.

Then, giving him her full attention, she said, "There is a bell on the tray." She picked it up and rang it. "Ring if you need anything."

With that she left the room, and Mr. Sturgis proceeded to eat.

On the road to Weymouth

They were making excellent progress since William had insisted they not waste any more time than necessary on sleep and they resumed their trip at daybreak each morning. Moreover, at consistent intervals, he had the horses changed, which meant they could travel longer distances each day. Now their only problem, as Richard saw it, was that Darcy might be driving the servants too hard—not to mention the toll this regimen was taking on Darcy himself. Given Richard's occupation, he was used to going days with little sleep during manoeuvres, whereas William was not. Moreover, it was obvious that his cousin's energy had been diminished, perhaps in part because he had already spent so many sleepless nights since Elizabeth's injury.

"Darcy, if you keep to this pace, we may arrive sooner, but I fear you will be too exhausted to do anything once we do." William threw him a look that spoke to his determination not to be deterred. "I understand your motivation, but Elizabeth will be best served if you return to her in good health."

"Let me worry about my health," William snapped.

Richard rolled his eyes and turned to look out the window. "It looks as though we are nearing Birmingham. Shall we not stop there to eat and stretch our legs?"

"We will stop when we reach the post inn between Birmingham and Cheltenham."

"At Worcester?"

"That is the one. We can eat whilst the horses are changed."

'Might I ask where you plan to rest tonight?"

"I hope to reach Gloucester."

"Napoleon could have used you when he marched across Russia," Richard mumbled under his breath.

"What did you say?"

"Nothing, Darcy. Nothing at all."

Chapter 30

Pemberley
The next morning

In the years since he had become Fitzwilliam Darcy's valet, Mr. Adams had often remained at Pemberley whilst the young master travelled alone or when he went off to attend university. This did not bother him in the least, for he knew the independent nature of the heir apparent and took no offense. Besides, George Darcy's elderly valet still resided at Darcy House in London and filled that role there whenever needed. Moreover, it gave Adams time to closely inspect his employer's closet, determining which clothes needed to be updated, repaired, or replaced, and to prepare for next season's wardrobe. It also gave him time to peruse the magazines filled with men's fashion plates that his cousin, a fellow valet in London, passed along once he had finished with them, to keep Adams abreast of the latest fashions.

All of that had changed with Lady Henrietta's arrival as the new mistress of Pemberley. Thereafter, Adams found it difficult to do his job when Darcy was away because the new Mrs. Darcy had a habit of cornering him and asking questions about her stepson—questions he chose to ignore. She was not easily dissuaded, however, and would act flirtatiously as though she thought that would gain his cooperation. The situation became so unpleasant that when Darcy returned to Cambridge for his senior year, Adams asked if he might go with him. Consequently, the valet wondered if Lady Henrietta would resume her former behaviour now that the master had left him behind at Pemberley again.

Fearing today would be the test of that, as Adams left his apartment to go upstairs, Mr. Darcy's words before he left for Weymouth played through his mind.

Since Colonel Fitzwilliam is accompanying me, and we hope to bring Mr. Sturgis back with us, you will not be travelling to Weymouth. We must have room in the coach to fashion a bed for him to lie upon, should it come to that.

He was still thinking of that when he encountered several maids in the hallway talking animatedly.

"Did you hear the news?" one asked.

"News?"

"Mrs. Darcy's maid has suddenly taken ill, and Mrs. Reynolds has sent for the physician."

Everyone knew that Pemberley's housekeeper normally dispensed draughts and such when someone was ill, for it was impractical and expensive to send for a physician for a cold or an upset stomach. Since Adams had come to admire Florence for her professionalism and devotion to her mistress, the news was especially disturbing.

"It must be serious if the physician was summoned," another maid ventured. "And we all find it odd that Florence, who is never sick, seemed perfectly fine last evening."

As the maids walked on, Adams' thoughts flew to Mrs. Darcy. *With Florence sick, who is attending her?*

Hurrying upstairs, he entered through William's dressing room and quickly crossed to the French doors in the bedroom. Pulling back the curtains, he breathed a sigh of relief to see the mistress sitting on the balcony. Glancing to the clock on the mantle over the hearth, he realised it was past the hour that Mrs. Green usually came to visit. Unable to shake the feeling that something was not right, he pulled a cord to summon a servant. Not long afterwards, there was a knock on the bedroom door.

Opening it, he found a footman standing without. "Did you ring?"

"I did. Please go downstairs and inform Mrs. Reynolds that

Mrs. Green is not here for her usual visit with Mrs. Darcy, and since Florence is ill, the mistress is all alone."

The man nodded and left. Trusting the housekeeper would rectify the situation soon, Adams decided to keep the mistress company until a maid arrived.

Walking onto the balcony, he said, "Good morning, Mrs. Darcy."

Elizabeth, who was lying on the chaise, shaded her eyes to look in his direction. "Adams, I thought you left for Weymouth with my husband."

"No, ma'am. At the last minute, it was decided I would stay here so there would be more room in the coach should Mr. Sturgis be able to return with them."

"I know my husband will be thrilled if Mr. Sturgis is well enough to travel...we all will."

"I agree."

Adams looked as though he wished to say more, so Elizabeth asked, "Is there something else?"

"I wondered if I might solicit your assistance with some changes I wish to make to Mr. Darcy's wardrobe."

Elizabeth smiled broadly. "Are you asking me to conspire with you regarding my husband's clothes?"

"I prefer to say *influence*. It is my hope you will use your influence to help him see beyond his usual black suits, white shirts, and cravats."

"I have to say I believe you have done an admirable job of keeping my husband well-dressed. He looks very handsome in his clothes as it is, and he wears a bit of colour in his waistcoats."

Adams beamed. "I do my best."

"Moreover, I am a firm believer that one should wear what pleases them and not what someone else favours," Elizabeth continued.

Adams' smile vanished.

"Be that as it may, I am not opposed to seeing Mr. Darcy in more colourful clothes."

"All I ask is your permission to suggest that he seek your opinion."

"You have it. I shall be glad to give my opinion if he asks."

"Excellent. Might I show you the clothes I will suggest he add to his wardrobe? They are featured in the latest fashion magazines I have stored in Mr. Darcy's dressing room."

"Of course."

"It may take a few minutes for me to locate them."

"Take your time," Elizabeth said with a broad smile. "I am not going anywhere."

Just as Adams disappeared, Lady Henrietta and her maid slipped into Elizabeth's bedroom via the servants' corridor. A glance at the balcony confirmed that their target was still there and alone, just as Sarah had reported earlier. The potion she had managed to slip into Florence's food last night had worked perfectly, eliminating that maid's interference. Moreover, Sarah had caught Clancy whilst Elizabeth was asleep and locked him in a shed to keep him out of the way.

Spying the breakfast tray filled with scones and a pot of tea, Lady Henrietta walked over and touched the pot. "Excellent!" she whispered. "It is still hot." She held out a hand. "Give me the laudanum."

Sarah reached into her pocket and brought out a small vial. She watched as Lady Henrietta took it and slipped it into her pocket.

"With any luck, I can slip a few drops into a cup of tea. Once she is drowsy, I shall help her take a tumble from the balcony."

"Should I wait in here?"

"No. Return to my bedroom."

As soon as Sarah left, Lady Henrietta picked up the tray and walked onto the balcony. Setting it down on the table next to Elizabeth, she said, "I heard that your maid was ill and thought I would see if you needed anything."

Surprised to find William's stepmother catering to her, Elizabeth was too dumbfounded at first to answer.

"I noticed you had barely touched your food. You really

should eat if you wish to regain your health." Whilst she talked, Lady Henrietta took a plate and placed a scone and some butter upon it. Offering it to Elizabeth, she asked, "Would you like me to pour you a cup of tea to go with this?"

"No, thank you. I had a cup earlier," Elizabeth said, holding up her almost empty cup. "And I am not hungry. Besides, there is no reason for you to think you must attend me."

Lady Henrietta forced a smile. "In actuality, I thought that since Georgiana, Fitzwilliam and Richard have abandoned us, you and I might be company for one another until Georgiana or the men return."

At that moment, Adams walked out of Mr. Darcy's bedroom with an arm full of magazines. For a brief moment, he and Lady Henrietta each froze at the sight of the other.

She was the first to recover, saying haughtily, "Can you not see you are interrupting, Adams? Return to whatever it is you do when Fitzwilliam is away and leave us to our conversation."

Before Adams could reply, Elizabeth said, "In fact, before you came to offer your help, Adams and I were discussing Fitzwilliam's wardrobe. If you will excuse us, we will resume that deliberation. I am certain you have other things to fill your time."

Furious, Lady Henrietta turned on her heels and stalked off. Elizabeth watched through the window in the sitting room as she passed through there and exited into the hallway. Then she turned back to the valet.

"Now, sit down and show me what you would like to see Fitzwilliam wear next season."

Lady Henrietta's bedroom

As she entered the room, Lady Henrietta picked up the nearest vase and threw it at the hearth. If her curses were not enough evidence of her displeasure, the fact that she had destroyed an antique porcelain vase certainly was.

"Wha...what happened?" Sarah asked.

"That fool, Adams! I assumed he was on his way to Weymouth with Fitzwilliam. Why did you not inform me he had been left behind?"

"I...I had no idea," the maid stuttered.

"I pay you well to know everything that happens in this house," Lady Henrietta retorted. "Had I known he was still here, I would have had you dose his food along with Florence's. As it is, that dim-wit ruined the perfect opportunity to rid Pemberley of Elizabeth forever!"

Suddenly the door opened, and Lord Hartford walked in, shutting the door quickly behind him. "I suggest if you do not want the entire household to know your business, Rietta, you lower your voice."

Watching as she rolled her eyes, he added, "What has you in such an uproar?"

"Inept servants!" Lady Henrietta replied, glaring at her maid. Then she added, "Go let Clancy out before someone finds him and wonders who put him there!"

As Sarah escaped into the servants' corridor, Lord Hartford asked, "What terrible crime did she commit?"

"It is not what she did, it was what she *did not* do! I had no idea that Fitzwilliam's valet was still here. Just as I was about to drop laudanum into Elizabeth's tea, that idiot barged onto the balcony babbling about the latest fashions! Sarah should have known he did not leave with Fitzwilliam! She should have warned me!"

Lord Hartford signalled once more to be quiet. "I am not going to ask what you planned to do after you gave Elizabeth the laudanum, but could you not have dismissed Adams?"

"I tried, but Elizabeth made it plain I was the one who should leave."

Despite himself, Lord Hartford laughed aloud, which made her even angrier.

"My plan was perfect! The vicar's wife was not able to come, and Elizabeth's maid was too sick to get out of bed. I was alone on that balcony with her when that dolt appeared out of thin air!"

"I suppose you will try again."

"Not in that manner. Eliminating the vicar's wife and Elizabeth's maid a second time would be too obvious."

"Were I you, I would take that as a sign. You should give up the idea of punishing the Darcys."

"Well, you are not me, and I see it as a sign that I must move on to a more ambitious plan—one that will require your help."

Lord Hartford shook his head. "You know that I am not a violent man. I could never—"

"No one is asking you to do it! Have the gypsies handle it."

"I...I have no idea—"

"Be careful, David. I tolerate you because you are the only relation I have left, and thus far, you have proven loyal to me. Do not betray my trust."

"Why do you believe I have any influence with gypsies?"

"Did you think I would forget? You were about seventeen, and you were angry with your father, so you told me how he provided the gypsies in Liverpool with horses, clothes and guns to act as highwaymen. After each robbery, he hid them in the woods surrounding Spelling Park until the law gave up searching and looked elsewhere. I can only imagine how much his share was if he was willing to take such chances."

"That ended when father died, which is one of the reasons I am without funds."

"Did it? One of my spies followed you into Lambton the last time you went there alone. From his description of the men you met, I believe they were gypsies. And directly after meeting with them, you called on a jeweller in Sheffield and sold some jewellery. That, along with reports of highwaymen on the road from Lambton to Liverpool gives me every reason to believe you are carrying on your father's legacy."

Lord Hartford knew he had been caught. "What I said is partially true. Father died during my last year at university, and shortly afterwards the leader of the gypsies died as well. I had heard nothing from them until six months ago when Tomas, their leader, contacted me. He said that he needed a way to make money quickly."

"That is nothing new. What was his great need?"

"His people, the Romani,[12] gather every four years to pass laws and elect leaders. The next assembly is in Spain in the spring, and he believes he can be elected their leader if he is there. What little money he has raised from selling trinkets, picking pockets and telling fortunes has not been enough to buy passage on a ship; thus, he asked if I would help him and his brother become highwaymen like their father. Since I was in dire straits and did not wish to trouble you for more funds, I agreed to help them and share the spoils."

"I do not care if he wishes to become King of England! Find him and tell him if he takes care of Elizabeth for me, I will make it worth his efforts."

"As long as she stays at Pemberley, she will be safe."

"Let me worry about that. Once we have an agreement, I will make certain she has reason to leave."

"One other thing. Captured women and children are valuable bargaining tools at their gatherings, so Tomas will not kill Elizabeth. He will sell her."

"I do not care what he does with her!" Lady Henrietta said, throwing up her hands in frustration. "So long as she never sets foot in England again, I will be satisfied."

"How will you pay him? You said your funds are limited."

Lady Henrietta pulled a necklace from her décolletage, revealing a diamond pendant. "This was a wedding present from Lord Wharton and is worth two thousand pounds. If the gypsy does what I ask, I will sell it and give him half the money when the ship sails with Elizabeth. The other half will be given to his brother after I receive a letter from Portugal proving they have arrived. The brother can always sail on a later ship."

"I cannot imagine Tomas turning it down."

"Good! Then go find him."

"I cannot find him; he finds me. I will get a message to meet

---

12 **Romani** – the information about the Romani people was created for this story and is not meant to represent any actual persons or events. Nor is the portrayal of the Romani in the story meant to paint all of them with the same brush. Just as in every nationality, there are good and bad.

them in Lambton once they have accumulated enough jewellery to sell."

"Then I suppose I have no choice but to wait!" Lady Henrietta declared crossly.

As she walked over to pour herself a drink, Lord Hartford was already thinking of an alibi to use when Elizabeth went missing. Knowing Fitzwilliam Darcy's reputation, not to mention that of his cousin, Colonel Fitzwilliam, he had no intention of being subject to either man's suspicions or wrath.

After tending to Florence, Dr. Camryn went to Mrs. Reynolds' office to give her a report. The housekeeper looked up to see the physician peeking in the door, and she motioned him inside.

"Will Florence recover?"

"I believe she is past the worst."

"Thank God! I have not seen anyone that sick in a long time."

"She will need to rest in bed until her strength returns; however, I believe three to four days will be sufficient."

"Have you determined the cause?"

"Florence appears to have been given too much of a draught meant to cleanse the bowels. There are a number of folk remedies that can do the task, but if administered in large quantities, they can prove fatal. Do you have any idea who might want to incapacitate her?"

"One comes to mind."

"Might I suggest that you increase the number of servants watching Mrs. Darcy, at least until Mr. Darcy returns. Let him decide what is to be done after that."

"I will never forget that Mr. Adams had to remind me that she was alone, so I have already taken those steps." Tears formed in the old housekeeper's eyes. "I must face the master with that on my conscience."

Dr. Camryn, who had known Mrs. Reynolds for years, patted her hand gently. "Agnes, do not be so hard on yourself. You were distracted by Florence's precarious state, as was I."

"Yes, but it is my duty to protect Mrs. Darcy, and I failed."

"Mr. Darcy is fortunate to have you. I do not believe anything could dim his good opinion of you."

Mrs. Reynolds smiled. "You were always a flatterer, Robert Camryn." Then, making a shooing motion with her hands, she said, "Be on your way. I shall send for you if I need you."

"Goodbye, Agnes."

Weymouth
Willowbend Hall
Three days later

Despite encountering a line of thunderstorms, rendering the roads muddy and dangerous and requiring the horses to be changed more often, William pushed the coach to keep up a furious pace, and he and Richard arrived at Weymouth just before dark on the fifth day after departing Pemberley. Richard suggested they stay at the inn in Weymouth that night, but William would not hear of it. By the time they reached Willowbend Hall, clouds were hiding the moon, and the driver could not see farther than a few feet in front of the coach.

Still, once at the manor house, they were warmly welcomed by the servants of Willowbend Hall. Since dinner had just been served, it was decided that the drivers, footmen and postilions would occupy some of the empty rooms in the servants' quarters downstairs, making it simple to feed them in the servants' dining room.

Mr. Steadman, the head groom, announced he would drive the coach on to the stables, where several grooms were waiting to help care for the horses. Once he left, Mr. Keagan asked Darcy's men to follow him downstairs. As the light of the butler's candlestick dimmed and the sound of footsteps faded, William turned to enquire about Mr. Sturgis.

"According to Dr. Parker, he is doing remarkably well," Mrs. Keagan answered. Then she smiled. "But I imagine you would rather ask him yourself."

"I would, indeed," William said, "if he is awake."

"He should be. I just delivered his dinner tray." Mrs. Keagan lifted the chamber-candlestick she was holding. "Follow me."

As she ascended the grand staircase, Mrs. Keagan kept up a steady stream of chitchat about the last time the master had visited Willowbend Hall, how she missed Lady Anne, and how well the portico looked now that Mr. Sturgis had had it repaired.

William exchanged amused glances with Richard. "I had forgotten how beautiful Willowbend is."

"Oh, it is not as grand as it once was," Mrs. Keagan declared, "but, it is still lovelier than most of the homes in Weymouth."

The Keagans were just as William remembered, and he felt a twinge of regret for not having visited since his beloved mother's death. The thought of being here without her had kept him away, and he was not certain, even now, if he could stand many days at Willowbend without her presence.

Suddenly, the housekeeper stopped and knocked on a door. "Mr. Sturgis?"

"Yes?" came a reply.

She opened the door and peered inside, "Mr. Darcy is here to see you, sir. Do you feel up to it?"

Sturgis, who had been eating, sat up straighter and set his tray to the side. "Of course!"

As William and Richard walked into the room, both men seemed to relax upon seeing the steward. William went straight to the bed, reaching to shake the hand he was offered. "You cannot imagine how pleased we are to see you, Sturgis, and to hear that the physician thinks you are doing remarkably well."

"Yes. Dr. Parker said that he may let me walk about my room tomorrow."

"Excellent!"

Richard leaned around William. "I do not mind saying you had us worried, old man."

Mr. Sturgis, who had always exchanged quips with the colonel, smiled. "I was worried, as well. Apparently, had the blackguard who tried to kill me had better aim, I would be six feet under now, instead of here, speaking to you."

"Remind me to drink a toast to his poor coordination," Richard said.

All three men laughed before William's brows settled back into furrows. "I want to discuss what you recall about the attack, but not tonight. Please finish eating. Richard and I wish to change clothes and sample some of Mrs. Beatty's fare, too."

"You will find the food here comparable to Pemberley," Mr. Sturgis replied.

Mrs. Keagan moved the tray, placing it across the steward's lap again. "No need to ring when you are finished. I will stop back in for the tray after Mr. Darcy and Colonel Fitzwilliam have finished dining."

After leaving Sturgis' room, the housekeeper did not walk far down the hall before she stopped in front of the suite George Darcy used to occupy. To William it seemed unreal when she unlocked it, pushed the door open and stepped aside, saying proudly, "I hope you find everything satisfactory. If you need anything—anything at all—you have only to ring."

As William walked in, she turned to Richard. "Come, Colonel, let me show you to your room."

Chapter 31

Pemberley
One week later

After learning what had brought an abrupt halt to Mrs. Green's visits, Elizabeth gave the Greens the use of a horse to pull their carriage, which allowed the vicar's wife to resume her calls. Elizabeth's health was improving daily, and, eager to get more exercise, she circled the entire lake at least once a day, accompanied by Mrs. Green and Clancy.

Each time, they would stop to rest, feed the fish and enjoy the view from the pier. "Did you receive another love letter from Fitzwilliam yesterday?" Mrs. Green teased Elizabeth as she sat down beside her on the bench during their morning walk.

Recalling the words her husband had used to describe his agony at their being parted, Elizabeth blushed. "Yes, I did."

"If I recall correctly, he has not missed a day writing to you since he left."

"He has written every day, though for some reason, the letters he wrote during his trip arrived in two clusters; nevertheless, since he arrived at Weymouth, the delivery of his missives has been more consistent."

"I never thought Fitzwilliam a romantic man. He was always so shy and reserved, especially around women. James and I used to wonder if, despite what his Matlock relations expected, he would ever offer for anyone."

Suddenly sombre, Elizabeth pulled a bag of bread from her

pocket and began tossing crumbs to the fish. "I know we would never have married had he not been too much of a gentleman to allow me to suffer ruin. I owe him everything."

"Oh, my dear, I did not mean to open old wounds. You may have had an unconventional beginning, but Providence meant for you to marry Fitzwilliam. Of that I am certain. God knew you were just the one to save him from his stubborn pride."

"I believe it was he who saved *me*. Before we married, I prided myself on my ability to judge character." Elizabeth shook her head solemnly. "I could not have been less proficient."

Judith Green patted her hand. "That is what makes a good marriage—each partner complements or improves the other."

Suddenly, a large fish jumped into the air, splashing loudly when it fell back into the water, and Clancy began barking.

"Clancy has run off all the fish again," Elizabeth said as she stood. "Perhaps it is best we continue our walk. If I do not return before long, Mrs. Reynolds will send someone to find me."

"She feels a great responsibility to keep you safe whilst Fitzwilliam is away."

"There was a time when I would have objected to such precautions, but I have learned that people in authority have duties to perform and should be respected for doing them well."

As they continued their circuit around the lake, Mrs. Green asked, "Has Fitzwilliam mentioned when he might return?"

"No, but from the description of all that is left to do, I cannot imagine him returning soon."

Meanwhile, two of the four maids tasked with keeping watch over their mistress day and night were observing the scene at the lake from the balcony of a guest suite located just down the hall from the mistress' chambers. This suite, complete with two bedrooms and a sitting room, was to be the maids' post until further notice.

"I am not complaining, mind you," the younger maid, Clara, said as she selected a scone from a tray of food provided to break their fast, "but why do you suppose Mrs. Reynolds relieved us of our duties merely to watch Mrs. Darcy?"

"If you ask me, it has to do with Florence being so ill," the older maid, Martha, replied, pouring herself, then Clara, a cup of tea. "She was too sick to get out of bed for three days and at the same time, Mrs. Green was hindered from visiting the mistress. Mrs. Reynolds has been suspicious ever since."

"But Florence has resumed her duties, and she is very watchful of the mistress."

"As Mrs. Reynolds explained to me, Florence has duties to perform and cannot watch Mrs. Darcy every second of the day," Martha replied, "whereas we are charged with doing nothing else."

"I also find it peculiar that Mrs. Reynolds wants to know the instant anyone other than Mrs. Green or Florence enters Mrs. Darcy's suite. Makes one think she suspects someone might be up to something."

"Clearly, she does not trust Lady Henrietta."

"Clearly," Clara repeated. "I am pleased, though, that it falls to Rogers and the other footmen to follow Mrs. Darcy whenever she leaves the house. She walks so fast I could never keep up with her."

"We do have the easier role," Martha said. "Now, we had better eat quickly and retire. It will be time to swap places with Addie and Agnes again before we know it."

"Might I sit in Mrs. Darcy's room tonight whilst you walk the halls?" Clara asked. "I am afraid to go through the servants' corridor after dark, even with a candle."

"I would never have believed you afraid of the dark."

"I am not afraid of the dark. I am afraid of what is *in* the dark, like spectres."

Martha laughed. "Be honest—have you ever seen a spectre at Pemberley?"

"Once, after I delivered one of Mrs. Reynolds' tonics to Mrs. Darcy's room, I was returning to my quarters through the corridor when a light came towards me from the other end. Then suddenly it disappeared. It frightened me so badly I slipped into an empty guest room, crossed to enter the main hall through that door and returned downstairs that way. Since then, I rarely go through the servants' corridor."

"Oh, it was probably just another servant."

"No one in their right mind would walk those corridors after dark unless they have reason to," Clara continued, "and Mrs. Darcy was the only resident on that hall that night."

"Rumour is that Lady Henrietta's maid has been seen entering that corridor after dark," Martha teased. "Perhaps she was your spectre."

"With her dreary personality, she would make an excellent one," Clara replied with a smile. Then she added, "Look! They have started to make their way in this direction."

Martha followed Clara's gaze to the group who were indeed returning. "We had best hurry from the balcony. The mistress must not know we are occupying this suite."

Weymouth
Willowbend Hall
The study

Richard poked his head in the open door of the study to find the desk piled high with papers, but his cousin was not seated there. A quick glance around the room revealed William was standing near the windows with his hands clasped behind his back in silent reflection.

"I am not interrupting, am I?" Richard asked, stepping inside. "I can always come back later."

"You are not," William declared, returning to his desk. "Come in."

"Where is Mr. Sturgis? I thought he would be here."

"After he and I finished the paperwork regarding the repairs to the tenant houses, he went upstairs to change clothes. Today, all that remains is to ride out and see how the men we hired are faring. If they are doing a respectable job on the repairs, I see no reason not to let them build the new houses."

"Darcy, you have been driving yourself—and I dare say everyone else—like a madman since we left Pemberley. Even I admit that I am tired. Why not rest today and check on the repairs tomorrow?" Richard questioned, sinking into the chair in front of the desk.

"Staying busy helps me cope with being separated from Elizabeth. And the
sooner I finish here—"

"The sooner you can return to her," Richard interjected. Shaking his head in defeat, he asked, "Have you been able to sleep since we left Pemberley?"

"I find it impossible to sleep for more than a few minutes before having night terrors and waking up in a sweat."

"I imagine seeing your wife almost killed in front of your eyes would bring on night terrors."

"For weeks after she was injured, whenever I closed my eyes, I would see her being shot over again. However, since we left for Weymouth the dreams have changed."

"How so?"

"Now I dream that I have returned to Pemberley to find Elizabeth missing, and no one knows where she is to be found. I frantically search the house and grounds, and from the library window, I see her in the distance running down the drive towards the house. She is almost to the circular drive when a man dressed in black rides out of the woods and captures her. I hear his laugh as he carries her away on his horse, but I am helpless to stop him, for when I try to move, I discover my legs are shackled. That is when I wake up."

Richard let go a low whistle. "If being married brings on such hallucinations when you are apart, I shall continue to avoid that venerable institution!"

"I have had night terrors before, but they were always about things that had happened. I do not know what to make of this vision."

"Surely you know that your wife is safe as long as she is at Pemberley."

"That is the only thing keeping me sane at present."

Suddenly, Sturgis walked into the room dressed in riding clothes. "I am ready to accompany you, Mr. Darcy."

"Sturgis, you look just awful!" Richard exclaimed.

The steward smiled and looked down at his clothes. "This suit is very worn."

"I was not speaking of your clothes, old man," Richard continued. "I was speaking of the fact that you look deathly pale. Are you certain you feel well enough to ride?"

"Despite my appearance, Dr. Parker said I may ride if I feel up to it."

"He insists on going, but we shall take our time and stop the minute he grows too tired," William added. Then, changing the subject, he asked Richard, "Did you learn anything new whilst you were in town?"

"Only that the constable still has no idea who attacked Sturgis. No one remembers seeing any strangers in town that day or anything out of the ordinary. In fact, Constable Higgins said it is as though whoever did the deed came into town for that purpose and left directly afterwards."

"The attack may have had no correlation to Mr. Sturgis or Willowbend Hall," William added. "Unfortunately, there are men willing to rob anyone if given the right opportunity."

"But whoever it was never rifled through my pockets," the steward reminded William. "I always carry a few pence, and he did not take it."

"Perhaps the man who found you frightened him away," William replied.

"Perhaps."

"The constable did mention you met someone in town before you were injured," Richard said. "What can you tell us about him?"

"That lick on my head must have been harder than I thought," Mr. Sturgis said. "I had completely forgotten that I met with Lord Warden. He sent a letter here asking me to meet him in Weymouth about the sale of Willowbend Hall."

"How did he know it was for sale?" William asked.

"According to his lordship, rumours abound that it is soon to be on the market, so perhaps one of the servants mentioned it. In any case, Lord Warden said he was interested in purchasing an estate for his second son and wanted to confirm if the rumours were true."

"Lord Warden...Lord Warden," William repeated. "I recall Father mentioning a Warden Manor once, though I do not recall in what context."

"He appeared to be genuinely interested in the property. All he asked was a chance to make the first offer once it came on the market."

"I shall speak to him before I return to Pemberley," William said. Then he stood. "Are you certain you feel up to accompanying me, Mr. Sturgis?"

"I do."

"What about you, Cousin?"

"I think I shall stay here," Richard replied. "I wish to see if I can find the old path that leads to the beach and see if things have changed much since we were lads."

"I hope you learned your lesson the last time you and I went swimming."

"There is nothing wrong with swimming naked, Cousin. The problem arises when ladies choose to stroll along the beach at the moment one is getting out of the water."

"Well, should you decide to indulge, please be certain there are no females about. It is one thing for a boy to expose himself, and quite another for a man of your age to."

Richard laughed. "I have no intention of exposing this magnificent body, especially to the ladies—it might cause a stampede."

"In the opposite direction," the steward added cheekily as he followed William from the study.

Richard called into the hall, "Jealousy does not become you, Sturgis!"

Hearing Darcy and the steward laugh made Richard smile. He would do anything to keep his cousin's spirits up.

Pemberley
That night

Thanks to her maid, Lady Henrietta knew that Mrs. Reynolds had people watching Elizabeth like a hawk. The fact pleased her, since she believed the more the housekeeper focused on Elizabeth, the less opportunity she had to interfere with her concerns. Knowing that once Elizabeth was taken by the gypsies, things would come to a head quickly, Lady Henrietta was determined to take as many of the Darcy jewels from the safe as possible before Fitzwilliam returned.

"Are you certain Mrs. Reynolds and Adams are asleep?" she asked Sarah for the third time.

"As certain as one can be."

"What about the maids who are watching Elizabeth? Where are they at present?"

"One is in her bedroom, and the other is walking through the servants' corridor, just as they were last night. All the footmen are posted throughout the house, and I know what time they are to change guard."

Sarah watched as her mistress removed a small box from inside a chest, opened it and picked up two keys. Then she slipped the keys into a pocket of her gown.

"Let us pray that Fitzwilliam has not changed the locks to the study or the safe since George died," Lady Henrietta said. "It would be just like that insufferable man to think of that."

"He has been too busy trying to tame his new wife."

"Hopefully," Lady Henrietta replied. Reaching for a shawl, she added, "Bring the chamber candlestick and a flint. We shall light the candle once we are safely inside the study, and this shawl shall suffice to lay across the bottom of the door to keep any light from being seen in the hallway."

Sarah nodded, and soon she and Lady Henrietta were stealing through the halls of Pemberley in complete darkness.

Ramsgate
At the beach

All the students of the art academy had removed to the beach for a day of sketching, and their parents and guardians had been invited to go with them and participate in a picnic Mrs. Younge had planned.

Georgiana loved the beach, and had it not been for the presence of Lord Worley, she would have been content to stay all day. Though he was Mrs. Younge's companion, he stayed near her and Lady Esme most of the time. As it was, Georgiana and her friend soon tired of his attempts at conversation, and, hoping to be rid of him, they walked to the pier to sketch the people fishing there.

They had just begun their sketches when a fisherman drew a fish from the water and laid it upon the weathered boards of the pier. As he removed the hook and reached for a nearby bucket, it began to thrash back and forth and slipped from his hands. Out of nowhere a cat appeared, snatched up the fish and ran back down the pier towards the beach. The angry man ran after the animal, his shouts filling the air. The scene was so funny that Georgiana and Lady Esme laughed until tears were rolling down their cheeks.

Suddenly, a voice from behind said, "Miss Darcy, I see you will have to add the cat to your drawing."

Georgiana did not have to look to know it was Lord Worley peering over her shoulder. Closing her sketchbook, she said, "This is not what I planned to paint." Turning to Esme, she said, "If you are ready, we had best join your mother for the picnic."

As they began to walk away, Wickham grabbed Georgiana's arm. Not knowing her friend was being detained, Lady Esme walked on. Struggling to break free of Lord Worley's grip, Georgiana said firmly, "Unhand me, or I shall scream."

Wickham smiled wickedly. "And what do you think will happen? I believe Mrs. Younge will agree that she sent me to fetch you." Then he suddenly acted as though nothing was amiss and let go of her arm. "Run along now and eat. I shall be there shortly."

Georgiana rushed to where her classmates had gathered on

quilts to enjoy the picnic. As she did, she vowed to address her concerns about Lord Worley with Lady Esme's mother. That opportunity came after everyone had eaten and she, Esme and Lady Farthingham were resting in one of the gazebos provided for beachgoers to escape the sun.

Once her friend fell asleep, Georgiana asked, "Lady Farthingham, may I speak to you about something that is troubling me?"

"Of course you may, dear."

"I...I hesitated to say anything before now," Georgiana began, "especially since he is Mrs. Younge's particular friend."

"You speak of Lord Worley?"

"Yes. He has taken too great an interest in my art, and it makes me uncomfortable."

Lady Farthingham smiled condescendingly and patted Georgiana's hand. "I can see why it would."

"You...you can?"

"Yes. You are very young, and for a man of Lord Worley's stature and wealth to take an interest in your art—well, it has to be overwhelming."

Georgiana was thinking of how she could refute that assumption when Lady Farthingham continued. "Actually, Lord Worley spoke to me about your talent. Whilst he feels Esme will be a talented artist one day, he thinks you are ready to progress in your studies. If he appears to be overbearing, it is because he sees your potential and believes you do not."

"I have made it clear that I do not plan to pursue art as a career, but he will not be gainsaid."

"Perhaps you should listen to him, Georgiana. God gives only a select few the ability to change the world with their talent. Lord Worley assures me that you are one of the lucky few who could. Frankly, I believe you should discuss this with your brother before tossing the idea away."

Seeing she was not going to get any assistance from Lady Farthingham, Georgiana quickly went silent.

Pemberley
The study

After opening the safe, Lady Henrietta was shocked to find none of the boxes containing the Darcy jewels were inside. Spying all that was left—a letter and a small bag—she pulled them out. After quickly reading the letter to Lord Appleby from the bank, she opened the bag and poured the contents into her hand.

"Fitzwilliam knows!" she hissed under her breath. "He used the Darcy jewels for collateral on a new loan, and the bank discovered the counterfeit pieces."

"But if Mr. Darcy knows, why has he not confronted you?" Sarah asked.

"Most likely because he cannot prove I did it! And even if he could, he cannot prove that George had no knowledge of it."

"That is fortunate."

"Are you mad? He must be biding his time until he can toss me off the estate and deny me the living George left me." Lady Henrietta looked around as though she had forgotten where she was. "We must return to my suite right away. It will not do for that haggard old housekeeper to find us in here."

Chapter 32

Lambton
Several days later

Elizabeth was feeling so much better that she decided it was time to begin refurbishing her bedroom in colours more to her liking. Mrs. Reynolds had been pleased to order paint in the shade she wanted—fern green to match the sitting room—and with this in mind, Elizabeth asked Florence to go into Lambton to pick up swatches of cloth from the dry goods store so she might choose materials for new drapes and a counterpane. Whilst Florence was there, she was also charged with buying two more bolts of muslin to use for clothes for the tenants' children. Moreover, Elizabeth had asked Rogers to drive the maid there and back.

Since there were other maids and footmen watching their mistress, the two had no choice but to comply. As they made the trip to Lambton in one of the Darcy carriages, Florence was intrigued by a group of wagons parked in a circle in a clearing near the road. Each brightly painted wagon[13] looked like a small house with walls, doors, windows, steps and a stovepipe sticking out of the roof. Moreover, all manner of household items hung

---

13 **A vardo wagon** (living wagon) is a traditional horse-drawn wagon used by British Romani people as their home. Possessing a chimney, it is commonly thought of as being highly decorated, intricately carved, brightly painted, and even gilded. The heyday of the 'living wagon' lasted for roughly 70 years, from the mid-1800s through the first two decades of the twentieth century. For the purposes of this story, I have them appear earlier.

on both sides of the vehicles, including washboards, buckets, ladders, pots and pans. To Florence, those standing around the fire in the centre of the circled wagons looked as unconventional as their dwellings. Men and women alike wore vibrantly-coloured clothes and gaudy earrings, whilst the women added rows of bracelets and strings of necklaces to their attire. The long, black hair framing their dark-complexioned faces was held in place by jewelled combs and multi-coloured scarves, though Florence noted that even some of the men donned these same scarves in place of hats.

Leaning close so that only Rogers could hear, Florence whispered, "Who are they?"

"The Romani," the footman said quietly, "but most call them gypsies."

"So, they live in those wagons?"

"They do. They are nomads, and they travel from place to place, staying until told to move along."

Florence's expression darkened. "Should we be frightened of them?"

"I cannot say with certainty, but people say that though they pretend to be friendly whilst they sell their trinkets and tell fortunes, they survive by picking pockets and stealing. And if you believe the rumours, some say they kidnap children and sell them abroad."

At that moment Florence's eyes met the dark eyes of one of the men. Shivering under his cold stare, she added, "I would not like to encounter that one in an isolated spot."

"Aye," Rogers said, slapping the horses into a trot. "Neither would I."

Ere long they entered Lambton, and Rogers proceeded to the dry goods store, where he pulled the horses to a stop behind a carriage already parked in front of it. Climbing down, he turned to assist Florence to the ground.

"Do you need me to accompany you inside, or shall I wait here?"

Florence eyed the already crowded little shop. "Please wait here."

As the maid made her way into the store, Rogers climbed back into the carriage, leaned his head back on the cushioned seat, and closed his eyes.

Upon exiting the dry goods store, her arms filled with bolts of muslin, Florence's eyes were drawn to a scene across the street. Two of the gypsies she had seen earlier were standing next to a coach, conversing with a gentleman who, from behind, favoured Lord Hartford. As she watched, all three men entered the building where the post stages stopped. Dismissing the notion as improbable that Lord Hartford was the gentleman, she hurried on to the carriage. Finding Rogers asleep, she called his name loudly enough to wake him.

"Wha...what?" the footman murmured, sitting up straighter. Seeing Florence, he began to climb down from the carriage. "I must have fallen asleep."

After placing the bolts of cloth into the compartment below the seat, Rogers went to help Florence back into the carriage, but she resisted.

"I have not finished shopping. Mrs. Darcy fancies the fudge and caramels at the confectioner's shop, and I thought it might brighten her day if I brought some back."

"What a capital idea!" Rogers declared. "In fact, I could do with a bit of fudge myself."

Florence smiled. "I suppose a wee bit for you will not be too dear. I shall return when I have made my purchases."

An hour later

Mrs. Green had already returned to the parsonage, so Elizabeth was now settled on the balcony, enjoying the sun and the candy Florence had brought from Lambton. Whilst she did so, she re-read her favourite part of the letter that she had received from William just that morning.

Long before I reached the age of majority, I swore I would have a marriage based on mutual affection. What I envisioned, however, was so far removed from the paradise I have found in your arms as to be laughable. I truly had no concept of the delight to be had when two souls find their match. I love you with all my heart, body and soul, Elizabeth Darcy, and I cannot wait to be with you again.

Elizabeth brought the letter to her lips to place a kiss on it. *Nor can I, my darling husband.*

Suddenly, Daisy, the maid Elizabeth had met on her first day at Pemberley, was standing before her. In her hand was a letter and as soon as Elizabeth looked up, she thrust it towards her.

"What is this?" Elizabeth asked.

"Excuse me for interrupting you, ma'am," the young maid replied, nervously curtseying. "I was coming up the back stairway, and I saw it lying against a step. It was standing on the edge and unless one happened to be looking down, as I was, it could easily have been overlooked. I thought I should bring it straight to you."

"Thank you, Daisy. You did the right thing."

Daisy curtseyed again and was leaving just as Florence returned from the kitchen holding a tray with a fresh pot of tea. As she set it on the table next to her mistress, Florence, who was curious said, "I just passed Daisy in the sitting room."

Elizabeth quickly explained about the letter. "Oddly enough, it is from Georgiana."

Tucking William's letter inside the pocket of her gown, she broke the seal on her sister's missive and began to read. The longer she read, the more troubled her expression became. Suddenly she stood. "I must leave for Ramsgate as soon as possible!"

Stunned, Florence stuttered, "I...I do not believe Dr. Camryn will allow—"

"Whilst I appreciate Dr. Camryn's concern, he is not in charge of my life," Elizabeth interjected as she strode towards her bedroom. "Georgiana must come home immediately."

"Might I ask why?"

"My sister hints that a certain gentleman is making her feel uncomfortable, and I cannot allow that."

"Why not send word to Mr. Darcy and let him handle the matter?"

"My husband already has his hands full, and there is no need to impose on him when I sit idly by. Besides, it would take a week for a letter to reach him, and I can be in Ramsgate by then."

"Surely Miss Darcy will expect her brother to come since you are still not fully recovered from your injuries."

"This letter makes it obvious that Georgiana knows nothing about my ordeal, yet Fitzwilliam said he wrote to her shortly after it happened. From what she says, she has only received one letter—the one where I mentioned that Fitzwilliam was on his way to Weymouth. That would explain why she sent the letter here. She believes he is travelling."

"I distinctly recall placing your letters to Miss Darcy on the tray downstairs to be posted. It seems odd that only one reached her."

"Just as odd as this being the first letter I have received from her. Moreover, she refers to other letters that went unanswered. I will mention it to my husband as soon as he returns."

By then, Florence had followed Elizabeth into her bedroom, where her mistress was taking clothes from a chest of drawers and stacking them on the bed.

"I shall need my trunk."

Florence went into the closet to locate it. Being empty, it was not very heavy, so she dragged it out of the closet and across the carpet to Elizabeth.

"I shall begin packing whilst you locate Rogers. Tell him to have Mr. Wilson ready the coach, as I wish to leave first thing in the morning. And warn Mr. Rogers not to say a word about this to anyone, especially Mrs. Reynolds. I shall tell her myself."

As Florence turned to leave, Elizabeth added, "And do not let me forget to send a note to Mrs. Green. I need to inform her that we are off to Ramsgate."

"We?"

"Yes. You and Rogers will be accompanying me."

Lady Henrietta's rooms
Two hours later

"What do you mean, you lost a letter from Georgiana?" Lady Henrietta demanded.

Cautiously, Sarah took a step backwards before replying. "I make it my business to be downstairs near the hour for the mail to be delivered. Whenever I am noticed, I tell them I am on my way to the kitchen to fetch something—a fresh pot of tea or some biscuits. Today, I had no sooner discovered a letter from Miss Darcy amongst those on the table, when Mrs. Reynolds walked out of the dining room and in my direction. I barely had time to slip the missive into my pocket and walk on to the kitchen. Evidently, it was not placed inside my pocket properly, for by the time I brought the tray of tea to your sitting room, the letter was missing."

"Can I not count on you to do anything right?" Lady Henrietta hissed, throwing up her hands. "Did you even bother to look for it?"

"Of course. I retraced my footsteps, but I could not find it."

"You better pray that if it contained important news, one of your *friends* will find out what was in it and inform you."

"I am confident they will."

"For your sake, I hope you are right."

Ramsgate

Immediately upon placing the letter speaking of her unease with Lord Worley in the post, Georgiana began to have doubts. Had she said too much? Fluctuating between wishing she had not brought up the subject and wishing she had been more forthright, she was now flooded with self-doubt.

What if I am wrong? Even Lady Farthingham thinks Lord Wor-

ley's attentions are nothing more than attempts to convince me to take my talent more seriously.

Though she tried to recall the exact words she had written, Georgiana could not. Whilst these worries swirled in her head, she was distracted from the portrait of the pier that stood unfinished before her.

Monsieur Dupuy, however, had taken note of her idleness and silently slipped behind her. Now he moved forwards to whisper, "Miss Darcy, this is the last day to work on seascapes. Tomorrow we concentrate on portraits. I would suggest that you take control over what is occupying your mind and concentrate on your work."

Several nearby students, who had stopped to observe her chastisement, began to giggle. This made Georgiana blush and, unable to speak, she merely nodded. Not long afterwards, the bell rang, indicating it was time for luncheon. Laying aside her brush, she waited for Lady Esme since they always walked to the dining room together.

"I saw Monsieur Dupuy speaking to you," her friend murmured quietly as they filed out of the room. "I must say he did not look happy."

"He was not," Georgiana whispered in reply. "I was woolgathering when I should have been completing my painting."

"I have noticed you have not been yourself of late," Lady Esme continued. "Is Monsieur Dupuy's decision to extend the school for two weeks a problem? My mother is ecstatic about it."

"I would welcome the additional days except for Lord Worley's presence. I found him standing in the hallway outside my room very early this morning. When he tried to speak to me, I ignored him."

"Mother told me that you spoke to her about him. I tried to make the case that his attention is bothersome, even to me. Nonetheless, she argues that he is upset with you, for he feels you are squandering your talent."

"I have told him repeatedly that I am not interested in his sponsorship, but he will not take me at my word. It is very unsettling. In fact, in my last letter to my sister, I hinted as much."

Lady Esme's hand came up to cover her mouth. "That means your brother could already be on his way here to take you home."

"Brother is travelling to Weymouth presently, so I have no idea if he can. Besides, I only hinted at my dismay, so Elizabeth may not notice. In any case, please do not mention what we have talked about to your mother. She would be upset that I did not take her advice concerning Lord Worley."

"I will not say a word," Lady Esme said, making a show of placing her hand on her heart. "You may rely on that."

Willowbend Hall
The study

Richard had been asked to join his cousin and Mr. Sturgis to hear what transpired at the meeting with Lord Warden earlier that day, and as he waited for William to take his place behind the huge desk that once belonged to George Darcy, he suddenly recalled the last time he had stood in that same spot before his uncle. It was the day he and William were punished for tossing rocks off the cliffs to the beach below to garner the attention of a group of young ladies. Though it had been his idea and his cousin had refused to participate, both were disciplined. At the memory, he could not hold back a smile.

"Is something funny, Cousin?"

"I was just recalling the last time your father summoned me here."

"Not just you, as I remember," William said, shaking his head.

"It was not my fault that Uncle George always assumed you were involved in my tomfoolery."

"Even when I swore I was not," William added. "You were just fortunate that it was my father who learned of your deeds and not Uncle Edward."

"I agree. My father would have tanned my hide, whereas Uncle George was more inclined to talk me to death."

"How well I know," William replied. "We could go on reminiscing, but I suggest we put off talking about the past until we have addressed the present."

"I shall do my best."

"That is all I ask. Now, as for Lord Warden, I found him to be a pleasant person and an astute businessman. He remembered visiting Willowbend when my parents were first married and said he always considered it one of the finest estates in Weymouth. He wishes to be the first to tour it once the renovations are complete and to have the opportunity to make the first offer."

"How long will it take to complete all the repairs and additions you have contracted?" Richard asked.

"Sturgis and I estimate five to six months, and since I would like Sturgis to return to Pemberley with us, I will have to hire someone else to be in charge here."

"Whereas I would like to stay and see the job through," the steward interjected. "If you will allow it, I shall take precautions never to be alone when I travel into town."

"If you agree to take the carriage and at least two footmen when you do, I am of a mind to agree. After all, you know how I want things handled."

"I do not wish to encounter the miscreant who tried to kill me again, so what you ask will not be a burden."

"Let us pray that blackguard is miles away by now," William said.

"Does this mean you and I are able to return to Pemberley?" Richard asked.

A wide smile crossed William's face. "It does, though I must return by way of London and spend at least one night there. Still, we can be at Pemberley in six days...seven at most."

"Mrs. Darcy is not expecting you back this soon, is she?"

"No, and I want my return to be a surprise." William stood. "I will inform the Keagans that we are leaving and Mr. Sturgis is staying. If all goes as planned, you and I shall depart early tomorrow."

"No offense, Sturgis, but I will be pleased to see your smiling face through the rear window of Darcy's coach," Richard said.

"No offense taken," Sturgis said, grinning. "For I shall be glad to see yours inside of it."

Pemberley
Lady Henrietta's sitting room
Later that day

Just as Lady Henrietta lifted the cover from the food on her dinner tray, there was a knock on her sitting room door.

"Rietta, I have something important to tell you."

Recognizing her cousin's voice, she nodded to Sarah, who opened the door. There was no time to inform Lord Hartford of what she had just heard before he began speaking.

"Whilst I was in Lambton, Tomas contacted me. His clan had to vacate the woods behind my estate in Liverpool. They are currently on their way to Scotland, but for now, they are encamped nearby."

"What precipitated the move?"

"According to him, the local constable became suspicious upon seeing the women in town too often. He began asking questions about where they were camped; thus, Tomas decided that the women, children and elders should head north to Edinburgh. They have a lot of allies amongst the Scots in that area, and he planned to sail from that port in any case; however, they are still short of the money needed to purchase passages on a ship, so he, his brother and four other men were to stay behind and continue as highwaymen."

"Did you tell him he could take the entire clan anywhere in the world with what I am willing to pay for taking Elizabeth off my hands?"

"I did, and Tomas is keen to participate. I advised him to keep some of the women here as that would be less suspicious. He is to camp in the woods near Lambton, and I will contact him by leaving a letter at the post stage inn when we have a plan to get her away from Pemberley."

"You are not the only one with good news to share. Sarah

has an admirer in the stables who overheard Mr. Rogers tell the head groom that Elizabeth intends to leave for Ramsgate in the morning."

"For Ramsgate? Why would she do that?"

"I have no idea, and that is not my concern. What you must do is contact Tomas immediately because he needs to be ready tomorrow. Once you have done that, you must convince Elizabeth to let you be her escort."

Since he had planned to be in Liverpool when the gypsies carried out his cousin's scheme, Lord Hartford was unhappy to hear her proposal. "But...but that is not feasible. Elizabeth knows Darcy would not want me to escort her."

"No respectable woman travels unescorted! I will cause a scene by arguing the dangers of a woman travelling alone. Knowing Mrs. Reynolds, she will insist Elizabeth accept your offer. You know how to be convincing, David. Just look sincere when you tell her you are worried for her safety."

Defeated, Lord Hartford had no choice but to do as she asked.

Chapter 33

On the road to London from Pemberley

One day later, Lord Hartford found himself inside a coach on the way to London with Elizabeth and her maid. Though the decision to allow him to be her escort was clearly based upon Elizabeth's desire to appease Mrs. Reynolds rather than his appeal as a companion, it had pleased Lady Henrietta. Knowing what had been set in motion, Lord Hartford also convinced Elizabeth to use her husband's unmarked coach, arguing that highwaymen targeted vehicles with family crests. In truth, once Tomas commandeered their coach, being unmarked would make it harder to search for Elizabeth.

Unfamiliar with the route from Pemberley to London, Elizabeth had also taken his advice to go south to Leicester and then east to Peterborough where they would be able to take the Great North Road all the way to Town. Unbeknownst to her, they would never make it as far as Peterborough, for Tomas was set to strike their coach along an isolated stretch of road approximately ten miles past Leicester.

Leicester
Days later

The room at the inn had been comfortable enough, but Lord Hartford was restless all night due to his plans for the fictional robbery, which kept playing though his mind. By dawn, he was fearful he may not have given clear instructions to Tomas. Wishing to impress upon Darcy that he had tried to defend Elizabeth, he had insisted on being struck by one of the gypsies, allowing him to fall to the ground and feign injury. Recalling that discussion now, he wished he had made it clear that whilst he wished to be struck, he did not wish to be hurt.

Tomas had decided his brother, Nikolae, would be the one to search him and Elizabeth for valuables. To that end, Hartford had added a silver flask and his father's pocket watch which, in addition to his rings, would make it appear the robbery had been successful. When Nikolae approached Elizabeth to demand she hand over her wedding ring, Lord Hartford was to object and be beaten for interfering.

"Lord Hartford?"

The sound of Elizabeth's voice drew him back to the present. Realising he had been distracted, he said, "I apologise. Did you ask me something?"

"Will we make Peterborough today?"

"No, but we should be halfway there by nightfall. The next inn we will stay at is still hours away; however, I have always had my coach stop at the creek halfway there to water the horses and give them a short respite. We can all stretch our legs at that point…even Clancy."

Though he hoped to gain a smile from her with his quip about the dog, that did not happen. Most likely because he had been adamantly opposed to bringing the dog along in the first place. In the end, he had no choice but to relent when Elizabeth insisted that bringing Clancy would be good for Georgiana's spirits.

After he had answered Elizabeth's question, silence reigned again. In truth, she had said very little the entire trip, which came as no surprise. He had not had a decent conversation with Darcy's wife since she chided him for suggesting he join her morning walks. Glancing at Florence, who held the dog, he also wondered how she would react. Would she be too frightened to interfere, or would she try to protect her mistress?

All his speculations abruptly came to an end when their

coach was surrounded by six men on horseback, each brandishing a pistol or a rifle. Dressed head to toe in black, including black hoods covering their faces with holes cut out to allow them to see, they were a fearsome sight, and he was grateful to know the men behind the masks.

"Halt, or we will shoot!"

Clancy was barking furiously, so Elizabeth addressed Florence. "Please try to keep him quiet, or they may harm him."

As the coach gradually rolled to a stop, she quickly removed her wedding ring and dropped it into one of her half-boots, whilst Florence pulled her shawl over Clancy's head. The dog stopped barking and instead concentrated on struggling to break free.

"Get out of the coach!" came the next order.

"Do not panic. Just do what they say," Lord Hartford stated calmly. Opening the door, he stepped down with raised hands. "Take what you want, just do not hurt us."

Turning, he let down the steps and helped Elizabeth and then Florence from the coach. Meanwhile, two of the miscreants already atop the coach aimed their pistols at the servants there.

"Get on the ground and lie flat on your bellies!"

As Rogers, who was seated next to the driver, began to climb down, he pulled a pistol from inside his coat. Immediately, the butt of a rifle hit the back of his head, sending him tumbling to the ground. One of the highwaymen on the ground walked over and aimed a pistol at the footman's head.

Elizabeth ran towards Rogers, crying, "Please let him live!" As she sank beside him, however, the man standing over him pulled her back to her feet. Angrily, she confronted the one who was obviously the leader. "Surely you cannot object to my helping him!"

That person did not reply. Instead, a jerk of his head sent another blackguard leaping from his horse and inside the coach, where he began to search the vehicle. Whilst he did that, their trunks crashed to the ground and two others began rifling through them. Clothes, shoes, mirrors, hairbrushes and everything imaginable were tossed in the mud.

Though frightened, Elizabeth made it a point to study the perpetrators. Unfortunately, other than the fact that they were of varying heights, they were as indistinguishable as the horses they rode, which were all dark brown with no markings.

Meanwhile, one of the men, who had already searched Lord Hartford and found the items of value on his person, settled his attention on Elizabeth. As he stood in front of her, he remarked that she wore no jewellery and smiled wickedly. "You can either give up your jewels, ma'am," he said, running the tip of his pistol around the lace edge of her décolletage, "or I will be happy to look for them."

Elizabeth's chin came up, and she pushed the weapon away. "All that I have of value is the money in my trunk. Do you think you are clever enough to find that?"

Abruptly, she was pulled against his chest. "I am going to enjoy this!"

"Unhand her!" Lord Hartford cried, stepping forwards.

Instantly, the butt of a pistol impacted that gentleman's nose, knocking him to the ground. He lay deathly still, blood pouring from his nose and his mouth.

"You!" the leader abruptly declared, pointing his weapon at Elizabeth. "Board the coach!"

Florence started towards Elizabeth, intending to go with her; however, a burly man blocked her progress. "Not you, wench!" he roared. "Just her!"

Frightened to think what that might portend, Elizabeth stood frozen in place, prompting one of the villains to begin pulling her towards the coach. By then, Clancy had escaped Florence's shawl and was trying desperately to break free of her grip. Just as Elizabeth was shoved into the coach, the small dog broke loose and shot inside with her.

"Come back here, you mongrel!" one villain shouted, grabbing Clancy by the back of the neck.

"Unhand my dog!" Elizabeth demanded, kicking at the perpetrator as both fought for control of Clancy.

The leader ordered, "It may be worth money. Let the dog go, too!"

As soon as the door shut, Clancy was on his feet, licking her face. Elizabeth whispered, "Forgive me for not letting you stay behind, but I fear you may have to show me the way home if I get lost."

Elizabeth's heart was already racing, but it pounded even harder when the coach began to move in a circle. By chance, her eyes locked with Florence's just as the maid covered her mouth with both hands and began to cry. By the time the coach was headed back in the direction of Leicester, she saw Lord Hartford getting to his feet. As she watched everyone fade from view, the only thing she clung to was the fact that they were travelling towards Pemberley, not away from it.

With no one to turn to, Elizabeth prayed fervently. *Lord, please send someone along quickly to find the others and to alert the authorities. Grant me the courage to persevere until I am found and keep Georgiana safe until she is home once more. But, if this ordeal is not short-lived and William must be told, please help him to bear it. You know what misery he has borne since his mother's death. Pray have mercy on him...on us both.*

Not long after the coach carrying Elizabeth passed the inn at Leicester, it came to a halt. Several men jumped off and began to pull brush and broken tree limbs away from the side of the road, revealing a crude opening in the woods. Immediately, the driver took the hidden road, whilst others replaced the brush and limbs, effectively hiding it again.

As the horses made their way down this narrow path, Elizabeth's spirits sank. *How will they ever find me here?*

Ere long, they entered an opening where ruts left by heavy wheels suggested several vehicles had once circled a large bonfire, evidenced by the remains of charred logs. Moreover, in the clearing stood a string of horses—enough to replace those pulling the coach.

As the carriage rolled to a stop, the men began to remove their hoods, revealing their dark hair and swarthy complexions. It was then that another terrifying thought came to Elizabeth's mind. *If they do not care whether I can identify them, they must not intend to let me go.*

Whilst the horses were being changed, one of her captors entered the coach with a bottle that he promptly uncorked. Pouring what looked like water into a small wooden bowl, he set it on the seat beside Elizabeth.

"What is this?"

"Water. In case the dog is thirsty."

Releasing Clancy so that he might drink, the dog sniffed the bowl before beginning to drink. In a short while all the water was gone, but as he tried to return to Elizabeth's lap, his legs gave way.

"You have poisoned him!" Elizabeth shrieked, pulling Clancy into her arms.

"It is not poison. It is a potion to make certain he stays quiet. Now, it is your turn," he said, holding the bottle towards Elizabeth.

"You have my word that I will not make a sound."

"If you should, I will make it my mission to see that you sleep all the way to Scotland."

"If I give my word, I keep it!" Elizabeth said vehemently.

He closed the door and pulled down the curtains, and in seconds the coach began moving. Shortly afterwards they reached the highway, where they halted to repeat the process of uncovering and then concealing the hidden road.

With the curtains drawn, Elizabeth listened for the sounds of passing vehicles, praying that each belonged to someone searching for her and imagining that they would be ordered to stop, and she would be rescued. This was not to be, however, and hours went by before she heard one of the men atop the coach mention Derby, which was the last large village before reaching Lambton. Soon after they passed that village, when the man riding with her looked away, she peeked out the curtain to discover the coach was taking a similarly hidden road into the woods.

When it came to a stop, the man leaped out, let down the steps, and reached inside for Elizabeth. Holding Clancy, she ignored his hand and manoeuvred the steps on her own. Once safely on her feet, she turned to survey the area and was too stunned to speak. In the clearing stood several brightly painted wagons, each resembling a small house. Next to two of the wagons stood two women clad in garments so bright that Lady Henrietta's wardrobe would have paled in comparison.

One dark-haired beauty, who looked about her age, offered Elizabeth a slight smile before the glare from her companion bade her retract it. The other, who appeared to be several years older, might have been pretty, too, if not for the severity of her expression. At the sight of Clancy, that scowling woman declared, "I will not be caretaker for a dog, Nikolae! Get rid of it!"

Before Elizabeth could object, the younger woman replied, "I will see to the dog. You just keep to your wagon."

Suddenly, Elizabeth's trunk hit the ground. "Clean it out! Put everything in a sack!" came an order. Recognising the voice as belonging to the one she had previously decided was the leader, Elizabeth turned to study him. He was not only taller than the others, but his thin moustache put her in mind of the drawing of a villain she had once seen in a penny novel. "Leave nothing inside it or the coach when you abandon it on the road to Liverpool."

A sudden touch on her arm brought Elizabeth's attention back to the women. "I am Alafare," the younger woman said. Pointing towards a wagon, she added, "Come. I will show you where you will stay."

Once inside the wagon, Elizabeth saw that it contained more space than she could ever have imagined. Filled with many household items, a multitude of cubicles lined the walls. Whilst they continued to the ceiling on the right, on the left they ended half-way up where a bed was situated. At the end of the bed was a ladder that allowed one to climb into it or into the loft above.

"Tomas ordered me to keep you in the loft with your hands and feet bound with shackles," Alafare said.

"Tomas?"

"Our leader."

"The dog may stay with you, or I will tie him down here."

"I had rather he stay with me."

"Then let me hold him whilst you climb the ladder."

Having no recourse, Elizabeth allowed it. She was surprised, however, to see Alafare bury her head in his soft fur before asking, "What is his name?"

"Clancy."

"Try to be as quiet as possible, Clancy, or Teza will find a reason to get rid of you. Teza cannot abide dogs—not since she was bitten by one as a child."

"It must have been a horrific injury to cause such a strong dislike."

"It was. A man who believed we had raided his chicken house set his dogs on us."

Elizabeth was appalled. "I…I am sorry."

Alafare shrugged. "After a while, you become accustomed to it."

Elizabeth had no way of knowing that one of her prayers had been answered not long after she was whisked away. Merely half an hour later, a coach belonging to Lord Edwards happened upon the stranded members of the Darcy party and immediately transported them back to Leicester. Once there, the local constable was summoned and apprised of the situation. He promptly sent express posts to his fellow law authorities in the surrounding counties, including the Bow Street Runners[14] in London. That venerable institution kept records concerning all the violent crimes committed in the whole of England, which included mur-

14 **The Bow Street Runners** have been called London's first professional police force. The force originally numbered six men and was founded in 1749 by magistrate Henry Fielding. *Bow Street Runners* was the public›s nickname for the officers "although the officers never referred to themselves as Runners, considering the term to be derogatory." The Bow Street group was disbanded in 1839. https://en.wikipedia.org/wiki/Bow_Street_Runners

ders and kidnappings, immediately passing them along to their cohorts in Scotland and Wales.

To further hide his involvement, Lord Hartford made a show of sending an express to Mrs. Barnes at Darcy House in London. "There!" he declared, once finished. "Mrs. Darcy said Fitzwilliam planned to return home via London, so should he decide to leave Weymouth early, my express could arrive there before I do."

"You are not returning to Pemberley?" Florence asked. "Who will lead the search for Mrs. Darcy?"

"I would have no idea where to look. Besides, it is best to let the law handle such matters. I believe my nose is broken, and I wish to see my physician in Town. I will stay at my house in Mayfair and make myself available to answer any questions the authorities may have, or if it is not soon resolved, that Darcy may have."

Since the area around his eyes was already a darkening shade of purple and his nose had swollen to twice its size, Florence could tell his nose was likely broken. Secretly, she felt the injury was not severe enough since he had done little to prevent Mrs. Darcy's abduction.

"The innkeeper, who has known the Darcys for years, has agreed to loan you and the other servants a coach to use to return to Pemberley. Meanwhile, I was fortunate enough to have secured a ride into Town with Lord Porterfield. He happens to be on his way there and has generously offered to help me."

"How convenient for you."

"What did you say?" Lord Hartford asked.

"Nothing. Nothing at all."

On the road to London from Weymouth

The journey to Pemberley started with the same gruelling pace as the trip to Weymouth; however, Richard could not complain. He could not recall when he had seen Darcy in such good spirits, and even though the long hours of travel were tiresome, to see his cousin's smile gladdened his heart.

"So, is it your plan to reach Salisbury tonight, Cousin?"

"If not Salisbury, we shall get as close to it as possible. If our luck holds and it does not rain, we should be in London the day after tomorrow."

Richard peered out the window at the cloudless blue sky. "Hopefully the sun will continue to cooperate. I saw enough rain on the trip to Weymouth to last me a lifetime."

"I agree. I would not care if I did not see any more rain until after we reach Pemberley."

"Is Mrs. Barnes expecting you? You know how flustered she gets when you arrive unexpectedly," Richard said, laughing. "She acts as though it is a crime for you to visit your own house unannounced."

"Mrs. Barnes tries to keep the house immaculate and does not like surprises. And to answer your question, I sent her a letter, but we may be there before she receives it."

"Let us hope not."

"When we reach Town, I thought I might speak with your father. Now that he has had time to recover from the shock of my hasty marriage, I hope to regain his trust, if not his approval. What do you think?"

"It is certainly worth a try. I should like to speak to him first, however, just to determine his frame of mind. If he relents, Mother will follow. If you are fortunate, he may do so just to irritate Aunt Catherine."

William smiled. "It is useful that on occasion he likes to remind her exactly who is head of the family."

"I could not agree more."

Chapter 34

On a road near Lambton

It was still dark when a noise outside the wagon awakened Clancy, making him growl. This woke Elizabeth and she pulled the dog closer, cautioning, "Pray be quiet, or they may take you away."

She had no way of knowing if he understood; however, the animal instantly calmed. Meanwhile, the door to the wagon creaked open and footsteps announced someone had entered.

A man was speaking in hushed tones in a language Elizabeth did not understand, so she manoeuvred as close as possible to the end of the loft and craned her neck to see who it might be. At that same moment, Alafare raised a candle, illuminating his face. Recognising him as the man who had accompanied her in the coach, Elizabeth lay back down after he exited the wagon, hoping that Alafare would think her asleep and possibly leave the wagon without locking the door. That was not to be, however, for it was not long before her captor stepped onto her own bed and peered into the loft.

"It is time to leave. After I unlock the cuffs on your ankles, I suggest that you relieve yourself before our journey begins." She chuckled. "I possess a beautiful chamber pot that I set on the floor. It once graced the house of a countess in Liverpool. I told her maid's fortune in exchange for it, and to this day I do not think the countess knows what became of it."

Elizabeth was too focused on her aching extremities to be

amused, and as the clamps fell away from her ankles, she instinctively reached to stroke them. The full extent of the damage caused did not become evident, though, until she tried to pull her feet underneath her in order to hand Clancy down. The soreness was so severe that she cried out with the effort.

"I am sorry for your pain."

"Thank you for not binding my hands as well."

Alafare could not meet Elizabeth's eyes. "I will take Clancy for a walk to give you privacy. Once you have finished, open the door and set the pot on the ground. If you wish, you may leave the door open for some air until I return. In any case, remain in the wagon."

Once the door closed behind Alafare and Clancy, Elizabeth climbed down the ladder. Checking to see if the window shutters could be opened wider to see better, she was disappointed to discover they could not. Drawing the curtains securely, she followed Alafare's suggestion, then opened the door and set the pot on the ground.

The sun had not risen yet, but Elizabeth was able to distinguish the form of a man crossing from another wagon to the horses tied underneath a large tree. From his height, Elizabeth recognised Tomas, who suddenly stopped and looked in her direction. As he began swiftly walking towards her, she stepped back inside the wagon. Fortunately, before Tomas reached her, Alafare returned with Clancy trailing on a rope. Elizabeth listened anxiously as he angrily addressed that young woman in the same language Nikolae had used earlier.

After Tomas stalked away, Alafare picked up Clancy and handed him to her. "Stay inside," she ordered.

Eager to learn all she could about her captors, when Alafare returned Elizabeth pretended to have figured out her connection to Tomas. "Why was your husband so angry?"

"Tomas is not my husband. He is my cousin, as is Nikolae, who rode with you in the coach."

"Is Teza you sister? You look alike."

"No. She is Tomas' wife."

"You never answered my question. Why was Tomas so angry?"

"When he first spoke of shackles, I reminded him that you were a lady and had delicate skin. Wearing them constantly will create sores, just as they did with—" Stopping in mid-sentence, for a time it seemed Alafare was lost in a memory.

Suddenly, she continued as though nothing had happened. "I promised Tomas that I would restrain you with strips of cloth when you are not sleeping so as to give your skin a chance to recover. Tomas saw that I had not kept my word."

"Thank you for being so kind. I am sorry to have caused you trouble. I had just set the pot down when he saw me."

"There is nothing to be done about it now. No doubt he and the others will watch you even more closely, so please try to stay out of sight."

A knock on the door proved to be Teza, who handed a bag to Alafare and left without a word. Picking up a board standing against one wall, Alafare laid it across the cubicles on either side of the wagon. On that improvised table, she spread a cloth and poured out the contents of the bag—a small loaf of bread, a chunk of cheese and four apples. From her boot, she withdrew a small knife and began to slice the cheese.

"This will have to do, for there will be no fires today," she said as she worked. "I suggest that you eat even if you are not hungry. My cousin has intentions of going as far as possible today, and he will not stop until either the horses are too weary to travel, or it grows too dark."

Clancy whined, and Alafare pinched off a bite of cheese, feeding it to him. "You had best behave, too," she said, "or you may find yourself tossed into the woods."

Later, after the wagons had begun to roll, Elizabeth was banished to the loft again. Two tiny windows there with shutters that could be tilted open, were her only connection to the world outside. No one without could see inside through the small opening and she could barely see out. Still, she saw enough to recognise that they were on the main highway north to Sheffield and not the route that ran through the middle of Lambton and connected with the highway further north. Realising how close she was to Pemberley, the urge to cry was almost overwhelming.

Stop feeling sorry for yourself and try to think of a way to escape or, at the least, a way to help William find you!

A still, small voice prompted, *A trail would make it easier to follow you.*

A trail? Elizabeth looked down at her stocking clad feet and then at the half-boots she had been wearing when she was seized, which were now stuffed into a cubicle in the loft. Surely William would recognise the footwear he had personally ordered for her in London—blue leather with an intricate design carved into the toes and sides. Praying she was correct and that their wagon was the last one in the caravan, she tilted the window open as far as possible and forced one boot through the opening. Then she held her breath to see if there would be any repercussions.

As she waited, she recalled her wedding ring, which she had secured by tying it in one corner of the pocket in her gown after Alafare asked her to remove her boots. Checking for it now, she was relieved to find it still there. Meanwhile, the prospect of going all the way to Edinburgh had Elizabeth wondering what she would sacrifice after she tossed out her other boot.

If only I had access to the monogrammed hairbrush, comb and mirror that were in my trunk.

Intending to drop the other boot once she was certain they had passed Sheffield, she resolved to ask Alafare if she might have her things once they stopped for the night.

Pemberley

Mrs. Reynolds was poring over a recent inventory of household linens in her office when the sound of raised voices in the foyer caught her attention. Setting aside the inventory, she stood and headed towards the front of the house to reprimand whoever was disturbing the peace. Once she turned the corner into the foyer, however, her heart skipped a beat at what she found.

Mr. Walker was awkwardly patting a distraught Florence on the back, whilst two footmen carried an injured Rogers into the house.

"Take Rogers directly to his room," the butler ordered. "And, Soames, fetch Dr. Camryn immediately."

Soames, the front door footman, flew out the door just as Mrs. Reynolds came forwards. Attempting to control her trembling hands, she clasped them together tightly. "What happened?"

"The coach was attacked by highwaymen not long after they left Leicester," Mr. Walker replied.

The only visible sign of how that information affected the housekeeper was the hand that flew to her heart. "Mrs. Darcy?" Mrs. Reynolds asked.

"They...they took her!" Florence stammered, beginning to cry again. "I tried to accompany the mistress, but...but they would not allow it."

"What of Lord Hartford?" Mrs. Reynolds asked with little emotion.

"After we were interviewed by the constable in Leicester, Lord Hartford said he was going on to London with a Lord Porterfield," Florence replied. "I asked Lord Hartford why he was not returning to Pemberley to search for Mrs. Darcy, but he dismissed the notion as useless."

"That is not surprising!" Mr. Walker interjected angrily.

"There is much to do," Mrs. Reynolds said, her voice sounding nervous for the first time. "The master may already be on the road to London, but I shall send an express to Willowbend Hall in case he is still there. Darcy House must be notified, as well as Mr. Claridge."

At mention of the constable of Lambton, Florence said, "Mr. Claridge may already know. The constable in Leicester said he would notify all the local offices, as well as the Bow Street Runners in London. In addition, Lord Hartford boasted that he sent an express to Darcy House, just in case Mr. Darcy should arrive there before he does."

Mrs. Reynolds walked over to put her arm around Florence's shoulders. "Go to your room and try to rest. I feel certain that once he is made aware of what has happened, Mr. Claridge will come, and he will want to question everyone involved."

Florence began towards the door leading to the kitchen, intending to take the stairs there to her apartment below. Once at the door, she paused and turned. "Mrs. Reynolds?" The elderly servant looked in her direction. "Please let me know the minute you hear anything about Mrs. Darcy...anything at all."

"You have my word," Mrs. Reynolds replied.

Ramsgate
Younge's Art Academy

Having grown tired of Mrs. Younge's constant nagging, George Wickham planned a romantic dinner in a private room at the inn to assuage her worries and ensure her cooperation. It had not proven a success, however, for the entire meal had been punctuated with her voicing doubts about his plan to abscond with Georgiana Darcy.

"I do not like this one bit, George," Martha Younge declared, finishing the last bite of her dessert. "You said you could make Georgiana fall in love with you, and she would welcome the chance to elope. That has certainly *not* been the case. If anything, she dislikes you even more today than the day I introduced you."

Standing, Wickham pulled the plain woman from her chair and into his embrace, kissing her fervently. When he felt her body relax, he pulled his head back to look at her.

"I am doing this for us, Martha, though you do nothing but fight me every step of the way. Since that spoiled little brat would not give me an opportunity to win her over, surely you know I have no choice but to change directions."

"But Miss Darcy is not quite fifteen and—"

"My mother married at fourteen, and so have many others."

"Still, I do not wish to be involved in a scandal, and to involve Lady Farthingham in your plans will make it even more outrageous. What will my friends think once it becomes well known?"

"What friends do you speak of? In my opinion, the few I have met would rather see you eke out a living by teaching art to spoiled children than see you happily settled. You confessed that you are barely able to meet your expenses. Can you name one *friend* who would pay your debts if you could not?" Mrs. Younge went silent, prompting Wickham to declare, "I thought not!"

"I...I suppose you are right, George."

"I am right!" Wickham declared, kissing her so zealously that her knees began to buckle. "Now, just leave everything to me. I shall be very careful, for I do not want you to come under suspicion, either."

Martha Younge sighed. "Explain to me again how it will play out."

"Once the school term ends you will invite Lady Farthingham, her daughter, Georgiana, and me to a celebration dinner since they will be leaving the following day. Before dinner you will slip something into their drinks that will soon put them to sleep. When the others awaken the next morning, you will pretend to wake as they do. By the time Lady Farthingham realises what has happened, Georgiana and I will be well on our way to Gretna Green."

"And after that?"

"You have only to wait here until I send word that I have secured Georgiana's dowry. Then I will instruct you where and when to meet me. Most likely we will sail out of Southampton. Just be sure to have all your possessions packed and ready to board the ship."

"Oh, George!" Martha Younge cried, laying her head against his chest. "Are we really going to sail away together and leave all of this madness behind?"

"You can count on one thing, my love," Wickham replied, an unseen smirk crossing his face. "I will get what I want. I always have."

Near Sheffield

As the small caravan travelled north, Elizabeth watched for signs marking the next town. After spying one that said Sheffield, she tossed her other boot out the window. Again, no one took notice of her actions, and she thanked God they had not.

Once they stopped for the night at another clearing in the woods, a bonfire was lit, and soon the air was filled with the smell of something cooking in a large pot suspended over it. Not long afterwards, Alafare returned to the wagon with two plates of what Elizabeth knew as a ragout. She had little appetite, but she wished to avoid the loft and the shackles as long as possible, so she ate very slowly.

In between bites, she asked, "I...I was wondering if it would be possible for me to have the items that were in my trunk? There are things in there that I use for my toilet, such as my hairbrush and mirror, and the items I use to clean my teeth, as well as things that a woman has use for only once a month."

Alafare looked taken by surprise. "It had not crossed my mind that you might have need of them. As soon as I finish eating, I shall find Tomas and insist that they be returned."

"Thank you." Elizabeth thought this the perfect opportunity to find out more about her captors. "Why are we going to Edinburgh?"

"That is where Tomas plans to board a ship to the Continent. If my cousin can get to the next meeting of our council, he may be elected the leader of all the Romani."

"Surely he could have sailed from a closer port."

"A good many of my people are near Edinburgh, including a distant cousin who captains a merchant ship. His grandmother was Romani, so he understands us. Whenever we must sail to the Continent, he allows us to use his ship."

"Will you go?"

"No. Only Tomas, Teza, and Tomas' parents, who want to resettle in their ancient homeland before they die."

"I assumed I was taken for a ransom and would be freed as soon as it was paid, yet I find myself on my way to Edinburgh."

"I do not know what Tomas plans to do with you. He has not said."

Although she did not wish to show any weakness, tears slipped from Elizabeth's eyes at her answer.

Alafare was moved at the sight. "You will fare better with us than by staying here under the control of your callous husband."

"I do not know what you mean. My husband is a kind, caring man."

"Not according to the man who arranged your abduction. He told Tomas that should you stay in England, you were marked for death."

"My husband and I are very much in love, and if I was marked for death, it was certainly not by him. He will be devastated to learn of my abduction."

"Can any woman truly know a man's heart?"

"I can. My husband is the most honourable man I have ever known."

"It is obvious you love him."

"I do," Elizabeth said. Then, leaning forwards, she pleaded, "Please, help me to escape! I promise my husband will give you a sizeable reward if you do."

Alafare shook her head emphatically. "To go against the dictates of our leader means certain death. I may not agree with Tomas, but I must follow his orders." She stood. "It is time to lock your shackles again. Once I have, I shall do what I can to convince Tomas to return the contents of your trunk."

Realising she would get no further with Alafare, Elizabeth climbed the ladder to the loft and lay still as her ankles were secured once more. When her captor left the wagon, she closed her eyes, trying to recall how it felt to be in William's arms the last time she saw him.

Quoting what he had said to her in the same exaggerated Scottish burr, she was barely able to finish before breaking into sobs.

And fare thee weel, my only luve!
And fare thee weel, a while!
And I will come again, my luve,
Tho' it ware ten thousand mile!

North of Salisbury
An inn

Whilst travelling, William and Richard usually shared a suite with two bedrooms if one was available. Often the suite had a balcony on which to eat, relax and enjoy a bit of fresh air before retiring. Moreover, it was not unheard of for the cheaper rooms to be broken into whilst the occupants slept. Suites had more secure doors and locks and offered greater protection against that possibility.

Being a veteran of many campaigns, Richard was used to sleeping lightly, and sometime during the early morning hours footsteps in the sitting room that divided his bedroom from William's brought him instantly awake. Grabbing the pistol he kept beneath his pillow, he crept from the bed as quietly as possible and cautiously opened the door into that room. Poised motionless in the doorway, it was not long before he made out the figure of a man standing in the open balcony door.

"Stop right there!" he barked.

William swung around with his hands in the air. "Do not shoot, Richard!"

Richard's racing heart almost stopped. "Darcy, do you have any idea how close you came to being killed?"

"I imagine you will remind me of that from now until eternity."

Laying his pistol on a table, Richard crossed to stand beside his cousin, who had walked onto the balcony. "That is not amusing."

"I apologise. I did not realise my footsteps could create enough noise to awaken you."

"I am a soldier. The slightest of noises wakens me."

The sky was clear, a full moon illuminating everything in a silvery glow. The view was magical, and for a moment both were silent.

At length, Richard ventured, "More night terrors?"

William nodded.

"The same one?"

"Yes," William answered with a ragged sigh. "I have never been one to believe in signs or premonitions, but I cannot escape the feeling that all is not right with Elizabeth." Chuckling self-consciously, he added, "Then again, perhaps marriage had turned me into someone who imagines the worse with every bad dream."

"Far be it from me to belittle such things," Richard replied. "Before every battle, Sergeant Butler could tell from his dreams whether our strategy was sound, or it needed revising. It was eerie, but I learned quickly that he possessed an insight I did not, and I learned to adjust my course according to his premonitions."

"All I know is that these night terrors are driving me mad. I cannot wait to see Elizabeth and learn that all is well."

Richard clasped William's shoulder. "One cannot fault you for that. Fortunately, if all goes as planned, we should reach London tomorrow afternoon."

"It cannot come soon enough to suit me."

"Why not lie down and close your eyes? Get some rest, if not sleep. Maybe then you will not keep me awake from here to Andover with your snoring."

"Elizabeth has assured me that I do not snore. You, on the other hand, were forced to sleep in a separate tent the last time you were on manoeuvres because none of your comrades would share a tent with you."

"You would never have known that had I not been drunk!"

"Not only do I know, but everyone who was at White's that evening knows."

Richard sighed. "A sad state of affairs when a man cannot trust his own cousin to take him home before he makes a fool of himself."

"I learned long ago not to interfere when you decide to have a drinking contest with one of your army cohorts."

"And I managed to do a good job of it. I bested him, did I not?"

"You will get no argument from me there."

Chapter 35

London
The next afternoon

So anxious was William to get to Darcy House, he had the coach stop in front of the townhouse so that he and Richard could exit there instead of riding on to the back entrance. No sooner had they stepped out of the vehicle, however, than the front door of Darcy House flew open, and both Mr. and Mrs. Barnes hurried out.

This cannot bode well! Richard thought as he glanced over to gauge his cousin's reaction. William's face instantly assumed the Master of Pemberley mask he wore whenever he wished to appear in control.

When they reached the portico, Mrs. Barnes declared, "Thank God you are here!"

Without replying, William continued into the house before turning in the foyer to confront the housekeeper.

"Perhaps it would be best if you sit down, sir," Mr. Barnes ventured.

"I am a man, not a child," William replied a little too sharply. Seeing the butler flinch, he added, "Please tell me what has you so concerned."

Butler and housekeeper exchanged anxious glances before Mrs. Barnes began to explain. "Just two days past, a letter arrived for you from Mrs. Darcy. Then, this morning an express post from Lord Hartford was delivered. I was already worried that something was amiss when the magistrate of the Bow Street Runners called."

"George Fielding[15] was here?" William asked incredulously.

"Yes. He said he did not expect to find you in residence but wished to be informed the minute you arrived."

"Did he mention why?"

"He acted as though he was not at liberty to discuss it; however, I explained that Mr. Barnes and I had served the Darcy family for over twenty years, and it was imperative we know immediately if something had happened to any of you."

"And?"

"He stated that he had received a report of a coach being waylaid by highwaymen near Leicester." Mrs. Barnes' eyes dropped to her wringing hands. "Word is that it was one of your coaches, and it carried Mrs. Darcy."

"That is preposterous! Mrs. Darcy has no reason to be on the road!"

Richard came forward to clamp a hand on his shoulder. "Darcy, why not go to your study and read the letters. I shall join you there shortly."

Visibly shaken, William walked woodenly towards his study. After he turned the corner and was out of sight, Richard addressed Mrs. Barnes. "Hot coffee and some refreshments would be helpful. We have not eaten in hours."

"Certainly!" Immediately she disappeared in the direction of the kitchen.

Addressing the butler, he said, "Barnes, please advise the head groom that we may be leaving sooner than we had planned. In any case, the coach should be ready to leave at a moment's notice."

"And your trunks, sir? Should we bring them in?"

"Wait until I have spoken with Darcy."

---

15 **Henry Fielding** founded the **Bow Street Runners** in 1749. For the purpose of this story, I invented the magistrate George Fielding, whom I cast as the grandson of Henry. https://en.wikipedia.org/wiki/Bow_Street_Runners

After watching the butler rush away, Richard hurried to join his cousin.

Upon entering the study, Richard saw an expression of such deep anguish on William's face that it impelled him to caution, "Darcy, if this should be true, you must stay calm to be of any use."

Instead of replying, William tossed the letter from Elizabeth across the desk. Richard picked it up and sat down to read.

"Good Lord!" he exclaimed. "Mrs. Darcy was on the way to Ramsgate to rescue Georgiana from some blackguard trying to impose himself on her, and Fielding says her coach may have been commandeered by highwaymen near Leicester. What is next? A fire at Pemberley?"

William was busy reading the express received that morning and his voice was strangely emotionless when he looked up. "If Lord Hartford is to be believed, there is no ambiguity regarding Elizabeth. He maintains—" Richard watched his cousin's hands shake as he refolded the missive. "He maintains that my wife was taken by the highwaymen who robbed their coach."

Immediately Richard was on his feet. "That is absurd! Highwaymen do not relish being hunted down and hanged for kidnapping. They want money and jewels to support their way of life and to be left alone!"

"I have not the time to question their motive; I must find Elizabeth!" William declared, coming to his feet. A knock on the door caused both men to look in that direction. "Come!" William barked impatiently. Both were shocked when Viscount Leighton entered the room.

"Forgive me for interrupting, Cousin, but my head groom's brother works for the Bow Street Runners, and this morning he passed along a most disturbing account regarding Mrs. Darcy. I came here hoping to find it all a mistake."

"It is no mistake," Richard interjected. "Mrs. Darcy has been taken."

"Good heavens! How can Father and I help?"

"Father wants to help?" Richard repeated.

"Yes. When I informed him of what I had heard, he asked me to find out if it was true and, if so, to convey his concern and to offer his assistance, along with mine."

Though as shocked as Richard, William explained the circumstances that caused Elizabeth to strike out for Ramsgate, adding, "It would be a great burden off my shoulders if you and my uncle immediately leave to retrieve Georgiana whilst I begin searching for Elizabeth."

"Certainly," Leighton replied. "However, it will not take both of us to retrieve my cousin. Pray, let me stay and help in the search."

Noting that William was not himself, Richard took charge. "We must put a plan in place quickly before the clues to Mrs. Darcy's disappearance grow cold. Leighton, go to Father, inform him of Georgiana's situation, and ask him to leave for Ramsgate right away." To William he said, "Darcy, write down the particulars of the art school she attends there."

As William pulled pen and paper from his desk, Richard continued. "After you have met with Father, use your influence to find two comrades of mine who recently retired: Sergeants Kennedy and McKinley. I understand they still live in Town. Explain what has happened and tell them I will pay them well to join the search. If they agree, each is to recruit four or five reliable men to work under their authority. Meanwhile, Darcy and I will speak with the Bow Street Runners and Lord Hartford and meet you back here this evening, hopefully with Kennedy and McKinley."

"Of course!" Leighton exclaimed, taking the information from William and heading towards the door. Before he quit the room, he stopped to address William. "Darcy, know this. However long it takes and no matter what needs to be done, we will find your wife."

William was touched. "That gives me hope. Thank you." As soon as Leighton left, he said, "I cannot bear to think of Elizabeth in the hands of—" Unable to continue, he closed his eyes.

Knowing he must keep William's spirits up, Richard declared,

"Then let us be off to Mr. Fielding's office and discover what he knows that we do not."

In only minutes, William and Richard were being jostled about in the carriage as it travelled over the uneven bricks on the road leading to the Bow Street offices.

"What are you thinking?" Richard asked. There was a long silence before he received a reply.

"I was considering how quickly life can change. I did not realise it at the time, but the moment Elizabeth appeared on my doorstep in Cambridge my life took a new direction. It has taken us so long to find our way...to admit we are in love. And now—" His voice caught, and he cleared his throat in hopes of disguising it. "If God allows me to find her, I shall never take another day with Elizabeth for granted."

"Just keep the faith," Richard said.

Turning to look out the window to hide the tears pooling in his eyes, William murmured, "I am trying."

Near Sheffield

That morning, after unshackling her legs and bringing her food, Alafare had quickly disappeared. As a result, Elizabeth was unable to enquire why they had not broken camp and moved farther north. Now that the items in her trunk had been restored to her, she longed to toss more of them out of the window to mark their way to Edinburgh.

It was afternoon before her captor returned to take her for a short walk, and as they exited the wagon, Elizabeth ventured, "I expected we would continue north today."

"Tomas decided we should stay off the roads for a few days."

"Did he say why?"

"The men who drove your coach towards Liverpool returned this morning. Tomas had instructed them to come back through

Lambton and buy something in the village to see if there was any talk of your disappearance."

"Was there?"

"Apparently, you are the talk of the town. The constable has men searching all of Derbyshire."

Elizabeth was so heartened by the news that an expression of relief crossed her face. Seeing it, Alafare commented, "What will you do if you are not ransomed?"

"Do you still believe my husband is indifferent and will not pay? For that is a lie."

"No. I meant in case Tomas decides not to ransom you."

"Why would he not? Surely he needs the money to travel to the Continent."

"He was paid well to take you, and you may be worth more on the Continent than here. To certain men, women like you are highly valued as—" She shrugged.

"I would rather die than submit to another man."

"Do not let Tomas hear you say such things. He would delight in proving you wrong."

"Please, if you have ever loved a man, think of how it would feel to be parted from him forever. I love my husband dearly. Help me to escape, I beg of you."

Alafare's expression darkened. "You ask too much of me. Climb back into the loft; I must keep you bound until I return." She watched until Elizabeth had done so before pushing Clancy into the space with her. Quickly locking the shackles, she stormed out of the wagon and locked the door.

Suddenly, the thought of never seeing William again so overwhelmed Elizabeth that she began to cry. Clancy inched closer, eventually nudging with his nose the hands covering her face. At this, Elizabeth pulled him into her embrace, stroking his head.

"I know you miss home as much as I do. Perhaps God will answer my prayers, and we will be there soon."

London
Lady Henrietta's townhouse

As Lady Henrietta's cousin descended the staircase in the house he pretended was his own, Richard struggled to suppress a laugh. Sporting eyes blackened and almost swollen shut, an angry split on his lower lip, and a nose that appeared twice its former size, he looked nothing like the handsome rogue who was so popular at Lady Emma's ball. Glancing to William, Richard was not surprised to see that his cousin's expression was all seriousness, and he adjusted his mien accordingly.

"Lord Hartford," William said without offering to shake hands, "surely you are aware of why I am here."

"I was expecting you," his lordship replied, his voice somewhat affected by his injuries.

"Then I shall get straight to the point. I wish to know everything that happened after the highwaymen stopped my coach near Leicester."

"My injuries make it difficult to speak. I suggest you go to the Bow Street Runners' office and read the statement that I gave to them."

"I have already done that," William stated menacingly through clenched teeth. "And I was not satisfied with the account."

"Of...of course," Lord Hartford stammered. "Let us go into the library where we may talk freely."

Once he and his cousin entered the awaiting carriage in front of the townhouse, Richard declared, "It is just as you said! Lord Hartford's explanation changed from the account he gave to Mr. Fielding."

"I have found that liars often have trouble remembering their stories. Now he contends he was struck twice. Once for objecting when the blackguard threatened to search Elizabeth—purportedly that was when he was knocked nearly senseless—and again when he regained his wits, only to learn they were taking my wife prisoner."

"No one could ever convince me that after having his nose thumped, that cad raised a second objection," Richard hissed.

"Nor I. No doubt Elizabeth's maid will provide the truth once I get to Pemberley."

"I am pleased you decided ahead of time not to challenge Hartford. Let him believe he has fooled us whilst we have him followed day and night. That may reveal who else is involved, and if we are fortunate, lead us to Mrs. Darcy. In the meantime, I aim to dispatch a man to Liverpool to learn everything there is to know about Lord Hartford, past and present."

"I would stake my life that he is involved, and he acted in conjunction with my stepmother," William said.

"I agree," Richard said. "Still, in order to find your wife, we must let all those in question believe they have gotten away with their crime. Can you endure being in company with Lady Henrietta and Lord Hartford and still keep your resolve?"

"For Elizabeth's sake I must, but God help them if something should happen to—" William looked away.

"Your wife is more valuable alive. In fact, I expect a ransom note will be forthcoming soon."

William rubbed his tired eyes. "I am so fearful of losing Elizabeth that I cannot think straight. How does one begin to search all of England?"

"By taking one area at a time," Richard replied. "Let me handle the details. I trust the men I charged Leighton with finding to mount a thorough search. And since we know the highwaymen headed back towards Leicester, we will concentrate our efforts first from there to Scotland."

"I imagine that any ransom note would go directly to Pemberley, so I leave for there in the morning. Along the way I will speak with the constable in Leicester, post a reward, and question the innkeepers and merchants on that stretch of road. Perhaps someone saw or heard something that might help us find Elizabeth."

"I can direct the search from Pemberley better than from here. If you can wait until I can commandeer the men needed, I will accompany you. Leighton can stay in London and direct the search from this end."

"I cannot wait, Richard. I have another coach that you may use to join me."

"I understand. Hopefully, Leighton will find my associates today so that I may accompany you tomorrow."

For a long while William stared out the window at what had abruptly become a dismal place—Grosvenor Square. "Thank God you are here. I fear I might have gone mad had I been left to face this alone."

"I have watched you handle one adversity after another, beginning with your mother's death, Darcy. You have a good head on your shoulders and are much stronger than you realise."

"Am I? I used to think I was. Then Elizabeth came into my life. She taught me there are things more important than wealth, estates...business. Her love brought me to my knees, and without her, I am lost. Pemberley will never be the same if she is not there."

Having never heard his cousin speak about his childhood home in such a manner, Richard was stunned. At length, he replied, "We *will* find her. I promise you."

William nodded silently.

Ramsgate
Younge's Art Academy

George Wickham stood at the door of the classroom, watching as Georgiana Darcy stepped forwards to receive her diploma from Monsieur Dupuy, along with several awards she had won for her paintings at the art exhibit. A good many of the students' parents were in attendance, and everyone applauded politely.

Reaching into his coat, Wickham removed a small vial and handed it to Mrs. Younge. "Is everything organised? Did you arrange to have your cook leave early?"

"Yes. Lady Farthingham, Lady Esme, and Georgiana will be here promptly at eight tomorrow evening. I planned a simple menu that can be served from the sideboard and had my cook prepare a punch. I thought it would be easier to conceal whatever you plan to put in their drinks."

"How clever of you," Wickham said, giving her a wry smile. "Pour all of the contents of that vial into the punch and stir it well before serving. Just be sure not to drink any yourself."

Mrs. Younge swallowed hard. "It will not kill them, will it?"

"Do you think me dim-witted?" George huffed, before realising he had spoken too harshly. Switching to a charming smile, he added, "I would never chance anyone being harmed."

Face still burning from being chastised, Martha Younge did not reply.

"I need your key to Georgiana's room. Whilst we are in the dining room, my man will remove all her things to the hired coach. In that way, once she is asleep, I have only to carry her to the coach and be off to Gretna Green."

"How long will it take the potion to work?"

"I was told an hour, perhaps sooner."

Mrs. Younge nodded. "I pray the plan goes according—"

"No more prayers!" Wickham exclaimed. "Everything is going to go as planned, and soon we will be rich beyond our dreams."

"I do not wish for great wealth, George. I wish only to be with you."

"And you shall be, my love," he said, giving her a quick peck on the forehead. "Just keep reminding yourself of that if you begin to doubt again."

Darcy House
Later

As Richard and William entered the house, Mr. Barnes rushed forward. "Sir, Viscount Leighton is waiting for you in the library. He has two men with him."

"Thank God!" Richard declared as he and William walked in that direction.

Once in the library, Viscount Leighton stopped conversing

with the men to address his brother. "I had no trouble finding them, Richard. They were having a round of ale in a pub right beside your office."

"I should have known that is where you would find them," Richard said, smiling as he reached to shake first one sergeant's hand and then the other's. "They spent a goodly portion of each day in that pub when they were supposed to be at work."

"I do not think I would tease them too severely were I you," Leighton interjected. "After all, you need their help."

"They know it is not true," Richard replied. "Thank you for coming, men."

"Anything for you, Colonel," Sergeant Kennedy replied. "A man does not soon forget the one who saved his life."

"Aye, this is true!" Sergeant McKinley seconded.

Richard ignored the tribute. "You have met my brother, now let me introduce my cousin, Fitzwilliam Darcy." To William, he said, "Darcy, it is my honour to introduce two of the best men I have commanded in all my years in the army: Sergeant Kennedy and Sergeant McKinley."

"A pleasure, gentlemen," William replied as both men nodded, murmuring a greeting.

"It is Darcy's wife who is missing," Richard continued.

"Viscount Leighton explained that you need men to search for her and want each of us to recruit four or five others to serve under our direction," Sergeant McKinley replied.

"Colonel Fitzwilliam has great faith in you, so I am placing my faith in you as well. My wife, Elizabeth Darcy, was kidnapped just east of Leicester as she travelled to London." William went on to explain all that he knew of the incident.

"Rest assured that you and those you recruit will be paid well," Richard interrupted. "Try to fill your quota quickly. My cousin wishes to leave London tomorrow, and we would like you to follow as soon as possible. Leighton will be your contact here. He will handle the particulars of getting you to Leicester as well as paying your advances."

"Do you have any idea where the search will begin?" Sergeant Kennedy asked.

"My initial strategy is for you to take the road to Liverpool that begins at Derby. Sergeant McKinley will begin at Leicester and go all the way to Scotland. Every road, every farmhouse drive, pig trail or anything that looks wide enough for a coach to enter is to be searched."

"That will take some time."

"We are prepared for that possibility. If you find any clue—anything that raises the slightest suspicion—send a man to Lambton and ask for directions to Pemberley. That is Darcy's estate. He and I will be coordinating the search from there, and we want to be informed the instant you learn anything."

Sergeant Kennedy stood. "We had better get started, Sergeant McKinley." Both men said their farewells and exited the library.

"What do you wish me to do?" Leighton asked.

"We need you to remain in London and stay in touch with the Bow Street Runners. Open all of my correspondence," William said, "and if any of it pertains to Elizabeth's disappearance, send it directly to Pemberley via express post."

"What should I do about Georgiana?"

"Once she is in London, have her stay with your parents. She will be safe with them whilst I scour the countryside looking for my wife."

"As you wish."

Chapter 36

Leicester
Two days later

After learning from the constable in Leicester that no trace of Elizabeth or those who took her had been found, a very disappointed William and Richard were preparing to leave when a stranger approached their coach.

"Excuse me, sir," a poorly-dressed man of approximately forty said as he performed an awkward bow. "I saw the reward placard in the window and was told it was you who put it there."

"It was," William replied.

"I do not know if this has anything to do with the lady's kidnapping, but I did see something I thought strange whilst I was hunt—" Suddenly realising that he was going to confess to poaching, he took a different tack. "I meant to say, whilst I was *walking* in the woods several days ago."

"What did you see?" William asked.

"I…I could really use that reward you offered."

"What is your name?"

"James Finwall, sir."

"Well, James Finwall, if your information leads to my wife's recovery, you have my word the reward will be yours."

"Like I said, I was in the woods just north of Derby when I came across a camp of several wagons in a circle—the kind gypsies travel in. I know, for they come down this way every so often and then head back north a few months later."

"Did you happen to see a gentlewoman with them?" William asked.

"Because of a dispute I once had with one of their women, I did not wish for them to see me, so I hurried to leave the woods."

Curious, Richard asked, "What kind of disagreement?"

"I paid her to tell my fortune, but nothing she said came true. Next time I saw her, I demanded my money back. Out of the blue, two of the men with her attacked me. I was lucky to escape with my life."

"I fail to see how any of this relates to Mrs. Darcy's disappearance," Richard stated.

"I have not finished my story yet," the man protested.

"Then, finish!" Richard exclaimed. "We were about to leave!"

"After I got back to the highway, I noticed they had covered up the access to the road. It seemed odd that they would take the time to cut down limbs and brush and such, just to try to disguise a road."

"Would you be willing to show us where you saw them?" William asked.

"Certainly."

"Tie your horse to the back of the coach," William said. "You may ride with us to the campsite."

North of Sheffield

Elizabeth could not have been more pleased when the caravan resumed its journey, since there was little chance of being found as long as they stayed hidden in the woods. Moreover, whereas at one time she felt certain she could walk home if she managed to escape, she was no longer so sure. Lying in the loft for hours at a time had sapped her strength and rendered the shoulder that had suffered the gun-shot so tender that even climbing the ladder caused her pain. Her hopes now rested in being found by those searching for her.

Her discomfort had proved useful, however, for Alafare responded by shuttering the windows downstairs to prevent Elizabeth from seeing out or being seen, and now allowed her to ride in the lower portion of the wagon during the day. Even Clancy, who was always kept on a rope to prevent his escaping, was allowed to lie on Alafare's bed instead of staying in the loft.

As the caravan slowly made its way onto the main highway north, Elizabeth noticed a broken slat on one of the window shutters. Peeking through the tiny opening, she was able to determine that their wagon was once again the last one in the procession. Hurrying to the loft, she retrieved her silver-plated comb and forced it through the window. Saying a quick prayer that William would find it, she hurried back down the ladder, picked up Clancy and sat holding her breath until she was certain no one had noticed.

It seemed hours before the wagons pulled off the road and began to make another circle. Instantly after the caravan came to a halt, Alafare opened the door of the wagon, providing a glimpse of their location—an open field beside a creek.

"Tomas says we will stop only long enough to eat," she said. "When the food is ready, I shall bring you a plate. Remember, stay hidden so that he will not realise that you are not bound and in the loft."

After the door closed, Elizabeth heard the sound of the latch sliding into place. Moving to sit beside Clancy on Alafare's bed, she lay back, closed her eyes and allowed herself the rare indulgence of thinking about William. Since her abduction she tried not to dwell on thoughts of him, for it only made her more miserable. This day, however, she felt the loss so greatly that her memories would not be suppressed. Recalling how handsome he had looked the day he left for Weymouth, she began to ache for his touch.

The sound of the latch sliding open again brought her back to the present. Hurriedly standing, she stared at the door, expecting to see Alafare. Instead, Nikolae slipped inside the wagon and pulled the door shut. Though the look in his eyes made her fearful, Elizabeth was determined not to let it show.

"I have a proposal to make."

Instead of responding, she fixed Nikolae with a sharp look, lifting her chin in defiance.

"If you agree to be my woman, I will convince Tomas to give you to me instead of selling you on the Continent."

Abhorrence flooded her, but Elizabeth strove to remain calm. "I have a husband whom I love very much. Fitzwilliam Darcy is the only man I will ever have."

Nikolae grabbed one of her arms and twisted it behind her back. Instantly, Clancy was on his feet, growling and barking as he strained against the rope. Ignoring the dog, the gypsy hissed, "Are you so stupid you do not know that your husband hired us? He wants you dead!"

"My husband had nothing to do with this!"

Suddenly, Nikolae attempted to kiss Elizabeth, whilst she twisted her head first one way and then the other. With all of the noise Clancy was making, neither realised that Alafare had entered the wagon until she began forcing her way between them.

"Stop it at once! Let go of her!"

Without warning, Nikolae was grabbed from behind and dragged out of the wagon. He landed on the ground on his back with Tomas towering over him. "You knew my orders concerning the prisoner; still, you defied me!"

"Why is it your place to decide her fate?" Nikolae hissed as he struggled to get back on his feet. "What if I want her for myself?"

"I am the leader, and I will tolerate no dissent. She *will* be sold at the gathering, and you *will* stay away from her. Is that understood?"

Looking about the camp, Nikolae found no sympathy in the eyes meeting his. He picked up his head scarf from the ground, and stalked off in anger, beating the scarf against his thigh.

Giving Elizabeth a look of disdain, Tomas said to Alafare, "I will have Teza bring you a lock. From this day forwards, make certain it is on the wagon whenever you are away."

After everyone scattered, Alafare set the food she had brought for Elizabeth in front of her. Seeing that her prisoner made no effort to eat, she said, "You must eat, else you will grow so weak you may not withstand the trip to the Continent."

Elizabeth's hands sought her stomach. "Just the smell is making me queasy. I doubt I could keep it down."

"I shall ask if anyone has tea. That might help soothe your stomach."

Just as quickly as she had appeared, Alafare left. The sound of voices just outside the wagon compelled Elizabeth to lay her head against the door in an effort to hear what was being said.

"Here is the lock Tomas promised," Teza said. "Do not lose the key, or the lock must be broken off."

At length, the only sound Elizabeth heard was the lock being put into place. Realising that it added yet another obstacle to her escape, she fought not to give in to her despair.

Please, Lord, show me a way out of this predicament or let William find me before the ship sails.

In the woods near Derby

Mr. Finwall, William, and Richard had combed the highway for some time before they located the hidden entrance to the road the gypsies had taken into the woods. At the end of the road were the remains of a large fire in the centre of a circle of wagon tracks, proving that Mr. Finwall had been telling the truth about what he had seen. Whilst William and Richard walked over the area searching for clues, Mr. Finwall stood with his hat in his hand and a satisfied look on his face.

"It is just as I said, is it not?"

Engrossed in combing the area, neither gentleman replied, so Mr. Finwall went silent. Not long after, Richard stooped to pick up something off the ground. "Have a look at this, Darcy."

Finwall followed as William walked in that direction. Richard stretched out his hand. In his palm was what appeared to be an earring, though not like those worn by women of the *ton*. This one consisted of a brightly painted array of small seashells and wooden balls.

"One of the gypsy men was wearing that!" Mr. Finwall stated confidently.

Richard reached inside his coat to remove a handkerchief. Placing the earring safely inside the cloth, he folded it and put it back into his pocket.

"Keep looking," William said. "With any luck we might find something belonging to Elizabeth."

Sadly, though they scoured the camp for another hour, nothing more was discovered. At that point, William addressed Mr. Finwall.

"Thank you for coming forward to tell us what you saw. At present, nothing points to my wife being taken by the gypsies, but I will not rule out anything. We must resume our journey, so please tell me where I can contact you."

"I live at Crosby, east of Derby. Ask anyone there, and they will show you where I live," he answered, though he seemed reluctant to leave.

"You have my word that if it turns out that the gypsies had anything to do with my wife's abduction, you *will* be paid the reward," William stated.

With that the man seemed satisfied, and untying his horse from the coach, he mounted and rode away. As they watched him leave, Richard said, "I do not hold much stock in the theory that gypsies, or anyone else for that matter, would kidnap someone and then camp near the scene of the abduction. If it were me, I would wish to get far away as quickly as possible."

"On the other hand, perhaps they would be successful for that very reason. Whilst everyone is searching for highwaymen with fast horses, they could pass by undetected."

"Highly unlikely, but I see your point," Richard replied. "In any case, we cannot afford to rule anything out."

"I agree." Glancing at the place where his wife might have been only days ago, a lump formed in William's throat.

Seeing the misery in his eyes, Richard said, "We should get started. Before we head north, I wish to leave word at the inn in

Derby for Sergeants Kennedy and McKinley to keep an eye out for gypsies in addition to highwaymen."

The next day

Lord Matlock had set out to retrieve Georgiana the day he was charged with the task, yet his coach got only as far as Rochester before darkness prevented him from going any farther. Despite being forced to spend the night at an inn, his coach was on the road to Ramsgate by the time dawn broke. The result of this dedication was that Lord Matlock's vehicle pulled into the town of Ramsgate shortly after the sun set. Ordering the coach to stop in front of the local hotel, he addressed the footman who climbed down to open his door.

"Go inside and enquire about the location of Younge's Art Academy."

The footman nodded and then vanished inside the building, whilst the other footmen and the driver climbed down to stretch their legs. Not long afterwards, the first footman returned, going straight to the still open door.

"Sir, the proprietor allows it is straight ahead two miles on the right."

"Take me there immediately!" Lord Matlock ordered his driver.

All the servants remounted the coach, and the horses surged ahead at the first crack of the driver's whip. In a short while, they halted in front of a large, older house.

Exiting the coach without waiting, Lord Matlock addressed the two largest footmen he had brought along in case of trouble. "Lawrence...Brooks, present your arms and follow me."

Pulling pistols from their waistbands, both followed their employer to the building. Trying the door knob, Lord Matlock found it locked, and proceeded to pound on the door. The second the door swung open, he walked right past the woman who had opened it.

"Sir, I am Mrs. Joiner, the housekeeper for the academy," the woman began. "The school is presently closed. You will have to come back tomorrow if you wish to speak with the proprietor."

"I will speak with her now!" his lordship declared, giving the woman a stern glare.

Whilst this was happening, two maids and a footman appeared in an attempt to support the housekeeper. Nevertheless, they were no match for the men with Lord Matlock.

"I am afraid the mistress is giving a dinner party and cannot be disturbed."

Without bothering to reply again, Lord Matlock stalked towards the light visible at the bottom of one of the doors.

"Sir...sir!" the housekeeper protested, rushing after him.

Reaching the room, Lord Matlock flung the door open. It had barely had time to bounce off the wall when he realised the occupants of the room were in distress. At the dining table, a lady had tumbled from her chair onto the floor, whilst a young girl, still seated, was slumped on the table. Lastly, it appeared that the hostess might have been preparing to serve the next course when she collapsed into the chair nearest the sideboard.

Taking in the scene, the shocked housekeeper began giving orders. "Quickly, see if they are alive!" Grabbing the footman as he started to walk past, she commanded, "Fetch the apothecary!"

As the housekeeper and maids examined each victim, Lord Matlock was relieved to learn they were only unconscious. Glancing to the table, which had been set for five, he demanded, "Who is missing?"

Wide-eyed, the housekeeper scanned the room. "Miss Darcy and Lord Worley were here earlier."

"Where is Miss Darcy's room?"

"In the rear, on the second floor; however, I heard a coach go around the side of the building just before you arrived. I was on my way to see who it was when you knocked on the door. Do you suppose it is related to their disappearance?"

"I intend to find out," Lord Matlock replied.

As he marched towards the door, she raced to get ahead of him. "Follow me. I will show you the most direct way."

Lord Matlock and his men trailed the housekeeper through

the house and out a side door. "The gravel drive leads to where vehicles must park."

A horse whinnied somewhere in the darkness, giving Lord Matlock hope that they were not too late. Rushing down the drive, they arrived in time to see a man leap into a coach and close the door. One of the earl's men rushed to grab the lead horse, whilst the other climbed into the driver's seat, forcing the man there to leap off the other side. He vanished into the darkness just as Lord Matlock jerked the coach door open. It was too dark to see much of anything, but as the man within the coach scrambled to exit the other side, William's uncle reached in and grabbed hold of him. The moon reappeared from behind the clouds just as he pulled that villain from the coach, illuminating his face.

"George Wickham! I should have known you were involved! What have you done with my niece?"

Before he could answer, one burly footman grabbed Wickham from behind. "You had best answer his lordship before I break your neck"

"She...she is unharmed! Look inside the coach!"

Lord Matlock climbed into the coach, and this time he caught a glimpse of his niece's face. Georgiana, wrapped in a blanket, was lying across the opposite seat as though she were merely sleeping.

"Lawrence," Lord Matlock called. "Please assist me by carrying my niece into the house." To the man holding Wickham, he said, "Brooks, keep a tight hold on that blackguard. I intend to see him hang."

"You can rely on me, sir!"

Longbourn
Mr. Bennet's Study

Jane waited patiently whilst her father read the letter delivered to Longbourn only minutes before. It had come from Edward Gardiner, and she was eager to know if her uncle had heard from Elizabeth of late, for she had not. As she watched Mr. Bennet's face, his expression changed from delight to concern.

"Papa, is something wrong?"

For a moment it seemed as though he had not heard. Then he laid the letter down on his desk instead of sliding it across to her as he usually did.

"I must go to Pemberley."

"Has something happened to Lizzy?" Jane asked, her voice trembling.

"I need you to remain composed so that you may be of service to your mother once she hears why I must leave. Can you do that, Jane?"

Jane looked as though she was about to cry. "I...I shall try."

"It seems your uncle received a note from Mr. Darcy saying Elizabeth was on her way to London when she was taken by highwaymen. Mr. Darcy is hopeful of receiving a ransom demand, so he might recover her quickly; however, at the time of his letter to my brother, no ransom had been demanded."

Silent tears rolled down Jane's cheeks. "Surely with his connections, Mr. Darcy will be able to recover her."

"Let us hope that is the case. In any event, I must travel to Pemberley to do whatever I can."

"Oh, Papa, you are not well enough to travel that far."

"I will not stay here and twiddle my thumbs."

"Then I shall go with you."

"Whilst I would love to have your company, I need your voice of reason here at Longbourn. Your mother may be critical of Lizzy at times, but she loves her and will worry exceedingly until she is found. Having you here will be a blessing for her and for me."

"Whatever you think is best. I shall, however, tell Charles what has happened. I know he will want to help however he can."

"That is between you and your young man." Mr. Bennet stood. "Now, come with me to inform your mother."

"Yes, Papa."

Chapter 37

Pemberley
One day later

Frustrated that his efforts had yet to produce results, William grew increasingly short-tempered with everyone, including his cousin. Consequently, when Richard entered William's study, he braced himself for another outburst. What he had not prepared for, however, was the need to take cover from the ball of paper that flew past his head, hit the wall and dropped to the floor, joining others like it on the carpet.

"What the devil!" Richard exclaimed.

Busily searching for a sharp pen amongst the items on his ink stand, William looked up, declaring angrily, "I pay well to have someone trim my pens and evidently that person is not up to the task! How am I supposed to write if all my pens are dull?"

"I know you are exasperated, Darcy, but you must keep your emotions in check."

Throwing up his hands, William said, "Must I? We are no closer to finding Elizabeth today than when we learned she was missing!" He dropped his head in his hands. "She had barely recovered from her wounds, and God only knows what they may have done to her."

"It is my belief they will treat her like the prize she is. After all, why destroy their chance to enrich themselves by making you angry enough to hunt them to the ends of the earth for revenge?"

William sighed. "I also feel guilty because I could not help Georgiana."

"You cannot be in both places at once. Father can deal with the cad who is bothering Georgiana just as well as you could."

Silent for a time, at length William stood and began pacing. "Sometimes I think if I stay in this house one more minute I shall go mad! I have done so little to recover Elizabeth that I want to saddle Zeus and go after her myself!"

"In which direction would you go?" At William's pained expression, he added, "It is best that we wait here until we know for certain which way they are heading. As for having done so little? One has only to examine the map lying on your desk to refute that claim! You have kept a record of every parcel our men have searched thus far, and it covers most of Derbyshire and the surrounding counties."

"Yet we have nothing to show for it."

"That is no longer true," Richard replied, pulling an express he had received only minutes before from his pocket. He watched all the colour drain from William's face. "Brace yourself, Darcy. Sergeant Kennedy has located your coach."

"Eliz...Elizabeth?" he stammered.

"No one was found with the vehicle. It was abandoned along the highway from Derby to Liverpool. Some locals found it and took it to the nearest inn. They had already reported it to the constable by the time Sergeant Kennedy arrived."

"Liverpool?" William repeated. "Do you mean we have been concentrating on the wrong route all this time?"

"We have been searching that direction, too. Why else was Sergeant Kennedy in the vicinity?"

"Of course, you are right. I am so tired my mind is muddled. Since the vehicle was unmarked, how did they conclude it was my coach?"

"Apparently there was a small plate fixed beneath the lid of one cushion box, indicating it was built for George Darcy."

"I had forgotten about that." For a time, William seemed lost in thought. Then he said, "As soon as we talk to Florence, you and I shall leave to examine the coach."

"That will not be necessary. It is on its way here. Sergeant Kennedy ordered two of his men to deliver it whilst he and the others stayed behind to continue the search."

"What do you make of it?"

"In his letter, Kennedy said the coach was roadworthy, as were the horses. In addition, there were no tracks nearby to indicate another vehicle had stopped to pick them up. In my opinion, the location of the coach was merely a diversion. They wanted us to think they went in that direction."

William sank back down in his chair. He did not look up, and there was a slight tremble to his voice when next he spoke. "For days now, I have feared voicing what is on my heart."

"Afraid that saying it aloud would make it true?"

"Yes."

"You know that is foolishness."

William nodded. "Maybe so, still ..."

"Do not let fear have that much power over you. Tell me."

"I fear they never intended to let Elizabeth go. If they did, I would have received a ransom demand by now."

"Deuce take their intentions! We will find Elizabeth and bring her—"

A knock on the door interrupted Richard.

As Florence followed Mrs. Reynolds towards the master's study, she recalled the first time she met that gentleman. He had appeared so forbidding that she was nervous in his company from that time until after Mrs. Darcy was nearly killed by Toby Harvey. Upon witnessing his devotion to his wife following that unfortunate event, her unease had been replaced with admiration. Knowing how deeply worried she was about her missing mistress, she dreaded seeing first-hand how Mr. Darcy was coping.

Mrs. Reynolds knocked on the door to the master's study. "Come!" called a voice Florence recognised as Mr. Darcy's.

The housekeeper opened the door and stepped inside. "Florence is here, sir."

"Thank you. But first, how is Rogers today?"

"Dr. Camryn said he is doing remarkably well."

"Good. Good. Send Florence in please."

After being waved forwards by Mrs. Reynolds, Florence stepped into the room as the housekeeper stepped out. Instantly struck by how thin and haggard the master looked, she did not realise Colonel Fitzwilliam was also in the room until he rose to his feet when Mr. Darcy did.

The colonel pulled out a chair, which he manoeuvred in front of the desk, saying, "Please have a seat."

As soon as she was seated, the men sat back down.

"First, let me say I was relieved to hear you were safe after my wife was...after the abduction," William said.

Florence was not surprised he had difficulty speaking of the event.

"Mrs. Darcy thinks very highly of you," William continued. "I do not doubt you will be one of the first persons she enquires after once she is recovered."

"I regret that they would not allow me to go with her."

"I appreciate your devotion, Florence. Now, if you will, please tell Colonel Fitzwilliam and me every detail you recall about the trip."

Florence took a deep breath. "Mrs. Darcy was irritated that Lord Hartford had insisted on accompanying us and, without asking her, had informed the head groom that we would be travelling in the unmarked coach. He also objected to her taking Clancy."

"I had completely forgotten about Clancy," William said. "What became of him?"

"One of the highwaymen said he might be worth some money, so they took him, too."

Richard returned to the subject of the coach. "What reason did Lord Hartford give for taking the unmarked vehicle?"

"He held that coaches decorated with crests were an invitation to highwaymen," Florence answered, "but obviously that theory proved imperfect."

"Yet my wife agreed to it," William stated.

"After the mistress was pressured into accepting Lord Hartford's escort, he took over all the travel arrangements; that included the coach we would use and which was the best route to London. I believe Mrs. Darcy accepted Lord Hartford's plans just to stop him from talking, and because a change would have meant a delay." Florence lifted her shoulders in a shrug. "Perhaps I should not have said that, but the mistress told me often enough that she despised hearing him pontificate."

William could not hold back a slight smile at that assertion.

"Go on," Richard urged.

"Everything went unexceptionally until the morning we left Leicester. We had been travelling about an hour or so when we were surrounded by men on horseback."

"Did anything about them stand out?" William asked. "Their clothes, their horses—anything?"

"I recall thinking they all looked alike. They were dressed in black with black masks pulled over their heads. Even their horses had no distinguishable markings."

"What happened after you were stopped?" Richard asked. Florence related the entire ordeal, and when she had finished, he remarked, "So Lord Hartford was struck only once?"

"Yes, sir. The blow sent him straight to the ground. From where I stood, he appeared to be unconscious; however, I noticed he roused quickly enough after the coach carrying Mrs. Darcy began to drive away."

"Are you saying you think he was feigning unconsciousness until they left?"

"In my opinion, yes. And, he talked more about having his nose seen by his physician than about recovering Mrs. Darcy."

"Thank you, Florence," William said. "If you recall anything else, no matter how insignificant it may seem, do not hesitate to tell us."

Florence curtseyed and began to leave. Stopping at the door, she turned. "There is one thing."

"Yes?" William said.

"I could be wrong since they spoke very little, but I swear I detected an accent in the two men who gave orders."

"An accent?" Richard said. "What kind of accent?"

"I could not say for certain. It sounded as though they were from another country but had learned to speak English."

"Thank you, Florence. That will be all."

The maid nodded and exited the study.

"So, she confirmed what we already knew: Hartford changed his story about how many times he was struck," Richard said. "And, if the highwaymen had accents, that might point towards the gypsies."

"It might indeed."

"I believe with all the men we have on the road, someone will find a clue to Elizabeth's whereabouts soon."

"I tell myself that every day, yet each day brings only disappointment."

Richard walked over to the door. "Come! We are going for a ride."

"I need to stay here and—"

"Exercise is the only thing that will give you some relief." Richard tilted his head towards the door. "One hour and then you may take up your burdens again."

Before long, the cousins were galloping across the pastures of Pemberley.

Somewhere north of Leeds

Tomas had driven the caravan hard to make up for the time lost whilst they hid in the woods. By the end of the day, they had already passed through the town of Leeds and were close to Boroughbridge when they finally stopped for the night.

"I have never heard of Boroughbridge. Is it very large?" Elizabeth asked.

Despite her best efforts, Alafare had become fond of her prisoner. Knowing there was no way Elizabeth could escape, she had decided it could not hurt to answer her questions. Besides, she enjoyed displaying her knowledge of the area. "As I recall, it is nothing compared to Leeds."

When she had finished eating, she added, "It has been some time since I travelled this particular route to Edinburgh, but if memory serves, Newcastle will be the next town of import we will reach, though we must go through the small village of Darlington first. Darlington is even smaller than Lambton."

"How long before we reach Edinburgh?"

"At our current pace, I would think four days—five at the most. At about the same time the ship will arrive."

"What is the name of the ship?"

"It is called the *Dundee*," Alafare said. "It carries freight, for the most part, which means it takes days to unload and then they take on more freight."

"Why not travel on board a passenger ship?"

"As I said, a distant cousin is the ship's captain. He looks the other way if it is necessary." Elizabeth grew quiet, so Alafare asked, "What will you do when it comes time to board the ship?"

"I will not leave Scotland."

"I know you do not wish to listen to me, but I beg of you, do not oppose Tomas. He will kill you if you try to defy him."

"Losing my life would be preferable to living without Fitzwilliam."

Alafare sighed. "I do not know what to make of such devotion."

"I pray that one day you will."

Alafare picked up her empty plate and reached for Elizabeth's. "I must wash the dishes. Climb back into the loft until I return, and I will leave your shackles unlocked."

Once her captor left, Elizabeth climbed into the loft and reached for the piece of flint she had found and kept tucked away. Grabbing her monogrammed brush, she scratched *Dundee* next to her initials and drew a crude ship underneath that. Then she hid the brush where it would not easily be found.

Should I throw it out tomorrow or wait until we are closer to Newcastle?

Choosing to leave that decision until morning, she lay down with Clancy and waited for Alafare to return.

Ramsgate

Lord Matlock was relieved that Georgiana seemed well when she awoke the next morning, as were Lady Farthingham and her daughter, Lady Esme. Whatever George Wickham had used to disable his victims had left no permanent consequence other than an inability to recall anything about the evening before. Fortunately, the apothecary had pronounced all three ready to travel, and Lady Farthingham and her child had already departed for London.

Since Wickham had been arrested the night before by the local constable and whisked away to jail, Lord Matlock was on his way there immediately after assuring himself that Georgiana was well. In addition to questioning that villain, he had to decide whether he would transport Wickham to London himself or allow the constable, Mr. Brown, the honour.

Once at the jail, Wickham was brought into the office where Lord Matlock and the constable waited. He appeared dishevelled—his clothes rumpled, his hair uncombed, and his face unshaven. In fact, he looked more like a vagrant than the gentleman he pretended to be.

After being shoved into a chair, the constable addressed him. "First things first. What is your name?"

Glancing uneasily at Lord Matlock, Wickham answered, "I was born George Wickham, at Pemberley in Derbyshire."

"Your father was the steward at Pemberley, and you were born in the servants' quarters, you braggart!" Lord Matlock retorted. "Only George Darcy's mistaken generosity allowed you access to a side of Pemberley you should never have known."

"Mr. Darcy loved me like a son!" Wickham protested. "He provided me with a good education and raised me to be a gentleman."

"Proving one cannot make a silk purse out of a sow's ear! No gentleman would have plotted to seize my niece and force her into marriage to steal her dowry," Lord Matlock hissed.

"You are mistaken! I wanted to marry Georgiana because I am in love with her."

William's uncle came to his feet. "Enough lies!"

"Please allow me to ask a question," Mr. Brown said. The earl sat back down.

"Mrs. Farthingham referred to you as Lord Worley. Why is that?" the constable asked.

"That was Mrs. Younge's idea. She asked me to pose as the fictional Lord Worley for the purpose of meeting Miss Darcy. You see, she was merely a child when I left—" Seeing Lord Matlock's expression darken, he began again. "She was so young when I was escorted from Pemberley that I hoped by using another name she would not remember me."

"I think I have heard enough, Mr. Wickham," Mr. Brown said. "When the

apothecary informed me that he doubted Mrs. Younge had been drugged, as she claimed, we searched her office. I read the you had written her, and you have confirmed the wisdom of my decision to arrest her. No doubt she will continue to cooperate and agree to testify against you in exchange for being transported in lieu of being hanged."

Wickham appeared stunned to learn his accomplice had already been taken.

Immediately, he turned to Lord Matlock. "I am privy to other plots against the Darcys. All I ask is that you assure me in writing that I will be transported instead of hanged, and I will tell you all I know."

"What could be worse than scheming to kidnap my niece for her dowry?"

"Do you think Lady Henrietta an innocent in all of this? If you hang me, she will be free to carry out her plans to destroy the Darcys."

"Naturally you would blame someone else!" Lord Matlock exclaimed. "Take him back to his cell."

Wickham screamed obscenities as he was led away, prompting the constable to ask, "Have you decided what you will do?"

"Yes. I am taking charge of transporting Wickham to London. Rather than let that snake ride in the same coach as my niece, however, I will hire one to carry him and his guards."

"I will gladly sign his release. Just give me time to write down the charges filed against him. That way the magistrate in Town will have all he needs to detain him for trial. Meanwhile, what about Mrs. Younge?"

"I will leave it to you to transport her to London. It is Wickham's tongue that needs loosening with regards to George Darcy's widow, and I mean to do that on the trip back without making any agreement on transportation."

"As you wish."

Pemberley
That evening

Mr. Walker stepped inside the dining room where the colonel and Mr. Darcy sat, having an after-dinner drink.

"Colonel Fitzwilliam, there is a man at the door who says a Sergeant Kennedy sent him. He arrived aboard an unmarked coach and asked for you."

Throwing his serviette down on the table, William stood and hurried towards the door. "That must be our man."

Both Walker and Richard rushed to catch up with William and did so just as he reached the foyer.

A man approximately thirty years of age bowed as they approached. "John Corbin, at your service. Sergeant Kennedy hired me to help in the search for Mrs. Darcy."

"Colonel Fitzwilliam," Richard said. Then, tilting his head towards William, he added, "This is my cousin, Fitzwilliam Darcy."

"A pleasure, sir," Corbin said, performing a quick bow.

"If I understand correctly, you delivered my unmarked coach," William said, glancing towards the door. "I would like to have a look at it."

"Mr. Hyatt drove the vehicle on to the stables."

"Walker, see that Mr. Corbin and his associate are provided dinner and rooms downstairs," William said. "I shall send Mr. Hyatt up from the stables."

"If you will follow me," the butler said to Mr. Corbin.

It had not taken long for the cousins to realise it was too dark to properly search the coach, even with the help of lanterns. Vowing to go through it first thing in the morning, they began to walk back up the gravel path to the house. Suddenly, the clouds dissipated, and a full moon bathed the earth in a silvery glow. William paused in an opening between towering trees and looked up. He stayed in that position for some time.

Curiosity finally got the better of Richard. "Looking for a particular constellation?"

"Actually, I was wondering if Elizabeth is looking at these same stars tonight."

Richard reached to pat his cousin's back. "Despite my warnings about keeping control of your feelings, I cannot imagine how you are coping."

"When Mother died, the pain was staggering. Still, whilst I learned to live without her, I was comforted by one thought: I had survived the worst. Nothing life could hand me in the future could ever be that difficult." He took a ragged breath. "I could not have been more mistaken. Elizabeth has become a part of me…of my heart…my soul. It is as though I have been cut asunder, and someone stole the other half."

"I wish I had the ability to say something profoundly comforting, but I am not that talented. I swear you will be reunited with Elizabeth. I promise you that."

Unable to speak just then for the lump in his throat, William nodded.

"Come! We had best retire and get some rest, if not sleep. I feel in my bones that tomorrow is going to bring a breakthrough."

"I pray you are right."

William's bedroom
That night

Whilst William washed before donning his nightshirt, Adams walked into the bedroom, leaving the chamber candlestick for his employer's use. He reasoned that the open dressing room door would provide sufficient light to hang his employer's coat in the closet, and he was correct. As he closed the closet door, however, a pinprick of light on the opposite wall caught his attention. Frozen in place, Adams watched as the light suddenly vanished, only to reappear further down the wall. Knowing that the servant's corridor was behind that wall, his heartbeat quickened.

Acting calmly, he walked over to the chest that stood against the wall beside the panel into the corridor. Taking a fresh nightshirt out of a drawer, he pretended to study its suitability before abruptly tossing it atop the chest and opening the panel. Reaching into the darkness, he startled a woman, grabbed her by the arm and pulled her into the bedroom.

"Take your hands off me!" Sarah Perry demanded.

"You are in no position to give orders," Adams replied. "Suppose you explain what you are doing here!"

"I...I was on my way to Lady Henrietta's rooms. I must have lost my way."

"And, since you ended up here, you decided to peek through some holes you happened to find in the wall?"

"I know nothing about any holes."

William was wearing only breeches when he heard the commotion. Donning his previously discarded shirt, he busily buttoned it as he walked into his bedroom.

"What is she doing here?"

Adams, who still held a strong grip on the maid's arm, began to explain. "I was near your closet when I noticed a light shining through a hole in the wall. The light went out and then reappeared in another location. When I opened the panel to the corridor, I found her."

"Hand me the candle," William demanded.

Sarah complied, and William addressed Adams. "Tell me when you see light."

William entered the corridor and it was not long before they had located several holes in the wall. When he re-entered his bedroom, William was livid. Gruffly taking the maid by an arm, he addressed Adams. "Find three footmen and meet me at Lady Henrietta's suite straightaway."

Adams did as he was instructed, whilst William pulled Sarah into the hallway and began dragging her towards Lady Henrietta's suite. Reaching the sitting room, he tried the doorknob and, finding it unlocked, shoved the door open. Fortunately, the one he was looking for was sitting at a small table, finishing the last of her supper.

"How dare you have your maid spy on me!" William shouted as he flung Sarah towards her.

Used to lying with a straight face, Lady Henrietta purposefully took her time, slowly setting down her teacup before answering. "I have no idea what you are talking about."

"You know exactly what I am talking about!" William roared. "Your maid created holes in the walls of my rooms; Adams just caught her spying."

"Why would Sarah do such a thing?"

"Perhaps to know what happens in the privacy of my bedroom and report it back to you."

Suddenly, the scope of what the maid might have witnessed occurred to William. "I intend to learn the extent to which you have invaded my privacy, and God help you both once I have."

"Now, Fitzwilliam, surely you realise that a handsome man like yourself can inspire fantasies in young women, especially those who may never have a chance to marry. Is it so wrong to want to see what a man looks like naked?"

"I am not surprised that you would defend her. After all, she can testify that you were the architect behind it."

"Suppose we let Sarah explain what she was doing."

Sarah knew to parrot her mistress' lies. Dropping her head,

she murmured, "I was curious what a man looks like without his clothes—that is all. Truly, Mr. Darcy."

"She has become as accomplished a liar as you!" William retorted. "From now until I have time to deal with this treachery, you will remain in this suite whilst your maid is confined to a room in the servants' quarters."

"But...but surely you do not believe—"

"If I hear one more word, you will join your maid in the servants' quarters!"

When William turned, he found Mr. Walker and Mrs. Reynolds in the doorway. Three footmen waited quietly behind them, and he began issuing orders.

"Mr. Walker, have the maid taken downstairs. Place her under guard in one of the empty rooms. Have every panel into the servant's corridor accessible from this suite nailed shut, then post two footmen at this suite day and night. No one is to go in or out. Meals will be left at the door. Is that understood?"

"Yes, sir," Mr. Walker replied, motioning for the footmen to come forward.

"Mrs. Reynolds, bring up as many maids as you need to thoroughly search Lady Henrietta's rooms immediately. I especially want to see any correspondence you might find."

William marched back to his bedroom with Adams on his heels. "Tomorrow I would like you to lead the search for holes in the walls of the rest of the house. Though I want them sealed immediately, keep a list of where you find them."

"Yes, sir."

"And, Adams, make certain to check Mrs. Darcy's suite."

"Of course."

Chapter 38

Pemberley
The next morning

As they walked towards the stables in a knee-deep mist which would dissipate as soon as the sun came up, William informed his cousin of what had happened the night before.

Shocked, Richard replied, "I was in my dressing room when I heard loud voices, but by the time I was dressed suitably to open the door, I saw no one save the footmen standing outside Lady Harlot's suite. Seeing as how you were nowhere in sight, I went back inside my room, ate the supper Mrs. Reynolds sent up and retired."

"I was too upset to eat anything last night. In fact, I still have no appetite."

"I can only imagine. Tell me, though. Why did you not send the maid packing last night?"

"I intend to see her punished more severely than a mere dismissal. Hopefully, we will uncover indisputable evidence of Lady Henrietta's involvement in Elizabeth's disappearance, and I will have her and her maid arrested."

"I knew that shrew was devious, but I had no idea to what extent. To have her maid spy on you—"

"Every time I think about it, my blood boils."

"Frankly, I am glad you finally have Lady Harlot under guard. After Mrs. Reynolds' account of what happened whilst we were in Weymouth, I believed her quite capable of plotting to harm you, too."

"Yes, everything points to Lady Henrietta. Hoping she might provide us with a lead if she felt she was not a suspect, I held off; however, after what happened last night, I had no choice."

"I agree."

The sun was high by the time William and Richard completed their search of the unmarked coach. Disappointed that they had found no clues, as William was returning one of the padded cushions back in the coach, he caught sight of something hanging in the fringe along the front edge. The upholstery pattern was so vivid that it had been easy to overlook; however, once William realised what it was, his throat began to tighten.

Richard, who was speaking with the head groom, noticed the stunned expression cross his cousin's face. "What is it, Darcy?"

Without replying, William held up an earring made of brightly painted seashells and wooden balls. Richard pulled from his coat pocket the handkerchief containing the earring found at the campsite.

Holding that earring next to the one William had found, he exclaimed, "God help us! It was the gypsies!"

For the first time in days, there was hope in William's voice. "We must inform everyone involved in the search. Those strange wagons the gypsies have should not be hard to track once we know which direction they took."

"I agree," Richard said. "Let us send express posts without delay."

They had walked halfway through the gardens when Richard asked, "What time does the post normally arrive?"

"Usually between sunrise and ten o'clock. Why do you ask?"

"I expect to hear from Mr. Taylor any day. I asked him to keep me informed of his progress."

"Mr. Taylor?"

"The man I charged with investigating Lord Hartford."

As William and Richard went down the hall towards his study, a footman followed unnoticed. It was not until the cousins were seated around the desk that the servant knocked on the open door.

"You wished to see the post as soon as it arrived, sir."

William glanced at him. "Bring it in, please.

After placing a silver salver piled high with mail on his master's desk, the footman departed. William began shuffling through the stack, and since most of the letters pertained to business, he set them aside. Suddenly, he stopped to examine one more closely.

Tossing that one to his cousin, he said, "It is addressed to you in care of Pemberley."

Richard examined the return address. "Just as I predicted. Mr. Taylor has written."

Opening the letter, he began reading it silently whilst William watched anxiously. At length, he looked up. "You are not going to like this, Darcy."

William's eyes narrowed, though he did not speak.

"Mr. Taylor states that on his way to Liverpool, he stayed at an inn in Birmingham. Whilst there he met a gentleman whose father is presently the constable at Liverpool. At the mention of Lord Hartford's name, Mr. Taylor got quite a bit of information, including the fact that Hartford's father was under investigation before he died."

"For what?"

"The constable had begun to question whether Lord Hartford was involved with some gypsies he suspected were acting as highwaymen in and around Liverpool. He told Mr. Taylor that his father discovered that whenever this particular group—who came down from Edinburgh—was in Liverpool, they camped on land at the rear of Spelling Park. He was preparing to question Lord Hartford's father about the connection when that gentleman died unexpectedly."

William was too quiet, prompting Richard to say, "Nothing good ever comes from your silence. What are you thinking?"

"It is my fault that Elizabeth was ever subjected to Lord Hartford's company. I should never have agreed to let him—"

"Balderdash!" Richard interjected. "I refuse to let you blame yourself when it was Georgiana's idea to invite him to Pemberley."

"I could have refused to let him stay!" William stood. "I would like to force my lying stepmother to tell me the truth!"

"I understand how you feel, but we need to connect her to Elizabeth's abduction before she learns that we suspect her or her cousin. Did they find anything when they searched her rooms?"

William sank back in his chair, defeated. "The room was devoid of anything of consequence, which makes me think she has an excellent hiding place."

Pulling paper out of a drawer in his desk, he passed several sheets across to his cousin.

"I shall write to Leighton to inform him the gypsies absconded with Elizabeth and that Lord Hartford has ties to them. He can inform Mr. Fielding at the Bow Street office, who promised to inform law officials in outlying counties." William reached for a pen and set a bottle of ink on his desk. "Moreover, I will ask Leighton not to let Hartford out of his sight."

Richard reached for his own pen from William's ink stand. "After we have written our letters, you and I should call on Mr. Claridge. Surely, he will know if any gypsies passed through Lambton lately and which way they headed."

No sooner had those words escaped his lips than Mr. Walker appeared in the open door. "Sir, Mr. Claridge is here to see you."

"Ask him to wait in the library," William replied.

After Walker left, William said, "You never told me you were a soothsayer, Cousin. You mention Mr. Taylor, and a letter arrives from him. Then you mention Mr. Claridge, and he appears."

"It is a gift," Richard said, giving William a wink.

As soon as William and Richard entered the library, Mr. Claridge began talking animatedly without bothering to exchange pleasantries. "Mr. Darcy, I was delivering a prisoner north of Sheffield this morning when I spotted an item in the road that gave me pause. I would not have thought much about it, had I not seen what I believed to be its match alongside the road as I left Lambton. I brought the one in Sheffield with me, just to prove to myself that I was not mistaken."

Claridge reached into the pouch and produced two dust-covered boots. At the sight, William's face lost all colour.

"Do you recognise them, Darcy?" Richard asked.

Without replying, William removed a handkerchief from his pocket and walked over to the liquor cabinet. Pouring water on the cloth, he took one of the boots from the constable and began wiping off the dust. Soon the blue leather beneath it shone like new.

Swallowing hard, William murmured, "I ordered these for Elizabeth before we left London."

"Your wife must have tossed them out for us to follow," Richard exclaimed. "How clever!"

William turned to Mr. Claridge. "We have just determined that gypsies took Elizabeth. Did you happen to see them around the time she was taken? We need to know which direction they headed."

"I saw their camp outside of Lambton the week before she was taken, but never saw them leave; however, whilst I was in Sheffield, I overheard Mr. Hairston, the constable, talking to a farmer who claimed some gypsies had stolen three of his chickens when they passed through town. I understood this was only days ago."

William rang for a servant, and Mr. Walker answered. "Tell Mr. Adams to pack my clothes and those belonging to Colonel Fitzwilliam for an extended trip. Send a footman to inform Mr. Wilson to ready my coach and to saddle two stallions, but not Zeus or Titan. He is also to pick two grooms who ride well to go with us, in addition to the usual number of drivers and postillions."

After Walker rushed away, Mr. Claridge said, "I would like to go with you, but I believe you can travel much faster without me."

"I appreciate all you have done," William said.

With those words and a handshake, the constable disappeared out the front door.

"If we are to search the road for clues, we cannot ride inside the coach. The two of us and the grooms will take turns trailing the vehicle on horseback. It will be tiring to ride and keep our eyes on to the road, so I imagine we will exchange places every hour or two. Whenever the coach takes on fresh horses, we will exchange mounts with the inn."

"And the reason for not taking Zeus and Titan?"

"The post inns have on occasion hitched my horses to other people's vehicles. I imagine it is because mine are rested and they do not have spares available. Then, upon my return, they try to pass off inferior animals as belonging to me. I will not take that chance with Zeus or Titan."

"I see your point."

Whilst Adams was busy packing his trunk, William went towards Elizabeth's bedroom. Just as on the day he returned to Pemberley, a drowning sensation threatened to overwhelm him the minute he stepped inside the room. The mere sight of her things caused his heart to ache with a pain so fierce he feared he might die if she were lost to him forever. Closing his eyes, he allowed the faint smell of her perfume in the air to raise his spirits and strengthen his resolve.

Then, crossing to the chest, he removed two nightgowns, some stockings and a chemise. Carefully laying them on the bed, he glanced about for her slippers. Spying one peeking out from under the bed, he dropped to his knees and was pulling them out when he noticed a book. Picking it up, along with the shoes, he was immediately reminded of the journal he had found in the tree on Oakham Mount.

Sitting on the side of the bed, he opened it. Immediately he realised that though this journal was of the same type, it was not the same one. This journal began after Elizabeth's arrival at Pemberley. She had not written every day and usually only a line or two. Still it was an insight into her heart, so he began reading some of the entries.

May 28, 1812

For better or worse, I am here. Whether my husband has noticed I have changed, I cannot say. Nevertheless, I intend to do my best by word and deed to show him how much I regret my mistakes and how hopeful I am that our marriage will exceed his expectations.

June 4, 1812

Lord Hartford must think me a simpleton. Why else would he suggest we walk together every morning? Even if I cared for his company—which I do not—it would be improper, and I have no wish to make Fitzwilliam think I am fond of any man, save him.

June 6, 1812

Why will Fitzwilliam not listen to me? I did nothing to be attacked so cruelly at the ball, but it seems he has made up his mind to let Emma get by with her scheme and punish me.

June 7, 1812

At last our marriage is consummated. It was not as I had always dreamed, but at least my husband was not unkind. And now I have the hope of children to fill my lonely days.

Distraught to read about his former behaviour and hoping to find clemency, William flipped the pages until he found an entry after she was wounded.

June 27, 1812

William could not be more attentive, and I do not think I could love him more than I do at this moment. I can only echo what Mrs. Green said of her marriage—I would not trade the love William and I share for the unremarkable existence of most married couples.

He smiled. *Now, I am William to her.*

"I heard you and the colonel were leaving. May I be of service?"

Turning to find Florence standing in the doorway, he said, "I have no idea what Mrs. Darcy may need." His voice was so full of emotion that he stopped to glance away. "Would you put the items on the bed in a bag, along with several of her gowns and anything else you think she would like to have. I want to take a blanket and her pillow, too."

"Certainly."

As Florence rushed to the closet, William dropped a slipper. "I will get that," he announced, using the opportunity to return Elizabeth's journal to its hiding place under the bed.

Upon rising, he found Florence laying gowns next to a carpeted bag on the bed. Recognising it as the one Elizabeth brought to Cambridge, as he ran his fingers across the well-worn material, he suddenly found himself lost in memories.

When Florence spoke, it startled him. "Mr. Darcy, you asked me to tell you if I recalled anything that might help you find Mrs. Darcy. I thought of something that may be of no significance, but I found it odd."

William's brows furrowed. "And that is?"

"Just before we set out for Ramsgate, Rogers and I were going into Lambton when we passed some peculiar people. He called them gypsies. After I came out of the dry goods store, I saw two of them across the street talking to a gentleman that favoured Lord Hartford. I thought it odd that he would be talking to them…if it was actually him."

"You cannot say for certain?"

"No, sir. His back was towards me and directly they went inside the building where the post coaches stop."

"Thank you for telling me."

Florence nodded and went back to packing the bag.

Between Darlington and Newcastle
Two days later

Before leaving the wagon that morning, Alafare mentioned that their next stop would be Newcastle. Trusting that her prayers not to be taken into Scotland would be answered, Elizabeth was hopeful her captivity would be over soon. Though she had no idea if the items she tossed from the window would help locate her, she still tossed out her brush just before they reached Darlington. The mere act of defying her captors raised her spirits, though it did nothing to conquer her increasingly unsettled stomach.

It seemed the wagon swayed and jerked more than ever, and the constant jostling threatened to bring up what little she had eaten earlier. Holding to the sides of the wagon, Elizabeth gingerly made her way to the bucket of water at the front. Dipping the cup beside it into the liquid, she took a sip only to find the water was not helpful, for it was too warm. Spying the bowl that Alafare used for Clancy, she poured some in it and offered it to the dog. As he thirstily lapped it up, Elizabeth smoothed the fur away from his eyes.

"Poor thing. I know you are as tired of being a captive as I am."

Clancy stopped to lick her hand just as the wagon pitched from the effort to leave the road. Rushing to the window, Elizabeth discerned they were at a creek that passed under a bridge. Once the wagon came to a complete halt, she heard Alafare climb down from the driver's seat. For what seemed an eternity, silence reigned; then the latch on the door slid back and it opened.

"Keep Clancy on the rope and climb out," Alafare ordered. "Tomas has agreed that you may go down to the creek with me."

Surprised, Elizabeth grabbed Clancy and went down the steps. Taking a deep breath of fresh air, she closed her eyes, only to open them immediately at Alafare's reproof. "There is no time to waste. We stay only long enough to water the horses."

Elizabeth allowed Alafare to lead her to the creek, where large flat rocks bordered water so clear you could see minnows swimming on the sandy bottom. Alafare quickly divested herself of her shoes and stockings, then helped Elizabeth out of hers. Sitting on a rock and dangling her feet in the water, Alafare watched as Elizabeth stepped into the stream and waded out. Clancy, still on a rope, wiggled to be let down, so Elizabeth set him in the creek. Not long after, Teza joined Alafare on the rock.

"She is getting thinner," Teza said. "If Tomas notices, he will be angry. He will not get a good price for a scarecrow."

"Elizabeth's stomach has been upset," Alafare said, "She has trouble keeping down what she eats, but once she feels better, she will gain the weight back."

Hearing this, Teza took a closer look at Elizabeth. Having borne two children who were now with Tomas' parents in Scotland, she knew the signs. "She is with child."

Disbelieving, Alafare started to argue. "That cannot be. She said noth—"

"She does not know yet," Teza interrupted. "We were told she had no children.

This would be her first which means she may have no idea what her symptoms signify."

Stunned into silence, Alafare stared at the woman she had come to care about as she would a sister.

"If Tomas learns she is with child, he may decide to kill her since men seeking concubines at the gathering will pass her by," Teza said.

"Why not just let her go back to her family?"

"And risk being caught and hanged? She can identify all of us."

"Please say nothing until we are certain she is with child," Alafare begged.

The sounds of horses approaching interrupted their conversation. Immediately, Nikolae rushed to Elizabeth, clamped a large hand over her mouth and pulled her into nearby trees. Alafare picked up Clancy, who was unhappy to be jerked out of the water and angry at having his mouth held shut. Then, she followed Nikolae.

In short order, five men on horseback crossed the bridge towards them. At the sight of the gypsies, they reined their horses to a stop. Meanwhile, Tomas and the others had formed a line in front of their wagons, signalling the intruders should keep their distance.

Used to the idiosyncrasies of gypsies, Sergeant McKinley did not think their behaviour unusual. "Pardon the intrusion," he said. "We are searching for a gentlewoman who was kidnapped near Leicester a few days ago. We believe she was taken north in an unmarked coach. Have you seen any suspicious coaches on your journey or a woman who looked out of place with her companions?"

"We have not," Tomas answered curtly.

Seeing the distrust in the eyes of those he was addressing, Sergeant McKinley nodded. "We mean to water our horses and be on our way."

Crossing to the other side of the bridge, they did just that, and soon McKinley and his men were headed in the opposite direction, to Darlington.

Immediately, Tomas ordered Elizabeth back in the wagon. Once she and Clancy were secure, he addressed the others.

"Since the prisoner's family has men searching for her this far north already, we cannot chance taking her the rest of the way to Edinburgh over land. Instead, we will divert to South Shields[16] and board the Dundee there. Those sailing with us to the Continent will join us onboard the ship at Edinburgh."

William and Richard were getting close to Darlington when they happened upon a farm wagon blocking the road, the result of a broken wheel. Frustrated that they were forced to stop, Wil-

---

16 **South Shields** is a coastal town at the mouth of the River Tyne, England, about 4.84 miles (7.79 km) downstream from Newcastle upon Tyne.

liam dismounted and walked towards Richard, who had already dismounted and was sitting on a tree trunk.

Watching as his men helped the farmer push the wagon to the side of the road, William said, "I had hoped to be nearly to Newcastle by dark. This will keep us from reaching that goal."

"Perhaps this was meant to slow you—" Suddenly, Richard went silent.

Staring blankly at the other side of the road, he stood. "What is that?"

William looked in the same direction as his cousin. "I do not see anything."

"I swear I saw the sun reflect off something."

As Richard crossed the road, William followed. When the colonel began using the toe of his boot to search the weeds along the road, William did likewise in the opposite direction. William's back was to the colonel when Richard stooped to pick up a silver-plated brush. Seeing the initials entwined on the back, he called, "Look at this, Darcy!"

William rushed to take the item from his cousin. A lump formed in his throat as he recognised the present he had given his wife. At length, he recovered his voice. "Dundee. Might that be the name of whoever took Elizabeth?"

"It is certainly possible, but what is that carved beneath it?" Richard replied.

"It resembles a boat."

"A boat makes no sense, but, if it were a ship—"

"A ship named Dundee!" William declared. "And the nearest port is just past Newcastle, at South Shields!"

Fortunately, the road was soon cleared, and after the farmer refused an offer to take him on to the next town, William and Richard exchanged places with the grooms and settled into the cushioned seats of the vehicle, whilst the servants rode horseback.

"You do realise that if we had not stopped to help that farmer, we would not have seen the brush?" Richard said.

William, unconsciously tracing the initials on the brush, nodded. "It appears God used a broken wagon wheel to encourage me. I had begun to doubt if we were going in the right direction—we had come so far without another clue. This reassures me that we are on the right track."

"I have often thought God uses what we perceive as calamities to either turn us to a different path or reassure us we are on the right one."

William smiled wryly. "You sound like Reverend Green. Perhaps you should have taken orders."

"God never pointed me in that direction. He knew that would have been a disaster!"

As the cousins laughed, it was not lost on either of them that they had not found reason to laugh since they left London. Thus, it was with renewed spirits that they continued their journey.

Chapter 39

The next day

As it happened, William and Richard were able to reach Sedgefield, several miles past Darlington before it grew too dark to continue. Though not of the best quality, the inn there had rooms available, and it pleased William to be that much closer to Newcastle. At dawn, Richard was on his way to the stables to see if the coach was ready when he heard his name called. Turning, he recognised Sergeant McKinley coming towards him.

"Colonel Fitzwilliam!" the sergeant exclaimed. "What a surprise to see you here! I thought you were in Derbyshire."

"I take it you did not get my letter."

"As you suggested, when I left Derbyshire, I checked for mail at the post stop in Leeds, but I found none."

"It is likely waiting for your return, then. How far did you travel?"

"We were at Newcastle when it occurred to me that they might intend to board a ship, so we headed east to South Shields. Nonetheless, I found no one that fit Mrs. Darcy's description or that of her kidnappers on the lists of passengers for any of the ships in port. It was then I decided to retrace our journey in the opposite direction, lest I had overlooked something."

"My letter was to inform you that we now know it was gypsies who abducted Mrs. Darcy."

Sergeant McKinley looked astonished. "My word! We passed a caravan of those misfits only yesterday. It never dawned on me to suspect them, though we stopped to enquire if they had seen any suspicious unmarked coaches. I even went so far as to explain that a gentlewoman had been kidnapped near Leicester by highwaymen. They must have had a good laugh at my naivety."

"How many were there?"

"Five or six wagons and perhaps the same number of men. I saw only one woman, though."

"How far ahead are they?"

"I encountered them about two hours this side of Newcastle. If they kept up a good pace, they might have spent last night close to that town."

"We also suspect they may be heading to South Shields. Was there a ship in port called the *Dundee*?"

"There was! I overlooked it since I was told it hauled only freight."

"Can we make South Shields by tonight?"

"If we ride hard."

"We? You and your men must be exhausted."

"That is true, but my men and I are determined to search until Mrs. Darcy is found."

"You are a good man, McKinley," Richard said. "Have your men ready to leave as soon as I locate Darcy."

Lambton

Not having the funds for a private coach, Mr. Bennet had taken the local mail coach from Meryton. The trip took longer than he had anticipated. The crowded, uncomfortable vehicles had taken their toll on his body, most especially his previously injured leg, which ached constantly now. He had been forced to spend one night at an inn and caught a second mail coach the next day. Hence, by the time he stepped out of the coach in Lambton, he was relieved to have arrived.

Picking up the bags a handler tossed to the ground, he set his weary eyes on the inn across the street. There, he planned to have a cup of tea before enquiring about hiring a carriage to go on to Pemberley. As it happened, he was crossing the street when he caught sight of his brother's relations, Duncan and Sophie Gavin, who also appeared to be heading towards the inn. At nearly the same moment, they noticed him.

"Thomas Bennet, how is it that you are here?" Mr. Gavin asked, stepping forwards to shake his hand and take his bags. "The last word we had, you were in no shape to travel."

"Though my leg still troubles me a bit, I am able to get around quite well. After hearing about my Lizzy's disappearance, I thought I would go mad if I did not do what I could to help. I set out for Derbyshire immediately."

"We have been distraught ever since it happened," Mrs. Gavin said. "Lizzy has always been like one of our own."

"She thinks the world of you, too."

"We were going to the inn to have a cup of tea. Will you join us?" Mr. Gavin asked. "You can gather your strength whilst we tell you all we know about the matter."

Mr. Bennet agreed, and soon they were all seated at one of the small, circular tables in the dining room of the inn.

"The Reverend and Mrs. Green—you may remember that he is the rector at Kympton—are very close to the Darcys, and they have been keeping us informed," Mr. Gavin stated. "According to them, Mr. Darcy and his cousin, Colonel Fitzwilliam, left two days ago, heading north. Apparently, they believe the villains took Lizzy in that direction."

"The villains?"

"Gypsies! Mr. Darcy sent the Greens a note before he left, saying he is certain that gypsies kidnapped Lizzy and asking that they pray for success in finding her."

Mr. Bennet looked stunned. "I have not had any dealing with their kind, other than having my fortune told in my youth. I thought them more of a curiosity than a danger, but if they did take Lizzy, why go off with her? Why not demand a ransom and be done with it?"

"Mr. Claridge, our constable, asked the same question. It makes no sense. I imagine that is why Mr. Darcy said—"

Mrs. Gavin gave her husband a kick under the table, and he hushed.

Concerned, Mr. Bennet prodded, "What did Mr. Darcy say?"

Glancing uncomfortably at his frowning wife, Mr. Gavin looked down. "Mr. Darcy said he did not think they ever intended to ransom Lizzy."

Mr. Bennet studied the pattern on the tablecloth for far too long. At last looking up, he said quietly, "I must believe the Lord will restore Lizzy to us, else it would be too hard to bear."

Mrs. Gavin reached to pat his hand. "Rest assured that all of Lambton has been praying for her safe return."

"Are you going to Pemberley today?" Mr. Gavin asked. "If so, we can take you in our carriage."

"I had rather not impose on Mr. Darcy's staff, if he is not there. I will stay here at the inn until he brings Lizzy home."

"You will do no such thing!" Mr. Gavin declared. "We are family, and you will stay with us."

"You are too kind," Mr. Bennet replied. "I must admit that I much prefer your company to staying by myself and brooding over being too late to be of any help."

"We all feel helpless," Mrs. Gavin replied. "All any of us can do is pray for Lizzy's safe return, but I believe that is important, too." She stood. "Come! Let us return to the house. I imagine you have not had a decent meal since you left Longbourn. Our cook roasted a pheasant with vegetables yesterday and baked a cake. There is plenty left."

Mrs. Gavin kept up a steady stream of conversation until they reached their farm outside Lambton. Thomas Bennet thought it ironic that, had he been at Longbourn, he would have disappeared into his study to avoid such prattle. Oddly enough, today he found it comforting.

South Shields

Upon reaching the port city, Tomas led the wagons to the forest which began at the end of the street where the road curved to go down to the docks. Being in the seedier part of town, a collection of rundown pubs, crumbling gaming dens, brothels and outdated inns lined the left side of the street, whilst warehouses next to the docks lined the other. The businesses thrived on separating seafarers from their money.

At the forest, Tomas discovered the trees were so dense that each vehicle would have to separately thread its way inside. By the time the entire caravan was concealed, with each wagon on its own path, they were scattered throughout the woods and not within sight of one another. To Alafare, this seemed a sign from God that she had done the right thing by choosing to help Elizabeth after all. In planning their escape, the isolation would prove invaluable.

Early on she had started to regret her part in the abduction, but Alafare arrived at her present position following two recent revelations. One was hearing that the men they encountered at the bridge were searching for Elizabeth. From that, she concluded Mr. Darcy *was* trying to find his wife, which meant he had nothing to do with her abduction. The second was when Teza suggested that Elizabeth might be pregnant. It was one thing to separate a man and a woman, but something inside Alafare rebelled against separating a woman with child from the man she loved. Consequently, between their break at the creek and their arrival in South Shields, she decided she could no longer be a party to this misery.

As Alafare sat on the steps of her wagon desperately trying to think of a way to help Elizabeth escape, Tomas and Nikolae suddenly appeared. Each was holding the handle of a huge trunk, which they set on the ground next to the wagon.

"I have never seen a trunk that large," Alafare stated.

"This is not the type used to pack clothes for a trip from one town to the next. It is used to pack household items for shipment abroad," Tomas explained. He opened the lid and began pulling out wooden dividers, tossing them onto the ground. "Without the dividers, there is more room. We purchased three—two to use to pack the contents of my wagon, and the other for the prisoner."

"What do you mean?" Alafare asked.

"Our cousin insists that she be hidden from view when we board the ship. If there is a problem, he wants to be able to say he never saw her come aboard." He tossed the key to Alafare.

"Nikolae and I will carry the captive on board last. For now, we must locate the warehouse where imported liquor is stored and *borrow* two crates each of brandy and wine. Our cousin insists we provide him that for his assistance."

"In addition to paying for the passages!" Nikolae hissed.

"We have no choice; we are at his mercy," Tomas stated soberly. "After Nikolae and I have secured the liquor, we will help the others move the heavier items, including the trunks Teza is packing. At that point, I will send her to help you put the prisoner in the trunk. Can I trust you to have the woman drugged by then?"

"Do not worry. I will handle everything."

After Tomas and Nikolae left, Alafare rushed inside the wagon to talk with Elizabeth. Realising Elizabeth was still in the loft, Alafare climbed the ladder to peek inside and found her asleep with Clancy in her arms.

"Elizabeth?"

"Wha...what?" her captive murmured tiredly.

"Leave Clancy tied, and come down. We must talk."

Elizabeth did as she asked and soon was sitting on Alafare's bed as the gypsy paced in front of her.

"I have come to believe you. Your husband was not a party to your abduction."

Knowing there had to be more to this change of heart, Elizabeth asked, "Why do you believe me now?"

"Do you recall those men who stopped to speak to Tomas at the creek?"

"I do."

"Their leader told Tomas they were searching for a gentlewoman who was kidnapped near Leicester and was last seen being taken away in an unmarked coach."

A mixture of love and hope lit Elizabeth's face. "I never doubted Fitzwilliam's love or that he would have men searching for me."

"After Tomas told me they were looking for you, I realised someone had to have recruited them to search this far north and that someone had to be your husband." Deciding not to mention Teza's observation about her being pregnant, Alafare continued. "I have thought of a plan of escape. Come outside, and I will explain."

Alafare watched astonishment cross Elizabeth's face at the sight of the trunk. "Tomas says it is so large for it is used to ship household items overseas."

Instantly, Elizabeth knew what he meant to use it for. Her face paled as she replied, "I cannot abide being in small places. I would never survive."

"He said it would only be used to transport you on board, but do not worry! All we have to do is pack it with enough weight that he believes you *are* inside. He has already given me sacks of flour and other grain he is not taking aboard the ship. With the bags I have and a few heavy pans, we can convince them of it."

"Will they not look?"

Alafare smiled and held up the key. "I will lock it and tell Teza that Tomas has the key. When he and Nikolae come for the trunk, I will tell them Teza has it."

"How will you get Teza to leave us alone?"

"I have thought of that, too. I will say that Tomas wants her to go on to the ship and begin setting the cabin in order.

Elizabeth's expression fell. "You told me the penalty for disobeying Tomas is death."

"I do not plan to stay long enough to find out. Now, help me fill the trunk quickly before Teza comes!"

Soon afterwards, the trunk lid was closed and locked. Dropping the key in the pocket of her skirt, Alafare ordered, "Take Clancy and hide in the woods. Make certain he cannot make a sound. After you see Teza, Tomas and Nikolae head to the ship, come back."

Almost as soon as Elizabeth had disappeared amidst the trees, Teza arrived. She looked into the wagon. "Where is she?"

"Already in the trunk," Alafare answered. "Tomas returned for a steel bar to pry open a crate, and seeing that she was already unconscious, he put her inside. I am pleased, for she proved heavier than I thought."

Teza looked uncertain. "Where is the key?"

"Tomas took it."

Gazing in the general direction of other wagons, Teza said, "I suppose I should try to find him."

"Actually, he asked me to tell you to go on to the ship. He wants you to begin organising the cabin."

For a fleeting moment, Teza seemed poised to question her. Instead, she shrugged and began walking towards the ship.

It was less than a quarter of an hour later when Tomas and Nikolae came for the trunk. By then, clouds had covered the sky and the wind was becoming blustery. Given that evening was drawing near, the setting sun and tumultuous weather left a gloom in the darkening sky.

Tomas looked up. "It will rain soon." Moving to the trunk, he tried to open the lid but could not. "Give me the key."

"Teza has it."

"Where is she?"

"At the ship. She said she wanted to attend to the cabin."

Satisfied, Tomas picked up one end of the trunk. "Let us get this over with, Nikolae."

It was raining lightly by the time the men were completely out of sight, and Elizabeth's clothes were damp when she returned with Clancy. Seeing that Alafare had hitched the horse to the wagon and was sitting in the driver's seat, her heart clenched when Alafare ordered, "Hurry! We must be away!"

Despite her misgivings, Elizabeth handed Clancy to Alafare and climbed up to sit beside her. "I thought we would escape through the woods."

"You are too weak to walk far, and the rain will do you more harm."

"But this horse cannot possibly walk fast enough to evade capture."

"With any luck, we will get to the marketplace of South Shields before anyone notices we are gone. If we get as far as the pubs, we can hide amongst the revellers and, at first light, slip past the buildings to the town centre. Surely someone of consequence will listen to you once we are there." Elizabeth looked so vulnerable that Alafare patted her hand. "Trust me."

With a slap of the reins, the horse began to move. It was not long before they had left the cover of the forest and entered the street leading to the high-spirited horde a few hundred yards away.

On the ship

As soon as Tomas set the trunk on the floor of the cabin, he demanded the key from Teza.

"Alafare told me *you* had it."

Instantly, Tomas grabbed the steel bar he had brought to open some crates and pried the trunk lid open. Reaching inside, he brought out a bag of flour. Furious, he shouted, "Alafare has betrayed us!" Turning on Teza, he added, "And you must have known!"

Teza began backing up. "I...I swear I did not—"

Tomas struck her with the back of his hand, and she fell to the floor. Turning to Nikolae and the others in the room, he shouted, "I want them found now!"

"Vano and I tied our horses at the top of the ramp," one of the men said. "You take them; we will find more!"

They had passed more than half of the pubs, brothels and inns when Alafare leaned over the edge of the wagon to look behind. Seeing two men on horses galloping towards them she pulled the wagon to a halt. "Get down, Elizabeth and hide!

"But...but, what about—"

"Do it now!"

With no time to question further, Elizabeth did as she was told, jumping down with Clancy and running into an alley between two buildings. She stopped and peeked around the corner to watch as Alafare slapped the reins and the horse began walking again. It seemed only seconds before the two men on horseback passed her hiding place, giving her a good look at the one nearest her. *Tomas!*

After he and Nikolae brought the wagon to a halt about two hundred feet farther, Elizabeth turned to run to the back of the buildings only to stop at the sight of two, shadowy figures approaching from that direction.

"Wha've we 'ere!" one said, his words slurred by drink.

Clancy growled and struggled to break free. It took all Elizabeth's strength to hold him and keep him silent.

"Come to 'ave a bit o' fun, miss?" taunted the other.

Suddenly, that man broke and ran towards her. Fortunately, he was so inebriated that he fell flat on his face, and the other man stopped to help him get to his feet.

Elizabeth took the opportunity to slip out of the alley and, staying as close to the entrances as possible, hurried down the row of pubs. She had not gone very far when a door opened right in front of her, and a man and a woman walked out. Impulsively, she stepped inside the building.

Elizabeth stood still until her eyes adjusted to the dim lights. Once they had, she was alarmed to find the room filled with men playing cards whilst scantily clad women sat on their laps. Other similarly dressed women lined a staircase all the way to the floor above. Like those *ladies*, Elizabeth's hair had long since escaped its pins and was hanging almost to her waist.

The instant she had entered the room, silence fell, and everyone turned to stare. It seemed only seconds before one man stood and stumbled towards her.

"Here now, she's a pretty one. How much for her?" he shouted.

The way the rest howled at his remarks, they must have thought his bluster hilarious. Stealthily backing up in hope of getting out the door, Elizabeth found her escape blocked when another man walked in. This gave her harasser the opportunity to grab her arm, causing her to drop Clancy. He flew out the door just before it closed.

"I asked how much she will cost me!" the man shouted, to more shrieks of laughter.

Without Clancy, Elizabeth felt even more vulnerable. She began shivering as more men stood to join the cad who was taunting her.

The sun had set by the time William, Richard, and their men entered the town of South Shields. Not bothering to stop in the town proper, they followed Sergeant McKinley who was already familiar with the area.

That man halted at the top of the street that led to the docks, intending to ask if they should split into two groups. However, before he could speak, a woman's screams caught everyone's attention.

"There!" Richard shouted, pointing to a commotion midway down the street. Without waiting, he kicked his horse into a gallop, and everyone followed his lead.

As Richard drew nearer, he realised the woman on the ground was lying next to a gypsy wagon. Moreover, the man she was fending off *was* a gypsy, as was his cohort. Flying off his horse, Richard tackled the one assaulting the woman, pushing him to the ground. Meanwhile, Sergeant McKinley kept on until he ran down and captured the other man.

William's concern was strictly for the woman, whose petite size and dark hair made him fear it was Elizabeth. Jumping from his horse, he knelt beside her, crying out her name. Almost insensible from being beaten, Alafare did not reply. Gently William pushed the hair from her face and instantly realised it was not his wife.

"Take this woman to the wagon and do what you can for her!" he ordered another man in their party.

As the man bent to pick up Alafare, William started to stand. Before he could, however, she caught his sleeve. "Eliz...Elizabeth is here," she murmured, her voice weak.

"What did you say?" William asked, leaning closer.

"Elizabeth is hiding nearby."

William stood, shouting, "My wife is here! Search every building!"

Richard and Sergeant McKinley, who had already restrained the two gypsies, heard William's shout and left those villains lying in the mud under the watch of others in their party. As they hurried towards him, a small white blur flew past, barking wildly. Clancy did not stop until he leapt into William's arms.

"You would know where Elizabeth is!" William exclaimed. "Show us!"

Instantly, the animal jumped to the ground and headed back in the direction from whence he had come. As everyone ran after him, Clancy went straight to the brothel and waited until William and the others arrived to open the door. The first one inside, Clancy headed straight to where Elizabeth stood surrounded by men and latched onto the ankle of the one nearest her. That blackguard began hopping about, shouting, "Get him off me!"

William followed Clancy, shoving first one man and then another out of the way until he reached the one the dog had attacked. He struck that man with a solid right to the jaw, and when that cad crashed to the floor, pandemonium ensued. Customers and whores alike began fighting with those who had come to rescue Elizabeth. Fists, chairs and bottles of liquor went flying.

Totally focused on Elizabeth amidst the chaos, William backed her into a corner where he protected her with his body. When bottles began to fly, however, Richard worked his way over to them.

"I will protect you!" he shouted over the racket. "Get Elizabeth out of here! I will clear a path, so follow me!"

With his wife in his arms, William called, "Come, Clancy!" and followed Richard out of the brothel.

"I am going back in," Richard shouted, disappearing inside.

Carrying Elizabeth to the end of the building where light from the brothel shone through a window, allowing him to see her face clearly, William gently set her on her feet. Her clothes were dishevelled, so he removed his coat and settled it about her shoulders. Then, framing Elizabeth's face with both hands, he looked deeply into her ebony eyes as the rest of the world disappeared and a profound silence enveloped them. Pledging their love anew, their lips met in a passionate kiss.

After the fighting ceased, Richard stepped outside to check on his cousins. He intended to ask how Elizabeth was; however, finding her secure in William's arms, he chose not to disturb them.

Noting that Clancy waited patiently at their feet, he called, "Come on, boy! Let us see if Sergeant McKinley needs our help."

The dog followed Richard back inside, where they picked their way over unconscious men to reach the bar where McKinley was treating scrapes, bloody noses and cuts all with the same prescription—plenty of fine liquor.

"Join us, Colonel Fitzwilliam?" Sergeant McKinley asked, wiping blood from a cut over his brow with one hand whilst holding up an expensive bottle of brandy with the other.

Richard smiled. "You have persuaded me, Sergeant."

Chapter 40

South Shields

Gratified that Elizabeth had stopped trembling once she was in his arms, for a long while William was content to have his head rest atop hers whilst she buried her face in his chest.

Finally, Elizabeth looked up to murmur, "Did you get my letter? Is Georgiana safe?"

"Thanks to you, my uncle left for Ramsgate the very day I reached London and read your letter. By now she is securely in his care."

Elizabeth sighed wearily. "I am so relieved to hear it."

Silence reigned once more until William thought himself able to control his emotions. "My precious wife, I never dreamt how fiercely I would miss you until we parted. I could barely keep my mind on Mr. Sturgis' situation or the repairs needed for Willowbend Hall. All I could think of was you. Then to arrive in London and learn you had been taken—" His voice broke, and he buried his face in her hair.

"I know, my darling," Elizabeth said, placing a kiss over his heart through the fine lawn of his shirt showing above the waistcoat. "Without believing God would reunite us, I do not think I could have survived."

William captured her lips again, but this kiss was as tender as the previous ones were passionate. Lingering over every nuance of the kiss, he was savouring her response when, out of the blue, she drew back.

"I...I completely forgot! One of the gypsies, a woman named Alafare, was helping me to escape. When last I saw her, two gypsies were bearing down on her wagon on horseback. Have you seen her?"

"I have. She is about your size, so naturally when I saw her on the ground, I feared she might be you. Richard and Sergeant McKinley dealt with the men assaulting her whilst my attention was focused on the woman. It was only after I knelt on the ground beside her that I discovered she was not you."

"Was she badly injured?"

Noting the turn their conversation had taken, William stiffened. "Her injuries did not look life threatening, so I ordered that she be taken inside the wagon and tended to."

"I must go to her," Elizabeth said, turning to search the street for Alafare's wagon.

"Wait, dearest. Listen to me."

She turned back to face him.

"Gypsies are a peculiar people. They do not live by the same standards we do. Richard has had many dealings with them through the years. They care nothing for those outside their clan and have been accused of everything from robbery and assault, to the kidnapping of children to sell overseas. God only knows what they had planned for you. They never demanded a ransom, so apparently they did not intend to return you to me." William shook his head as though banishing the image that came to his mind. "If they had harmed you ..."

Seeing the pain in his eyes, Elizabeth stood on tiptoes to press a quick kiss to his lips. "They did not."

William closed his eyes in relief, pulling her back into his arms. "Thank God for that! Still, your circumstances would have only gotten worse the longer they kept you prisoner. Furthermore, it is my belief that the freighter *Dundee,* which is dockside already, was to be used to take you north in the morning."

"Yes. I was supposed to be in a trunk taken aboard the ship just before Alafare and I escaped."

"You see, I was almost too late. A day later and you would have been out of my reach. Most likely, I would have had to sail to the Continent to find you. All these reasons make me wary; I beg you not to ask me to trust any gypsy."

"But...but Alafare is different."

"She helped keep you a prisoner."

"She did, but only because she was told that you arranged my abduction. She believed I would have been killed had I stayed. Once she realised you had nothing to do with it, she tried to help me."

"Ask yourself why she would take such a chance. It is well known that gypsies who disobey their leader are dealt with harshly."

"All I know is that Alafare risked her life to help me, and I must speak to her."

"Elizabeth, you have been through an awful ordeal. I dare say you seemed traumatised when I carried you from the brothel. Clearly you have lost weight and are weak. Can it not wait until tomorrow?"

"I will not be able to sleep until I see her."

William tenderly ran the back of his fingers over her cheek. "It seems I am overruled. I will trust your judgement."

With an arm around her waist, he helped his wife walk towards the wagon. The door was open, and as they approached, the man taking care of Alafare came down the steps. Pulling a well-worn hat off his head, he bowed.

"Mr. Darcy...Mrs. Darcy. I am Clyde Mansfield, a friend of Sergeant McKinley." Then he addressed Elizabeth specifically. "Please let me say that it has been an honour to be part of the search for you, ma'am, and I am relieved that we have found you safe."

Elizabeth smiled as William replied, "My wife and I appreciate your help."

Elizabeth glanced nervously at the wagon. "How is she?"

"She was beaten, and when she fended off the blackguard wielding the knife, she suffered cuts to her hands and wrists."

"Poor Alafare! Do the cuts need stitching?"

"No, ma'am. I was a surgeon's helper in the navy and I have some experience recognising which wounds do. I applied an ointment and bandaged them. They should heal tolerably well if the bandages are changed regularly."

"Do you think her well enough to speak to me?"

"I believe she is, but she may have fallen asleep."

After nodding, Elizabeth headed into the wagon. Choosing to give her privacy, William conversed with Mr. Mansfield outside.

Cautiously approaching the one whom she had come to think of as a friend and who had almost died trying to help her, Elizabeth found Alafare lying on the bed with her eyes closed. She looked pale and lifeless, and for an instant, Elizabeth wondered if Mr. Mansfield's judgement was to be trusted. The young woman's lip was split, and she had suffered a deep gash over her brow. Even in the dim light of a single candle, discolouration had already become visible around her swollen eyes, her cheeks and her neck.

Alarmed, Elizabeth had turned to summon Mr. Mansfield, when Alafare murmured weakly, "Eliz...Elizabeth, is that you?"

Instantly at her side, Elizabeth pushed a stray lock of hair from the gypsy's face. "Oh, Alafare. I had to know that you were not—" Realising what she was about to say, Elizabeth stopped.

"Do not fret over me."

"I am so sorry you are suffering because of me."

Unsteadily, a bandaged hand reached out, and Elizabeth grasped it gently. "Never forget, it was what my people did to you that caused this."

"You had no choice but to follow orders."

"No. We all have choices," Alafare argued weakly. Men's voices drew her gaze to the scene outside the wagon. "I understand why you love him. Your husband...he is a kind man and very handsome."

"I love Fitzwilliam because he is an honourable man, not because of his appearance."

Alafare attempted to smile. "But you are not displeased that he is handsome."

Glancing at William, Elizabeth smiled. "No, I am not displeased." Turning again to Alafare, she grew solemn. "I plan to tell the authorities that you helped me escape and ask that you not be punished."

"I expect no favours. I took part in your kidnapping, and I deserve whatever punishment is given me."

"You risked your life to help me, and for that, you deserve leniency. Now, do not waste your strength arguing with me; try to rest. Fitzwilliam said we are staying here tonight, so I will speak with you again in the morning."

Alafare closed her eyes. "I am so very tired."

"Then sleep well, my friend."

Elizabeth waited until Alafare's breathing became slow and regular, then stepped out of the wagon. Several men had just arrived on horseback, and their leader was talking to the colonel. William was walking towards them, and as she started to follow, Mr. Mansfield stepped forwards to offer his arm.

"Mr. Darcy asked me to escort you, ma'am."

Knowing that William was still concerned about her safety, she placed her arm on his and smiled. "Thank you kindly."

Accustomed to being called to the seedier sections of town to arrest drunks, card cheats and countless unruly patrons, Mr. Powers, the constable of South Shields, responded immediately when informed of the brawl in progress at one of the brothels and brought three of his assistants with him. They arrived just as Richard hoisted a well-tied Tomas across the back of a horse and was about to do the same to Nikolae, who was still lying on the ground, being guarded by Clancy.

Seeing this, Mr. Powers rode directly to Richard, asking loudly, "What have we here?"

Wanting to clarify what had happened, William walked in that direction; however, before he could intervene or Richard could answer, Sergeant McKinley walked out of the brothel, followed by his men.

Immediately recognising his childhood friend from Kent, Mr. Powers exclaimed, "Charles McKinley! As I live and breathe! What are you doing this far from home?"

"I could ask the same of you, Powers!" Sergeant McKinley replied with a grin.

As the sergeant began to explain why he and the others were in South Shields, the constable's attitude changed with the realisation that this was not just another brawl. Consequently, Tomas and Nikolae were immediately taken into custody, with the constable issuing orders for his men to assemble a search party and look for the remaining gypsies. Richard offered their assistance, but upon observing how weary the men from Derbyshire appeared, the constable declined. saying he would handle the matter.

As for Alafare, Elizabeth intervened on her behalf with Mr. Powers and as a result, she was treated more charitably than the men. Still, the constable insisted that Alafare be taken into custody until he could sort out all the charges, whilst assuring Elizabeth he would have the local apothecary examine the woman once she was in jail.

It was a weary lot that headed into town to find lodging. Informed by the constable that Clarendon Hotel on the main street had superior accommodations, William ordered his driver there and the entire party followed. He insisted on paying for rooms, hot water and meals for all who had come with them, including the servants. For Elizabeth and himself, he secured the finest suite in the hotel—one which included a large bedroom, dressing room and sitting room. When told the dressing room had an oversized tub, he requested it be filled with hot water.

Since everyone was famished and the hotel needed time to heat such a large quantity of water, it was decided they would eat first. A private dining room was opened exclusively for their use. Before long, an array of delicious fare was brought in and placed on the sideboard, and not one person had to be persuaded to fill a plate and find a place at the dining table. Even Clancy was given some food in a bowl.

Whilst he ate, William noticed that his wife merely pushed the food on her plate from one side to the other. "Elizabeth, would you care for something else? I will gladly order whatever you desire."

Smiling lovingly at him, Elizabeth answered, "Do not worry, dearest. Apparently, my appetite has deserted me; however, I am certain it will return once I am home."

William took her hand and brought it to his lips. "I cannot wait to take you home."

Once they were alone in the sitting room of their suite, Richard having taken charge of Clancy, William placed his hands on her shoulders and turned Elizabeth to face him. "Darling, please let me send for the apothecary. Given what you have been through, it would ease my mind to be certain you are well."

"Dearest, I do not wish to be prodded and poked by a strange apothecary. All I desire is a hot bath."

Unwilling to press her further, he leaned in to place a kiss on her forehead. "Very well. Your desire is my command, my love."

Steering her to a comfortable, upholstered chair, he said, "I intend to act as your lady's maid. Please sit down whilst I make certain your bath is ready."

Elizabeth laughed. "If you manage to wash my hair and comb out the tangles without leaving me bald, I shall be amazed."

"Then let us pray that you are amazed, Mrs. Darcy." Capping his declaration with a quick kiss, William took a candle and disappeared into the dressing room.

William was astonished at the size of the copper tub that sat in the middle of the room. Larger than any he had ever seen, it occupied most of the space, so shelves had been added to the wall beside it to hold items necessary for a bath. It was already filled with steaming water.

As he removed his coat, waistcoat and cravat, William hung

each on a peg fixed on the back wall. Then, rolling up his sleeves, he went to get Elizabeth. As he neared the chair where he left her, he realised she was asleep, and, for a brief moment, he was content to watch the woman who owned his heart sleeping peacefully.

Still, not wanting the water to grow cold, he leaned down to whisper, "Mrs. Darcy, it is time for your bath."

Elizabeth's eyelids fluttered open. "I...I must have drifted off."

Helping her gently to her feet, he guided her into the dressing room and watched, amused, as her dark expressive eyes grew even wider.

"I do not believe I have ever seen so large a tub."

"Nor I. Perhaps it is time to replace the ones at Pemberley."

Whilst he talked, William began unbuttoning her gown.

"Wait!" Elizabeth reached into the pocket of her gown, pulled it inside out, and began untying a knot she had fashioned to keep her wedding ring safe. As she slid the ring back onto her finger, she sighed. "All is as it should be now."

Heart overflowing with love, William kissed her shoulder before beginning to work the buttons again. At the feel of his fingers, Elizabeth closed her eyes and let her head fall back lazily. "I had little chance to bathe when I was—"

Suddenly realising it would only upset her husband to hear details of her captivity, she went silent. When she spoke again, it was about something else entirely. "You may never get me out of this tub."

William pushed the gown from her shoulders and watched it float to the floor. Leaning down to place kisses across his wife's naked shoulders, he said, "That will make things difficult, for it is my intent to stay by your side all night."

"What a lovely idea!" Elizabeth exclaimed. "Join me! There is plenty of room."

In truth, William was finding it difficult to control his desire. Determined not to take advantage of his wife in her present state, he was uncertain he could keep that resolution if he joined her in the tub.

"I was teasing, Elizabeth. I plan to pour some water in the

basin and wash myself in that manner. You, however, will benefit by soaking in the hot water."

"You did say my desire was your command, did you not?"

William realised he had been ensnared. "I did."

"Well, my desire is for you to bathe with me."

Once he had removed all but her chemise, William gently guided Elizabeth to the only other piece of furniture in the room, a stool. "Sit here whilst I remove your stockings."

Sliding one stocking gently down her leg, he froze when he encountered the angry black and blue bruises surrounding her ankle. His face became an unreadable mask as he hurriedly checked the other ankle. Finding the same bruises there, he tenderly ran a finger over the evidence of her imprisonment.

"What caused this? You told me you were not harmed."

"In the beginning, I was forced to wear shackles on my hands and feet. Alafare removed them as often as possible, though, and by the time I was able to escape, I only had to wear them on my ankles at night." Seeing the pain in his eyes, she continued. "The bruises look far worse than they feel."

William's head dropped. "This is my fault. Had I not left you—"

"Hush, my darling," Elizabeth interrupted, framing his face with her hands and forcing him to look up. "What happened was not your fault, and I dare say we shall be separated many more times in the future. Such is life."

Standing, William pulled Elizabeth into his embrace, whispering, "Do you have any idea how ardently I love you?"

He kissed her again before pulling the chemise over her head and picking her up. As soon as he placed Elizabeth in the tub, she asked, "Will you wash my hair first?"

She sank below the water and came right back up. William knelt on a towel to do as she asked. Afterwards, he gathered her hair atop her head, securing it by wrapping a small towel around it like a turban. As Elizabeth laid her head back against the rim of the tub, she closed her eyes. "How in the world did you learn to wrap hair so well?"

"When Georgiana was a child, she and I often swam in a

small pond in the hills," William replied as he began to remove his breeches. "Mother showed me how to wrap her hair to keep her from getting a chill in the night air. You see, we often stayed out so late that it was dark by the time we reached Pemberley."

Now completely undressed, William stepped inside the tub and sat down facing Elizabeth. He was doing his best not to stare, when she lifted one perfect leg and began washing it. Willing his treacherous body not to react, William grabbed the pitcher, poured water over his head, closed his eyes and began washing his own hair. He had just finished rinsing off the last of the soap when Elizabeth turned completely around in the tub.

Sliding between his legs, she held a soapy washcloth over her shoulder. "My arms ache. Will you wash my back?"

William took a deep breath and let it go slowly. "Whatever you wish, my love."

After he had washed and rinsed her back, Elizabeth scooted back even farther, laid her head against his chest and arched her back in invitation for him to continue to bathe her. Unable to resist, he soaped his hands and slid them around to cup her breasts. As he gently explored each perfect globe, the centres hardened, and recalling his earlier resolve, he moved to wash her abdomen. Then, grasping the pitcher, he filled it with water, pouring it over her repeatedly until all traces of soap vanished. The minute he set the pitcher down, however, Elizabeth grasped his hands and brought them back to her breasts.

"Elizabeth, darling," William said, his voice rough with desire, "you had not healed completely before you were abducted and being held captive has obviously taken its toll. You are fragile. Perhaps it would be best if we wait until—"

"You said I could have whatever I desire," she murmured, "and I desire you."

William closed his eyes. Unable to fight his desire if she persisted in fulfilling hers, when he felt her stand, he looked up. She had stepped out of the tub, pulled the towel off her head and shaken loose her hair before turning to face him. Although she had suffered, he thought Elizabeth more beautiful than any nude in all the museums he had ever visited. Her body summoned him like a siren, and he surrendered.

Though William told himself to be gentle because of their long separation, their joining progressed swiftly from tender to urgent—each whispering words inspiring the other to new heights of passion. Afterwards, they clung desperately to each other as their breathing returned to normal. At long last, William lifted his head to look at Elizabeth. Eyes so dark and deep that he was instantly lost in them stared back. Then she smiled.

William could not resist collecting the kisses he had missed during her absence, and as each grew more passionate than the last, the intimate dance began again. This time, however, he moved slowly and deliberately, prolonging the tension. Not until the brink of bliss did he unleash a torrent of thrusts which succeeded in bringing them both to completion.

Elizabeth sighed as she felt herself floating back to earth. "William, had I known the pleasure to be found in your arms, I would never have resisted being married to you."

William nuzzled her neck, then kissed her there. "We have the rest of our lives to make amends for our failings, my love."

He attempted to roll over, but she pulled him closer. "Please stay."

"I worry that my weight is too much for—"

"Your love is what I need to heal! And, in truth, I love the feel of lying beneath you—of knowing that I am yours and that my body satisfies your desires."

Her words reignited William's passion, the evidence irrefutable as he pressed his hips against hers. "You satisfy me in every way possible, my Elizabeth."

Staring at his chiselled chest, Elizabeth ran her hands slowly down to his rock-hard abdomen, fingering the fine hair there. Feeling his stomach lurch at the gesture, she murmured, "I fear the flame inside me still burns. Dare I hope that you share the same struggle?"

"By now you must know, my darling, that I can never have you enough."

Elizabeth threaded her fingers through William's hair whispering breathlessly. "Show me."

Chapter 41

London
Matlock House
Two days later

Perkins, the Matlock's longsuffering butler, answered the door to see the now familiar form of Viscount Leighton. Since Mrs. Darcy's abduction, the earl's firstborn had spent more time at Matlock House than he had in the two years since his marriage to Lady Susan. It was no secret that theirs was a marriage of convenience or that after the wedding, he had begun to stay at his apartment in Town. He avoided his parents' company because his wife was always with them.

In fact, it appeared that whilst the viscount had little use for his wife's company, Lady Matlock delighted in it. "Thicker than thieves," Leighton had labelled them once in his presence, and were he asked, Perkins would have had to agree. None of the staff thought well of the high-minded Lady Susan who treated all the servants with disdain, even those in positions of authority.

"Good morning, Viscount Leighton. If I may say so, sir, it is good to see you again."

The viscount smiled at the man he had known all his life. "It is good to see you as well, Perkins. Is my father already in his study?'

"He is. Would you like me to announce you?"

Leighton had already begun walking in that direction. "There is no need. He is expecting me."

Once at the study door, Leighton knocked and waited for an answer.

"Come!"

Entering the room, Leighton could not repress a smile when his father looked up. Taking the chair directly in front of his father's desk, he began speaking. "It was just as Wickham said, Father. The townhouse in Mayfair does not belong to Lord Hartford. It belongs to Lady Henrietta."

"I am certain George had no idea. Before they married, we discussed what few assets she would bring to the marriage, and he said she had no property. It just goes to show: there is no fool like an old fool when it comes to conniving women."

"Since Wickham was right about the townhouse, I wonder if what he said about Lady Henrietta's plan to destroy Darcy is true as well."

"I confess that is one claim I do not comprehend. As George's widow she has a good living. Why destroy the means of her livelihood?"

"I imagine it would depend on why she hates the Darcys. Did Wickham disclose that information?"

"He swore she never divulged it to him."

"And you believe him?"

"He is trying his best to avoid hanging. For that reason, I believe he is being truthful about the things he has divulged."

"There is more. After receiving a letter from Darcy about the link between Lord Hartford and the gypsies, I asked the Bow Street Runners to take that blackguard into custody, even accompanying Mr. Fielding to the Mayfair townhouse where we caught Hartford packing for an extended trip. According to the housekeeper, he spoke of booking passage on a ship to the Americas."

"I cannot fathom how that villain thought he would escape. Fitzwilliam would have had him tracked to the ends of the earth, if necessary."

"I agree; however, Hartford is not very clever. He even seemed surprised to see us at his door. Moreover, once he was in custody, I explained our presence to the housekeeper, and she showed us where Lady Henrietta kept her correspondence when in Town.

That was when I discovered that woman has hidden bank accounts."

"Hidden accounts?"

"Yes. They are in the name of Lady Wharton."

"Lord Wharton was her first husband. How much money is involved?"

"As best I can tell, over twenty-five thousand pounds."

As a grin spread slowly across his face, Lord Matlock leaned back in his chair. "Her property became George's when they married, and since the townhouse and bank accounts were not settled upon her in his will—I should know, as I was the executor—they now belong to my nephew. There is not a court in England that would rule otherwise."

"Which would serve her right. Fitzwilliam is convinced Lady Henrietta instigated the kidnapping of his wife," the viscount said. "Therefore, Mr. Fielding hopes to trick Hartford into implicating her."

"How?"

"By telling him Lady Henrietta *has* been implicated in the kidnapping and pointed the finger at him, swearing it was his idea. With any luck, that may loosen his tongue."

"I tried to warn George that woman was nothing but trouble, but he would not listen."

"Fortunately, it appears my cousin will recover part of the money Uncle George took from Pemberley because of her."

"Fitzwilliam deserves every farthing of it! When George died, it was a great shock to him to learn how far in debt Pemberley was. I do not know if I could have handled the estate as well as he has done, especially since Catherine opposed his every move."

Both men were silent for a time before Lord Matlock asked, "How long has it been since you heard from Fitzwilliam?"

"Almost a sennight ago—right before he and Richard headed north."

"Is it still your plan to travel to Pemberley?"

"It is. There is so much to tell Darcy that I had rather do it in person. Besides, Mr. Fielding wants to send two Runners with me to escort the perpetrators to London."

"When do you leave?'

"In the morning. Please say nothing to Georgiana. She may insist on accompanying me, and I believe Fitzwilliam needs to deal with Lady Henrietta before his sister returns."

"I agree," Lord Matlock said. Then he added, "Georgiana has always been too fond of that woman for my taste."

"That is understandable. My cousin missed having a mother, and Lady Henrietta is excellent at deceit."

"I understand why Georgiana is fond of her; still, it irritates me that she was never told of that harridan's true character."

"Fitzwilliam thought it best to wait until she was older; however, now he will have no choice but to expose Lady Henrietta. That should put an end to any admiration Georgiana may have felt."

"It should. In any case, tell my nephew that I would like to see those involved in Mrs. Darcy's abduction brought to justice in London. My solicitor is well known in the courts here—his uncle and cousin are judges—and he assures me that all involved can stand trial as a group, saving Fitzwilliam time and money. Of course, Wickham will have to be tried separately for his actions."

"If we are fortunate, we can link Lady Henrietta to Wickham's and Hartford's crimes, assuring that she will never be set free...if she is not hanged first."

"Hanging women is a beastly affair, but unfortunately, it becomes necessary to punish severe crimes as a deterrent. It is Fitzwilliam, though, who will have the final say in her punishment."

Leighton stood. "I have to be on my way. I must stop by Darcy House and check the mail before I return to my apartment and begin to see to the packing."

"Inform me as soon as you hear anything."

"I will."

Pemberley
Lady Henrietta's sitting room
The next day

At last, Lady Henrietta had a plan. There was only one way out of her room, and that was to walk right past the footmen guarding her door. She planned to do that disguised as a maid. Studying the two maids who alternated bringing her meals, she was pleased to note that both were approximately her height, though each was a good deal heavier. That detail would make it possible for her to wear a gown underneath the uniform as she escaped. It was the perfect plan. She would drop a bag containing a few clothes and shoes out a window, walk out of the room and collect the bag once she exited the house.

Several days prior, she had asked that her dinner tray not be retrieved until the next morning, using the excuse that she preferred to eat dessert just before she retired. This ensured that after exchanging places with the maid, no one would enter her room until the next morning. Fortunately, the groom Sarah had always trusted was the night watchman at the stables, and with the funds she had secreted, she felt certain she could bribe him to ready the gig and drive her to Lambton. From there, he could disappear just as she intended to do.

I will be on the early mail coach to Derby before Mrs. Reynolds finds out I am missing.

The sound of a key turning in the lock announced the arrival of dinner, and Lady Henrietta turned to face the door just as the maid entered. After setting the tray of food on the table, the maid closed the door as usual.

"Would you like me to help you undress and don your nightgown, Mrs. Darcy?"

"I would, but I am not certain I have a clean gown. It seems my laundry has not been a priority for Mrs. Reynolds of late."

The maid went straight into the bedroom. As she approached the chest, she said, "I brought clean ones up only yesterday."

The second the maid pulled open the drawer, Lady Henrietta struck her on the head with an iron that stood near the hearth, and the woman crumpled to the floor, unconscious.

I must act fast!

Pleased to find the uniform had few buttons, Lady Henrietta stripped it from the maid easily. Then, she removed a cord from the drapes and used it to bind the woman's hands and feet before stuffing a stocking in her mouth to keep her quiet. After rebuttoning the uniform, Lady Henrietta pulled it over her head, satisfied that it successfully hid the gown she was wearing. Lastly, she brushed out her hair and fashioned it into an ordinary bun, donned the maid's cap and pulled it down over her forehead as far as possible.

Hurrying to the door, Lady Henrietta took a deep breath and opened it. Keeping her head down, she calmly walked past the footmen who were conversing and down the hall to the staircase leading to the rear of the house. Once on that floor, she peeked down the hall. Seeing a footman, she waited until he went in the opposite direction; then she flew out a door into the gardens. Relieved to see the customary torches had been lit about the yard, Lady Henrietta stopped to catch her breath before dashing off to find the bag of clothes. After locating it, she ran all the way to the stables.

The rectory

Mrs. Green was not surprised to find the Gavins on the porch when she opened the rectory door. They had been frequent visitors since Elizabeth's disappearance, always eager to hear of the latest developments in the search. She was surprised, however, to find they had brought someone with them.

Judith Green exclaimed, "How good to see you both again!" She then smiled at Mr. Bennet as though awaiting an introduction.

"I hope you do not mind that we brought our houseguest along," Mr. Gavin said. "This is Lizzy's father, Thomas Bennet of Longbourn. And this is Mrs. Green, Thomas."

"I am delighted to meet you, Mr. Bennet. I only wish it were under different circumstances," the rector's wife said, stepping aside to wave them past. "Do come in."

"Yes...well...I have hope that my daughter will soon be restored to us," Mr. Bennet replied solemnly. Then, with a wan smile he added, "It is good to finally meet you. My Lizzy mentioned you and your husband often in her letters."

"We think the world of Elizabeth," Mrs. Green said. Then she called out, "James, come and see who has arrived."

In mere seconds, there was the sound of a door shutting and footsteps heading in their direction. As soon as James Green entered the foyer, his face lit up.

"Judith and I were saying just this morning that the Gavins should be here today." He reached to shake the hand Mr. Gavin offered.

"This is Thomas Bennet...Lizzy's father," Mr. Gavin announced as the two shook hands. "He came to help search for Lizzy, but Fitzwilliam and Colonel Fitzwilliam had already gone north by the time he arrived."

"I am pleased to meet you, sir. Your daughter talks of you often."

Mr. Bennet's smile broadened, and he shook the vicar's hand with renewed vigour. "I was just saying to your wife that my daughter wrote of how kind you and she have always been. I appreciate that more than you will ever know."

"It is not hard to be kind to Elizabeth," Mrs. Green broke in. "She is a precious girl...I should say woman. After all, she is married now."

"We came to see if you have heard anything more," Mr. Gavin interjected.

"In fact, Mrs. Reynolds sent a note this morning. We had decided to drive out to your farm this afternoon, if you had not come," Mr. Green replied. Seeing the eagerness on each face, he quickly continued. "Mr. Darcy sent word that Elizabeth has been recovered in South Shields. She is in good health, and they are on their way home."

Mr. Bennet gasped. "South Shields? Good heavens! They

could have taken her aboard a ship, and God knows where she would have ended up."

"Tis true," the vicar said. "Thank God she was found before that could happen. I truly believe it was His doing that Fitzwilliam discovered so quickly who took her."

There was agreement all around, and Mr. Bennet asked, "Do you have any idea when they will arrive?"

"If I calculated correctly," Mr. Green replied, "they should arrive either tomorrow or the day after. In any case, as soon as we are notified, we will inform you."

"I would appreciate that very much," Mr. Bennet said. "I cannot wait to see my Lizzy again."

"Of course, you cannot," Mrs. Green replied. "Now I hope that all of you will join us for refreshments. I baked some ginger biscuits, and they are especially good with a cup of hot tea."

Boroughbridge
An inn

Richard sat on the balcony of his room, waiting for the world to awaken, when he heard a soft knock at the door. Crossing the room, cup of coffee in hand, he cracked it only wide enough to see who was in the hall.

"Darcy," he said, stepping aside and swinging the door wide. "Come in." William walked past him. "I thought I would not see you for at least another hour." Looking into the hall once more, he added, "And what became of Clancy? He is usually the first one up."

William walked straight to the balcony where a steaming pot of coffee occupied a table between two chairs. "I awoke and could not go back to sleep, so I slipped out of bed so as not to wake Elizabeth. As for Clancy, he opened his eyes and, seeing it was only me, went back to sleep."

"Clever dog," Richard teased.

"Once I was dressed, it dawned on me that you would be

awake and would have charmed some maid into bringing you a pot of coffee by now. It seems I was correct."

As William poured himself a cup of the hot liquid, Richard chuckled. "Can I help it if the ladies find me irresistible?"

"I suppose it does come in handy at times," William said, smiling before he took a sip of the coffee and sat down.

Once settled in the chair, William looked about. Everything as far as the eye could see was blanketed by the grey haze that settled over the land just before dawn. "Boroughbridge is just as I remembered."

"I am not surprised. You were here just two days past."

"I was speaking of when I was a child. I was about seven years of age when Father took me to Newcastle on a business trip. We stayed at this very inn."

"Boroughbridge does have a country charm about it. I have often passed through here on business for His Majesty."

For a time, they were silent, each enjoying the warmth the coffee provided against the cool morning air. At length, Richard said, "I am relieved you asked Sergeant McKinley to continue his employment by helping to transport the gypsies back to London for trial. I will sleep more soundly, knowing he and his men are assisting Constable Powers."

"I am thankful that McKinley agreed. I know he and his men are weary. God knows we all are."

"Your offer was certainly generous, Darcy. I dare say all those who helped in the search for Mrs. Darcy will receive excellent compensation for their assistance. Will paying them so well be hard to manage, given Pemberley's current financial situation?"

"If I could, I would pay them more. Still, the consolidation of the loans will allow me to pay as promised."

"I only raised the issue because I have a little in savings that I could put towards the expense, if you need it."

William clasped Richard's shoulder. "Thank you, Cousin. I shall keep that in mind should my funds sink too low before I am able to sell Willowbend Hall."

The sun had just peeked over the horizon when Richard

broached the subject that had been on his mind since the day Elizabeth was recovered.

"Darcy, I feel I must ask. How is Elizabeth faring…truly?" Before William could answer, he continued, "Oh, she smiles at the right times and always says she is well when I ask, but she does not act the same as before. Obviously, she has lost weight and is quite pale, but it concerns me that she sleeps so much—not just at night, but all day in the coach—and still complains of fatigue. I wonder if you should send for an apothecary before we resume our trip."

The words had barely left Richard's mouth when William's expression fell, and a hand flew to his forehead. He squeezed it as though staving off a headache and replied sombrely, "I stay in torment over her condition. She rebuffs my entreaties to see an apothecary or a physician, insisting she will see Dr. Camryn once we are home."

"Do you think it wise to wait?"

"I cannot bear to force her to do anything against her will. Not after what she has been through."

"That is understandable. May I ask, did you tell her about the letter found in Tomas' pocket—the one incriminating Lady Henrietta and her cousin?"

"Since I plan to deal with my stepmother as soon as I get home, I had no choice but to tell her."

"And what was her reaction?"

"She expressed concern only for Georgiana."

"I worry about how this will affect Poppet, too."

"As do I."

"If we push the horses a bit harder, we could reach Pemberley by late tomorrow."

"This evening I will make a decision on whether to proceed farther, based on Elizabeth's health."

"I agree. Her health should direct your decision."

Chapter 42

Peterborough

Viscount Leighton could hardly believe his eyes. After going to the stables to confer with his driver before continuing north, he walked back inside the inn to settle his bill and discovered that Lady Henrietta was ahead of him at the desk. Darcy had written that he had confined his stepmother to her rooms until his return, so evidently, she had escaped. Leighton was not entirely surprised, given her past resourcefulness.

Meeting the eyes of the two Bow Street Runners silently waiting for him to conclude his business, he tilted his head towards Lady Henrietta, alerting them that this *lady* was relevant to their case. The Runners had the power to make arrests, and he meant to make certain Lady Henrietta went no further. With her back to him, she had no way of knowing that her luck had run out, and as a Runner moved to stand on either side of Leighton, he waited whilst she continued to argue, as discreetly as possible, with the innkeeper.

"What do you mean you will not ask the gentleman in room three? I am a respectable lady, and it is hardly my fault that my coach lost a wheel stranding me in this miserable place." Guardedly sliding several crowns across the desk, she looked left to right before adding, "Any respectable gentleman would be proud to see me to London safely."

The innkeeper's eyes followed the coins before he looked back at her. "I have no idea how you arrived upon my doorstep, ma'am. You have no coach in the stable awaiting repairs, and you arrived without even a maid. This establishment does not condone impropriety, and the gentleman in room three is a married man. Furthermore, I will not importune any of my customers when the post coach will be along shortly. Might I suggest that you purchase a ticket for it?"

"Do you know who I am?" Lady Henrietta hissed, still trying to keep her voice low. "I am George Darcy's widow. My husband was a customer of yours for years before he passed, God rest his soul. I often stayed here with him."

The innkeeper looked up from his ledger where he had begun to write. "Oh, I have fond memories of Mr. Darcy…and his first wife."

"You sodden old fool! See if I ever stay at your establishment again!"

Lady Henrietta turned and bumped right into Leighton, her eyes growing bigger than saucers as she recognised him. Pasting a disingenuous smile on her face, she nodded her head in acknowledgement. "Viscount Leighton! What a delight to see you again."

"The pleasure is all mine, I assure you," Leighton said calmly. Then, glancing to the men standing beside him, he added, "Arrest her."

As the Runners stepped forward to escort William's stepmother towards the coach, now situated in front of the inn, Leighton said to the innkeeper, "That *lady* will never bother you again, Mr. Thompson."

"I never thought her a lady," the innkeeper replied with a smirk.

Leighton suppressed a smile. "Let me settle my bill and get back on the road. I hope to make Pemberley by tomorrow."

"Please tell Mr. Darcy that my wife and I continue to pray for Mrs. Darcy's safe return."

"I hope that by the time I reach Pemberley all our prayers will have been answered."

Pemberley

William's coach had made excellent time for the last two days, mainly due to a scarcity of rain, and as they approached the towers and the imposing gate that marked the entrance to Pemberley, he was pleased it was still daylight. As usual, Elizabeth lay on the seat, her head on a pillow in his lap. Though he hated to wake her, he felt certain she would want to see the view from the ridge.

Leaning over, he softy said her name. She stirred and sat up.

"We are almost home, dearest. Would you like the coach to stop at the crest?"

Elizabeth nodded. "I would." Then, meeting Richard's eyes, she blushed. "I must have fallen asleep again."

"You did," William said, "but you needed the rest." To Richard he said, "Please alert the driver."

Richard did as William asked by tapping the roof with his sword, and shortly after, the coach pulled to a stop at a place with a breath-taking vista of Pemberley. Without waiting for a footman, William opened the door and stepped out. Then he helped Elizabeth to her feet, placed an arm around her waist, and guided her towards the rise.

At the view of her home, Elizabeth murmured softly, "I thought I might never see Pemberley again."

"I would never have stopped searching for you, my love," William whispered. "Pemberley could never be the same without you."

Closing her eyes, Elizabeth leaned back into him. "I cannot imagine it without you, either."

Knowing this moment was sacred to them, Richard remained in the coach and kept Clancy from following. Still, he found it hard not to stare at the couple so clearly in love. He had witnessed many people in unhappy marriages, his parents and Leighton included, and had grown jaded towards that venerable institution, yet witnessing the devotion shared by William and Elizabeth provided a sliver of hope.

Perhaps if I found a woman like Elizabeth...

His musings were cut short when the couple returned to the coach, and they all proceeded towards the manor.

Meryton
Longbourn

After being praised in every way possible by Mrs. Bennet since he stepped inside Longbourn two hours past and having listened to Lydia and Kitty argue over which colour ribbons to trim their bonnets with since tea was served, Charles Bingley was ready to participate in a rational conversation.

Waiting until her mother stopped babbling to take a sip of tea, he broke in. "Jane, since this is the first sunny day in ages, I should like to take a turn in the garden with you." Glancing to his future mother, he added, "That is, if you do not mind, Mrs. Bennet."

"Oh, no, no!" Fanny Bennet gushed. "You and Jane need time to yourselves. Do not let us hinder you."

After they had strolled to the far end of Longbourn's flower garden and settled on the stone bench situated beneath a tree, Bingley said, "I cannot tell from your mother's demeanour...is Lizzy any closer to being found?"

"Mama easily forgets Lizzy is missing when she has company," Jane said resentfully. "Sometimes her cheerfulness is more than I can bear."

Charles slipped an arm around her shoulder, giving her a small squeeze. "I am sorry, my love. I did not mean to cause you pain."

"It is not your fault, Charles. You have every right to be bewildered by Mama's joyful attitude. I know I am."

"Since she cut short what you were saying about your father's letter, would you continue now?"

Jane's face crumpled as tears filled her eyes. "Papa said that Mr. Darcy and Colonel Fitzwilliam had headed north before he arrived. They are following some gypsies they believe took my sister. Papa is optimistic they will find Lizzy and bring her home soon."

Bingley reached into his coat, pulled out a handkerchief, and handed it to Jane. "Do not cry, sweetheart. If anyone can find your sister, it is Darcy! And having the colonel's help makes it even more certain. That man knows nearly every law enforcement and army officer of import in the whole of England. If he seeks help, he will get it."

Jane dabbed at her eyes with the handkerchief. "That is a comfort to hear."

"You said your father plans to stay in Lambton until Lizzy is found. Will that create a hardship for your mother?"

"Mother has little to do with running the estate. Papa left Mr. Hill in charge of what must be done whilst he is away."

"Mr. Hill...the butler?"

"Yes. Years ago, Papa employed a steward, and Mr. Hill, who was only a footman at the time, trained as his assistant. Papa decided to do without the services of the steward about the same time our former butler died. Mr. Hill moved to the butler position, and he and our housekeeper married not long afterwards. Still, Mr. Hill often helps Papa with estate matters."

"I am relieved to hear it," Bingley said with a faint laugh. "I thought to offer my services, but to be truthful, I have no experience. Darcy had been instructing me, but after his father died, more pressing problems took precedence."

At the expression of apprehension on Jane's face, he hurried to add, "Do not worry, my dear. Darcy said that once I purchase an estate, he will be glad to advise me."

"It is good that Mr. Darcy is such a kind man. Lizzy always says so in her—" Jane began to sob, so Charles patted her back.

"I cannot bear to think of my sister being held against her will or what cruelty she may be suffering."

Seeing Mrs. Bennet and Jane's sisters standing at the windows, Charles refrained from kissing Jane, instead saying, "I cannot bear to dwell on that, either. That is why I try to focus on how happy everyone will be once she is recovered."

"I shall endeavour to do that as well."

Pemberley

Though one of the guards at the gate had ridden ahead to alert Mrs. Reynolds that the coach was on its way, there was still chaos in the household as the result of Lady Henrietta's escape. With Mrs. Reynolds and Mr. Walker both issuing orders, the Darcys' coach rolled to a stop at the bottom of the steps before everything was ready. Nonetheless, the housekeeper and the butler walked out onto the portico to greet the Darcys as though nothing was amiss.

William waited until a footman opened the door and let down the steps before exiting the coach and handing Elizabeth out. Knowing how fragile she was, he placed his arm around her waist and guided her towards the steps. Upon seeing her look down and hesitate, he instantly swept her off her feet.

"William!" Elizabeth said with a grin. "I am perfectly able to walk up the steps."

"Indulge me," he said, giving her a wink. "I neglected to carry you over the threshold, so I am correcting that omission today."

At the portico, the housekeeper and butler simultaneously expressed their happiness at having Mrs. Darcy home, and Elizabeth was able to declare, "It is wonderful to be home," before William swiftly entered the house.

Once in the foyer, instead of setting his wife on her feet, he continued towards the grand staircase, giving orders as he went.

"Mr. Walker, send a footman to fetch Dr. Camryn straightaway."

"Yes, sir!" the butler replied.

At the flick of Mr. Walker's hand, the nearest footman flew out the door. Then, William addressed the housekeeper.

"Mrs. Reynolds follow me please." Once she complied, William started up the stairs. "I want hot water brought up for Elizabeth, myself and Richard to bathe."

"Water is already being heated, sir."

"Excellent! Please ask Mrs. Lantrip not to use heavy spices for dinner this evening. Elizabeth has had an upset stomach."

Elizabeth, who by now was used to William's protective manner, looked over his shoulder at Mrs. Reynolds and rolled her eyes. The housekeeper stifled a laugh.

Unaware, William kept speaking. "Please send up a pot of tea straightaway, along with toast, butter and jam. That should suffice until dinner is served. Oh, and make certain to send the same refreshments to Richard's room and to the quarters of those who accompanied us. We have not eaten in hours."

"Yes, sir."

Florence stood on the landing, and once they had passed, followed them to the suite. When they reached the door to the sitting room, Mrs. Reynolds opened it whilst William carried Elizabeth inside. Only then did he set his wife on her feet.

Elizabeth smiled at her maid. "Florence, I was relieved to learn that you had been unharmed."

"Thank you, ma'am," Florence replied. "I was so happy to hear that you were found safe."

"William said that Rogers was recovering nicely before he left," Elizabeth said.

"Rogers has fully recovered," Mrs. Reynolds interjected.

Suddenly, a maid appeared at the door. "Pardon me, Mr. Darcy, but the footmen have brought up the hot water. Would you like them to fill Mrs. Darcy's bathtub first or yours?"

"Mrs. Darcy's."

The maid curtseyed and disappeared. The sound of footsteps in Elizabeth's dressing room announced that her bath was being readied.

"Elizabeth, do you not think it best to bathe quickly and have a bite to eat before Dr. Camryn arrives? Doctors are not easy to endure, especially not if one is hungry."

Elizabeth smiled at his teasing. "You make a good point. Come with me, Florence."

Once she and Florence had left, Mrs. Reynolds closed the door to the hallway. "Sir, may I have a word with you?"

"Of course."

"I hate to be the bearer of bad news," the housekeeper began, her gaze dropping to the carpet as she began wringing her hands. "Especially since I was the one in charge of keeping Lady Henrietta confined."

William's brows furrowed. "Go on."

"She is not here. She has escaped."

"Deuce take that harridan! How in the world did she manage that?"

"By overpowering a maid, donning her uniform, and walking right past the guards at the door. This happened two days ago at dinnertime. We did not discover she was missing until the next morning. Apparently, one of the new grooms readied the gig, drove her to Lambton and then disappeared himself. The gig was found behind the building where the post coach stops, and according to witnesses, a lady wearing a veil bought passage on the early coach to London."

William looked livid. "I will notify the Bow Street Runners immediately. If Lady Henrietta is in England, we will find her. We already have men at every seagoing port should she try to leave by ship. We can merely instruct them to change their search from Elizabeth to Lady Henrietta."

"So you will not be leaving again?"

"No. My place is with my wife, especially when she is unwell."

"What of Colonel Fitzwilliam? Should I plan for his departure?"

"My cousin is exhausted, and I will not have him chase after her, either."

"This is my fault. I am so very sorry."

"You are wrong. The fault is mine. I underestimated my step-mother's cunning. I should have had her locked up downstairs, like her maid. I take it *that* woman is still with us."

"She is, Mr. Darcy."

William was silent for a moment. "Do not say anything to Elizabeth or to Richard. I shall inform them."

"Yes, sir."

William reached out to place a comforting hand on the housekeeper's arm. "Do not fret about it. I am certain Lady Henrietta will be caught ere long and then she will suffer for having had my wife kidnapped."

"May I ask, do you have sufficient proof to convict her?"

"Yes. The leader of the gypsies had a letter in his possession. It is in her handwriting, and it implicates her and Lord Hartford."

The long-time servant nodded. "It may not be charitable to say, but I shall be proud to see both of them pay."

"So shall I."

Richard watched an angry William stalk back and forth across the sitting room, mumbling to himself. Obviously, his cousin was worried about what the doctor might find, but he was also livid at being ordered from Elizabeth's bedroom. Had Florence not fetched him to intervene, Richard feared his cousin might have carried his criticism of the doctor too far.

Now that they were ensconced in the sitting room, Richard opened the bottle of brandy he had brought from his room to ease his cousin's nerves. "Sit down and I will pour you a drink."

"I can drink standing up, thank you."

"You must calm down, Darcy. Besides, all this pacing is giving me a headache."

"I apologise for giving *you* a headache," William said, his tone dripping with sarcasm.

"I do not deserve your hostility."

William stopped pacing to face his cousin. "Forgive me. You are correct. Of all people, you do not deserve to be ill-treated. It is just...I am so worried that—"

He turned away and Richard walked over to pat him on the back.

"Life is too short to think the worst until it is unavoidable."

Instantly, the door to Elizabeth's bedroom opened and Dr. Camryn walked out, his bag in hand. William tried to determine the seriousness of Elizabeth's condition by the look on his face, but the doctor's expression was unremarkable.

"Will you excuse us, Colonel Fitzwilliam?"

"I had rather Richard stay."

"Very well," the doctor said, motioning to a chair. "Please, sit down."

William's first instinct was to argue, but Camryn's bearing compelled him to obey.

"Mr. Darcy, I do not believe your wife's symptoms portend anything serious."

"Let me see if I understand correctly. You are saying that not being able to keep food in her stomach is not serious?" William asked irritably.

"It is not...if one is with child."

Richard almost laughed aloud at the expression that crossed William's face.

William stuttered, "Eliz...Elizabeth is with child?"

"The nausea, especially in the morning, a lack of courses, and her fatigue are all symptoms. If her recollection of when the symptoms started is correct, she should feel the quickening in about four weeks. That is the best confirmation that a woman is with child." Dr. Camryn removed his glasses, placed them inside their case, and tucked them in his bag. Snapping it shut, he added, "I believe her to be nearly two months along, so early March will begin her confinement. For now, I will prescribe a soothing tonic to help settle her stomach, and I recommend that she eat small meals and nothing too spicy." The doctor smiled knowingly. "Otherwise, the activities you and she have enjoyed in the past may continue as long as she feels well enough."

Taking no notice of his last statement, William reached to shake Camryn's hand. "Pray forgive me if I was too severe with you earlier."

Without waiting for absolution, William rushed into his

wife's bedroom and closed the door. Richard walked over to stand by Dr. Camryn.

"I cannot tell you how relieved I am that Darcy is going to be a father. My cousin's life has been so ill-fated these last few years that I feared the worst concerning Mrs. Darcy's health."

"I was a witness to much of his misery, so I am glad to be the bearer of happier news this time."

"You seem confident of Mrs. Darcy's condition."

"I am, but I advise couples to wait for the quickening to be certain."

"I understand."

That night

Sliding aside William's nightshirt, Elizabeth snuggled closer and placed a kiss on the hard planes of his chest. "Are you as thrilled as I am about the baby?"

"Remember, Dr. Camryn said we could not be certain until—"

Elizabeth lifted her head to look into William's eyes as she interrupted. "I know he must be careful not to raise expectations, but I feel certain that I am with child. So, tell me honestly, are you happy?"

Though William was thrilled at the prospect, the fear of losing Elizabeth in childbirth was equally strong. Unable to separate the two, he could not say as much to her.

"I can think of nothing more wonderful than knowing you are carrying my child."

Elizabeth smiled, kissed the warm skin of his chest again, and laid her head there. "I pray it is a boy. Having an heir first will take the worry away."

"I care not if it is a boy or a girl, my love. Pemberley is not entailed, so we can leave it to a daughter as easily as a son."

"I understand, but a man needs a son, and girls need an older brother. I want at least six children, so I have plenty of time to bear girls."

Amused, William repeated, "Six?"

Elizabeth raised her head again. "You do not want that many?"

William cupped her face and brought her lips to his. "I want as many as the Lord sees fit to send."

Elizabeth kissed him again, deepening the kiss as she entwined her fingers in his hair.

At length, he rolled over so that she was beneath him. "Sweetheart, perhaps we should refrain—at least until you are in better health."

"Dr. Camryn said the nausea and tiredness should end soon, and I will begin to gain weight. And when I asked, he said we should not be afraid of marital relations as it will not hurt the baby."

"You asked him that?"

"Knowing your penchant for keeping me safe, I felt I had no choice."

William laughed.

Tenderly, Elizabeth brushed the hair from his forehead. "I believe we should heed his advice. What say you?"

"Far be it from me to disregard the doctor's orders."

Chapter 43

Pemberley
William's bedroom

To the Master of Pemberley, nothing compared to waking up in his own bed in his ancestral home. Furthermore, to wake up with his wife in his arms fulfilled every dream William had harboured since he was old enough to consider his future. Today would have been a perfect day had it not been for the task that lay before him—seeing that those behind Elizabeth's ordeal were brought to justice.

Dawn had broken an hour ago, but rather than rise early as was his wont, William lingered in bed so as not to awaken Elizabeth. She had been so weary by the time they reached Pemberley that she had napped until nearly the dinner hour and retired early, only to reawaken when he entered the bed around midnight. It was then that she asked his thoughts on having a child and assured him that the doctor had sanctioned the continuation of their conjugal activities—not that he had been too difficult to sway. Still, he was responsible for keeping her awake long after that.

Reaching to brush a stray hair from her forehead, he smiled when her nose twitched. Small, turned-up, and with a sprinkling of faint freckles, it was one of the things he had always loved about Elizabeth. Most women of means would never be caught outdoors without a parasol or, at the very least, a bonnet, so freckles were uncommon amongst the ladies of the *ton*.

A flutter of lashes drew his attention to her eyes. Black lashes hid equally dark orbs that never failed to mesmerise him. Having been lost in their depths many times, William considered the fact that before Elizabeth, no woman had ever captured his attention with merely a look.

Your eyes communicate your soul, my darling. Love or hate, desire or loathing—everything is there if one only cares to look.

A knock on the door interrupted his musings. Having left instructions not to be disturbed, an irritated William slipped out of bed, donned his robe, and hurried across the room. Upon opening the door, he was about to upbraid Adams when the concerned look on his valet's face stopped him short.

"Sir, please forgive the interruption, but it is imperative you dress immediately."

"What demands my attention this early?"

"Viscount Leighton arrived moments ago."

"My cousin is here? I thought him still in London."

"Well, sir, he is here. Furthermore, it will surprise you to learn who accompanied him."

"Tell me."

"Lady Henrietta, and as you can imagine, she is not pleased."

"Where is Richard?"

"Colonel Fitzwilliam is downstairs already. It was he who insisted I wake you. He asks that you join them in the library as soon as may be."

William glanced at Elizabeth. "Where is Florence?"

"She is in the kitchen preparing a breakfast tray for Mrs. Darcy."

"Send a footman to tell Florence I do not want my wife disturbed. She can bring the tray up after her mistress wakes of her own accord."

"Very well, Mr. Darcy."

"After you have done that, please wait for me in my dressing room."

"Yes, sir." Adams bowed and left.

William gingerly sat down on the edge of the bed and leaned

over to place a soft kiss on Elizabeth's forehead. To his chagrin, her eyes opened.

"What time is it?" she asked sleepily.

"It is still early, my love. Go back to sleep. I have business letters I must write and post. You may send for me once you wake, and we shall break our fast together." Placing a gentle kiss on her lips, he added, "Now rest."

Her lashed fluttered, then closed.

The library

When William walked into the library, he half-expected to find Lady Henrietta holding forth as she had often done in the past. Instead, only Richard and Leighton were there, and they were conversing so intently that they did not hear him enter.

"Where is that woman?" William asked.

"She is being guarded by two Bow Street Runners in the blue drawing room," Leighton answered. "I wanted to speak to you before you interview her."

"Runners? Here?"

"Mr. Fielding thought it worthwhile to send two of his men along, just in case you had discovered sufficient evidence to have Lady Henrietta arrested. Richard informed me that you have."

"She escaped from a locked room," William said. "How the devil did you find her?"

Viscount Leighton recounted the story he had told Richard only minutes before, adding, "It was merely a piece of good luck that we crossed paths."

"I prefer to think of it as divine providence," Richard interjected. "Recompense for sins and all that." Then he held up a letter. "Leighton also brought this letter from the fellow I hired to investigate the fake jewellery. It holds proof that Lady Henrietta was the one who had the Darcy jewels exchanged for paste."

"I am not surprised," William said, "but how will that information serve me? After all, as Mrs. Darcy, she had the right to—"

"He enclosed the receipt for the switch, Cousin," Richard interjected. "It is dated after Uncle George's death, which means she no longer had the right to do anything with the Darcy jewels. In addition to having Mrs. Darcy kidnapped, Lady *Harlot* is a thief."

"At this point, I would not be surprised to learn she is a foreign spy," William hissed. Then an expression of fear crossed his face. "The plan was for you to wait in London, Leighton. Is your presence here a sign that something has happened to Georgiana?"

"Heavens, no! Georgiana is well, I assure you," Leighton replied. "She is with my parents, just as you wanted. I came because there is so much to say regarding her situation and George Wickham that it would have taken forever to put it down on paper. And, knowing your penchant for asking questions, I thought it best to explain in person."

At the mention of Wickham, William's face settled into a scowl. "What does that blackguard have to do with Georgiana?"

Immediately, Leighton related what had transpired at the art school. When he mentioned Wickham had implicated Lady Henrietta, however, William came to his feet.

"I shall see both of them hang!"

"That is a fitting punishment," Richard said, "but there is one thing you may want to consider first."

"And what is that?" William snapped.

"Do not misunderstand me. I think both those reprobates should hang, along with Hartford and the gypsies; however, Georgiana has considered that harridan her mother for several years now. I have to wonder what effect it will have on her if she learns Lady Henrietta is to hang."

William took a deep breath before letting it go loudly. "Until now, I kept the truth about our step-mother from my sister. It is past time Georgiana learned not all people are what they seem. It will be a hard lesson, but thank God, she has a sister to confide in now. If anyone can help a heart to mend, it is Elizabeth."

"I raise the subject only because judges often consider the injured party's wishes at sentencing," Richard added.

"I will keep that in mind."

"There is more, Darcy," Leighton said. "Whilst investigating Hartford, I learned the Mayfair townhouse he occupied actually belongs to Lady Henrietta. Moreover, she has accounts in several banks worth more than twenty-five thousand pounds in the name of Lady Wharton. Father is adamant no court in the land would disagree that the townhouse and the accounts passed to Uncle George upon their marriage and to you upon his death. And, you know how well-versed Father is in the law governing inheritance."

"It is only fitting you recover some of what Uncle George squandered on that strumpet," Richard added. "Just think! You might not have to sell Willowbend Hall after all."

"For the present, I want to focus on why Lady Henrietta set out to destroy my family," William said. "Lord knows she and I were never friends, but to hurt Georgiana, who thought the best of her, and Elizabeth, who was never unkind, is beyond the pale."

Richard walked towards the door. "Do you mind if we accompany you and hear what she has to say?"

"Not at all."

Richard winked at Leighton. "I would not miss this for the world!"

After entering the drawing room, Leighton introduced the Runners to William before their host continued to the windows where Lady Henrietta sat on a sofa with her back to them. As he walked around so he could face her, William discovered that not only were her hands tied, but a handkerchief had been stuffed in her mouth. Raised brows directed at Leighton asked the question on his mind.

"Since her arrest, she has done naught but scream at the top of her lungs about the injustice of it all," Leighton replied. "Frankly, I got tired of hearing it; thus, the gag. Remove the cloth yourself, and you will see."

William did just that, and a string of profanities filled the air before Lady Henrietta hissed, "How dare you treat me in this manner! If your father were alive, he would be ashamed of you! And what do you think Georgiana will say once she hears of it?"

"My father should have been ashamed to marry you and bring you into this house! As for my sister, Georgiana will understand once she hears that you were the instigator of George Wickham's scheme to kidnap her, and it was you who had her sister abducted!"

"If that fool Wickham did anything to Georgiana, it was not at my direction. I tried to tell him she was too young to take to Gretna Green. If he did not listen, it was because he coveted her dowry. He always has."

"And I suppose you also deny hiring the gypsies who took Elizabeth?"

"Why should I? You must have proof, else I would not have been arrested. I heard Mr. Walker tell the viscount that Elizabeth is here. Is that correct?"

"It is."

"Then I was not successful," she said disappointedly. "I hoped your grief over her disappearance would be the tragedy that finally brought Pemberley to its knees."

William's hands formed fists as he flew towards her. Only the quick reaction of Richard and Leighton, both struggling to restrain him, kept the two separated.

"You sorry excuse for a human being!" William shouted. "As my father's widow, Pemberley would have provided you a decent living for the rest of your life. Yet you would destroy all of that in order to kill those I love!"

"A decent living! What do you know of living decently? All your life you have had everything handed to you on a silver platter."

"You wish to destroy me because I am wealthy?"

"I wish to destroy you because I despise you. All of this," she looked about the room, "should rightfully have been mine! I should have been the heir to Pemberley, not you!"

"Are you insane?"

"When she met George Darcy, my mother was Lady Mary Abercrombie of Winfield Park in Sussex and barely eighteen years of age. It was the year she came out, and for months after they were introduced, he squired her to every dinner party and ball London had to offer, to all the popular plays and recitals. He made no secret of how smitten he was, raising not only *her* expectations, but those of family and friends. Then, at a dinner party given by Lord and Lady Matlock, he met Lady Anne Fitzwilliam. Though he was practically engaged to my mother, George Darcy discarded her like a used shoe to pursue your mother! I suspect her dowry had a great deal to do with it, for my grandfather had fallen on tough times and my mother's dowry was modest. In any case, your father broke my mother's heart, ruined her life, and thereby ruined my own life."

"Surely my father was not the only man willing to offer for your mother."

"After she was publicly humiliated by George Darcy, any suitors she had vanished into thin air. My grandfather was too ill to challenge your father, so his solution was to insist that she accept the next man who offered for her regardless of who that might be. His only thought was to lessen the family's mortification."

"Do you expect me to feel sorry for—"

"Sorry! Which of our misfortunes would you feel sorry for? That my mother was forced to marry a philanderer? That Lord Carmichael, my worthless father, gambled away every cent of her dowry before he was killed in a duel two years later? Or perhaps you would feel sorry that his estate was entailed to a distant relation upon his death and Mother was left with only a few hundred pounds a year? Or could it be that you feel sorry because my grandfather's estate was entailed to the male line as well, so when he also died, she no longer had a home?"

"You seem to imagine that you are the only one who has ever suffered hardships."

"Spoken like a true Darcy!" she hissed, coming to her feet. "The fact is, I married Lord Wharton—a man old enough to be my grandfather—at the tender age of fifteen because I needed the old fool's money to care for my mother. Moreover, I felt certain he would soon die and leave me with the resources to go after you."

"You mean my father."

"I certainly do not! Why would I marry that shell of a man, when you were young, vibrant, and handsome? You cannot possibly know how degrading it was to give myself to Lord Wharton, and I had no intention of tethering myself to another old man. Unfortunately, after Lord Wharton died, you would not give me the time of day, so I settled for George."

"You married my father just to exact revenge?"

As she talked, Lady Henrietta progressed stealthily towards William. "As she lay on her death-bed, I promised my mother I would destroy the Darcys for what they had done to us."

Wishing to distance himself, William turned to walk away when suddenly Lady Henrietta's hands were free. Picking up a marble figurine, she raised it above her head and lunged at him.

Richard reacted instantly, wrestling the weapon from her grasp and shoving her to the floor. Hearing the commotion, the Runners rushed back into the room in time to restrain Lady Henrietta whilst she kicked and screamed more obscenities.

"Tie her with ropes, not cloth!" Richard ordered. "And this time make it tight!" Once that was done, he added, "Take her downstairs and lock her in one of the empty servants' apartments. Until we leave for London, I want two men guarding her day and night."

As she was being dragged down the hallway, Lady Henrietta shouted curses. By the time she was far enough away to barely be heard, William was drained. Crossing to a liquor cabinet, he poured two fingers of liquor into a glass and drank it in one swallow. Then he turned to his cousins. "I have no doubt the entire household heard that witch's insults, so I must see to Elizabeth. Help yourselves to the brandy."

Once alone with Richard, Leighton said, "After listening to that woman's vitriol, I believe it will take more than one glass to settle my nerves."

"An entire bottle would not be enough!" Richard declared wryly, "But it will be a start."

A balcony

William returned to Elizabeth's bedroom to find her awake and enjoying the sunlight on the balcony. Seeing him, she smiled. "I was hoping you would come soon; I am famished."

He walked over to give her a quick kiss atop her head. "I shall ring for Florence and tell her that you are ready to eat."

"Tell her that *we* are ready!" Elizabeth replied cheekily. "After all, you promised."

"So I did," William said, giving her a wink. "I shall be right back."

Knowing Elizabeth as he did, he was certain she would have questioned him if she had heard Lady Henrietta's rantings, so he decided not to say anything about that woman's presence until later.

After their meal, William noticed Elizabeth shivering. "You are cold, my dear," he said. "I shall fetch you a blanket.

Before Elizabeth could protest, he was already entering the bedroom. Going straight to the blanket that always lay over the back of the settee, he had just picked it up when Florence opened the door leading to the sitting room.

Dropping a curtsey, she said, "Sir, the Reverend and Mrs. Green have arrived and are in the foyer. They are asking to see Mrs. Darcy. Mrs. Darcy's father is also with them."

William was not certain whether to be happy for Elizabeth or fearful of her father's opinion of him. He was pleased, however, that the Greens had accompanied Mr. Bennet. "Ask them to come up, please."

Walking to where Elizabeth sat, he spread the blanket over her legs and tucked it in. "Elizabeth, Mr. and Mrs. Green are here to see you."

"I am so glad. I have missed them very much."

"And your father is with them."

"Papa...here?" Elizabeth said excitedly, beginning to stand.

"Stay as you are, sweetheart. You are still weak and can greet them just as easily sitting down. I shall have some chairs brought out so that everyone can sit with you."

Elizabeth acquiesced and followed William's progress with her eyes as he went back into the bedroom. After ringing for a footman, he was waiting in the sitting room when the Greens appeared in the open doorway.

"Fitzwilliam!" Mrs. Green declared, rushing to throw her arms around him. "James and I had to come and see for ourselves that Elizabeth is home."

"She is thrilled that you have come," William replied. "Please, go on to her through the bedroom."

As Judith Green rushed towards Elizabeth, James Green stepped forward, taking William's hand and shaking it firmly. "Fitzwilliam, Judith and I are so thankful that you were able to find Elizabeth and that she is well." Continuing, he motioned a reticent Mr. Bennet to come forward, "Please allow me to introduce Elizabeth's father, Thomas Bennet. He arrived in Lambton just after you and Colonel Fitzwilliam left to go north."

William extended a hand. "I am very pleased to see you again."

Accepting William's sturdy hand, Thomas Bennet shook it vigorously. "Pleased hardly describes how I feel to greet the man who rescued my Lizzy in more ways than one." Mr. Bennet's hand then flew to his heart. "You have this father's gratitude."

William's whole expression changed with his smile. "I prefer to think it was Elizabeth who rescued me by accepting my hand. Now, since she is aware that you are here, let us not keep her waiting any longer. Follow me, please."

To say that Elizabeth was excited to see her father would be an understatement. She cried tears of happiness the entire visit. Seeing the joy in her countenance affected William deeply, and he vowed to share their lives with Elizabeth's family as much as possible.

After a short while, when it appeared the Greens were preparing to leave and take Mr. Bennet with them, William said, "I insist that you stay, sir. Your place is here with your daughter. Where shall I send for your luggage?"

"I am afraid my bags are at the Gavins' farm. They decided to wait and see Lizzy tomorrow."

"I shall send a servant after them," William replied. "Please stay with Elizabeth whilst I escort Reverend and Mrs. Green downstairs and instruct my housekeeper to prepare a room for you."

After saying farewell to the Greens, Elizabeth reached for her father's hand. "Sit down, Papa. I have something important to tell you."

As soon as her company had gone, and Mr. Bennet had complied, she said excitedly, "Doctor Camryn said I should wait for the quickening before I tell everyone, but I just know it is true! I am going to have a baby!"

Mr. Bennet's heart swelled with pride along with a tinge of heartache whilst his eyes pooled with tears. Of all his children, Elizabeth was closest to his heart, and it had been bittersweet to have lost her to marriage at the tender age of eighteen. Still, he knew full well that he could not have chosen a more suitable husband for Elizabeth than Fitzwilliam Darcy.

She looked at him tenderly, asking, "Has my news made you unhappy, Papa?"

"Do not let these tears fool you, child. I could not be happier. May I suggest, though, that we keep the news from your mother for as long as possible. Once she learns of it, she will hasten here to give you the benefit of her knowledge on the subject."

Elizabeth laughed. "I had already thought of that, Papa. For now, only you and Jane will know...and Mr. Bingley, of course. Jane shares everything with him."

"So tell me, what does your husband have to say about becoming a father?"

"William is over the moon with happiness."

"From your letters, I know he is a kind, generous man, and I look forward to knowing him better."

"Once you do, I know you will love him as much as I."

"Maybe not quite that much," Mr. Bennet teased. "But observing how he cares for you, I am inclined to like him a great deal."

"Oh, Papa! It is so good to have you tease me again. Thank you for coming."

"I always intended to visit once my leg was sturdy enough to carry me. Despite your letters, I had a niggling fear I might have made the wrong decision by sending you to Cambridge. Now I am reassured that Providence set everything right by bringing Mr. Darcy back into our lives."

Elizabeth nodded. "God has truly blessed me by giving me Fitzwilliam for a husband."

"I may be prejudiced," Mr. Bennet added, "but I think Fitzwilliam has been equally blessed."

As William walked the Greens to the front door, he stopped in the foyer. "I believe having her father here will lift Elizabeth's spirits."

"I could not agree more," Judith Green replied. "Elizabeth's face fairly glowed when she saw him."

"It is wonderful to see her happy after all she has endured," James Green said. Then he added, "Remember to call on us if you need anything, my boy."

"I will," William replied. "And thank you for being there when we needed you."

"You both are dear to us," Mrs. Green replied. "We could do no less."

Too emotional to reply, William merely nodded. Watching until the couple he embraced as parents went through the door, he composed himself and went to locate Mrs. Reynolds.

Chapter 44

On the road
September, 1812

As they made their way to Meryton for the wedding of Jane Bennet to Charles Bingley, William could barely suppress a smile as he listened to the banter between his wife and his sister. There was a time when he feared Georgiana would never recover from the shock of learning that her stepmother was not what she had seemed. Without his wife's presence in their lives, he shuddered to think of how it may have affected her gentle nature. As it was, Elizabeth was able to coax his sister from despair, and by the time sentences were announced for the perpetrators, Georgiana had recovered sufficiently to handle the results.

Georgiana begged William to petition the court for transportation to Australia for Lady Henrietta, which he did; however, the court refused to grant it, declaring her crimes were too serious to waive the severest punishment, which was death by hanging. Lord Hartford and George Wickham were also sentenced to hang, whilst Sarah Perry and Mrs. Younge were each given ten years in Newgate Prison for their parts in the crimes. The hangings were carried out immediately following the trial.

With Elizabeth's intervention, Alafare was released. Refusing any help other than the money William gave her for helping Elizabeth, she sailed to the Americas to begin a new life. Teza was sentenced to be deported, with the understanding she would be imprisoned for life if she ever set foot on English soil again.

William had thought Teza deserved prison as well, but Elizabeth pleaded for mercy since Teza's two children had already lost their father, and he relented. Tomas and Nikolae were killed trying to overpower their guards whilst being transported to the courthouse from the jail. The other gypsies involved disappeared into thin air, abandoning their wagons in the woods of South Shields to slip over the border into Scotland.

All these things played through William's mind as he watched one of Elizabeth's hands slide to her swollen belly. Immediately on guard, he enquired, "Is anything wrong, sweetheart?"

Used to his increased vigilance since Dr. Camryn confirmed she was with child, Elizabeth smiled. "All is well. It is just that your child wishes to make his presence known. Perhaps the jostling of the coach is not to his liking."

"We should stop and rest."

Their hands were entwined, and Elizabeth brought his hand to her lips for a kiss. "I am perfectly fine, dearest."

A fascinated Georgiana watched from her perch on the opposite seat. "I am so excited I am to be an aunt!"

"You have such a good rapport with the tenants' children that I know you will be an excellent aunt," Elizabeth said.

"Oh, I do so want to be useful!" Georgiana continued. "It will be wonderful to have a baby in the house, will it not, Brother?"

William smiled and nodded, though the niggling thought of losing Elizabeth in childbirth crossed his mind once again.

Noting the look upon her husband's face, Elizabeth changed the subject. "Was it not considerate of Charles to move the wedding to before Michaelmas[17] to ensure I could stand up with my sister?"

"Very kind, indeed," William replied. Left unsaid was that he

---

17 **Michaelmas term** —Regarding Oxford University, an eight-week term usually after the fest of St. Michael, September 29. For the purposes of this story I chose October 10th as the beginning of the school term since that date was most often shown in the years near 1812. http://www.regencyre-searcher.com/pages/schoolterms.html

had suggested as much to Bingley, for he was concerned about Elizabeth travelling in the latter months of her pregnancy.

"Look!" Georgiana cried suddenly, pointing out the window on her left.

Elizabeth leaned over to see a rock tower standing amongst trees in the distance. "That is all that remains of a castle which once stood on that very spot," she replied. "Which means we are close to the road that turns to go through Meryton. Once we reach the village, I will point out all the places I have been telling you about, Georgiana."

"Perhaps Brother will allow us to stop at the book shop when we reach Meryton," Georgiana said, her brows rising in question.

"I fear I would never get either of you back in the coach," William chuckled. "There will be ample time to visit the village once we are settled at Longbourn."

"And remember, Georgiana," Elizabeth said, "if we wait, we shall have more time to search for treasures."

William groaned, prompting Georgiana to laugh before she turned to Elizabeth. "Did I hear you say that Mr. Bingley's entire family is to stay at Longbourn?"

Seeing her sister's anxious expression, Elizabeth asked, "Yes. Does that present a problem?"

"It is only...I do not understand Miss Bingley. I met her only once when I was visiting William at Cambridge. Afterwards, she assumed we were great friends and wrote to me. I asked Brother to tell her I was only allowed to correspond with girls my age."

Elizabeth suppressed a smile. "Shall I tell you a secret?" At Georgiana's enthusiastic nod, she continued. "My sister Jane is the sweetest person in the world, and even she thinks Miss Bingley is peculiar."

Georgiana's face lit up. "I am glad I am not the only one who thinks so."

William took it upon himself to change the subject. "I have to wonder how we will all fit at Longbourn. It would be no great imposition for us to stay at the inn."

"Mother would never hear of it!" Elizabeth declared, laughing. "Besides, I told Papa we wished to be placed on the top floor, which is normally used for guests. It is less noisy than the family floor below...or it will be until the Gardiners and their children arrive."

As William cringed secretly, Georgiana asked, "Am I to stay on that floor with you?"

"Yes. I requested that you be given the room directly across from ours. It was recently redecorated. Moreover, I asked Kitty to share the room with you. In that way, you will not feel as though you are all alone in a strange house. I am sure you and she will become great friends."

Naturally shy, Georgiana tried to smile as she nodded.

Their welcome to Longbourn could not have been more enthusiastic. Mrs. Bennet waxed eloquent about her happiness at having a son of Darcy's calibre, and she mentioned it half a dozen times before he, Elizabeth and Georgiana were able to escape to the privacy of their rooms. Using the excuse that they were tired from their journey and wished to rest until dinner, they escaped the balance of Mrs. Bennet's effusions until being summoned to eat.

As William feared, dinner proved a boisterous affair with the sisters and their mother all talking at once. Whilst he and Georgiana watched in bewilderment, Mr. Bennet seemed amused. Therefore, after dinner William jumped at the invitation Elizabeth's father offered to accompany him to his study. Consequently, he spent the rest of the evening in relative quiet, whilst his wife and sister dealt with the rest of the Bennets.

One happy circumstance was that the Gardiners and Bingleys were not expected until the next day, so what Elizabeth had said proved true—the floor their rooms were on was blissfully quiet that night. Happily, Kitty and Georgiana were compatible, so that solved the matter of William's sister's trepidation, and had it not been for Mrs. Bennet knocking on William and Elizabeth's door well after they had gone to sleep to enquire what time he wanted to break his fast, they might have slept soundly all night.

The next morning

As it was, a still sleepy William woke early the next morning and rode to Oakham Mount to hide something and returned before anyone discovered he was missing.

Later, when Elizabeth opened her eyes, she could see through the window that it was dawn, even though the room was still mostly dark. Reaching to touch William, she found his side of the bed empty and promptly sat up. When her eyes became accustomed to the dimness, she made out his form sitting in an upholstered chair next to the bed.

"William, why are you up so early? Surely you do not wish to be in Mama's company so soon."

At the sound of her voice, William's eyes flew open. "Actually, I could not sleep, so I dressed in anticipation of having you accompany me to Oakham Mount once you awoke. I wish to relive the first time I saw you."

Elizabeth slipped out of bed and rushed across the cold floor to sit in his lap. William's arms encircled her as she snuggled against his chest and he buried his face in her tangle of curls.

"Who would have thought you a romantic? I certainly did not—at least not when we first met."

"What *did* you think of me then?"

Elizabeth did not wish to revisit her prejudices. "I thought you the most handsome man I had ever met." She felt rather than heard him stifle a laugh. "And I was very attracted to you, despite knowing you would never be interested in someone like me."

"I was a fool not to recognise your worth even then. I was, however, captivated by your high-spiritedness and your beauty."

Elizabeth pulled back to look into his eyes. "All my life I felt as though I was nothing special, particularly compared to Jane. You have always made me feel beautiful. Thank you."

"It is the truth, my love. You are the most beautiful woman of my acquaintance."

His declaration was rewarded with a passionate kiss, and

when it ended William whispered, "If we are going to Oakham Mount, we must leave before our family rises, else they may want to go with us."

"Quickly! Help me dress."

The world was still cloaked in a foggy mist when they left the house. Having no idea that William planned to ride, not walk, to Oakham Mount, Elizabeth hesitated when he began to guide her towards a horse already saddled in the paddock fence.

"You know how I feel about riding."

"I will not take a chance on having you walk that far, especially when most of it is uphill," William replied. "Trust me. This animal is docile; you will be safe."

Resigned, Elizabeth was surprised that the animal stood perfectly still whilst William lifted her to its back and quickly mounted behind her. Sliding an arm around her waist, he pulled her close against his body, and they proceeded to exit the paddock.

It was not long before the mist began to vanish, and Elizabeth found herself enjoying familiar vistas from a new vantage point. By the time they reached the summit of Oakham Mount, rays of sunlight were bursting through a line of trees on the horizon, and for a brief period of time they watched the earth come to life in the valley from atop the stallion.

After he dismounted, William set Elizabeth on her feet, took her hand, and guided her towards the tree she had once considered her sanctuary. Sinking down on the well-worn trunk, Elizabeth glanced around. "I have missed this place," she murmured. "It holds so many good memories."

"It holds a special memory for me as well."

Elizabeth looked puzzled. "How can you say that? I treated you horribly when I discovered you here with my journal."

William smiled lovingly. "All I remember is that I fell in love for the first time in my life at this very spot."

"And I had no earthly idea."

"Actually, I had no idea at that point, either. It was only with retrospection—when I could not get you off my mind—that I realised a sprite of a girl in Meryton had stolen my heart."

As he talked, William surreptitiously tipped over some rocks he had stacked against the tree just as they had been years ago. Something wrapped in burlap and tied with string stood out on the ground. Immediately, it caught Elizabeth's eye and she stood to pick it up.

"What have you done?" she asked, beaming from ear to ear.

"The only way to find out is to open it."

Pulling the string, Elizabeth found a journal inside and brought it out. Similar to those she had used in the past, this journal had her husband's name embossed in gold on the front. Opening it, she discovered only one entry, and that was dated the day they left Pemberley for Meryton. She read it out loud.

September 15, 1812

I am looking forward to escorting my beautiful wife to her childhood home to attend her sister Jane's wedding. This will be the first time I have visited Meryton since I met Elizabeth during the Christmas holiday of 1810.

What a fortuitous gift that meeting turned out to be, for she became my wife and soon will bear our first child. God has blessed me with someone I love more than life and a future filled with joy, love and devotion. I want for nothing.

By the time she had finished reading, Elizabeth was blinking back tears and found it hard to speak.

William hastened to say, "When you were missing, I stumbled across the diary beneath your bed. It was wrong of me to read your private thoughts, but I missed you so much that I was unable to refrain. When I read in your own hand that you loved me, it brought me such joy that I wished you to experience that same joy. I know that I am not a great writer, but I hope by recording my thoughts often in this journal, it may help to remedy that failing. I intend to keep it in the top drawer of my desk, and since you have a key to the study and the desk, you may read it whenever you desire."

Elizabeth threw her arms around him, laying her head on his

chest as she hugged him tightly. "Oh, William, I will be honoured to read whatever you write in this journal." Then, pulling her head back to look up, she added, "I love you so much that words fail me."

A fierce kiss followed, gradually progressing until William found it necessary to reclaim control. "We should return," he murmured breathlessly. "If we reach Longbourn and our room with no one the wiser, we can lock the door and feign still being asleep whilst we indulge in other pleasures."

Elizabeth smiled. "I shall not complain if you press the horse to go faster on the way back."

Fortunately, the couple was able to enjoy the pleasures of the marital bed before insistent knocks on the door bid Elizabeth to answer from where she lay beneath her husband.

"What is it?"

"Mrs. Bennet sent me to ask if you want a tray sent up," Mrs. Hill replied.

"That will not be necessary. Tell her we shall be down shortly," Elizabeth replied.

The sound of footsteps going down the hall made it plain the housekeeper had retreated. Seeing the smile playing on William's lips, she teased, "Are you going to let me up, Husband?"

"Do I have a choice?"

Elizabeth giggled. "Not unless you want Mama to return in Hill's place."

When at length William and Elizabeth entered the dining room, they were met by a wry smile from Mr. Bennet. Having just finished eating, he immediately folded his newspaper, stood and retreated to his study. Jane smiled warmly and greeted her sister and William whilst Kitty and Lydia did nothing but giggle.

Georgiana, who appeared to be unaware as to what was funny, smiled benignly and bid them good morning.

After acknowledging everyone, William and Elizabeth had just taken their seats when Mrs. Bennet, who was hoping to gain a compliment, said to William, "May I assume that you slept so soundly, Mr. Darcy, because your accommodations were adequate?"

"Indeed," William answered, trying to keep a straight face. "We found the room most comfortable."

Subsequent sniggers from the youngest Bennets were cut short when Mrs. Bennet declared, "Lydia, Kitty, come with me. I have some embroidery that needs to be finished."

Both girls groaned and complained, though each followed their mother into the parlour.

Later, when everyone had removed to the parlour, the sounds of a coach traversing the gravel drive caught their attention. Mrs. Bennet threw down her embroidery to rush towards the front door.

"Jane, dear! It must be Mr. Bingley! Come at once!"

Naturally, Lydia and Kitty followed Jane from the parlour. Even Elizabeth went to the door and peered down the hall, causing William to motion for Georgiana to come as he walked over to stand beside his wife.

Mrs. Hill opened the front door at the first knock and found Charles Bingley, his sister Caroline, and Louisa and Bertram Hurst standing on the portico.

"Oh, Mr. Bingley!" Mrs. Bennet cried from behind the housekeeper as she pushed Hill aside and took her place. "How good it is to see you again! Please, everyone, come in!"

Introductions were made, though from her perch in the doorway Elizabeth noticed that Caroline Bingley's nose wrinkled in disgust when her mother asked if they had eaten. Charles replied they were so famished they had stopped to eat at the inn in Meryton. Though Mrs. Bennet was obviously disheartened to hear it, still she instructed Mrs. Hill to show the guests to their rooms. Dutifully, Caroline followed the servant up the stairs, as did Louisa and her husband.

After greeting Jane, Charles noticed the Darcys and walked towards William with an outstretched hand. "Darcy! I am so pleased that all of you came."

"We would not have missed your wedding for the world," William replied, shaking Bingley's hand.

"Elizabeth and I were about to walk into Meryton to show Georgiana the village. Would you and Jane care to join us?"

Charles turned to Jane, who smiled and nodded. "It seems that we would."

"Excellent. Do you wish to change clothes or go as you are?"

"I shall not take the time to change." Then Bingley leaned in to say quietly, "Perhaps we can escape without Caroline if we leave now. You know she is a sycophant where you are concerned."

William grasped Elizabeth's hand. "Perhaps now that I am married, Caroline will flatter someone else."

"I would not rely on that," Bingley said with a laugh. "Though I will do my best to control her."

Ere long, both couples and Georgiana were walking the trail that led to Meryton. Mrs. Bennet refused to let Lydia, Kitty and Mary go with them, insisting that they stay behind to entertain Caroline and Louisa when they came downstairs.

Meryton

Whilst the women were in the millinery shop, William stood outside with Charles, who was explaining where he and Jane would reside once he returned to Cambridge. Suddenly, John Lucas walked down the street towards them. Bracing himself for what his former friend had in mind, William was shocked when Lucas stopped, bowed and said, "Darcy, I have given you no reason to hear me out, but I pray that you will be kind enough to listen."

William's eyes flew to the shop window where he saw that

Elizabeth was busy with her sisters. Glancing back to Lucas, he waited in silence, and Lucas took that as a sign to proceed.

"What I did to you...and to Elizabeth...was unconscionable. The lies I told were not only irrational but heartless. I almost caused irreversible harm, and I pray at some point you and she will find it in your hearts to forgive me."

Then he turned and went back the way he had come.

"I would never have thought Lucas had the mettle to face you after what he did," Charles murmured.

"Please, say nothing about this to Elizabeth," William said. "I will tell her when the time is right."

"Of course."

The wedding
Two days later

The nuptials went according to plan, and nearly all the Bennets' neighbours attended. William could not have been prouder to take his place next to Bingley for Elizabeth was standing up with Jane and, in his estimation, she looked as beautiful as the bride. She wore a new, lemon-coloured gown with an ecru-coloured lace overlay, created by her modiste in Lambton. It featured a green vine with yellow flowers embroidered along the neck, sleeves, bodice and hem, and its Empire style made it almost impossible to tell Elizabeth was with child unless she rested her arms upon her belly, which she had begun to do. Even then, William thought her lovely.

Before the ceremony began, he looked about the chapel to see if Lucas was in attendance. Though he spotted the rest of the Lucas family, John was not seated with them. He had not told Elizabeth about Lucas' apology and had no reasonable explanation why, other than he had conflicting emotions about their shared past. He would tell her; he was just not certain when.

Afterwards, a majority walked from the church to Longbourn to participate in the breakfast Mrs. Bennet was hosting. Despite her flaws, she was known throughout Meryton as an excellent hostess, and the house was soon filled to capacity with guests, all enjoying a variety of foods so vast it impressed even Caroline Bingley.

As the breakfast was coming to an end, William spied Lucas in the far corner of the parlour. He was standing next to a door that led outside and when their eyes met, Lucas looked as though he might be considering escaping. In the end, however, he remained where he stood.

Elizabeth, who was standing beside William, noted his worried expression. "What is wrong, darling? You look as though you have seen a ghost."

"Is there somewhere we can talk?"

Taking his hand, Elizabeth led him through the crowd and into the hall between the parlour and the kitchen. From there she led him to a door past Mr. Bennet's study. That door opened to reveal a large supply room and once they went inside she turned to face him, smiling wickedly.

"And what is your plan now that we are alone?"

Instantly she was caught in his embrace, and before long, began to mould her body to his as he poured his love into a kiss. When the kiss ended, she teased breathlessly, "Surely you do not mean to take me in this closet with all of Meryton outside the door?"

"No. I…it is just—"

"Just say it," she said, running the back of her hand tenderly over his cheek.

William confessed everything. He even admitted he was unsure if he wanted to forgive Lucas or to see her grant him forgiveness. "I…I am afraid your former familiarity might make you wish to—"

"Oh, my darling!" Elizabeth cried, standing on tiptoe to place a comforting kiss on his lips. "John was never anything to me but a friend. I can forgive him because he is not essential to my happiness. He will forever be someone who taught me I was acting like a spoiled child instead of a woman."

William smiled wryly. "I have changed my mind. I do wish to take you in this closet."

"May I propose that we go back to the parlour where you will find my father and listen whilst he makes sport of the neighbours instead? Meanwhile, I will locate John and inform him that whilst we both have forgiven him, we think it best to continue as indifferent acquaintances. Then, as soon as Jane and Charles leave for their trip, I will inform Mama that I am tired and wish to rest. Of course, you will see me to my room."

William embraced her again, whispering in her ear, "Have I told you today how much I adore you, Mrs. Darcy?"

"Yes, but you have permission to tell me again."

Chapter 45

Pemberley
March 10, 1813

The Mistress of Pemberley had been so uncomfortable the past two months that when labour began the previous evening, it seemed the entire household sighed in relief. All, that is, but the Master. William had been on pins and needles for months and as his wife's confinement neared, the anxiety took its toll on his normally steady nature.

As it turned out, Richard happened to arrive for a visit that same day, which was fortuitous, since no one dealt better with William's outbursts than he, and lately the master tended to blow everything out of proportion. This included the fact that Dr. Camryn was out of town when Elizabeth's pains began, which left the midwife, Mrs. Posey, in charge of the birth. Though William assumed the woman knew her trade, she was not one to explain her actions, and that, combined with the fact that he expected answers to his questions, had led to several clashes already. Moreover, as the night wore on, Elizabeth's labour progressed at such a snail's pace that by daylight the sound of her cries had worn William's patience razor thin. As a result, he often escaped to the sitting room to compose himself before returning to her side.

Mrs. Reynolds had stayed up all night, as had Mrs. Lantrip. They provided a ready supply of hot tea and coffee, as well as sandwiches and biscuits for the master and his cousin and offered their support to Elizabeth. Whilst Richard had appreciated the fare, William had partaken of nothing save the coffee. Florence had been with her mistress all night, mopping Elizabeth's forehead with a cool, wet rag and providing sips of water whenever William was not available.

Only the Greens' arrival at first light significantly aided Richard's efforts to calm his cousin, who had just entered the sitting room again. With her first glance, Judith Green had discerned William's anger was born out of his fear and convinced him to stay with her husband and Richard whilst she attended Elizabeth. He had agreed, with the understanding that as soon as he had composed himself, he would return.

During William's exile, Dr. Camryn arrived at Pemberley. He was shown directly to Elizabeth's bedroom by Mrs. Reynolds and a short while later entered the sitting room, intending to speak to William. Immediately, he was challenged.

"Why did you leave town knowing Elizabeth was near her time?" William demanded. "When you were here last, I expressly asked you to stay close by."

"Now, Fitzwilliam," Reverend Green began to say, only to be interrupted by the doctor.

"Mr. Darcy, your wife is not the only woman in England having a baby. I was called to Chesterfield to deliver the child of a woman in her forties who has suffered through a difficult pregnancy. I am pleased to say that she and the child survived, which is fortuitous since she has four other children who need her. As for Mrs. Darcy, she is young and healthy, and frankly, I see no rationale for your attitude since Mrs. Posey was available."

"One would think you would show less concern for a woman who has borne several children than for one who is having her first," William declared. "From all I have read, statistics prove that a first birth often ends with the mother's death, if not the child's, too."

Recalling why William would be so fearful, Dr. Camryn's attitude softened. "May I suggest that many of the articles presently being published concerning childbirth have no foundation in reality. It would serve you better to listen to those, such as myself, who have brought many children into the world."

When William did not reply, he continued, "Now, as for your wife, her pains are about five minutes apart, which means the child should be born within the hour."

William's face drained of all colour.

"Sit down!" the doctor ordered. As he complied, Camryn addressed Richard. "A brandy might be of help, Colonel Fitzwilliam."

In seconds, Richard was pouring two fingers of brandy for his enervated cousin. As he walked over to hand the glass to William, Camryn added, "Gentlemen, I leave it to you to supervise Mr. Darcy. I have a child to deliver."

Having said that, he disappeared back inside the bedroom.

Bennet Fitzwilliam George Darcy made his entrance into the world less than half an hour later. The doctor pronounced him nine pounds, if an ounce, and his robust cries alerted everyone in the entire household of his arrival, especially his father, who jumped to his feet and rushed to the bedroom door before suddenly halting. It seemed like forever before the door opened, and Judith Green emerged, smiling from ear to ear.

"Congratulations, Fitzwilliam. You have a perfectly healthy son."

"Eliz...Elizabeth?" William stammered.

"Elizabeth is well."

William broke into a wide smile, turning to announce to Richard and James Green what they already knew. "I have a son!"

"Congratulations!" they declared simultaneously.

Turning back to Mrs. Green, William asked, "May I see them?"

"Dr. Camryn has not quite finished, and once he has, Elizabeth wants Florence to help her into a new gown and brush her hair. She wishes to look presentable before you see her."

"Elizabeth could never be anything but beautiful in my eyes."

"I suggest that you tell her that when you see her. Now, for the time being, just sit back down until you are summoned."

The reverend came forward, slapping William on the back and teasing him that his life was about to change forever as he guided him to a chair. Richard returned to the tray of liquor and began pouring a drink for everyone present.

"Come, let us all celebrate this august occasion," he declared. "Join me in a toast to Darcy's heir!"

It was almost an hour later when the door to the bedroom opened again and Florence came out. "Mr. Darcy, the mistress wishes to see you."

Florence did not have to say it twice. As William rushed into the bedroom and shut the door, Richard handed her a small glass of brandy.

"I...I should not—" Florence began, only to be interrupted.

"Of course you should!" Richard said. "After all, how often is an heir born at Pemberley?"

Florence conceded, accepting the glass. "You are absolutely right. To the heir!" she declared, draining the glass far too quickly for someone who rarely drank spirits. Immediately she began to cough whilst those watching tried not to laugh.

"A word to the wise," Richard teased. "The first two fingers are the deadliest."

Once William entered Elizabeth's bedroom he stopped to take stock of all that was happening. The doctor was washing his hands, whilst the midwife removed instruments from a clean towel and placed them in the doctor's bag. Several maids were rushing about, whilst Mrs. Reynolds stood at the servants' door, admonishing them to hurry. The sheer curtains on the canopy over the bed were partially drawn, making it impossible to see Elizabeth, so he hurried over to the bed and pulled them aside.

Not expecting Elizabeth to look so beautiful after her ordeal, he lost all ability to speak upon seeing her. She was dressed in a fresh nightgown with pink roses embroidered over the bodice and sleeves, whilst her loose hair was held back with a matching pink ribbon. Though obviously exhausted, she was gazing at the babe suckling at her breast with unabashed love and when she saw him, she smiled. William fought to contain his emotions.

Removing the child from her breast, she turned him so that William could see his face. "What do you think of our son?"

Sitting beside her on the bed, he leaned in to examine his child. The baby's lips continued to suckle though the source of his nourishment had been detached and when a small bit of his mother's milk trickled down his chin, William gently wiped it away. Softly running finger tips over the baby's fine, dark hair, he said, "I think him beautiful, for he favours his mother."

Elizabeth returned the baby to her breast and as she gazed at him, her eyes became misty. "I think him the spitting image of his father and I am proud of that. My prayer is that he will grow to resemble you in every way, especially your sense of honour and integrity."

William rewarded her words with a quick kiss, adding, "Whilst I shall pray he inherits your intellect and temperament." Abruptly, his expression became solemn. "Elizabeth, I do not possess the vocabulary to adequately thank you for giving me this child. The pain you suffered to bring him into the world—"

"Was forgotten the moment he was born," Elizabeth interrupted, gently pushing a stray lock of hair from William's eyes.

"Just know that you and Bennet are my world."

"I do, sweetheart," Elizabeth said, "for you and he are mine."

William grasped her free hand, bringing it to his lips for a kiss. "It appears that we have settled on his name."

"I think we have," Elizabeth said, looking down at her son. "Welcome to the world, Bennet Fitzwilliam George Darcy."

By then the babe was asleep, so securing the blanket about him, Elizabeth held him out to his father.

William protested. "I...I have not held an infant since Georgiana was born. Perhaps we should wait until I have more—"

"There is no time like the present, Papa!"

Once Dr. Camryn had finished and was ready to leave, he walked over to William, who stood by the French doors holding his sleeping son whilst Mrs. Reynolds assisted Elizabeth with a draught mixed into a cup of tea. The doctor pulled back the edge of the blanket to see the baby's face.

"Congratulations on the birth of your son, Mr. Darcy."

"Thank you. I am indebted to you for safely delivering my wife of our child," William stated. "Moreover, I apologise for my comments earlier. I was out of line."

"No need for apologies. You said nothing that other concerned fathers have not said already."

Sheepishly, William nodded. Then, he said, "Mrs. Green said you pronounced my son and Elizabeth both healthy. Is that true?"

"It is. Mrs. Darcy is in excellent health for what she has endured, and the babe is perfect." The doctor laughed. "There can be no doubt as to his parentage; he is not a small fellow by any stretch of the imagination. In fact, I would not have been surprised to have discovered your wife was carrying twins. I find it remarkable that someone so petite managed to carry a child that large to full term and have a safe delivery. She must have been quite uncomfortable most of the last two months. I will also add that seldom have I seen a woman of her age so fearless once labour began."

"My wife is remarkable," William agreed. "May I ask how I can assist her recovery?"

"Because of the size of your son, I would have her rest in bed longer than most women—say, at least a fortnight."

William chuckled. "Knowing Elizabeth, that may be impossible."

"If she takes on too much too soon, her body could pay. She needs to recover fully before she assumes her role as a mother and the Mistress of Pemberley."

"Of course."

"I will allow her to walk about for a quarter of an hour every other hour; otherwise, she should be in bed."

"I understand."

"Have you hired a wet nurse?"

"I had Mrs. Reynolds engage one, though when I mentioned it to Elizabeth, she insisted she will nurse our child."

"Knowing Mrs. Darcy, I am not surprised," Dr. Camryn said wryly.

"May I suggest that she feed the baby when she is awake and have the wet nurse take over when she retires."

"I shall try."

The doctor patted his back sympathetically. "That is all any man can do."

One week later

The house had just begun to settle into a steady routine with the newest Darcy when Elizabeth's entire family arrived without notice. It was not a total surprise; after all William had sent an express post the day of Bennet's birth inviting Elizabeth's family to visit. Still, he had hoped that by mentioning the doctor's admonition that she remain in bed for a fortnight, they would postpone their trip until Elizabeth was back on her feet. Falsely, he had believed good sense would prevail.

Alas, Mrs. Bennet had not inherited good sense. Not only did she and Mr. Bennet come, but they brought all of Elizabeth's sisters, including Jane, whom they fetched from Cambridge, and Elizabeth's Aunt Phillips from Meryton. Moreover, once she learned that the Gardiners were visiting the Gavins in Lambton, she insisted that Mr. Darcy invite them and their four children to stay at Pemberley as well.

If William wondered what his servants thought about his new family who filled the house with boisterous chatter and outlandish conduct—such as when Mrs. Reynolds had to admonish Lydia and Kitty for chasing the Gardiner children through the priceless artefacts in the sculpture gallery—today he would wonder no more. As it happened, when he passed the door to Mrs. Bennet's bedroom, which had been left ajar, he heard two maids discussing that very subject. Irritated at being summoned by Elizabeth's mother for the third time to change the sheets on the bed because she found them not soft enough, they were expounding on the Bennets' behaviour. Though just as exasperated as the maids, William made a mental note to mention their conduct to Mrs. Reynolds, knowing she would handle the matter. After all, though the Gardiners' children were better behaved than Elizabeth's two youngest sisters, for his wife's sake he would not allow any of the servants to disparage them.

Elizabeth was delighted to have her relations visit Pemberley, for she relished the chance to introduce Ben, as he would be called, to her family and to exhibit her skills as the Mistress of Pemberley. Though upset with how little she was supposed to be on her feet, she strove to make the best of the situation by having her family gather in her bedroom often whilst she reclined in bed.

Mrs. Gardiner's presence was especially valued, not only because she was very dear, but having reared four children, her aunt had plenty of advice to offer regarding infants. Clever enough not to ask any questions in front of her mother, Elizabeth was still subject to Mrs. Bennet's unsolicited advice, which seemed designed to show how little her daughter knew.

On this day, four days after the Bennets' arrival, when William walked into his wife's bedroom, Mrs. Bennet spontaneously began to pontificate on the correct way to feed her grandchild.

"Lizzy, you must not let Bennet dawdle at the breast!" she declared decisively. "Keep him awake and force him to finish. If he will not, have the nanny put him to bed. If he wakes in a short while wanting more, let him cry. It will not take long for him to learn to drink his fill whenever he is brought to you and that will save you from wasting so much time feeding him."

Once she had said it, the smug look on Mrs. Bennet's face

confirmed she thought herself clever. The shock on Mrs. Gardiner's face and the scowl on William's, however, made it plain that they disagreed.

"I do not mind feeding Ben for as long as he wishes," Elizabeth pronounced.

Mrs. Bennet seemed poised to argue with her, so William interrupted, "Elizabeth, may I have a few minutes of your time?"

Mrs. Gardiner, Mrs. Phillips, Jane, Kitty and Georgiana stood to leave, but it took William adding "alone" to get Mrs. Bennet on her feet. Once they were alone, he crossed to where Elizabeth was sitting propped up by pillows, feeding their son, and sat down on the bed beside her.

After he gave her a kiss and then Ben, Elizabeth lay her hand against his cheek tenderly. "Pay no attention to Mama; I do not."

"It is a mark of maturity that you have not let her opinions affect you. At present, I cannot boast of that same maturity."

"Surely you jest," Elizabeth teased. Then she added, "You wished to speak to me?"

"I pray that you will take what I am about to say in the spirit it is intended."

"Do not worry, my love. I know you have a kind spirit."

"When we stayed at Longbourn, I could not help but notice that after a while certain members of your family drain your strength. The doctor cautioned that stress is not good for your recovery or for Ben's welfare. So I took the liberty of speaking with your father, the Gardiners and Georgiana about providing you with a short respite from most of our company—some peace and quiet, if you will. They all agreed with my motivation, but I leave it up to you to decide if we implement the plan tomorrow or not."

"Peace and quiet," Elizabeth repeated. "That sounds lovely." Then a crooked smile creased her face. "What do you have in mind, husband? Trapping my mother, Kitty and Lydia in the cellar and pretending we cannot hear their cries?"

William laughed. "Nothing so dramatic! I simply asked Georgiana if she would persuade Mary, Kitty and Lydia to join her in the conservatory to practice painting with oils. We have all the necessary supplies, and if your sisters are willing, she can instruct them in the techniques she has already mastered. Mrs. Gardiner plans to ask your mother to accompany her into Lambton to purchase materials to sew a gown for Ben and, once there, insist that they visit the Gavins. Mr. Gardiner volunteered to take his children to the lake to fish. Cook can prepare a picnic basket, and I will send two maids and a footman along to assist with the youngest. This will leave only you and Jane to talk to your heart's content."

"You left out Papa," she teased.

"Your father will be lost in the library, as usual."

"I do not know what I did to deserve you, William!" Elizabeth exclaimed, leaning forward to bestow a kiss on his lips. Ben lost his grip on her breast in the move and began to cry. After guiding him back to the nipple, when he instantly quieted, his parents smiled.

"I am afraid that you have it backwards, sweetheart," William said.

"Have what backwards?"

"I am the one undeserving of you." His pronouncement earned him another kiss, howbeit this time Elizabeth drew his mouth to hers so as not to disturb their son again.

"I take it that you agree then?"

"Oh, yes! A thousand times, yes!"

Days later

The day after Elizabeth's family departed found Mrs. Reynolds entering the mistress' bedroom to discover it empty. She walked out onto the adjoining balcony and was scanning the lawn when Adams came through the doors that led to Mr. Darcy's bedroom. He was focused on beating the dust from a pillow that matched the upholstered chair and did not immediately notice the housekeeper. When he finished, he looked up.

"May I be of assistance, Mrs. Reynolds?"

"I am looking for Mrs. Darcy. It is time to administer another draught. It may be the last of the batch, but I wish to follow Dr. Camryn's instructions and have her take it all."

"I imagine you looked in the nursery."

"I did. The nanny said that Mr. Darcy took the baby, and I assumed he brought him here."

Adams walked to the rock wall surrounding the balcony and, leaning forward, peered to the right as usual. "If Clancy is to be believed, they are in the garden."

"Clancy? What has he to do with it?"

"You may not have noticed, what with all the hullabaloo surrounding Mrs. Darcy's family, but he disappeared the second they arrived. Clever fellow, if you ask me."

Had Adams been any other servant the housekeeper would have been obligated to chide him for that remark, but Mr. Darcy's valet offended whomever he pleased, and the master indulged him. Besides, more often than not she agreed with Adams, though she could not say as much. The valet continued talking whilst she listened.

"As soon as the Bennets left, the pup reappeared, heading straight to Mrs. Darcy. Now that she can walk about, he trails her everywhere. Since I just saw him retrieve a ball in the garden and rush towards the pond, I assume she and Mr. Darcy are there."

Adams was surprised when Mrs. Reynolds did not excuse herself immediately. Instead, she said, "I think I shall leave the draught until tonight."

Bestowing upon him a rare smile, she left him standing on the balcony alone.

For what seemed the hundredth time, William took the ball Clancy dropped at his feet and tossed it as far as possible. Wiping perspiration from his brow, he declared, "Evidently Clancy is so pleased to be free to run that he has no idea how tired I am."

Taking a seat next to Elizabeth, who was sitting in the swing under the gazebo holding Ben, he noted how wearily she smiled.

Slipping the babe from her arms, he said, "Here I speak of my tiredness whilst you do so much more and never complain. Let me hold him, my love."

After laying the sleeping infant in his lap, he was soon predictably lost in admiring his child. Once he began softly tracing Ben's features with a fingertip, Elizabeth threaded her arm through his and laid her head against him.

"He is an angel."

William tried not to smile. "Perhaps we should make a note of that in our journals. In that way, once he reaches the age to act contrary, we can fondly recall a time when he was truly angelic."

"Do not be so cynical. I intend to write that I am certain Ben will never behave like anything but an angel, no matter his age."

"If he does, you can always force him to read your journal."

Elizabeth's delightful laugh was accompanied by a punch on the arm.

Clancy returned to sit at their feet and William slowly began to rock the swing. In the silence, Ben's soft breathing was the only sound to be heard.

"I ask God every day," William murmured at last, "why I have been blessed with such happiness...with you and Ben...when many men will never experience half the joy I know."

Elizabeth nodded in agreement. "At least we are not foolish enough to believe we will never face any hardships, so let us strive to cherish the moments when we are completely and incandescently happy, such as now."

Ben became restless, so William brought him up to lie on his chest. Kissing his forehead, he tucked the child safely under his chin and patted his back.

"If I have nothing more than you and Ben for the rest of my days, I shall be content."

Leaning over to receive his next kiss, Elizabeth murmured, "As shall I, my darling."

Finis

Thank You For Reading!

I hope you enjoyed *Proof of Love – A Pemberley Tale.* It was fun exploring the love story between a younger Darcy and Elizabeth—so much fun, in fact, I have decided to do something I have never done—write a sequel.

Journey of Love – A Pemberley Tale will be my next endeavor, and I hope to have it finished in early 2019.

As always, I would love to hear from you. You can send me an email at DarcyandLizzy@earthlink.net or you can always find me on my forum DarcyandLizzy.com/forum. If you join the forum, you'll find stories posted by a host of JAFF writers whose names I'm sure you'll recognize. Prior to publishing, I always post my newest book there.

If you would like notifications when my books are published or when I begin posting them on the forum, please send an email to this address and tell me you wish to be added to the 'Notifications' email list: BrendaBigbee@earthlink.net. I will never share your information, and I promise you will not be inundated with irrelevant emails.

Finally, if you are so inclined, I would appreciate it very much if you would review this book. You, the reader, have the power to make a book more visible by leaving a review.

Again, thank you so much for reading *Proof of Love – A Pemberley Tale.*

With gratitude,
Brenda Webb

Printed in Great Britain
by Amazon